THE TILTED WORLD

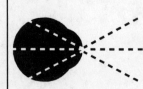

This Large Print Book carries the
Seal of Approval of N.A.V.H.

THE TILTED WORLD

TOM FRANKLIN
BETH ANN FENNELLY

WHEELER PUBLISHING

A part of Gale, Cengage Learning

GALE
CENGAGE Learning®

Detroit • New York • San Francisco • New Haven, Conn • Waterville, Maine • London

GALE
CENGAGE Learning

Copyright © 2013 by Tom Franklin and Beth Ann Fennelly.
Wheeler Publishing, a part of Gale, Cengage Learning.

ALL RIGHTS RESERVED
Wheeler Publishing Large Print Hardcover.
The text of this Large Print edition is unabridged.
Other aspects of the book may vary from the original edition.
Set in 16 pt. Plantin.

LIBRARY OF CONGRESS CATALOGING-IN-PUBLICATION DATA

Franklin, Tom.
    The tilted world / by Tom Franklin and Beth Ann Fennelly. — Large print edition.
        pages ; cm. (Wheeler publishing large print hardcover)
    ISBN-13: 978-1-4104-6501-6 (hardcover)
    ISBN-10: 1-4104-6501-2 (hardcover)
    1. Married people—Fiction. 2. Orphans—Fiction. 3. Floods—Mississippi River Valley—History—20th century—Fiction. 4. Large type books. I. Fennelly, Beth Ann, 1971– II. Title.
PS3556.R343T55 2013b
813'.54—dc23   2013037203

Published in 2014 by arrangement with William Morrow, an imprint of HarperCollins Publishers

Printed in the United States of America
1 2 3 4 5 6 7 18 17 16 15 14

*For Nolan
and
Nat and Judith*

AUTHORS' NOTE

During the winter of 1926 and spring of 1927, record-level rains tested — and bested — the poorly engineered levees along the Mississippi River and its tributaries. There were many small floods, many deaths, and still the rains worsened. By March 1927, a thousand miles of levees, from Cairo, Illinois, to the Gulf of Mexico, were in danger of collapsing, and thousands of refugees were being housed in temporary camps. All along the river, armed guards were trained to fight floods and saboteurs. But no training could prepare them for the big flood when it came, on Good Friday, 1927. The levee at Mounds Landing, near Greenville, Mississippi, collapsed, and a wall of water one hundred feet high and with twice the force of Niagara Falls scooped out the Delta. It flattened almost a million homes, drowning twenty-seven thousand square miles, sometimes in up to thirty feet of water, and the water remained for four months. Over 330,000 people were rescued from trees, roofs, and levees. At a time when the federal budget was around three billion dollars, the flood caused an estimated one billion dollars' worth of property damage.

In addition to permanently changing the landscape of the South, the great flood of 1927 permanently altered race relations and American politics, causing hundreds of thousands of African Americans to migrate north, ushering Herbert Hoover into the White House, and cementing the belief that the federal government — which had done nothing to help the flood victims — should create an agency to prevent emergencies and assist recoveries. Despite these legacies, and despite being considered by many to be the worst natural disaster our country has endured, the flood of 1927 seems largely forgotten today.

The Tilted World is an effort to reinhabit that era. Although the historical background is as accurate as the authors could manage, the town of Hobnob is a fictional creation, as are its inhabitants.

Prologue

April 4, 1927

Dixie Clay was squelching through the mud along the creek's swollen banks, shooing mosquitoes with her hat, when she saw a baby coffin bobbing against a sycamore snag. For a second the idea that her son, Jacob, buried two years back, might have come home nearly collapsed her. She dropped her hat and her rifle and plunged into the stream. She was crashing hip-deep through the foamy, coffee-colored water when she got hold of herself. It wasn't Jacob in the coffin. Wasn't, in fact, a coffin. She slowed and trudged closer and saw that the box had rivets on metal bands, that it was a small steamer trunk, a hat trunk.

Sounds could carry for miles, echo weirdly, in these wooded hollows, but the last thing she expected now was men's voices. And that they reached her over the hissing, fumbling stream meant the men were yelling. Her husband, Jesse, wasn't supposed to be home this afternoon. She reversed direction in the swirling creek and fought equally hard to reach the bank and stumbled out, waders filled with water.

It was a quarter mile back to the house and she ran it, glad she'd borrowed an old pair of Jesse's trousers and glad too that she'd brought the Winchester. Dixie Clay was light of foot but the rains had swamped their hundred acres and shin-deep mud pulled and slurped at her boots. As she ducked pine branches and dodged a black-berry thicket, she could hear Jesse's voice, though not his words, and the voices of perhaps two others. A few years back cus-tomers sometimes came right up to the house, but Jesse stopped it, didn't want her talking to men. Anyway, they didn't sound like customers.

When she crested the ridge, she dropped to her stomach, but the back door of the house was clear. They must be out front. She started down the gulley, terrified when her foot slipped on wet leaves, releasing a cascade of pebbles and pinecones. She went on more carefully and kept to the dense, shaded woods as she made her way around to the front gallery. The voices were clearer now but she still couldn't see their owners.

She was about two hundred yards off and to get closer she'd have to leave cover to dart to the stand of tulip poplars at the far end of the clothesline. She was halfway there, low and fast, when she heard a gunshot.

She flung herself at a poplar and crouched, heaving.

Now the voice, unknown to her, grew louder. "You want I should just kill you now?"

A mumble in reply.

"Then shut your piehole."

Dixie Clay was determined to move closer. Then she heard a staccato clacking. A rattler, she thought. But it was early April and rattlers should still be underground. Unless the rains had choked them out? She took a breath and forced herself to look down. Her trembling fingers were knocking her wedding band against the barrel of the Winchester. *Dix,* she told herself. *Dixie Clay Holliver. Steady now.*

She worked her way among the slick poplars and finally hunkered close enough to look down the slope, past the moat where the scraggly rosebushes had drowned, onto the front gallery. There was Jesse, sitting in the rocker, and beside him two men stood, one early twenties and clean-shaven, nosing his handgun into a shoulder holster. The other, older, bearded, wore a homburg hat and leaned against crates of whiskey stacked on the hand truck.

At first they were strangers, but then she remembered a few days back, how she'd been standing at the counter of Amity's store, testing the weight of different ropes, when she sensed a man at her side. She didn't turn. "I wonder if this will hold shut a busted valise," he said, and snapped a rope between his hands. She pretended the comment wasn't addressed to her and moved down the counter toward the fishing lures, letting Amity swoop in. Still, Dixie Clay felt his eyes. She was a small woman and men liked that, liked too her brown curls and the constellation of freckles across her nose. But she felt no pleasure in it. Long had it been since she'd thought of her legs as good for something other than walking to the still, her arms for something other than stirring mash. That day, exiting the store, she'd seen the man leaning against a car, talking to another — talking about her, she could tell. Maybe if she'd looked them over instead of hurrying away, she would have realized what they were. But she hadn't. The rain had brought plenty of strange men to town, some working as sandbaggers, others as engineers, or journalists, or National Guardsmen patrolling the levees for saboteurs.

And now it had brought these two revenuers. Dixie Clay crouched, her heart galloping, and peered through the scrubby azaleas that footed the poplar copse. Jesse looked small, like a naughty schoolboy. His arms were folded behind his back and through the rocker slats and she guessed he was handcuffed. Handcuffed, but not shot. His lemon-yellow shirt still tucked in.

"But if we come back here," said the younger agent, tapping a Lucky Strike from its pack, "with a newspaper writer?"

The older man shook his head, but the younger continued. "How did those Jackson fellas get their pictures in the paper? You wonder how?" He paused to pinch the cigarette between his lips and light it with a match. "They called the damn paper, that's how." He exhaled and dropped the match to the boards. "They don't hack open kegs of giggle juice out in the country by theirselves with no one standing by. No sir. They telephone the paper. Then they tie a goddamn necktie. Brilliantine their hair. And only when the tripod's up do they make like Jack Dempsey."

Dixie Clay willed Jesse to look at her, to

communicate what she should do, but if he knew she was there, he gave no sign. He stared out, chin raised. From that distance, his eyes looked black, not different colored as they were, the right one blue and the left green.

The older man crossed his arms and propped them on the handles of the hand truck, then propped his foot on the metal bar. He was shod with brogans, not boots, so there wasn't a weapon there, and Dixie Clay could see he wasn't wearing a shoulder holster. Beside the front door rested a shotgun. Perhaps that was his only one. "You want your mug in the paper so bad?"

"Don't you?" said the younger agent. "Give your wife something to crow about at Temperance? Besides, it'd be good for the campaign. And fetch us a raise, I bet." He brought his cigarette to his lips and glanced at his partner. "Think of us out yonder" — he jerked his cigarette in the direction of the still — "whiskey spraying up from a dozen barrels, us with our axes raised. And it's a big still, bigger than the one they found in Sumner, I promise you that, and those collars ain't paid for a restaurant steak in a month."

"No phones out here. We'd have to drive in, call the paper, drive back out, take better part of an hour."

"Then we'd best get going before it gets dark. I'll fetch the car."

For the first time Jesse spoke. "Gentlemen —"

With that the older man whirled and backhanded Jesse so hard that the chair rocked on its rails, balanced for an impossible moment on the curved tip, and then careened forward again.

Dixie Clay hadn't aimed, hadn't meant to fire, but the shot blasted from her gun, and the men on the gallery leaped and she leaped too. They dropped low, the bearded one scrambling behind the crates of whiskey and the other diving behind Jesse. Dixie Clay looked down, shocked, at the Winchester. Now they'd be in even more trouble. And she certainly wasn't willing to shoot these revenuers to save Jesse. At times, in fact, she'd entertained the dream of shooting him herself. No, not shooting him, just getting him gone. Disappearing him, bloodlessly, and at a distance.

As if reading her mind, Jesse hollered into the eerie ringing birdless silence. "Boys! Don't shoot yet. I know you got 'em behind the crosshairs" — Dixie Clay saw the two men exchange a glance — "but don't kill 'em till we see if we can't work things out."

15

Jesse turned his face to the man using him for cover — "Now, if you ever want to see your picture in the *Delta Democrat,* you'll drop your gun and unlock these cuffs. Unless you favor the obituary section."

Across the porch the older man was gazing at his shotgun by the door, a full eight feet from where he crouched behind the whiskey.

Jesse noticed and pressed on. "Just one of you with a weapon at hand, and I got me four godless shiners aiming at your tenders. So drop your gun and uncuff me."

Instead, behind her husband's rocker, the young man's elbow flashed and a handgun snaked up and pressed itself to Jesse's jaw. The agent yelled, "Give yourselves up and I won't blast him to hell, like I've a mind to. We'll take y'all in nice and peaceful."

Jesse tossed his head back in what looked like merriment. "Hey, now," he told the revenuers, his voice droll, "that threat ain't worth a pinch of coon shit. These fellas don't care if you kill me. It'd just mean one more slice of the whiskey pie for them. And as for you?" Jesse made three quick clucks with his tongue. "They might shoot you just for target practice." He commenced to rocking as if it were a Sunday afternoon filled with nothing more pressing than shelling peas. A fist flew up from behind to steady the rocker and Jesse's chair stilled, but his body seemed at ease and he crossed his feet with their two-toned boots.

"Yup," he continued, flexing his foot, then circling his ankle. "They're bored and ornery. Sharpshooters from the war, that's who I've got working for me. Just itching to trade some lead." Jesse lifted his chin and called to the woods, "Hey, Clay! Show 'em how you beat the kaiser!" He paused, surveying the gallery. "Hit the pie plate!"

On a cord from the ceiling, she'd strung a tin pie plate and filled it with birdseed. Now she aimed the Winchester. *Clay. Dixie Clay. You can do this. Are you not that girl who won the blue ribbon for down-the-line single-barrel clay pigeon shooting, back when you wore pigtails?* She remembered the years of hunting alongside her father, remembered shooting a panther out of a pin oak. She visualized that shot, and visualized this one. She squeezed the trigger. The pie plate rang and danced on its cord and the birdseed exploded, then bounced on the floor and rolled still. She used the diversion to scuttle behind the sassafras, the last shelter before the downhill slide to the front gallery forty feet away.

"Hah!" Jesse yelled, watching the pie plate

17

jangling. "Now it's getting fun. Tell you what," he said, addressing the revenuers and starting to rock again. "Let's have us an exhibition. Yuh-huh. It's Four-Fingered Fred's turn." For a second Dixie Clay was so caught up in Jesse's fiction that she expected this phantom beside her.

Jesse continued, "Freddie, you big galoot, see if you can strike that there pack of Lucky Strikes."

The revenuers looked at it, lying flat where the younger one had dropped it. Dixie Clay aimed at the red circle that centered the green package, calmer, feeling again that electric connection of gaze to target, as if her eye fired the gun, not her finger on the trigger. She shot and the package did not explode in a flurry of confetti. She'd aimed low, though the hole in the floor wasn't more than an inch off. Not a bad shot, all told.

"Ah, Fred, Fred, Fred, I guess you needed that fifth finger to make that shot. Bit sloppy there, Fred. Your unlucky strike, I guess. Well, Bill, it's up to you." Jesse made a show of considering possible targets. "Tell you what, Bill. Tell you what I need. I don't like the homburg hat."

Dixie Clay looked to the older man's hat, sticking a few inches above the stacked cases of whiskey. Jesse continued, "Don't care for the crease running down the middle, see. All the gentlemen nowadays know it's the smoother, rounded bowler that's in fashion. Bill, I need you to take that crease out of our chum's hat for him."

Behind the sassafras, Dixie Clay didn't move. Shoot the hat off his head? Surely Jesse didn't —

Jesse was talking again, his voice still humored, and only because they'd been married for six years could she hear the strain in it. "Yup, I need a little haberdashery for this gentleman sporting last season's fashion, cringing yonder behind the hooch we worked so hard to cook. You do that, Bill, and then, Bill, then maybe your brother Joe can trim the man's whiskers." Jesse angled his mouth to stage-whisper to the younger agent still holding the handgun to Jesse's jaw, "We like our revenuers well groomed." Jesse turned back to the woods. "Now, Bill —"

"All right!" the bearded man snarled. "You got us." He jerked his head to his partner. The younger man tossed his revolver, which skidded across the floorboards. Then he shouted toward Dixie Clay, "I'm reaching for keys, you hear?" and he bent his face to where Jesse's hands were cuffed behind the slats of the rocker.

Freed, Jesse sprang up and lunged for the younger man's pistol and then rose and backed to the door to grab the other's shotgun. He aimed them at their owners. For a moment all three stood like stiff actors waiting for the curtain to fall.

"Alrighty then." Jesse smiled, white teeth beneath the wings of his black mustache. "I'm taking these feds to town, see if we can't come to an agreement. Y'all see any shenanigans, you got my permission to shoot. Otherwise, it's business as usual." Jesse put his foot on the grain bin beside the door and tucked the handgun in his bootleg. Then he waved the shotgun at the men and gestured at the gallery steps. They walked down and Jesse stooped beside the rocking chair where the handcuffs were dangling and threaded them through the slats and pocketed them and followed. "Well, well, well," Jesse said to their backs as they splashed across the yard. "Where'd you hide your paddy wagon?"

Dixie Clay didn't hear the answer but saw Jesse nod his glossy dark head as he marched them west, down the drive to Seven Hills. The sun was an orange smear behind the clouds at the crest of the ridge, and Dixie Clay watched until they disappeared and the colors of the sky leached after them. So Jesse would bribe them. Jesse would bribe them, and that would be the end of it. Nothing would change. She leaned her forehead against the puzzle-piece bark of the sassafras and let out her breath in a shaky stream. The damp bark smelled like root beer; she'd forgotten that. A string of sweat ran between her shoulder blades, down her backbone. She leaned there until the peepers set up their evening song around her.

She pressed off the trunk and decided to pick her way down to the stream to fetch her hat and see if the steamer trunk was still there. She half stumbled, half slid her way to the front gallery and sat on the steps to peel off her waders. When she stood, she returned the chair to its correct angle. Then she went inside to fetch the lantern, every key she could find in the house, the Disston handsaw, and the bent-nose pliers. She grabbed a heel of bread and a hard-boiled egg for her supper and, after giving the mule his, she climbed the ridge again and forged her way to the stream and found her hat.

The trunk was still caught in the snag and she hoisted it to the bank, bruising her thighs and drenching herself all over again. It was dark now and she sat the lantern atop the trunk and tried every key in the lock, hoping one would have the magic silhouette, but key after key refused. Nor could she pick the lock with the pliers. She'd almost resorted to the Disston when she spotted one last key in her sack and inserted it and heard the tumblers give. Inside, there was a dry chamois leather sack and she loosened the drawstring and drew out a mandolin, a bowl-backed beauty carved of mahogany.

She left the trunk yawning open on the spongy bank and took the mandolin with her, plucking a few strings as she walked, musing on its worth. In truth she wasn't of a mind to sell it, though neither she nor Jesse could play.

She wished he would come home, tell her he'd settled the matter with the revenuers safely. But it wouldn't occur to him that she was frightened. Well, Jesse had said it was business as usual. And because her business was moonshining, and because at her back the moon was fixing to shine, it was time to go to the still.

CHAPTER 1

April 18, 1927

The overhanging roof of the general store where federal revenue agents Ham Johnson and Ted Ingersoll hitched their horses was tin, so at first they didn't hear anything but the rain, endless marbles endlessly dropped. They were quick about the hitching, keeping their heads down, water coursing off their hat brims. And even when they began climbing the stairs and heard the faint wailing over the rain, they weren't sure what they were hearing, for then came the shock when they realized the sacks of flour they'd glimpsed on the floor of the gallery as they'd ridden up were wearing boots. They weren't sacks of flour lying on a black tarp but two bodies in a thin scrim of dark blood.

Then the men had drawn their sidearms, were vaulting the final steps, Ingersoll's boots slick in the blood, half a step behind Ham. The bodies lay facedown and Ham kicked their guns off the gallery, and then he and Ingersoll flattened themselves on either side of the door, pressing against the bead board. Ham nodded and they were through, into the dimly lit store lined with shelves and a glass display case on the left. Ingersoll took one aisle and Ham the other, both men scuttling low, meeting at a row of barrels.

Whatever noise they'd heard had stopped, but Ingersoll turned. There was a door to a storeroom. And then that noise began again, ratcheting up, a climbing squall.

"I sure hope that's a cat," Ham said.

The baby lay in the middle of the room, on its back, wailing and flinging its arms and legs. About ten feet away, facing shelves stocked with cartons, lay another form on its side, black suspenders marking a Y over the shirt dark with blood, above apron strings dark with blood. Ingersoll kept his gun, a Colt revolver, on the front entrance while Ham darted to the figure and toed the shoulder, rolling it on its back, the head thunking on the wood floor. He was maybe seventeen, a rifle a few feet from his head. Ham didn't bother to kick it away because when the boy's eyes opened behind crooked, blood-speckled glasses, you could tell he was done for. Ingersoll scanned the store in front, the room behind. How much blood a bag of a body could release when punctured. It was puddled all the way to a back door and running out the crack beneath. Another arm of blood reaching toward where the baby lay screaming. Ingersoll kept his gun trained at the door but backed closer.

"Son," said Ham, leaning over the boy. "What happened here?"

The boy's eyes tracked slowly to Ingersoll and then back to Ham. "Looters," he said. His *t* was crisp, likely a Scot.

"What's your name?"

"Colin . . . Stewart."

"Colin, we're going to get you and your baby to Greenville, to the hospital."

"Not my baby."

"It's okay, your baby is fine. We'll take him along, we'll be careful, have him looked at —"

"Not my baby. Looters. Looter baby. I shot 'em. Looters."

Ham and Ingersoll exchanged a look, and when they turned back to the boy, his lower lip was jerking. He spat an indistinguishable word and bloody foam flecked his chin.

"Jesus," said Ham, and holstered his gun to slide his hands beneath the boy's shoulders. Ingersoll did the same to lift the boy's ankles and he felt light, perforated. Ingersoll began backing toward the door, head turned to steer around the baby and down the aisle, blood dripping off in splatters. They were out on the gallery again with its loud roof and dead looters and Ingersoll was aiming for the steps when Ham called his name. Ingersoll turned and saw the boy was dead. He'd seen enough death to know it when it came. The body was sagging between them and they lowered it to the gallery beside the other two.

"For Christ sake," Ham said, and removed his hat and raked a hand through his bushy orange hair, the heel of his palm leaving a blotch of blood on his forehead, reminding Ingersoll of Ash Wednesday, the sign of the cross. "What the hell will we tell Hoover?" Ham asked, and gazed beyond the overflowing gutter of the gallery roof to where the rain striated the world into needles.

They'd gotten their current assignment just a few hours ago. The day had been earmarked for R&R, but Commerce Secretary Herbert Hoover, now in charge of the Red Cross and overseeing flood relief for President Coolidge, had nixed that. First, Hoover's men had telephoned Jackson's Edison Walthall Hotel, where they'd just checked

26

in, and summoned them to the train station. Hoover was crossing the flood region in a Pullman sleeper, dispensing relief and making sure to be photographed at each stop. It was quite a task, controlling — or acting as if he could — the record-high Mississippi. Twelve hundred feet of levee at Dorena, Missouri, had collapsed two days prior. One hundred and seventy-five thousand acres flooded. To calm the rest of the country, the River Commission had blamed Dorena, implying its levees were shoddy, subpar: "There has never been a single break nor a single acre of land flooded by a break on a levee constructed according to Government specifications." But there had been, and there would be. Just looking at the river could tell you that.

So Ham and Ingersoll had gone to the station, where a Negro porter wearing a white jacket and cap ushered them into the smoking car and told them to wait. What seemed like a few minutes later, the porter was shaking Ingersoll awake and the train was stopping. He and Ham were led to Hoover's Pullman, mostly filled with a polished mahogany desk. They stood before it and declined a drink and watched through the windows the frenzy of loading and unloading on the platform. Ingersoll had never met

Hoover, though he'd seen — the whole nation had seen — the newspaper photo of Hoover giving the first public demonstration of the television. He'd delivered a speech from his office in Washington, and two hundred miles away, at the Bell Telephone Laboratory in New York, men stood before a glass box and saw Hoover in his double-breasted black suit, and when his lips moved they heard his voice. It said, "Human genius has now destroyed the impediment of distance."

Ham lifted a folded newspaper off the desk and held it out to Ingersoll. Below CHAPLIN ASKS FOR DIVORCE AND NATION FEARS FLOOD was a photo of Hoover taken the day before in Memphis, the river gauge behind him at record level, HOOVER PROCLAIMS LEVEES WILL HOLD.

"He's gonna be our next president," Ham said, which was what Ingersoll had been wondering.

They'd been partners for eight years, Ham his commanding officer for a month at the ass end of the war, and they'd gotten along well enough, though when the war ended they fell out of touch. Ingersoll drifted around New York, sitting in with some bands in Harlem, though the blues wasn't near as tight as what he'd known in Chicago.

He'd been at it maybe a year when Ham strolled in, saying what a coincidence, saying he'd been strutting down 142nd Street when the siren call of Ingersoll's A-minor guitar lick siphoned out of the Club De Luxe. "Let's team up," Ham told him as they pissed outside the club, facing the rising sun, after a dozen pints of lager. Ingersoll didn't remember agreeing but left with Ham later that day. One of the dancers had taken a fancy to him and apparently her boyfriend, the club's owner, former heavyweight champion Jack Johnson, was planning to pay Ingersoll a visit.

It was 1920 then, the "Noble Experiment" still young, the revenuers its noble heroes. In January of that year, 1,520 agents were commissioned and paid fifty dollars a week. But even 1,520 clean agents couldn't patrol eighteen thousand miles of coastline and borders, and they didn't stay clean for long. Which was when the Prohibition commissioner got the idea to train a few pairs of mobile agents, who wouldn't be assigned a single jurisdiction, wouldn't get the chance to get chummy with the mobsters. The commissioner started with Ham, whom he'd known in the war and found "clean as a hound's tooth," or that's what Ham told Ingersoll. Wherever things got out of hand, the pair would be sent, mysterious, ruthless, unbribable.

But over the years they'd grown weary. In fact, the whole nation had grown weary, watching Volstead create more drinking, more crime, minting mobsters, crooking a finger to opium and cocaine. Although Ham and Ingersoll earned one hundred dollars a week now, they were itching to get out, had even trained a few sets of replacements. But when the still busts went bad, or when an undercover agent got nabbed, they were the pair the commissioner wanted. And now the commissioner had lent them to Hoover.

Hoover was everywhere in the news these days. Ham had said he was looking to capitalize on the success he'd had feeding the starving Belgians and decided a disaster closer to home would make his name. By March, Hoover had managed to get Coolidge to proclaim him chairman of a special committee of five cabinet secretaries to coordinate rescue and relief, a post that gave him authority over the army and navy. Right away he commenced with his massaging of the press, the photo shoots and statements praising his leadership attributed to various sources. In the weeks that followed, he announced that since he'd taken over, there'd been no flood casualties, no levee sabotage, no looters, no Negro levee workers shot, no refugee camp problems, and that, by God, there'd be no great flood. All of which was either untrue or unlikely.

The engine's whistle blasted, signaling departure, and Hoover entered, wearing a burgundy smoking jacket with tassels hanging from the sash. He told the men to take a seat, they were along for the ride.

"Sir," Ham protested, even as he sank into a leather club chair facing Hoover's desk. "Our stuff's still in the hotel back in Jackson."

"Yes, yes, but you'll be compensated."

Ingersoll didn't doubt it but pictured his guitar in a locker in the Peabody Hotel in Memphis, where he'd stored it three assignments ago. His fingertips were losing their calluses, that was how long since he'd strummed her.

"There's a town, a little town," said Hoover, spinning his chair to face a small bookshelf secured by a chain, "on a bend in the river." He lifted a large leather volume and swiveled back to them. "Hobnob Landing." He balanced the book on his left palm and licked his right index finger and began flipping pages, pausing to lift a pair of spectacles to his nose. "It's a modest town, Hobnob, 'bout three thousand folks," he continued, spreading the page and scanning. "Small farms, mostly corn. Some river trade, some railroad business. Hilly, not good cotton country." He looked at them over his spectacles. Bad cotton country meant good moonshining country.

He made a little cluck with his tongue and stabbed the spot with his finger, then angled the book toward them. "There. Two officers have gone missing."

"How long?" Ham asked.

"Two weeks."

"Jesus." Ham shook his head. "Who?"

"Little and Wilkinson. Know 'em?"

"Yeah," Ham said. He and Ingersoll had trained the younger one, Wilkinson. A bit of a hothead, but solid.

"Think they could be bought?"

"No. I don't think so." Ham paused as if remembering. "No."

"Well, they're bought or they're dead."

Neither Ingersoll nor Ham replied.

"Problem is, boys, I'm responsible for this area now, and I can't have any bad press coming out of it." Hoover swiveled the chair around to slip the atlas back in its slot, then faced them again. "These agents have wives, and these wives have questions, so I can only hold off on this for so long. Pretty soon I'm going to have to announce these agents were killed."

Ham nodded.

"Only thing that could make it better?"

"Announcing you've found the killers?"

"Bingo," said Hoover. "Listen, they were onto something big. We don't know what, exactly, but Wilkinson had told his wife they'd be in the papers for busting this still. Unfortunately, he didn't tell her where the damn thing was. So I need you two to go in there and find it. And, better, I need you to figure out who all is connected. Get me names — buyers, distributors, crooked police, whatever. I want to break a big story, so big the two dead prohis are just a foot-note, got me?"

They nodded.

"But the one thing I don't need? *Four* dead prohis. So use caution," Hoover continued. "Tensions are high there, and not just because anybody involved with the moonshine is running scared. The whole place is divided. Apparently, Hobnob was offered a tidy sum by a group of New Orleans bankers, cotton merchants, who approached the levee board, offering to buy out the town."

"Buy out the town?"

"Indeed. Offered fifty grand to let its levees be dynamited. Hobnob is weak because of that big horseshoe bend, levees in danger of bursting anyway. If they were to burst, that would take the pressure off the levees down south, save those big columned mansions in the Garden District."

Ham gave a snort.

"So it started out as a straightforward business arrangement," Hoover went on. "Let us dynamite your levee that's probably gonna blow anyway, and you all get a fresh start."

"And it ended up?"

"Human. The people of Hobnob jumped at the offer, but then they couldn't figure out how to divide the money. Some had more property. Some had better property. Some had no property at all. You can imagine the squabbles. In the end, they couldn't agree, and the bankers withdrew their offer." The secretary removed his glasses and put his thumb and index finger to the bridge of his nose. "Now we're worried about saboteurs."

"Like Marked Tree." It was the first time Ingersoll had spoken, and perhaps he shouldn't have, as Hoover glanced at him above the tent of his fingers. Four saboteurs from across the river had been shot while planting dynamite on the Arkansas side, and now Ingersoll guessed that Hoover had tried to keep this out of the papers.

"Yes," said Hoover. "Exactly like Marked Tree."

He rose and walked to the window and looked out while the men chewed on what he'd told them, the train rocking as it gained speed. "The Corps has sent men to Hobnob, engineers and levee guards. Which gives you an in — you're just more engineers sent to examine the levee — but it's gonna be harder to get people to talk. They're suspicious."

They nodded, though Hoover had his back to them. It was raining so hard that water was running down the inside of the glass, and Hoover removed a pocket square and wiped a swath free. The drowned landscape clacked by, rows of shriveled cotton combed by water. "Don't linger. Infiltrate, telephone me for the go-ahead, bust the still, and then get out." He turned to face them. "I'm giving you a week. Then I'll have to announce the missing prohis. Don't let me down."

"Yes, sir."

He walked to a coat tree and untied his sash and slipped the smoking jacket off and exchanged it for an army coat. Thumbing the buttons through their holes, he added, "We'll be pulling into Greenville soon, and

I can't have you disembarking when I do, in front of the newspapermen with their flash-bulbs. They'd blow your cover."

"How will we get to the town, then?" asked Ham.

Hoover shrugged. "You're enterprising gentlemen. I expect you can rustle up some horses."

Neither acknowledged this.

"Well?"

"Mighty wet for horses," Ham said.

Hoover reached for a golden cord scalloping the wall over the window and pulled. A buzzer went off and the porter opened the door.

"Oliver, these gentlemen will be departing."

"Here?" Ham asked, incredulous. They were nowhere near a town.

The porter pivoted and was gone. In a moment the train's brakes squealed, like something punctured.

Hoover slid open his desk drawer and lifted two cream envelopes onto the leather blotter. Neither man reached so Hoover picked up the envelopes and walked around the desk and placed one in Ingersoll's hand and thumped him on the back and then did the same for Ham.

"You served in France," he told them,

which caused both men to look up. "At the end of the day, this is just another war. A war against men who think they are above the law. And a war against Mother Nature."

The door opened again. Hoover picked up his spectacles and an envelope from the stack on his desk and turned it over to examine the return address. "They're ready."

"Luggage, sir?" asked the porter.

"None to speak of." He slid a brass opener into the envelope. "This war," he said, levering the opener, "is the one I'll ride all the way to the White House." He looked at Ham over his spectacles. "And I'll bring my friends with me."

Ham nodded and stood and Ingersoll followed, looking back at Hoover unfolding his correspondence. The porter held the door and they stepped onto the metal grating between the cars, both clasping their hats against the sidewindering wind. Beneath their feet the clacking had slowed and the blurry fields grew definition, shriveled brown claws where cotton should have been. First Ham, with a grunt, and then Ingersoll jumped out into the scrolling world of mud.

At the first farm they passed, they asked where they could buy two horses, and the farmer said, "I'll sell you two horses and throw in a farm to pasture them on, too." Ham said no, just the horses, and they barely had to lighten their Hoover envelopes for the two ribby roans.

Now on the gallery Ham surveyed the three bodies, the clerk faceup and the looters facedown, and shook his head. "Goddamn it. They were looting for boots." A lidless box beside the bigger body held nothing but cardboard boot lasts. Blood had soaked the bottom of the box and had climbed halfway up the sides.

Ingersoll knelt and turned over the other figure. A woman. The baby's mother. She wore trousers, dark hair pulled back behind a man's hat. Her mouth hung open and she was missing a few teeth. Her stomach was open, too, where it had been shot. Beside her in the blood lay a paper sack, a rip revealing a box of puffed wheat.

"Probably drunk," said Ham, but without conviction. The flood had made regular folks desperate, and desperate folks down-right reckless. Reckless, jobless, hopeless. You can't be hired as a corn sheller when the corn's been drowned.

"We'll send the police back when we get to Hobnob," Ham said, patting the man's pants, and then the woman's. He stood. "No papers, no wallet. Don't imagine they're from around here. Gypsies, I guess."

Ingersoll heard the baby again, wailing. It was a terrible sound. He stood.

As if to head off any crazy thoughts, Ham said, "Let's go, Ing. We've delayed too long already."

"Ham."

"Let's go. Now. They got telephones in Hobnob."

"Ham, we can't leave it."

"Well, we sure as hell can't take it. You heard Hoover. One week to find the still."

"But leave the baby?"

"What? We should nursemaid the infant while the killer goes free?"

"No, but . . ."

"It's not our problem, Ing."

"It's an orphan now, Ham."

Ham's gray eyes met his and relented. "Oh, for Christ sake. Fine. Fine. But I don't like it."

Ingersoll turned and entered the store again, Ham behind him, and they crossed their bloody footprints back to the storeroom and stood above the baby. It wore a shred of diaper. It had stopped crying but made wavery, raspy breaths. The men leaned over it.

"What do you think we should do with it?" Ham asked.

"Do with it?" They watched the baby kick. "I think we should pick it up."

"Be my guest."

Ingersoll hesitated, then squatted to lay down the Colt he'd forgotten he was carrying and rubbed his hands on his thighs and crab walked closer, his knees cracking, and inserted his big hands stiffly beneath the baby. The cloth was wet. No wonder the little fella was unhappy. "Ham," he said, "go get me a diddie. Got to be one here somewhere."

"Jesus, Ingersoll, go get one yourself," Ham said, but he was already walking toward the door.

Ingersoll lifted the baby to his shoulder, both of them so wet they couldn't get much wetter, he figured.

"Bingo," called Ham.

A blue box flew into the room and skidded to Ingersoll's feet. He turned it over to read, in small cursive, *Kotex*.

"It'll absorb just the same," Ham yelled.

"Try again," Ingersoll yelled back.

And then, "Wait, here we go." Ingersoll stuck his arm up in time to catch the package of diddies. He put the baby down and it started crying again. Ingersoll was unpinning the soggy cloth, with difficulty, pins so goddamn small, when Ham walked up, pulling on a taffy, grinning at the spectacle. The heavy slab of wet diddie fell open and the baby straightened his little legs as he screamed, an angry red acorn of a penis vibrating.

"Least we know he's a Junior now," said Ham.

Ingersoll yanked a cloth from the brown paper package and made several attempts to wind it through the baby's legs and then he figured close enough and pinned it loosely. He picked the baby up with straight arms and held him out from his chest.

"What now?" asked Ham. "You're the orphan expert."

They decided the matter quickly, Ham agreeing to push on to Hobnob, find them lodgings, search for the moonshiners, while Ingersoll doubled back to Greenville. He'd drop the baby off in an orphanage; town of fifteen thousand, had to be one somewhere. But first he'd visit the police station, better to do it there than Hobnob if they wanted to stick to their story of being levee engineers.

"I'll say we're just some fellas that needed chewing tobacco and had the bad luck to arrive after the shoot-out," said Ingersoll.

"Talk like that and they'll know you're a fed," said Ham. "Most folks would call that good luck."

They picked out supplies, Ingersoll filling his saddlebag with two cans of Pet evaporated milk for the baby and a bag of fried pork skins and a Nehi soda and two cans of tuna for himself. Then they went outside past the dead couple and collected their guns and Ham flung his saddlebag over his horse and took the reins and hoisted himself up with a grunt.

"Ditch it fast," he said, jerking a thumb toward the baby on Ingersoll's chest, "and get to Hobnob. I know you like that colored music, but don't stay for no Greenville jamboree. Only thing them poor niggers are playing these days is shovels and picks."

He kicked the horse to a trot and it flung back two crescents of mud that Ingersoll turned to take on the shoulder, shielding the baby. He watched Ham ride away, patting Junior in time to the hooves, feeling like a discarded wife, husband gone off to fight Hoover's war.

CHAPTER 2

Dixie Clay stepped onto the covered gallery of the Hobnob mill and shrugged off her slicker and untied the strings of her hat and held it dripping away from her body. She pounded the door, but rain guaranteed that neither her pounding nor any answer to it would be heard. So she put her shoulder to the swollen wood and shoved: it whooshed and she stumbled into the gloom, sending up a few puffs of flour. There were several groups of women seated around the roller mill. They looked up but none acknowledged her. They turned back to the work of their hands.

Dixie Clay pushed the door closed against the roar of the rain, and scanning the room she saw, to her right, the unmistakable backside of Amity Tidwell oozing between the slats of a high-backed chair. She was sitting with three others before a pallet stacked high with sacks of cornmeal, covered with branches. Dixie Clay hung her coat and hat on a nail and stood wordlessly behind Amity, who looked up because the other women had stopped talking. "Dixie Clay," said Amity. "Many hands make light work. Pull up a chair." But there wasn't a chair left so Dixie Clay hauled over an upturned grain bin. When she sat, her head was a foot lower than the others'. She felt like a child whose indulgent mother lets her sit with the grown-ups though she stifles their gossip.

Amity instructed her to select branches of the same size from the pile of willow saplings and to weave them through the thicker switches already laid on the pallet. They were making fascine mattresses to buttress the riverbank, trying to siphon some of the rage out of the waves smashing into the levee where Hobnob hugged the river's horseshoe bend. Dixie Clay watched the plump, ringed fingers of Amity and imitated them with her own smaller, work-nimble ones. The conversation that had ceased now picked up, the women talking about the flooding in Arkansas: five thousand people in Forest City without homes or food; six thousand refugees in Helena. The state newspapers had been told to downplay the flood but someone had fetched the *New York Times* from Memphis last week and it passed from hand to hand in the mill. When it came to Dixie Clay, she read, "Seven more die in flood along the Mississippi. . . . Additional levees broke today on both the Missouri and Illinois shores. . . . Somebody's house passed through Memphis today en route to the Gulf of Mexico." She was glad to pass the paper on.

After a while, the women moved to local news: the alligator that had swum into the Neills' chicken coop, the oak that had crashed through David Gavin's roof. Talk drifted to the mill itself. The farmers had no corn to be ground up for meal. Last summer had been the rainiest they'd ever seen. It rained all March, so farmers got only light plantings in the ground, and it rained all June so they got little harvested. The miller himself was a sandbagger now, though Dixie Clay preferred to remember him standing beside the millstones with his fists on his hips, his eyebrows and mustache battered with cornmeal.

Talk meandered to their husbands, levering rain-heavy sandbags up the levees. Dixie Clay didn't add to this conversation. Nor did they expect her to — they knew that when she rode home with a sack of cornmeal, warm and damp and laid over the pommel, she wasn't frying corn pone or feeding chickens. "I prefer my corn in a jar," Jesse liked to say. Many of these women hated her because they thought she was married to a bootlegger. But she wasn't just married to one. She was one. She imagined telling them, just to enjoy their sputtering shock.

"Last time I braided willow saplings," said Lettie Ball, organist of Hobnob Baptist, "it was to beat that rascal son of mine, who'd gone and —"

"Which one?" asked Dorothy Worth. "Eli or Arlis?"

"Lord, Dorothy, you know my Eli is so sweet you get a toothache just looking at him. No, it's Arlis, wild as a june bug on a string. And this day I'm talking about, you remember when the Washington County fair was just fixing to start, 'bout July first of last year —"

Dixie Clay let their voices braid above her head as the switches braided through her fingers. She'd forgotten how women's talk could harmonize women's work. She remembered the pneumatic player piano owned by the mayor in Pine Grove, Alabama. At the Christmas party, it played a ragtime, the black and white keys depressing as if by ghostly fingers. Now Dorothy was telling a story on her son who worked for the bridge tender. Over the keening of wind and rain, the story and the lulling affirmative "uh-huhs" of the women were hole punches in the paper scrolling in the wooden piano, pulling the work along. Dixie Clay had never learned to play much piano herself, though her mother had begun teaching her before dying when Dixie Clay was ten. Her household after that was just her father and her brother, Lucius, and certain aspects of her education had fallen away, but she rarely felt their lack. The Irish neighbor, Bernadette Capes, had sent for Dixie Clay when it was time for canning or quilting, so Dixie Clay learned those skills firsthand. To learn the rest, she read a lot.

A new woman came in with a gust and lifted off a rain bonnet and held it dripping at arm's length to give Amity a quick kiss and move on down the table. People selected their seats carefully, because the bid to flood the town had divided them into Flooders versus Stickers. Dixie Clay hadn't heard about the bid until after it had fallen through, but Jesse had been right in the center of things, as usual. He had friends and customers in New Orleans, and it was Jesse who brought the bankers' proposal to the town meeting. Later she'd asked Jesse which way he'd been leaning when the offer was still on the table, and he'd lifted the bottle of Black Lightning he'd been drinking and said, "You think I wanted to dynamite my money-printing factory?" Dixie Clay would have sided with the Stickers, too, if anyone had asked her opinion. Not that she didn't thrill to the idea of a fresh start, this whole rotten town underwater. But Jacob's grave: that was what she couldn't imagine losing.

Again the door to the mill opened and conversations paused until it shut against the roaring rain. This time it was Bess Reedy, a Sticker, who would pay Dixie Clay no never mind. About two years back, Bess's husband had been drunk and pissing into the river when he'd fallen in and drowned. He'd been drinking Black Lightning, sold to him by Jesse.

"What's the level?" another Sticker asked Bess.

"Fifty-two feet."

"And the flood crest still upriver." She shook her head. "How long till it reaches Hobnob?"

"They say two weeks. Lord help us all."

Bess touched Amity's shoulder as she passed.

Well, if Hobnob snubbed Dixie Clay, Dixie Clay snubbed Hobnob. When she and

Jesse were first married, she'd come to town every once in a while. Then she got tired of waiting for a baby to quicken in her and she took over the shining from Jesse, and after that she was too busy. She cooked the shine, and Jesse sold it, and it worked fine that way for a while. And then Jacob was born. Jacob and his necksweet. Jacob and his milk-breath. And then she didn't shine as much, and still didn't go to town. Why would she go to town? She had Jacob's tiny fluted nostrils; she had the tender depressions on his temples where his pulse throbbed; she had his toes like ten shelled peas, each one delicious. But Jacob — Jacob didn't last three months. She'd bundled his tiny body — he looked sunburned, the scarlet fever rash like sandpaper on his arms and legs, redder behind his knees, knees so tiny her thumb and forefinger could meet around them — and hitched up Chester and rode to Hobnob. When she got there, Jesse was gone, to Greenville, said the Chinese green-grocer, who was a customer. Greenville: thirty-five miles north. And not immediately afterward nor now could she recall how she got from Hobnob to Greenville. She must have ridden in someone's car. The time after Jacob's death was full of holes.

What she recalled was knocking at the gar-ish painted door of Madame LeLoup. A light-skinned Negress answered, wearing a blue flapper dress that stopped at her knees.

Dixie Clay realized that she must speak. Seemed like days, maybe weeks, since she'd spoken to anyone but Jacob.

"I'm here for Jesse Swan Holliver."

"Never heard of 'im," the Negress said.

"Jesse Swan Holliver. My husband. He has different-colored eyes."

"Ain't nobody here like that. Ain't never been."

"Please," Dixie Clay asked, and then "Wait —" as the Negress started shutting the door. Dixie Clay held up the bundle, Jacob wrapped in the baptism gown she'd made from her wedding dress, though the child hadn't been baptized.

"Lord," said the woman. "Lord." She blessed herself and said that she'd bring the husband down. And she had.

Now Dixie Clay flinched to feel a hand on her shoulder, Amity's warm palm pulling her back to present. Amity angled her shoulders to address Dixie Clay privately as the women's conversation shifted down the table.

"Jesse know you're here?" she asked in a low voice.

"I reckon he'll guess. Can't work Sugar

50

Hill when there's no sugar. Can't even check the traplines."

"Traps washed away?"

"Traps and animals both. Beaver dams sunk. Minks drowned. Rabbit burrows collapsed. So I figured, might as well do something useful."

They wove in silence for a few minutes. "Any word?" asked Amity, barely above a whisper.

"Word? About what, the flood crest?"

Amity's fingers stilled. "No, about the Prohibition agents."

The two that had come to her house? How could anyone know about that? "Amity, what are you talking about?"

"Surely you know, Dixie Clay. Two Prohibition agents were undercover in town, and they've gone missing. About two weeks ago. It's being investigated."

Amity was studying her, Dixie Clay struggling to control her face.

"Never reported back to the agency," Amity continued. "Last place they were seen was here."

Mercifully, Amity's attention was called away, and Dixie Clay bent to the floor, gathering discarded branches and trying to breathe. The day after Jesse had marched the revenuers away from their property,

51

she'd waited for him on the dock of the Gawiwatchee. He puttered up in his boat around noon and threw Dixie Clay the rope and she caught it and tied a bowline knot and cinched it around the post. While he climbed onto the dock she watched to see if he had been drinking — he had — and if the boat had been christened a new name. This past year it had been the *Teresa,* then the *Cheri,* and now it had been the *Jeannette* for four months, and still was. She knew without anyone telling her that these were the names of women he'd run with.

He lurched past her onto the uneven dock. "Jesse," she started, her voice thin. She called again, louder. He stopped but didn't turn.

"What?" he said, spitting the *t.*

"Last night, after you left with the two men, the revenuers . . ."

"What, Dixie Clay, what?" He turned then, his blue eye and green eye both squeezed with anger. She said nothing and he began walking toward the house. But this was her chance. If she didn't ask now —

"Jesse!"

He whirled. "Jesus H. Christ on a Popsicle stick, here you are harassing me before I've even had my breakfast."

"But, Jesse —"

He took two rapid steps toward her and raised his hand and she stepped toward the edge of the dock. She was lifting her arms toward her face when he slipped on some fish scales and skidded and dropped to a knee. He pushed to his feet and began scraping his two-toned calfskin boot against the dock piling. And just like that, the anger was directed at the dock, which he cursed, and his workers who'd cleaned fish there between whiskey deliveries. Finally he kicked the boot off and said, "I'll take dinner in town tonight. Have this cleaned up by the time I get home," and teeter-tottered up the path to the house in one sock foot and one heeled boot, heeled to make him appear taller. He moved into the trees, hissing ". . . sicka this small town."

Jesse hadn't come back after dinner, and Dixie Clay couldn't stop thinking about the agents. What if Jesse's bribe wasn't big enough? What if they came back when she was in the still, alone? She'd taken her Winchester with her everywhere.

But the agents wouldn't be coming back. They hadn't been seen in two weeks. Last seen in Hobnob. By her and then by Jesse.

"Ouch!" Amity dropped the branch that had pricked her and stuck her plump pointer in her mouth. She studied Dixie

Clay, then withdrew her finger and seemed to address it. "Jesse might not be too keen on you being here. He's getting his sugar today. He phoned from the store yesterday. It's coming from New Orleans by tug."

"New Orleans," said Dixie Clay, and shook her head. Even now, he wasn't slowing down.

"Woman on the phone said, 'What you need five hundred pounds of sugar for? Cotton candy?' "

Both women gave a low chuckle. Amity continued, "Tugs have been coming along the river too fast, sending waves against the sandbags." She selected a willow branch and began to weave it. "Randy Yates and them are all worked up about it. They telegrammed the Port of New Orleans saying tell the barge line that if they can't control their speed, we will. Saying the next boat that comes through at thirty-five miles per hour better have two pilots, as they intend to shoot the first one."

"Lord God. They sent that?"

"Anonymous they did." Amity lifted a willow branch, found a kink in it, then discarded it by her feet. "So Randy Yates and Jim Dees and some others have spread a few miles down the levee."

"Amity, won't the sugar go to you first,

for the store?"

She smiled wryly, carding the woven branches with her fingers. "Whiskey before cake." She angled her backside on the chair to rejoin the larger conversation.

When the mattress was finished, two women lifted one end, and Dixie Clay took the other. She was twenty-two and just over five feet tall but strong from lifting twenty-five-pound sacks at the still. The three women half hoisted, half dragged the mattress to the wall to stack it with the others, then stood brushing their hands against their skirts.

Dixie Clay was the first to hear the rifle fire and she held her hand up and the women stopped chatting and then they all heard the shots. With a grunt, Amity heaved from her chair and bustled to the riverside door. The others followed, funneling onto the loading dock. By the time they'd gotten outside, the shooting had stopped, the tug just coming into sight as it sloshed around the horseshoe bend with an angry blast of its horn.

"But it's not even going that fast," said Amity. "Thirty, at the most."

They watched the tug slow even more as it exited the horseshoe, muscling down the river, dragging two parabolas of smoke. It sounded its horn again as it drew abreast, the captain in profile red and jerky, very much alive. The tug passed them, blasting its horn a third time to warn small craft that it approached the Hobnob dock.

"Don't know why they fired," Amity said, "but they fired above it. I guess Randy and Jim were just feeling ornery. Or maybe having a pissing contest, you know." She shrugged.

The dock trembled beneath them. It abutted the levee, the giant wall of earth thirty feet high, with another few feet of sandbags on top. In normal times, the river's natural banks were almost a mile from this levee, so when you climbed to the levee top, you looked down to see the berm, then the barrow, which functioned as a dry moat fifteen feet deep, a pit from which the red earth had been excavated and carted in wheelbarrows to build the levee. Then you gazed over the wide flat batture, planted with willows, and a few separate channels that paralleled the main river, serpentining around small temporary islands. Then the Mississippi itself, almost a mile wide, and on the far side, Arkansas. That was normal times. But the river had started gobbling up the batture in January, closer every time you looked. And the whole town was looking as the river absorbed its channels, swelling and fattening, covering the batture, then filling the barrow pit, then climbing the levee foot by foot. Now it sloshed and surged at the top where the sandbaggers raced against it.

The men on the levee had slowly straightened to watch the tug and now stood blinking, their fists pressed into their lower backs, the sky gauzy and low, like a rafter cobweb Dixie Clay yearned to knock down with a broom. The tug, now out of sight around the curve, gave a last blast of its horn, and then they heard only the rain again, which was what had passed for silence these last months. Dixie Clay thought how they'd all forgotten the sound of not-rain, the way they'd forgotten the smell of not-rot. No, they didn't smell it, none of them, not the fetid mud, the festering crawfish mounds, the bloated cow washed down from Greenville and caught in their bight, nor, deeper, inalienable: their own flesh rotting. Beneath their sodden boots, the webbing of their toes scummy white and peeling in layers.

Here was the question everyone was asking: When will it stop? And here was the answer everyone was giving: It can't go on forever. But the answer had a lilt and sounded like a question.

Now, as if the sky had read their thoughts,

as if it'd stepped back and regarded their puckered upturned faces, it thundered a laugh and redoubled its efforts, pewter skewers hitting the men full in the face. Without protesting, they slid their fists from their backs and bowed down to the sodden sandbags once more.

Amity turned and the others followed her inside and resumed their weaving. But not Dixie Clay. She walked through the mill and lifted her hat and slicker from the hook and exited, knowing Jesse's men would be getting his sugar off the tug and that someone would have told him where she was. So she was waiting on the gallery but still jumped when she heard the bray of her name. Jesse had ridden up alongside the mill. His hat in the rain, his face obscured behind that dripping veil, just a pale oval and the dark smudge of mustache. Beneath him the bay mule, Chester, laden with tightly tarped sacks of sugar. She was glad the women were inside and couldn't see this, her tightly tarped shame.

Jesse rode to the porch steps and slid off Chester and held the reins to her.

"Jesse," she said, walking closer. The rain was loud and he didn't even look up. She stood on the second-lowest step and glanced behind, but no one had followed her.

"Jesse," she said, almost shouting to be heard, and reached across the saddle to put a hand on his glove. "Two prohis have gone missing. The ones from our house — where did you take them?"

"Get on," he yelled.

"When you left our house, where did you go?"

"Dixie Clay, get on —"

"Not till you tell me what happened —"

"I bribed them, okay? I paid 'em so much they up and headed to Biloxi. That was two weeks ago. Probably blew it all at the casinos by now."

She watched his lips spread under his mustache, and his teeth, even through the rain, showed white, and she realized it was a smile and his attempt to charm her.

He thrust the reins into her hands. "Now get on with it," he yelled, and gave Chester a wet slap on his flank. Dixie Clay scrambling to swing her leg over, Jesse already turning away.

She pulled her collar tight against her neck as Chester plodded down Broad Street, his hooves spackling her skirts with mud. She would have to think about her next step. Maybe the police, but she must be careful. The captain was in Jesse's pocket. She could find someone else to report Jesse to — but she'd better be certain of her accusation first. There wouldn't be a lot of careful investigation, Jesse just one more moonshiner they were happy to send to prison, Jesse's wife the same but with the scandal and the jeers.

When Chester reached a break between buildings, she craned her head to gauge the men's progress on the levee. Will it hold, will it hold, will it hold? That was the other question asked a thousand times a day. She couldn't discern the workers' faces in the slanting rain, just limbs rising and falling, looking like nothing so much as the furious scrambling of ants building their hill. Most of the limbs were dark-skinned: the sharecroppers in cotton country all around them had been trucked here, slept at night on a barge tied to the levee. Some of the limbs wore white and black stripes: prisoners from Parchman.

Dixie Clay stopped behind the Tidwell store and yelled for Amity's husband, Jamie, to come out. She unloaded a sack of sugar and left it slumped against the wall, but because she cared little for issuing awkward explanations or receiving awkward thanks she was back around the corner by the time she heard the door.

Chester knew the route home without

even a nudge. Before Jesse had bought the Model T, this same bay mule had taken him to Hobnob from Sugar Hill several times a week. She withdrew her rain-chilled fingers into her sleeves and slumped into the saddle. She rode past the town square with its courthouse and jail, its Farmers' Bank and Lund Pharmacy and Collins Furniture and Hobbs and Son Undertaker and Amos Harvey Furniture with its Victrolas cupping their ears to the glass to listen for a pause in the monotonous song of the rain. They plodded past the stolid stucco McLain Hotel, but Dixie Clay turned the mule before reaching the Vatterott Rooming House, a place she avoided. That's where they had stayed the night Jacob died. After she'd found Jesse at Madame LeLoup's, they'd ridden back to Hobnob in his Model T, and Jesse took a room at the Vatterotts'. He sat Dixie Clay, holding Jacob, on the bed and told her he was going to order the coffin. He removed Jacob from her hands then. Just lifted him right out. When he came back a few hours later, she was still sitting on the white chenille bedspread, staring at her empty hands. Their room was on the alley side, not far from the speakeasy. Later, lying in bed, Dixie Clay heard the horns slide their brassy song. She pretended to sleep so Jesse could sneak away.

In the morning, they drank coffee in the dining room and when they went back to their chambers, they found that Mrs. Vatterott had lain out a black dress, and Mr. Vatterott a dark tie and jacket. So, like children playing dress-up, they walked to church, where a tiny maple coffin lay on the altar. The preacher and the soloist and Hobbs the undertaker were the only people there. Words were said and "Nearer My God to Thee" sung and then Jesse lifted the coffin (the size of a toolbox) and carried it to the churchyard, Dixie Clay following and tripping on the dress. She didn't listen to the words spoken there, either. She was thinking of how Jacob liked to suck his three middle fingers. That little slurping sound. How he liked to grab a handful of her dark curls while he nursed. The preacher, a stranger, had never laid eyes on Jacob. She couldn't imagine why they permitted an unbaptized baby to be buried there. Likely the preacher was thirsty.

After the funeral, she and Jesse had walked back to the rooming house, where she saw Chester tied to the post beside the Model T. They stood in front of the hotel, Jesse turning his hat in his hands as if a eulogy might be embroidered on the label. They

62

watched the mule lower his muzzle to the weeds poking out of the slats in the gallery. Dixie Clay was aware of being stared at by both the people on the street and the ones in the parlor.

She spoke at last, saying, "Reckon those traps need emptying, before the coyotes get there."

Jesse hadn't answered and after a moment she continued. "Reckon I better ride home and see to 'em, and to the still."

She turned and began the business of unhitching the mule, then reached down for her satchel before she remembered she'd come to town with nothing in her hands but her stiffening son.

At her back, Jesse said, "I'll follow on directly in a day or two, once business here is tied up."

She nodded and fit her shoe into the stirrup and swung up.

Jesse spoke again. "Dixie Clay, hey, you go on, take the Model T. I know you know how. I know you've always wanted to. I'll — I'll take the mule this time."

She merely yanked Chester's head toward the road and gigged his flanks.

Jesse called out to her back. "Dixie Clay. Dix. There will be more babies."

She gigged the mule harder and was gone.

It was April when Jacob died and it was April now, but a stranger looking through her eyes wouldn't guess she traveled the same road, mud choked, deeply rutted, washed out altogether in spots. A sort of phantom road sprang up alongside the first, cutting through the forest where a giant elm, struck by lightning, had toppled, or where a buggy had mired in the mud and the furious owner up and left it after a vicious kick or two. Today, if she didn't get stuck and have to haul the mule out herself, the seven miles down Seven Hills would take over two hours, and it'd be dark when she arrived. This ride two years ago would have taken an hour. Not that she'd been in a hurry to find her house empty of everything but signs of how much life it'd once contained.

As she rode with her shoulders hunched against the rain she thought that if she'd lived in a different kind of place, she might have been spared the worst of that homecoming. If she'd had a sister, or a friend like Patsy McMorrow back in Pine Grove, or a neighbor like Bernadette Capes. Neighbors, not these squinty, rifled men (here she passed Skipper Hays's house, a bootlegger who drank too much of his product to have enough to sell), men as skittish and inarticulate as the game they trapped. A sister, friend, or neighbor would have come to strip the baby bunting and remove the cotton dresses she'd made, each with a J in blue embroidery floss. Instead, after that mule ride home, she'd stood in the doorway and stared. On the floor had been the soft cloth that she'd used to wipe Jacob's sick — when he'd still take enough of her milk to get sick on, before he turned away from her leaking breast. Before he began panting, and she saw first the White Strawberry Tongue she'd heard of, pale with raised red bumps, which progressed exactly as she'd heard it would to the beefy Red Strawberry Tongue.

She must have dropped the cloth as she'd fled with him. Balled on the floor, it was studded with flies. She kicked and the flies lifted, swirled, resettled. The air was rank — milk she'd left on the counter. She'd known that as soon as she got the still running, she'd have to put things to rights, get down upon her bones and scrub. She was twenty then and knew that all that lay before her was work and more work until she died. So far, she hadn't been wrong.

Now Dixie Clay swerved the mule off Seven Hills to skirt a tree that had fallen even since her ride into town. It was an elm, with a squirrel's nest that had been ripped like a paper sack as the branches bounced against the ground. But maybe, she told herself, the squirrels had felt themselves falling and leaped to safety. The key was to know when you were falling.

Around the tree she was in sight of the last hill, beyond which was the turnoff to their house, a drive you came upon quickly, as Jesse had intended. Of course Chester knew to turn. Pines crowded the drive, low limbs forcing Dixie Clay to duck, and once she didn't dip her head enough and a shaggy forearm knocked what felt like a gallon of cold water down her back. But there was the house, a black bulk against the navy sky.

She'd hated Jesse that day two years ago for saying there would be more babies — as if Jacob could be replaced — although some part of her knew, too, that that was what she'd been waiting for. But Jesse was wrong: there'd been no more babies. He stayed in town more and more, coming home only to load whiskey to fill the orders that he wrote in his pretty script in a little ledger he kept in his breast pocket. She knew now she'd never recover from Jacob's death. That's what Jesse had never understood: she didn't even want to. She'd known, too, for the first time, that her mother had been lucky to die in childbirth, still one with the baby dying within her.

She led Chester past the house to the barn and unloaded the sugar and peeled the wool blanket from his back and began to curry his coat. He gave a little whinny and she scratched his long black ears. She wondered — when was the last time she and Jesse had lain down together? Would she even want that? As she dumped a scoop of grain into the mule's bin and watched him sink his nose in, she tried to imagine Jesse kissing her, the tickle of his mustache on her lips. But when she thought of kissing, she thought only of Jacob. Suckling, his hungry mouth working, his eyes squeezed in pleasure, his long eyelashes two dark zippers.

My husband is a murderer, she thought. It tasted true.

She wondered when she'd see him next. Jesse kept a room, she knew, at Madame LeLoup's, paid for with cases of whiskey. Her whiskey. She remembered again the painted door, the whore in the short blue dress who'd opened it and brought Jesse downstairs, how she'd opened the door again after Jesse had gone back up to get his things. The woman was staring at the street when she said, "I done lost three."

For a second, Dixie Clay didn't know

what she was talking about.

"Three babies," the woman said. "I done lost three. All three."

Dixie Clay knew now that the world was full of secret sorrowing women, each with her own doors closed to rooms she wouldn't be coming back to, walking and talking and cutting lard into flour and slicing fish from their spines and acting as if it were an acceptable thing, this living. But there wasn't the least thing acceptable about it, Dixie Clay thought as she bent to grab the corners of a sack of sugar and, with a flip, hoist it over her shoulder. Not the least, and she made her way by memory up the path to the darkened house.

CHAPTER 3

If folks thought it strange to see a mud-coated man with a mud-coated baby sleeping on his shoulder riding past the crowded storefronts of Greenville, they gave no sign. Probably they'd seen lots stranger these past months, and they'd see stranger yet if the levee blew. At the lumberyard, men were listening to the radio tell of record levels on the Tennessee River, Chattanooga flooded, sixteen dead. Ingersoll asked a man pricing a boat kit where he could find the police station. The man removed the nail he was holding in his mouth to point.

Ingersoll hitched his horse at the station and lifted Junior to his shoulder and mounted the steps with dread. On the hour-long ride into Greenville from the cross-roads store, he'd realized how strange and suspicious his story sounded. But it turned out that the story — and the bodies — had beaten him to town. A pretty dark-haired receptionist directed him to the officer who took his report: Ingersoll was just a fella who wanted chewing tobacco and had the good luck to arrive at the store after the shooting was over. The officer was only half listening, kept one ear cocked to the loud fellow behind him offering a dramatic story of the shoot-out. There were no tough questions for Ingersoll, just name and place he could be reached. Levee in Hobnob, he answered. I'm an engineer.

The officer yanked the paper out of the typewriter. "You're done," he said, and pushed away from his desk.

"How do I find out where the baby's parents were from? Do they have any kin?" Ingersoll asked the blue back walking away.

"Consult a crystal ball," the officer threw over his shoulder. "We're a little busy here."

The reenactment was still going on behind Ingersoll so he joined the rear of the circle, beside some reporters waggling their pencils along their pocket notebooks. It seemed the dead Scottish clerk hadn't been alone at the store after all — he'd been out back, helping a deliveryman unload crates of ginger ale. The driver was saying how the clerk had been backing into the storeroom when he surprised the looters, who must have figured they had the place to themselves. So the

70

clerk shot at the looters and they shot back and the driver went to get help.

The driver didn't mention the baby at all, and Ingersoll figured he probably took off as soon as he heard the shooting. Switching the baby to his other arm, Ingersoll thought how sad that Junior would grow up in a world lousy with cowards and fakes.

A door opened from the rear of the station and a clerk poked his head through. "Coroner says he's done with the gyp corpses!"

The deliveryman snapped his fingers. "Hot diggity! Let's go look! Come on, boys."

The group scrummed away like a many-tentacled creature. Ingersoll could hear them chattering through the door and down the steps. He bet neither the driver nor those others had served. If they had, they'd have seen enough bodies to last a lifetime. Many lifetimes.

When he looked up, he was standing alone in the middle of the room. The dark-haired receptionist was studying him.

"You look lost, big fella," she said.

"I suppose I am."

"What're you looking for?"

"I guess I'm done here" — he glanced around as if expecting to be contradicted —

"so now I gotta find some officer to give this baby to."

"Judson!" she called out, swiveling on her chair, but Judson was punching his arms into his rain slicker. "Mrs. Allen, I'm heading to the coroner's," he said, and slipped out the door.

"Hmmph," she said, swiveling back around. "Well, I guess it just needs to get to the orphanage. It ain't far. I could take it when I get off. 'Course that's not till five."

Ingersoll raised his eyes to the clock, quarter past three. "I can take it there," he said.

A man walked by and dumped some heavy folders on the receptionist's desk, and Ingersoll looked to see if the thump had woken the baby. It had but he didn't cry, just blinked and turned his head.

The receptionist rose from her chair. "Girl or boy?"

"Boy."

"Can I hold him?"

Ingersoll shrugged. "Sure." She began walking around her desk, but then he felt a warmth on his thigh, a strange warmth that began cooling and he looked down and saw a dark wet patch on his slightly less wet dungarees.

When he looked up, the receptionist was

grinning. "I believe you've been baptized."

"I gave him a fresh diddie," he said, a touch of defensiveness in his voice.

"Sure you did, sugar." She lifted the baby from his arms and held him away from her crisp green dress. "But you didn't pin it on tight enough to keep anything in it. Now, let's see what we can do."

Ingersoll said he'd fetch a diddie from his saddlebag and trotted to get it, and when he came back she was kneeling beside a bench and had the baby naked on a blanket. She took the diddie and cooed to the baby as she lifted his heels in one hand and with the other wound the cloth. Ingersoll tried to memorize the dance of her fingers. When he was a child at St. Mary's Foundling Home for Boys he'd diapered the occasional baby, but he had since forgotten the ins and outs.

Now Mrs. Allen was nimbly pinning the cloth. "Poor baby," she said to Junior. "This big silly man didn't get you *near* secure enough." She gave Ingersoll a wink and then sat the baby on the blanket. "Now then," she told Junior, peering into his face, which was dirty. She must have thought so too because she reached into her cleavage and tugged out a little lace hankie and licked a corner and wiped his cheeks.

It occurred to Ingersoll that some of the

speckles on the baby were mud, but some were blood, most likely. This poor kid. And about to be dumped at an orphanage.

He'd been deciding something. *If she smiles, she's the one.*

"That feels better, doesn't it?" she asked the baby. She smiled.

So it was meant to be.

"Ma'am — Mrs. Allen — this baby's got no family now. This baby needs a mother."

She turned and then what he was asking dawned on her and she hooted. "A baby? Lord, wouldn't my Jeffrey love that. We got three already."

"Three kids?"

"Three babies. Triplets, six months old. Faith, Hope, and Charity. And they got a big sister, who's three. And Jeffrey's got two big boys from his first wife, who died when she took the Spanish flu. I'll never get to the picture show if I keep taking in children, you reckon?"

"Yes, ma'am. I reckon. I reckon so." He bent to lift Junior onto his shoulder. "Do you — do you know of a family that might feel otherwise? Nice folk?"

"Well . . ." She stepped closer and patted the baby's fanny. "He is a little lump of sugar. My friend Stacie Andrews got the baby fever all right, can't hardly stand to walk by a baby without smelling of its head, but she's gone back to her people in Starkville, 'cause of the flood, you know? So, hm, I'll have to think on it. Because these are strange times." She slipped her hankie back into her dress opening and then drew upright. "Oh," she exclaimed. "You don't think nothing's wrong with it, do you? On account of having gyp blood and all? Oh Lord, you might as well carry that child along to the orphanage."

She looked up at Ingersoll and read something in his face. "Aw, hon, I'm sure someone will come along soon who falls for that little fella. How could they help it, right?" She laid her hand on his elbow, holding the baby. "Right?"

"Right."

"Especially when they see how good and tight his diddie is?"

She was trying to tease with him. But he couldn't. "I thank you. Good-bye."

"Anytime, hon. You come chat with me any old time."

On the street he got directions from a boy selling toy boats and then he and the baby were aback the roan horse and riding toward the orphanage.

The building was one street over from the levee, visible through the rain-stripped trees.

Ingersoll dismounted and, holding Junior in one arm, tied the horse to the wrought-iron fence, which creaked when he opened it. The baby swiveled his head to see where the noise came from, so Ingersoll closed and opened the gate again for the baby's entertainment. Or maybe, thought Ingersoll, he was stalling.

The three-story brick building, set back from the sidewalk behind a concrete path, must have housed a few hundred kids at least. The orphanage where Ingersoll'd grown up was much smaller, just an extension of the convent where the nuns of St. Mary's lived. As he walked toward the steps he saw a brass plaque beside the door. "Greenville Home for the Friendless," he read. He didn't like "friendless" but supposed it accurate.

He rapped on the door and there was no answer, so he twisted the brass bell and still no answer. He leaned his face to the fan window but couldn't see through the lace curtains. Where were all the kids? All the shouting? Finally he heard footsteps and a man opened the door with a child-size tuba under one arm.

"You're here for the icebox?"

On the ride over, Ingersoll had prepared a dignified statement for when he handed the baby to the nuns, but now those words had vanished.

"Isn't there — Isn't this — ?"

"You're looking for the orphanage?"

Ingersoll shrugged, the baby on his shoulder lifting with the gesture.

"Oh, right, right, right," the man said. "Okay then. Wait." Here he raised himself on his toes to peer over Ingersoll's shoulder — "Excuse me" — and put two fingers to his lips and whistled, and both Ingersoll and the baby flinched. A Negro in a newsboy cap pushing a hand truck turned up the path.

"Yeah? Okay, we can take the infant," he continued, not looking at Ingersoll, and then laid a hand on his arm to move him aside and address the Negro as he passed, "Come on in, it's out back." He turned his focus on Ingersoll at last. "But we've moved. Had to. Water in the boiler room. Levee breaks, we can't evacuate 437 kids with just six pneumatic nuns and a mongoloid house-boy, hey? So we upped and moved the whole kit and caboodle" — he gestured with the tuba — "to Leland, got an old hospital there where we're housing everybody. Kinda nice, actually. Got a swimming pool. I'll be heading back there this afternoon —"

A crash, like a wardrobe turning over,

came from behind him. He yelled over his shoulder — "Clint, use your noggin" — and turned back to Ingersoll. "I can take her with me when I go."

"It's a he."

"I can take *him* then. Just leave me whatever paperwork you got, if you got any, and its belongings, and lay it on a pallet in the music room."

Ingersoll was already backing down the stairs. "I gotta get the papers and, uh, little dresses and things."

The man nodded. "Sure, sure, sure. You want to leave it now and come back with the papers?"

Ingersoll was on the walk. "No, thanks."

"All right. I leave at four. Have that baby here and I'll take it in the Chrysler."

Ingersoll turned toward the gate and raised his arm. As they hurried down the path, the baby rested his head on Ingersoll's shoulder, as if knowing he'd dodged a close one.

Junior liked riding the horse, which the farmer had said was called Horace. "Horse?" Ingersoll had asked, and the man had repeated the name. He'd come with a Hamley Formfitter saddle and Ingersoll held Junior snug between his stomach and

the pommel. Junior found his fingers en-
twined in wet mane and gave a happy yank.
They rode through the mud of Main Street.
Ingersoll hadn't articulated any plan yet, or
made any admissions, but when he saw a
drugstore on the next corner, he tugged the
reins. As he swung off the horse, he ac-
cidentally dislodged a brimful of rain from
his hat into the baby's face and wondered if
he would cry. There was a moment when
Ingersoll thought he wouldn't. It would be
fine. But then Junior opened a quivering,
square mouth, drew in his breath, and
began to wail. Christ Lord, this baby was
loud.

"Shh, now," he told the baby, jiggling him,
patting, begging, "shhhh," wiping Junior's
wet cheeks with his wet sleeve, which accomplished nothing other than making the
child madder. His nose was bubbling snot
and when Ingersoll tried to pinch it off, it
clung to his fingers until he shook his wrist.
The baby was crying harder now, kicking
his legs. How could something so small
make such a racket?

He somehow hitched the horse and carried the screaming baby, hipping open the
door. Inside, all the faces swung toward
him, a dozen folks in the aisles and a dozen
more at the soda fountain. He froze, drip-

ping muddy water beside the front counter with its patent medicines and sweets, unsure he could do what needed to be done here. The baby was screaming louder, somehow, snot smeared across his face, into his eyebrows even. He was so loud Ingersoll could barely think. *Gotta get some food, some* — he searched for the word — *pabulum into this baby fast,* so he read the signs hanging from the ceiling until he saw INFANT CARE and made for the aisle and scanned the complicated packages, the baby red-faced and shaking.

He heard a voice from the row behind: "Who is torturing that poor child?"

He thought, *The hell with it,* and was striding to the door over his own mud puddles, knowing leaving wouldn't solve anything, when he noticed the tree of ball suckers on the counter. He grabbed one and bit off the cellophane and popped it in the baby's mouth. Junior quieted instantly, his lips stilling around the red candy, eyes wide.

"That's better," Ingersoll said in a low voice. He looked at the tears still on the baby's cheeks and thumbed them away. Junior gave a little shuddering breath that bubbled his lips around the sucker, and then settled down to the serious business of eating the hell out of it. Ingersoll watched, relieved the screaming had stopped, and thinking maybe he could do it now, could buy the complicated packages.

A tall, aproned man appeared at his elbow. "A penny," he said.

"For my thoughts?"

"For the sucker," the man said, and Ingersoll heard a tittering from the ladies at the soda fountain.

He shifted the baby to the other hand and unbuttoned his back pocket and pulled out the damp cream envelope and withdrew a twenty and slapped it wetly on the counter. "Get me everything a baby needs," he said to the clerk, who was gazing at the Andrew Jackson like he'd never seen one before. "No," Ingersoll continued, spinning the tree of suckers as the baby watched, then plucking a matching red one for himself, and again biting off the cellophane, "get me" — he popped the sucker in his mouth — "*two* of everything a baby needs. And when you're done, come find us over here." He gestured with the lollipop to the only vacant stool. "We'll be relaxing, enjoying our hors d'oeuvres." Ingersoll strolled over and sat, crossing his ankle on his knee, resting the baby in the triangle his legs made. He held the sucker to the baby's mouth, occasionally twisting on the stool for Junior's diversion, until red syrup had fanged down the baby's chin and his shirt was lacquered to his chest.

By this time, the clerk was totaling up the packages at the counter. Ingersoll plucked another damp twenty from the envelope. "Garçon," he said, "fetch Junior some new duds, too."

They couldn't reach Hobnob before nightfall after the time spent at the drugstore, so Ingersoll decided to camp. Just before dusk, back on the horse and carrying Junior in his new red union suit, Ingersoll came upon a farmhouse with boarded-up windows and no lights anywhere. Out back, darker yet, an old barn. Ingersoll rode there and yoohooed and then pushed the door open. Inside was tight and dry, smelling pleasantly of old hay and faintly of manure. There was a Massey Ferguson tractor with a cracked leather seat and a rusted baler. If he'd thought to buy a camper's lantern at the hardware, he could've shined it into the rafters, but it was just as well he didn't, guessing bats hung by their toes, cloaked in their wings.

He led the horse inside, and it walked directly to a stall and began pulling hay from a dusty bale. In the fading light, Ingersoll peered into the recesses of the barn and saw a pile of thin twisted wood, probably cuttings from vines, maybe muscadines, and decided to build a fire. He needed both hands to do it, though.

"Guess I should lay you in a manger, huh," he said to Junior, but instead placed his hat on the dry hay and then lined the hat with a blanket. He lowered the baby, Junior's little ass a snug fit in the dome, and arranged Junior's arms along the sides, like he was in a soaker tub. It was the second time that Junior had enjoyed this particular perch. A few miles back Horace had gotten his leg stuck in the mud, so Ingersoll had dismounted and placed Junior in the up-turned hat and squatted and grabbed the horse's leg and pulled with all his might, the mud yielding with a greedy and an-guished slurp.

"Let me get this fire lit and I'll fix you a bottle," he said now.

The baby said something back, something like, "Eb we bod," and kicked his legs, which rocked the hat a bit but not so much it would overturn.

Earlier, when he and Ham had split up and Ingersoll was doubling back to Green-ville, the baby'd started fussing in his arms. Ingersoll was drinking his orange Nehi soda and it occurred to him that Junior was thirsty too, but he couldn't give the baby the Pet milk because he'd neglected to get a can opener at the crossroads store. He figured he'd buy one at the next place but the baby fussed louder so Ingersoll held the glass bottle to the baby's mouth and Junior gummed it but didn't drink, almost like he didn't know how. Ingersoll tilted the bottle and the soda flowed into his mouth and then out the sides as his eyes widened. Ingersoll took the bottle away, but Junior flapped his gums wetly. So Ingersoll poured little sips as they rode, between sips for himself.

He stacked some of the vines in the center of the barn. With his thumbnail he flicked fire from a match and lit a cigar and then a pile of the vines. Before long the baby was sucking on his bottle and the fire was popping and smelling mildly of fruit, and he stretched his legs toward the flames and his boots began to steam. He warmed a can of beans and mashed a few beans for Junior with his knife and crouched beside the hat. The baby didn't seem interested and kicked and gave a little grunt, like he was uncomfortable, so Ingersoll leaned forward to adjust him in the hat and Junior burped, right in Ingersoll's face, a burp that smelled like Nehi soda, not sour at all. It must have cleared some room because after that Ingersoll was able to poke the beans in and the baby gobbled them down.

After dinner he smoked the rest of his cigar and wondered where Ham was, if he'd found some suspects. Ham would've expected him tonight, would be annoyed with the delay, especially with Hoover giving them only a week. Junior yawned, wrapped in his jail blanket, small flames reflected in his glassy eyes, and Ingersoll wished he had his guitar to play them a little Bessie Smith in place of a lullaby. He sang a couple bars of "I Ain't Got Nobody," and Junior swiveled his head to watch Ingersoll's mouth, then turned back to the fire when it popped, pointing a crooked finger as a spark rose. His eyes seemed heavy and Ingersoll decided to change him. He laid out the blanket and got the pin open pretty well this time and powdered and diapered the baby, who didn't cry but lifted his hand to suck his wrist. Ingersoll rocked back on his heels to survey his success, nice tight diddie, baby all ready for sleeping and pinkrosy in the firelight, and admitted to himself that some small part of him was considering keeping the baby.

But that was crazy. Wasn't it? Ham would

be waiting, and a moonshiner desperate enough to have killed two agents already.

First thing tomorrow he'd find Junior a new home, a fit home, with good parents. It shouldn't be difficult. Despite what that receptionist had wondered, there was nothing wrong with this baby. Ingersoll had seen about every inch and Junior was a pretty little fella, no bad parts.

Which hadn't been the case with Ingersoll, in St. Mary's Foundling Home for Boys. Which is probably why he'd never been adopted. He'd gained this insight one day when he was six. One of his earliest memories. He was standing beside Sister Mary Eunice at the third-floor window and pressing his forehead against the chilled glass to see two orphans, brothers, go home with new parents. Sister Mary Eunice was stroking his hair, and together they watched the woman climb into the carriage and then reach her arms out, and the man passed her the blanketed bundle that was their new baby. Her arms withdrew the bundle back into the darkness of the cab. Then the man turned and lifted the other boy, three years old, his skinny legs dangling out of his short pants, and placed him in the carriage, and then the man climbed in himself. Sister Mary Eunice sighed. "Two more of God's children have a home tonight."

Ingersoll knew the sisters had decided to keep the siblings together. He'd heard them speak of it. Most people wanted only one child and they wanted it to be a little bitty baby. The sisters knew there would be takers for the baby but the three-year-old would be harder, so they'd bundled them as a package, hoping someone would want the infant enough to take the brother, too. They'd been right.

Ingersoll fogged the glass with his breath so he couldn't see the carriage drive away. "Sister?" He leaned against her leg. "What was I like as a baby?" He'd never seen a photo.

"Ah, you were lovely. A lovely lad. And you still are."

"I mean, what did I look like?"

"You were my handsome Teddy. My handsome dimpled Teddy. Would you care for bread and butter?"

In the kitchen, at the butcher's block where she sliced his bread, he kept on. Something made him keep on. "But what did I look like?" There must have been a reason his parents didn't want him.

Sister did her considering sound, the whispery insuck of breath that she did when presenting the record books to the monsignor. She must have decided something, because she sat down beside him on a wooden stool.

"You were a special boy. You looked special, too. You had a strawberry mark, Teddy, my love."

"A what?"

"A strawberry mark. A mass of tissue, blood vessels really, that bunched up under your skin, on your cheek. Up by your eye."

As she said this, Ingersoll's fingers floated up to stroke his cheek, and even as they did he knew what she said was true, that his fingers had spent a lot of time on that place, and while his skin was now smooth there, his fingers remembered when it was bumpy and begged to be caressed. He did it to fall asleep. He remembered it like he had never forgotten. He'd suck his right thumb while rubbing his pointer finger over the lumpy-bumpy.

"Is that why they left me here? My parents?"

"No, no. No. Well . . . I don't really know, Teddy." She buttered a slice of bread for herself, too, and told him that the mark, a *hemangioma* was the fancy word, grew on his cheek until it squinched his eye a bit. The sisters were worried it would compromise his sight but the doctor said it wasn't hurting him, just a cosmetic imperfection, and nothing to be done about it. It stopped growing when he was around ten months old and merely stayed the same size and color for a few years.

"Like a strawberry?"

"More like grape jelly," she told him.

He lowered his bread. He wondered what ugly thing he'd done to deserve an ugly mark. "Why don't I have it now?"

"We prayed over it. We prayed that the Lord would see fit to take it from you, and he did. It started fading when you were about four, and by the time you turned five, there was no sign of it."

"But why did he give it to me in the first place?"

"Ah, Teddy. I always thought he kissed you there. He left the imprint of his kiss on your cheek as a sign that he would let me keep you for a while."

And she did keep him. He lived at the orphanage until he was sixteen and six foot three and enlisted, shipped off to fight the Krauts.

Now, in the barn, the fire was nothing but coals. He watched the baby sleep, Junior's breathing easy in a way he felt his could never be, or never had been. *My God,* thought Ingersoll, *this month I've seen six dead bodies, including the ones at the cross-roads store. Your mother and father.*

This was no life for a baby. All the short-lived jobs, all the short-term rentals. Everything about him was temporary. He couldn't even parent a guitar.

The baby deserved someplace stable. Yes, he'd find some family for Junior tomorrow.

Ingersoll bunched some hay under his jacket for a pillow and lay down on his side, sliding the hatful of baby to his chest and curling around it, to keep him safe and warm.

CHAPTER 4

Dixie Clay woke past noon, and even waking she noted that the world sounded different from when she'd retired at dawn. As she swung her feet off the bed and into rubber boots, she looked out her window. The rain lashing Hobnob had slowed, now just fat drops plopping from greasy-looking leaves. By the time she was drinking instant coffee in her kitchen, the sun was coming out. This had happened a few times since the big rains had started in November, but Dixie Clay no longer ran to the door. She didn't look for a rainbow. No, she no longer hoped, merely waited for the rain, and when it came, falling harder than ever, as if it'd shored up its strength in the interval, she took a bitter comfort in being right.

Meanwhile, she'd roam a bit. If she didn't go out during breaks in the storms, she rarely saw light at all, as otherwise she was sleeping. Or it was dusk and she was doing chores, getting ready to work the still. Or it was dawn and she was warming up after working the still, rocking before the fire, wrapped in the Circle of Hearts afghan that the Pine Grove Knitting Society had made for her wedding gift. So tired that, without Jesse to cook for, breakfast and dinner were indistinguishable, Cream of Wheat, a whip of beef jerky. She'd grown as stringy and tough as late-season game, had lost the soft swell in her chest and tummy where she'd used to pillow Jacob. She made another cup of Red E — she preferred brewed coffee, but brew a pot just for herself? — then emptied the five pans trembling with last night's roof leaks.

There was another reason why she didn't shine when the sun did — Prohibition agents in low-flying aircraft. She'd become attuned to their hornet's buzz. Her still was camouflaged, and so was Dixie Clay — she wore brown among the trees plastered with leaves. Now she yanked on a pair of Jesse's old trousers. Once she'd been in the garden pinching worms from the corn tasseling out, and a navy seaplane had swept so low that she ducked, the corn blown into italics all around her. When she raised her head she saw the plane's shadow, like a cross, belly over her house, and she got the heebie-jeebies. She described all this to Jesse the next day in the drive where he'd squatted beside the Model T to patch a tire, his peach silk necktie flipped over his shoulder.

"The plane barnstormed the house like Lindbergh," she said.

He removed his boater and hung it on his kneecap and wiped his forehead with his peach pocket handkerchief and then turned back to the lace-on grommets. "Them boys were just having some fun with you. Don't worry, Dixie Clay. They're on the payroll."

Perhaps. But they couldn't *all* be, could they?

So she'd avoid the still today and instead scout the Gawiwatchee. The stream was usually about twenty feet wide, bordered by slick mossy shelving rocks that trapped pools of whirling minnows. It was fast but shallower than it looked due to a ridge of midstream sandbars that beached boats. That's why the Indians called it Gawiwatchee, meaning "Place Where the World Tilts." Or so Jesse'd said. He'd also said that a hundred years ago the river pirates of Crow's Nest, an islet north of Natchez, would paint false markers on the rock banks of the Mississippi to indicate that the Gawiwatchee was a passable channel. When the boats beached, the pirates would slaughter the crew, slicing open their chests and filling them with rocks and sewing them shut so the bodies would sink. And then the pirates would steal the boats and cargo and disappear.

That seemed like an awful lot of trouble to go to get rid of bodies, though. What would she do if she had two bodies to get rid of? If she were Jesse, that is? Assuming there *were* two bodies. Every afternoon as she fetched her Winchester — she never left without it now — she vowed to go to the police, but every evening found her trimming Chester's hooves or bringing him a new salt block, then heading to the still. To do nothing meant — well, it meant letting Jesse get away with murder. But to go to the police meant prison, where *he'd* be murdered. Sure as eggs are eggs, as Jesse would say. Sure as God made little green apples.

Would Jesse have dumped the bodies on their land? Two days prior she'd spotted a trio of wheeling buzzards and hurried to their shadows gyroscoping the ground but found only an Appaloosa horse wedged between shoals in the Gawiwatchee. A few days dead. Probably slipped off the levee where it was being worked in Greenville. She hoped it had broken its neck in the fall, that it hadn't merely hurt itself, hadn't tried to clamor and hoof helplessly up the sliding walls of mud before being swept away.

Dixie Clay poured the last of her coffee down the sink and tucked a stale biscuit in the pocket of the trousers. Then she slung the rawhide strap of her Winchester across her back and exited by the kitchen door, avoiding the still as she headed toward the Gawiwatchee. The walk was shorter than it used to be, because the moiling and nonsensical stream had leaped its banks and kept spreading, spreading, now maybe sixty feet across. It was blood-red due to swirled clay, full of downed trees, snags that river folk gave names to, planters and sleepers and sawyers and the trees, called preachers, that submerge and then spring back up. Two pecan trees, yoked, pierced the water — where Dixie Clay used to hang laundry after washing it in the stream. She hadn't used that line in years, not since Jesse had bought her the Thor Electric Washer, first one Hobnob had seen. Now she dried her laundry near the house, but she hated to see the line hyphenated above the water, something rudely interrupted.

In addition to searching for the revenuers, Dixie Clay liked to check the stream because, though the traps were drowned, storms sometimes brought surprises. Two weeks ago, that mandolin. Before that, a Flying Arrow Jr. Wagon, the wood warped but all four red enamel wheels working. Dixie Clay cleaned it and used it to transport jars from still to storage shack. Before that, she found a frilly white waterbird in her last remaining badger trap. The bird looked sewn of snowflakes, or what she had seen of snowflakes in *National Geographic*. Dixie Clay would have freed it, let it fly back to — what place was exotic enough — Timbuktu, Constantinople? But it had snapped its neck on the spring-loaded door. So all she could do was fold its wings and lift it out and carry it home, where she identified it in her field guide: a great snowy egret. Like Dixie Clay, it didn't belong in these parts.

As she walked the muddy banks, high-stepping to pull her boots free and scanning the water for the sinuous ribboning that decried a snake, she remembered leaving her wedding. Held in the backyard of her father's house, with all of Pine Grove picnicking on tea sandwiches. She and Jesse had sat for the photographer, and then Jesse had loaded her trousseau in the bed of his wagon — the same light and speedy wagon that had bounced away singing in its traces three years earlier when she'd sold him her bundle of skins.

Without a mother to advise her, Dixie Clay had duplicated the trousseau recommended in *Ladies' Home Journal:* six pairs of sheets, two dozen pillowcases, three dozen tablecloths, three dozen napkins, all finished with neat hemstitching. For dress — she had this memorized — "personal linens embroidered with the bride's maiden initials, one smart dress of serge, one afternoon frock of georgette crepe, one dark suit with several gay colored blouses." She'd packed some books — Meredith, Swinburne, and Hardy — her mother's Bible with the family tree inscribed on the flyleaf, the medal she'd won for the county's best Spencerian penmanship, the clover pin from the 4-H club. She'd packed her bell-end, hickory-handled hammer. It was small, child-size, really, but with a good head-to-handle ratio, perfect balance, practically swung itself. She wouldn't have traded it for Thor's. So practiced was she that she didn't even have to look as she balanced a pecan on its flat end and swung, crack. Pick out the good sweet meat, the nestled halves like tree brains, she'd always thought.

She'd packed those items, and the gift from her papa of a pearl bracelet, but her wrist was so small that she'd had to make a fist to keep it from sliding off, which made her appear angry in their wedding portrait. Dixie Clay had packed as well the books her father had given her, *Husband and Wife, The Physical Life of Woman,* and *Getting Ready to Be a Mother.* They would stay the night in the Thomas Jefferson Hotel in Birmingham.

The leave-taking went too fast, the wedding guests throwing rice and hooting, her brother shooting his pistol in the air, her father looking stricken despite his smile, spilling punch down his shirt. She twisted on the bench for a last glimpse of his red kerchief as Jesse pulled the wagon onto the road. He held the reins loosely and sat relaxed while he chatted about Hobnob, Mississippi, population 3,244, where he'd built his house — "Our house," he corrected himself — which sat seven miles off from the town square, in corn country, not cotton country, this rocky, hilly pocket of the river. One hundred acres of wooded hills bordered by a stream. Three bedrooms, the house had. One a nursery. He reached across the wagon seat to give her hand a squeeze.

The town's full name was Hobnob Landing, nestled where the Mississippi doubled back like a black racer fixing to bite its tail.

The Chickasaws had camped there because it was a good launch for canoes, Jesse said, the high sediment load causing a braided river where several smaller channels joined the main one. The Indians were long run off, but the slow and churlish meander bend still had enough sandbars to beach unwary craft. The town grew up around the docks where the men did their repairing and trading. There was always such a ruckus of quarter boats and showboats and puffing, hooting, grinding steamboats with rattling paddle wheels — the old wild river filled with black thumbs, gamblers, hustlers, and medicine men, Jesse said, with what struck Dixie Clay as a nostalgic sigh — that it became a place to hobnob.

"Of course," he said, "the river has been mostly straightened out." He jigged the reins to steer around a dome-backed turtle. "Corseted, you could say. All those government levees, river can't change its course anymore. Neither can the rivermen. They've straightened out, too." As he talked she listened, but she was also admiring his red lips beneath his upturned glossy black mustache. It was like a bow, his face her wedding present. He wore a dove-gray cloverleaf lapel jacket with a gray-and-black checkerboard tie. His black curls were tucked under a snap-brim hat, gray with a black band. Even the black ears of the bay mules, Chester and Smokey, seemed part of his getup. So pretty he was, she gazed at him and not the road. He glanced at her and smiled. He looked like someone used to being looked at.

Jesse had told her that after his father died of Spanish influenza, he'd left Louisiana and skipped around from Arkansas to Alabama, trading skins, but had decided that he'd settle down by the time he was twenty and start building a future. And he was about to turn twenty.

It was the first Dixie Clay had heard that he didn't plan to keep fur trading. She pondered on it, then asked, "What will you do with yourself?"

In answer, Jesse reached his right arm around Dixie Clay's small waist and slid her close. He nuzzled his lips below her ear, and his ticklish mustache made her squeal and rippled gooseflesh along her forearms.

"Jesse, quit now." But she was smiling. "You're giving up trading?"

"Can't keep traipsing around forever."

"But what will you do?"

"Make a name for myself."

"But how?"

"Don't you worry, pretty li'l wifey. Ole

Jesse has a plan."

Wifey. She liked — loved — the sound of it, but a car was coming and Dixie Clay elbowed Jesse's hand from her waist. He turned his head to watch the car pass and whistled. "That's an Austin," he told her.

She'd never heard of it.

"Austin 20 touring car. Know how much one of those will set you back?"

She shook her head.

"Six hundred and ninety-five dollars."

Dixie Clay craned her neck, but the car was gone in a cloud of red dust. It was too much to even consider.

The mules' ears, which had pricked forward as the car approached, softened again into the floppy rhythm of their walk. She'd always liked mules, their boxlike upright hooves, less prone to cracking than horse hooves.

"I aim to have a car before long," he said, glancing over to see if she was impressed. She was. *My ambitious husband,* she thought.

"I've stayed at the Thomas Jefferson before on business, you know," he said. "Uh-huh. Before Prohibition you could get oysters on the half shell and champagne. Now, you're lucky to get fruit cocktail with marshmallows." He snorted. "But I know folks. We'll have some fun." He told her the hotel had a blind pig around back.

"A blind pig?" Her father drank black-berry vinegar on ice, not whiskey, though he kept a jug for company. Once he'd of-fered it to Jesse, who declined, and when Jesse'd departed that night her father had patted him warmly on the back, and she'd been proud. "Aren't blind pigs . . . danger-ous?"

He laughed. "Not with me around. The owner — he's the bee's knees. Stores his hooch in a secret room under the staircase. You need a long, thin metal key, long as your femur, inserted into the particular whorl of a particular eye in a particular beam of that oak staircase, and the whole thing swings open. Ali Baba, baby," he said, and laughed again.

Later she'd wonder why she didn't wonder how he knew so much about the storeroom. At the time she'd been too intrigued to question. *My worldly husband.* His eyelashes were so long they fringed a shadow on his cheeks.

"Wanna know how you get past the boun-cer?"

She nodded.

"Code words. You go behind the hotel, down the alley, and knock on the metal door. A grate slides open and you say the code. Last year it was, 'Joe sent me.' This year, you say, 'I'm here to see a man about a dog.' "

He smiled at the thought of it, and she smiled to see him smile, teeth white as sugar cubes.

He added, "The Jeff has nineteen floors, and a moorage mast to tie down zeppelins."

She nodded, feeling that she too needed to be tied down, or happiness would float her away.

That night, as it turned out, they never needed the code words. They had plenty of entertainment in the honeymoon suite. And though she'd been a good student, she didn't need the things she studied in the books her father gave her. Jesse was teacher enough.

Dixie Clay was sixteen then, and it was their sixth anniversary last month when she'd found the great snowy egret, and she knew now that neither one of them would be floating away anytime soon. Well, she'd become a businesswoman, no time for nickel romances. The field guide concluded by noting that the egret's frothy tail feathers, aigrettes, were desired for women's hats. So she plucked it raw and sent them through Jesse to the milliner, who gave her twenty-five cents apiece.

At the Gawiwatchee today she found no exotic bird, no wagon, no mandolin. And no sign of the revenuers, no homburg hat worn by a cypress stob, no magpie nest bearing a revenuer badge like a family crest. If only she could ask Jesse what had happened and trust he'd tell the truth. Could it be she'd been mistaken, assumed the worst? Like mistaking a mandolin case for a baby coffin.

She thought of the mandolin on her front gallery and decided to head back. As she slogged out of the marshy lowlands, she found some huge, bulbous, ocher-colored toadstools that gave a satisfying powdery puff when she kicked them, which she did as far up the ridge as she could. This little game must have distracted her because she was almost at the house when she realized she smelled tobacco. Jesse didn't smoke. He didn't like the smell trapped in his mustache. Dear God, not more revenuers. She reached over her shoulder to grasp the Winchester. She felt weary. Scared, but also weary.

Above the blood-drumming of her heart, she heard something strange — not men yelling, or dogs barking, or guns firing, but singing:

Gee, but it's hard to love someone
When that someone don't love you.

Dixie Clay began to creep forward, staying low. The smell of smoke got stronger as she snuck around the side of the house. When she pulled even with the front gallery, she could see an unfamiliar roan horse tied to her postbox. She leaned her head from behind a clump of holly bushes, but the gallery was shrouded by pines and all she could see was a muddy cowboy boot propped on the rail. It was wagging with the music, which was coming from her mandolin. The tune changed, the voice deep and unafraid:

Trouble, trouble, I've had it all my days.
Trouble, trouble, I've had it all my days.
It seems that trouble's gonna follow me to
    my grave.

If this was a lawman, it was the damnedest damn lawman she'd ever seen. But it wasn't a customer either — a customer would know better. The boot wagged on until the last note died.

"Well," asked the voice, "how'd you like that?"

Dixie Clay started. *He's spotted me,* she thought. But then there was another sound:

a high sliding three-note wail. She knew it for what it was. A baby. What kind of drunk brings a baby to a bootlegger's? And why was it crying? She sprang from the bushes and aimed her rifle at the boot.

"Hands up!" she yelled. "I got my gun and I'll shoot you dead." She couldn't see much as she half ran, half slid down the gulley, just knees and then a torso, arms held in the air, the mandolin between them. She scrambled up the steps, sighting down the rifle the whole time. When she reached the top, she saw the rest of him: a big man, his long right leg bent, boot on the rail, his left angled open, ankle on knee, and, in the opening, a bundle. A bundle with a spastic arm: a bundle of baby. The man's chair was balanced on its hind legs, and as he appraised Dixie Clay he let the front legs bump down. He started to lower the instrument so she yelled, "I said, hands up."

He straightened his arms again, a corner of his mouth curving with a quick siphoning dimple, which disappeared as she trained the gun on his heart.

"What are you doing here?"

He tilted his head beneath his brown hat as if sizing her up. "I came to bring you a baby."

"A baby?"

"Yeah."

"You came here to bring me a baby?"

"Yeah. I came here to bring you a baby. This here baby. A real American-style baby. Bona fide A-one cowboy, too. Likes the open road, Nehi soda. Loves the blues." The baby gave another cry and the man shrugged. "Well, usually he does. That was Bessie Smith. Your husband play?"

She said nothing, trying to gauge what type of crazy she was up against. She glanced around to make sure he was alone. To the side of the gallery, where she'd stuck a few measly rosebushes that had since drowned, was a collage of broken glass. She'd left a Dr. Pepper bottle on the wooden crate, saving it for the refund. Why would he smash her bottle?

"You want a baby?"

She couldn't figure out his angle. He didn't appear to have a weapon. He had a strange way of saying his *r*'s. He wasn't from around here. She glanced behind her: no one. "You're . . . fixing to give your baby away?"

"Not *my* baby," he said. "His mama's dead. Daddy dead. Baby shoulda been dead, too, but I found him and for some fool reason decided to carry him around till I could nab him another mama. Can I lower my mandolin now?"

"You mean *my* mandolin," said Dixie Clay.

He grinned and lowered his arms and set the instrument gently beside his boot.

She kept the gun trained. He slid a ring from his left hand and set it down beside the mandolin — no, not a ring, the bottle neck of the Dr. Pepper, which he'd been using as a slide. But who wears a broken bottle with a baby in his lap? The man leaned forward to lift a cigar from the porch rail, gave it three quick bellows to bring it back to life. He turned it to verify that its end was aglow. Satisfied, he took a longer puff and replaced it on the rail. Then he blew out the smoke in a slow stream, his dark brown eyes looking up at Dixie Clay.

"Well?" He lifted the bundle from between his knees and turned it to face her in the lingering smoke. "You want this baby?"

She studied it as it dangled. Hard to tell girl or boy. It was still fussing, kicking its legs a bit. It was dirty. Where its diaper cloth sagged, its belly was whiter than the rest of its torso. The man's huge hands were dirty, too, fingernails rimmed brown, covering the baby's rib cage. The baby kicked harder, and the diaper slid an inch down its hips. The man turned the baby around and set it back in the crook of his knee and began to tug the cloth higher. "I had him in some clean duds," he said, "but there was an accident." To the baby he added, under his breath, "Now don't you go wetting on me again."

Dixie Clay studied the man now, slab shouldered and rough looking, muddy dungarees plastered halfway up his legs, red Henley shirt open at the collar, in need of a shave. And a haircut. Brown shag poked from his misshapen leather hat. He looked up then and caught her looking, and she lifted the gun, which had sagged a few inches.

"Listen," he sighed, "you don't want this baby, fine. Fine. I'll find someplace better. But I gotta find it quick. The woman at the store said start with you."

"Woman at the store? What woman at the store?"

"Big woman. Maybe fifty. Gray hair. Lots of rings."

"Amity."

"Whoever. She said you're in the market for a baby."

Dixie Clay looked and looked but didn't say a word.

The baby gave another protest, not quite a cry, but not quite not a cry.

"Aw, hell," the man said, and lifted the baby from beneath with one hand, reaching for his cigar with the other. "Gotta be an orphanage in Leland, or Indianola." He stood.

"Give it," she said, quick.

"It ain't an it," he said, drawing up to his full height. "He's a boy." He addressed the baby now: "Ain't you, Junior?"

"Give it." She held out one hand. "Give it here."

He tilted his head at her again. "You want him, you put your gun down and come get him."

She did. She leaned the gun on the rail and crossed the gallery to where he was dangling the baby toward her. She slid a hand behind his back and another beneath his diaper and lifted him out of the man's arms. The cloth felt damp and must have been chilly. But the baby felt solid, good and solid. She guessed him about six months. He didn't have that newborn tremory head. He looked like he might sit up okay, secured by her afghan, say. She brought him to her chest and patted his back a few times and he slowed his fussing. Then she wanted to see his face so she lowered his head to the crook of her elbow. He had a swirl of downy dark hair. His eyes were closed beneath the faintest ridge of eyebrows. His face was dusty except where tears had cleared a path. He opened his eyes and suddenly she was being pulled into them, blue-gray eddies that held her fast. She closed her own eyes to break the spell.

Her voice was breathy when it came. "What's his name?"

"Don't know. Don't know he got a name. I guess it's up to you to choose him one."

She looked up then and saw he was standing close, looking down at her and the baby. She stepped back, toward the gun, and folded the baby into her chest. "How do I know you're not gonna come back for him?"

"Because you'll shoot me dead if I try?"

She allowed herself a little smile. "Yeah," she said. "Because I'll shoot you dead if you try."

It was his turn to smile now, and she saw the quick flick of dimples through his unshaven cheeks. "Well," he said. "Let me give you Junior's gear." He walked down the steps and crossed to the horse. He flipped open the saddlebag and pulled several cans and packages into his arms and crossed back to the gallery and stacked them beside her door.

"Okay then. I guess I'll push off." He touched two fingers to his hat brim, then inspected them and held them up to show smudges from the wet leather. But Dixie Clay was already turning away. She was patting the baby, walking inside, crooning him low words.

Not till the next morning, when she drifted onto the rain-loud gallery with the dreaming baby in her arms, would she spot against the rail her forgotten gun. And the cowboy's cigar, also forgotten, a half-moon singed into the rail where he'd left it smoldering when he rode away.

CHAPTER 5

It wasn't hard to figure out the place Ham would pick to stay. The first boardinghouse Ingersoll passed was too remote, reeked of cabbage, and cobwebs tethered the single rocking chair to the wall. He rode on to the levee and saw the McLain Hotel, a broad-shouldered terra-cotta thing that would have a good view of the levee from the top floor, but there were no vacancies. He continued to the square and found the Vatterott Rooming House, three stories, valises beside the door, wet towels hanging out of the upstairs windows like tongues. Inside, the matron recognized him from Ham's description and said his room, the Bluebird Suite, was ready. She hoped he'd appreciate it, she said, because to free it she had to kick out two Flemish engineers. Mr. Johnson, she continued, was booked in the Cardinal Suite next door. Would Mr. Ingersoll like to inspect his room? He would, he would. So he lifted his knapsack — sagging and light without the clanking jars of baby food — and followed Mrs. Vatterott as she climbed the stairs. Her nylon stockings sagged around her ankles like shedding snakeskin, and he reflected that the trend for shorter skirts was not a universal good.

Mrs. Vatterott opened the door painted with a bluebird, a room clean and simple with a chenille bedspread and a washbasin and a stack of nappy-looking towels. There was nothing Ingersoll wanted more than to topple across the bed like a giant elm, falling into slumber, waking three days later with a beard and craters in his face from the pompoms. And then a bath, a bath that would last another three days, water so hot his toes would turn crimson as soon as they hit. Then those Brillo pad towels buffing him dry, then clean clothes. Then the barber with his warm lather and beaver bristle brush while the voices of men, voices unurgent, unthreatened, and slow, threaded through his ears, his eyes closed behind the warm lemon-scented washcloth, and all this to be followed by a rack of beef ribs as long as a xylophone.

Mrs. Vatterott was still standing in the hall. "Well? Anything I can bring you?"

"I'm heading out," he told her, the vista

of pleasure scrolling closed like a school-house map. "But if you could rustle me a cup of coffee, strong coffee, I'd be grateful."

"Strong? Strong is the only kind we brew, here at Vatterotts'. I brew chicory coffee. I'm from New Orleans, you know. My granddaddy opened the ball with Lafayette."

This was meant to impress him, so he whistled, and she smiled and turned away. What did impress him was the chicory coffee, so scalding strong he thought it almost might burn away thoughts of the baby and that feisty, curly-haired girl he'd handed him to. He'd liked her freckles, and the way her blue eyes speckled with other blues, so they matched the freckles. Dixie Clay. That's what the shop matron had called her. Dixie Clay. What a name.

Ingersoll was looking for McMahon's diner, where Mrs. Vatterott said Ham would be, and thank God because Ingersoll hadn't eaten since that morning when he'd split a can of peaches with the baby. He turned right out of the boardinghouse and down one side of the square, past Collins Furniture and a shoe repair, and turned left to continue along the east side, toward a well-lit, noisy corner where cars nosed in like cows at a trough. As he passed the diner window, he saw a man's hand resting along the high, rounded red banquette, fingers thick as roman candles and tufted with orange hair. *Ham, you son of a gun. Hope you ordered me a steak.*

When Ingersoll hung his hat and coat and approached, he saw another man, a small man whose black hair didn't clear the high banquette, smoking his cigarette and leaning into Ham, like an old friend, but Ingersoll had never seen him before and bet Ham hadn't known him long either. Ham had a way of encouraging intimacy, of making you feel you'd known him for years, and only when you *had* known him for years, like Ingersoll, did you realize you hardly knew him at all.

Ingersoll could tell from the rhythm of Ham's voice that he was building to a punch line, so Ingersoll slowed.

Ham was using his Jewish accent. " 'Oy vey, I wasn't blessing myself, I was just making sure everything is still here' " — and Ham pantomimed an exaggerated sign of the cross — " 'spectacles, testicles, wallet, and watch!' "

Ingersoll smiled, not at the joke, which he knew, and not at Ham's skill, which he expected, but at Ham's unquenchable raspy guffaw, a guffaw Ingersoll had appreciated ever since he'd met Ham in the war nine years ago, though in the trenches a laugh like that could get you shot.

Now Ham looked up and, still laughing, waved him over, and with his leg under the table he scooted a chair out for Ingersoll.

"Ahhhh," Ham said, the laugh winding down, thumping his barrel chest twice, "ahh. Ing, this here's my man Jesse, whose father fought in the Third, at Argonne. Jesse, meet Ingersoll."

The man half rose from the table and plucked his napkin from his shirt, which was the color of an egg cream, a color Ingersoll'd never seen a man wear. He guessed that the long camel hair coat on the rack had been removed from this man's shoulders. Ingersoll had endeavored not to brush it with his own sodden coat, noticing as he shrugged it off something like cottage cheese on the lapel — the baby's spit-up, clotted in the seams. Jesse's handsome coat most certainly had never worn epaulets of vomit.

"Glad to know you," Jesse said, gesturing toward the chair. He was a few years younger than Ingersoll, midtwenties, but the thing you noticed was that his eyes were two different colors.

Ingersoll nodded and sat down and opened a menu. The two men looked at him, but he was too hungry to say hello, much less tell a joke.

Ham must have sensed this because he put a finger up and a pretty waitress appeared almost immediately, pitcher in hand.

"We're ready to order, darling."

"Shoot."

"I'll have a ham omelet," said Jesse.

She nodded. "And for you gentlemen?"

"Two steaks, well done," Ham said.

The waitress nodded and turned.

"Ma'am?" said Ingersoll. "You didn't take my order."

The waitress slowly turned back, glancing at the three to see if there was a joke. "The gentleman said two steaks."

"He did. That's his order. I want two steaks, too."

As the waitress walked away, Jesse said, "They got fine boiled okry, too. But it's so slippery I'm scared that when I get up, I'll leave it in the chair."

And there came Ham's guffaw again, Ham not noticing that nearby diners turned at the boom of it, or not caring, if he did notice. Jesse too laughed, throwing back his head of brilliantined black hair, which shined almost blue beneath the lights. Ingersoll would find everything funnier after the steaks.

The waitress brought glasses of water and Ingersoll nearly lunged for his and was three gulps in when he realized it wasn't water. The muscle ringing his throat pinched, and then he was sputtering moonshine all over the menu. Ham's thunder laugh and Jesse's too and Ingersoll was red-faced coughing and red-faced embarrassed and even the waitress was giggling and Jesse reached to give her fanny a pat. Through his tearing eyes, Ingersoll saw that their fingers clasped briefly before she pushed Jesse's hand away. He wondered if Jesse had a wife in some big house on Broad Street convinced her husband was at prayer meeting.

Ingersoll held his napkin to his eyes and forced the cough to die in his throat. "Sorry," he croaked. "I thought it was —"

"We know what you thought," said the waitress. "Now, let me get this out of your way" — she dangled the menu so the whiskey dripped from the corner — "before we get another display of Yankee table manners." She pranced off, the apron bow framing her backside.

"I like a dumper with a little motion to it," said Ham. "Looks like a sack of puppies under that skirt."

Jesse laughed and Ham laughed and Ingersoll took another sip, and now that he knew what he was drinking, he drank with pleasure, the whiskey smooth as if it'd burbled out of the first spring thaw, between snowdrops and crocuses and little hopping birds. "Damn," he said, and holding the glass up to appraise its clarity, again, softer, "damn."

"I'm guessing if you'da known 'bout this hooch, you'da hurried on last night," Ham said. "Split a bottle," he said, nodding to Jesse.

Jesse lifted a roll from his bread plate. Ingersoll glanced around, hoping to see a waiter hustling toward him with tongs outstretched.

Ham lowered his voice. "I wouldn't mind knowing where a fella could get his hands on some more. Fella who's mighty thirsty."

Jesse looked at Ham as he brought the roll to his lips and bit.

Ham continued, "Mighty thirsty indeed. Thirsty enough to drink about a dozen cases."

Then the waitress's arm swooped around his face with a plate of ham omelet.

Merciful God, that was fast, thought Ingersoll.

"Ketchup, please, Connie my pearl," said Jesse, looking up, and Connie said, "It's right here in my apron, gimme a sec." Her other arm held two plates, one in her fingers and the other balanced on her forearm, and she transferred that one to her free hand and began lowering Ham's heavy double steak.

Jesse reached into the apron and said, "Oh, I'll just help myself to what I want, don't mind me," and rummaged there as she squealed and shimmied, Ham's eyes gleaming as he watched the frisking, Ingersoll smelling his steak just out of reach and feeling saliva channel his tongue and thinking how strange it is when something you hear about your whole life happens: his mouth was watering.

At last Jesse got his ketchup and Ingersoll his steaks, decidedly smaller than Ham's. "I'll take two more," he nearly shouted at the waitress's back as she turned to bring more whiskey. Then he lowered his head and tucked in and didn't say anything for a long time. Which was fine: Ham might finally have met his match in terms of loquaciousness, a word Ham had taught him. The men watched as Ingersoll sawed a giant bite and forked it in.

Ham said, "He's so hungry he could eat a buttered monkey."

Jesse said, "He's so hungry he could eat the ass end of a rhino."

They clinked glasses and drained them while Ingersoll kept eating. He didn't even look up until the first steak was gone. Then he was able to slow down, to nod and laugh — men like that craved an audience, and besides, one and a half steaks and three whiskeys in, he felt like laughing. The second plate of steaks arrived and Ingersoll remembered last night's can of beans that he'd shared with the baby and he reckoned both of them were eating better now. He took a deep breath to clear some room in his stomach and kept eating as the men spoke of Coolidge, cars, and coochie.

Jesse circled his glass in the air. More whiskey arrived. *We're good and drunk now,* thought Ingersoll. *We're drunk and good.*

"Ham," said Jesse. "How come you come to be called Ham? That short for anything?"

Ingersoll gave up on the fourth steak and pushed his plate away and laid his fork down. He loved this question. Never once had he heard Ham give the same answer. Last time someone'd asked, they were in a speakeasy in Fort Smith, Arkansas, and Ham had told a tale about being named after Hamlet, from Shakespeare, because his mama had married the man who'd shot his daddy and Ham'd grown up unsure if he should seek revenge and had begun opining to a skull as his only confidant.

Now Ingersoll leaned back in his chair and stretched out, crossing his long legs under the table.

"Well," said Ham, catching Ingersoll's eye, "funny you should ask. Nope, not short for anything, and not long either. Ham for Ham. Ham 'cause when I was born, I smelled so good, so good like a sweet little piggy that ate nothing but acerns and brown-eyed Susans, and the porcine smell even spurted out the top a my head, and they'd pass me around in church, all the womenfolk taking a drag off me, then falling out and fainting."

Ingersoll was grinning and shaking his head.

Ham's accent was pure Kentucky now, which happened with whiskey. "Yep," Ham continued after a swallow, "smelled so sweet that people used to get hungry when I'd waft by on the breeze. Smelled so sweet" — Ham laid a hand on his chest and belched — "Daddy used to fret I'd convert folks to cannibalism."

Ingersoll was chuckling now, and Jesse.

"Poor old Daddy, how he had to beat them dogs away. Coyotes howling outside my room all night." Ham leaned in. "This one time? I was about eighteen months,

Mama walks in my room and says it was three big rats sitting there on the rails of my baby bed, gazing down at the hammy feast lying asleep before them, rubbing they little fists together."

Even Ham was laughing now, and then gave up trying to finish the story, holding his shaking stomach and laughing, a sheen of sweat on his red red face.

"Ahhhhhh." He sighed himself out of the laugh at last.

Connie appeared to refill their glasses. "Drink up," she told them. "Somebody's got your check."

Jesse leaned slightly out of the booth to raise a finger in the direction of the police captain's blue hat.

Ingersoll's reach for his glass was a little off. *Lord Jesus but I am drunk,* he thought. *Shouldn't be, but I am.* He was thinking of the way the baby had lounged in his up-ended hat by the fire last night, leaning back to watch the flames. Mellow, like a tired old cowboy soaking in hot springs after rounding up cattle. And now Ingersoll was thinking how empty his hat must feel with nothing in it but the hook.

It had been a strange few days. When he'd ridden away from Dixie Clay's, he'd asked himself, *What is it I'm feeling? There must be a word for it.*

At least he wasn't the only one in his cups. Ham was blinking slow, drunk blinks. But Jesse was a marvel — he couldn't weigh as much as Ham's thigh yet he'd matched them glass for glass.

As if to confirm what Ingersoll was thinking, Jesse dabbed the corners of his mouth with his napkin. "Damn fine meal. I feel fitter than a butcher's dog." He tossed the napkin onto the table and leaned toward Ham. "Alrighty now," he said. "What's your real name? *What* Johnson?"

"I'll never tell," Ham said.

"Come on."

"Bigger and meaner and more famous men than you have wanted to know."

Jesse swished a last swash in his glass and drained it and set it down. Quietly: "Not meaner."

The place had emptied of its dinner rush and now only one other table was occupied, a couple of drunk engineers scowling over their charts, the hopeless task of keeping the river at bay.

Jesse selected a toothpick from the holder and sat back against the booth, angled toward Ingersoll, who wondered was it dawning on the man that Ingersoll hadn't said more than a dozen words.

"How 'bout it, Ing?" Jesse said. He was the kind of fella who'd use a nickname as soon as he could.

"How 'bout what?"

Pointing to Ham with the toothpick. "What's his Christian?"

Ingersoll shrugged. In the kitchen, someone dropped a plate and cursed.

"I reckon it's time," said Ham, "to get back to bidness. Now, this whiskey is the finest I've had outside Kentuck, bonded or no. And I'm thinking a man like you, who makes dinner bills vanish and pretty waitresses bat their eyes like toads in a hailstorm, might know how to get some more."

Jesse lifted the knife beside his plate and tilted it, smiled to inspect his white teeth. He flicked his thumb beneath the right wing of his mustache to curl it, then flicked the left. "Love to oblige you, boys," he said, lowering the knife to the table. "But I don't know nothing about nothing."

"That so," said Ham.

"That so. And even if I did, why would I trust a fella won't tell me his real name?"

"All sorts of reasons to trust a fella."

"Such as?"

"A taste of the take."

"Thought you fellas were engineers."

"Engineers is what we be. But with expen-

126

sive tastes."

"That right?"

"Got me a blue-book octoroon named Sappho in a house of ill repute in Storyville. Smokes moota with her coochie."

Jesse leaned forward, eyes boyish and bright. "Liar."

"No lie. She opens her whorehouse window and lowers a basket and the banana vendor packs up a big bunch of those Chiquitas, and a little moota in the bottom, rolled up to smoke. My gal Sappho can French inhale, blows smoke rings with her coochie lips. It kills me, every time. Can't stay away. Even if her room always smells like rotting bananas." Ham shrugged philosophically. "But such talent don't come cheap. Costs me ten dollars. Wanna do her in the mirrored parlor? Costs extry. Wanna see her with her friend, Miss Carmen Brazilia of the Mule Skinner's Whips? Costs extry. So you see even a distinguished engineer got to have some extry extry."

Jesse nodded, removing the toothpick from between his lips and dropping it into the ashtray. "You have a point. Ten dollars is a lot."

"Yeah, well" — here Ham jutted his jaw out and scratched his sideburns — "she charges by the inch."

All three laughed, Ham the hardest.

"So if you find out the distiller of this here whiskey," Ham continued, "wants a partner with ties to vast engineered metropoli scattered across this great nation, you tell him to come find us."

"Oh, will do, will do." Jesse gave them a keen look with those queer eyes of his. "Gentlemen," he said, and pushed his chair back and stood, "this has been a most enlightening meal. We'll see each other soon, I trust." He reached and shook hands with Ham.

When Ingersoll extended his hand to shake, he bumped his whiskey glass, upsetting it. He snatched for it and the whiskey flung in the air and splattered down on his hand.

"Well, will you look at that," said Jesse. "Man's getting his date drunk."

Silence while the joke touched ground. And then Ham's huge guffaw, table shaking as he pounded it with his fist, and Jesse too throwing his head back and hooting. Ingersoll mopped his hand with a balled-up napkin and waited for the laughter to die. It took a good while. At last Jesse, still chuckling, made his way to the door, passing the table Connie was wiping down. He leaned close and whispered something that made her laugh too. She straightened, and all three of them watched Jesse proceed to the coatrack and slip into the camel hair and place his hat on his black hair and flick the brim. He withdrew his umbrella from the stand and opened the door, the bells ringing. Under the awning, he dipped his head to open the umbrella, then pushed off into the blustery night.

Ingersoll was exhausted. It hit him just that fast. "Let's go," he said, thinking of the rooming-house bed, and Ham nodded.

Then Ingersoll leaned over and picked up Jesse's glass, a half inch of whiskey left, and he drained it. "Huh."

"Water?"

Ingersoll nodded.

CHAPTER 6

The whole first day, she was skittish with
the baby. She didn't even realize she was
expecting someone to whisk him away —
the dead mother, risen from her grave, or
even the cowboy who brought him — until
she decided to trim the baby's fingernails,
bendy but so sharp they'd scratched his
cheeks. She put her curved scissors to his
inch-long finger and had to make herself
squeeze. Holding her breath. One, two,
three, four nails done, then his pinkie
twitched and she pinched it and a tiny smile
of blood appeared and immediately she
glanced at the door. But no one came to
take him, leave her orphaned. The child was
squalling so she picked him up and sucked
his little finger and shushed him, holding
him against her shoulder and patting him as
she executed her loose-legged bouncy walk,
the one that had worked on Jacob.

The bouncy walk came right back. The

baby calmed. Later, to trim the rest of his nails, she put his fingers one by one in her mouth and nibbled them smooth.

And so she grew to know him through her mouth. Through her nose and ears and fingers. He dirtied his diddie and the mess got all up his back and she bathed him, worked her wet cloth into his wrinkles and crevices, lifted up his chin to suds out the grimy beads. He didn't like the bath, she could tell the sensation was new, and he fastened desperate eyes on her, so she sang to him about arms as she swirled the washrag over his arms, sang to him about toes as she flossed between his toes. He fell asleep afterward and she had the strange experience of missing him, though he was right there. She hovered over the nest of blankets she'd made on her bed, and at one point he was so still she held a finger beneath his nose to make sure he was breathing. She wanted to study him from every angle. *When have I had this feeling before? Oh yes — falling in love . . .* She didn't mind the rain, which she wore like a cloak pulled tight around them both.

She named him Willy, for her father; Jacob had been named Julius Jacob Holliver, for Jesse's father. She wished her father could meet Willy soon, though Jesse had never allowed her to go home to visit. She didn't want to think about Jesse now, worried he wouldn't like her having a baby. But she couldn't give him back. Wouldn't even know how to. It was too late.

Each hour brought her discoveries. The first was that he was happiest on the move. He'd woken squalling from his nap and kept squalling and she knew he was hungry. The strange-talking cowboy (where do you come from if you talk like that? Not Alabama or Mississippi, that's for sure) had given her some strained peas and oatmeal, and she offered them, but he didn't seem interested. She thought maybe he was thirsty. The cowboy had also said the baby liked Nehi soda, but that was crazy, and besides, she didn't have any. She made him a bottle of Pet milk with a bit of sorghum molasses, but he wouldn't take it. He cried when she held him and cried when she pinned on a fresh diddie and cried when she put him down on a pallet. She picked him up and he paused to burp then resumed crying. As the wind outside deepened from a whimper to a howl, he met it and raised it, opening his mouth impossibly wide (Dixie Clay thought of a snake she and Lucius had once surprised in the corncrib, disengaging its jaw to swallow a rat). The baby was good and angry by then, his eyes squinched, face a red fist, arms flailing, his tongue vibrating like the clapper of a bell. Dixie Clay decided to fetch him some cow's milk from the nearest neighbor, Old Man Marvin, so loyal a customer that his teeth had about rotted. Marvin could be counted on not to gossip, and her instinct was to preserve the secret of Willy for a while. Certainly Jesse should learn about the baby from her.

But first she had to check the still, so she bundled Willy against the rain and ran with him pressed against her chest. She tried not to jostle him. He stopped crying, though the way was rough and rooty.

When she got to the still, the mash was bubbling and she needed both hands free, to lift the heavy lid and stir the wooden paddle. She rested the baby on the thumper keg while deciding what to do. She didn't want to lay Willy on the floor because she'd seen a coachwhip there a few weeks ago. Her feeling was that if snakes got in her house, well, she had no choice but to kill them, but when she was in the woods, she was in their home, and she let them be. But now she was uneasy about the coachwhip, its black body tapering off into gray and then creamy white at the tail. She remembered stories from her girlhood about the coachwhip chasing children by putting its tail in its mouth and rolling like a hoop. It would loop their feet, trip them, and then whip them bloody with its tail. She knew all this was hogwash then and knew it more so now, but still she hesitated. And that's when she realized Willy'd been lulled to sleep on the rumbling, hiccuping thumper keg.

Which was how William Clay Lucius Holliver became a moonshiner. A moonshiner, six months old on that day of April 19 (she had declared this to be the case when she realized he couldn't have a birthday if she didn't choose one).

Dixie Clay did buy milk from Old Man Marvin and then on second thought rode back and bought the cow outright. Her name was Millie, and Dixie Clay put her in the stall next to Chester and he sniffed at the partition and pawed his hoof. Four years back, when she'd begun to shine, she'd let all the farm animals go, first the cow, then the sheep and chickens, no time to tend them, no need for what they could give. But Chester — this she'd never tell Jesse, he'd laugh at her, but was true nevertheless — had grown melancholy. She scratched his withers and then leaned her forehead on his shoulder. "We both have some company now, Chet," she whispered.

Buying Millie was maybe the first time she'd spent any of the moonshine money (what need had she for frippery when she kept a raccoon's hours?). It felt good, so unexpectedly good, that the next day she tucked her son (her son!) inside her apron and buttoned her raincoat over him and rode him into town, where she bought baby supplies at Amity's store. Amity was helping another customer and Dixie Clay kept Willy hidden, but her packages made Amity curious enough to follow her outside. Finally, after Jamie had loaded her mule and gone back inside, Dixie Clay opened her coat to Amity and lowered the top of her apron, revealing Willy's face, chubby lips open in slumber, drool darkening Dixie Clay's green blouse.

"An angel," Amity whispered. Amity herself had never had a child. "What did Jesse say?"

"He hasn't seen him yet."

"Oh, Lord."

But then Jamie was calling Amity inside and Dixie Clay was glad to ride away from Amity's ridged brow. They headed home and Willy seemed happy on Chester with her arms around him, and happy tucked into her apron front while she unloaded her purchases, and happiest of all that evening on the thumper keg. Her William. Willy. Willy-boy.

Who wasn't happy was Jesse, arriving home the next day with red eyes and a dent in the Model T and, she saw as he strode past, a tear in his calfskin coat. He didn't even notice the baby at first, propped in a peach basket balanced on the Energex vacuum sweeper she was pushing over the rug. But after a nap and a bath, Jesse came out for dinner wearing a new navy pin-striped shirt and smelling like spicy oranges and was taken aback to find a peach-colored baby in the peach basket. Questions, and more questions. No, Dixie Clay didn't know the man, the baby bringer, or where he came from. And no, Dixie Clay didn't know his business in Hobnob, or how he found the house, or where he went when he departed. And no, she didn't even know his name. And, no, she wasn't very smart.

At this point they were finishing their pork chops.

"What did he look like?" Jesse asked.

"I don't know. Tall. Shaggy." Dixie Clay cast her eyes up, remembering. "Maybe thirty, maybe not quite. Red shirt, muddy dungarees."

She stopped when she saw Jesse snap his head back, and she figured he knew the man, but didn't know what that meant.

"What did he do when he brought the baby? Did he look around?"

"No."

"Ask questions? Seem curious? Try to buy whiskey?"

"No. He just wanted to find the baby someplace to live."

Jesse lowered his knife and pushed his plate back and said, "Bring it here."

Dixie Clay lifted the basket of sleeping baby and tipped it toward Jesse. The evening light filtered soft through the rain-running window and lit up Willy's skin, his peach fuzz hair. He was beautiful. She wanted Jesse to say so. She was hungry to hear it. *Say "beautiful," Jesse.*

Jesse studied the baby, then said, "Well, well, well." He slowly refolded his napkin and tugged it into its ring and placed it beside his plate. "I suppose he'll be company for you," he said, looking up at her. Dixie Clay realized she was holding her breath, and she let it out. Jesse surprised her and compounded it by giving a wink of his blue eye, and a grin: "Just don't let it slow you down none."

Dixie Clay nodded and turned toward the kitchen with the basket and had the impulse to give a little leap through the doorway,

137

like a vaudeville dancer. She smiled at the thought, then sliced the jelly roll for Jesse.

And Willy didn't. Slow her down, that is. He had his days and nights mixed up, but so did she. He got fussy in the early evening before it was time to go to the still. But so did she. She calmed them both with the bouncy walk back and forth across the gallery.

The night that Jesse said Dixie Clay could keep Willy, she gave him the bouncy walk and sang what little she knew of the cowboy's song, "Trouble, trouble, trouble, I've had it all my days," then fell to humming. Maybe she'd take some moonshine money and buy herself a Victrola and some records, some Bessie Smith. Back and forth on the gallery, humming and bouncing and humming as the sky grew dark and her boot soles made a scuffing percussion on the floor.

When Willy fell asleep on her shoulder, she stood and moved to go inside, and when she opened the screen door, a bright flash beside her made her duck. A hummingbird, its needle nose caught in one of the screen's tiny squares. So small. So furious. Dixie Clay waited for it to work itself free, its wings in their blurry panic sounding like Jesse's boat's outboard motor. After a moment of watching, with one hand on Willy's back to steady him, she propped the door open with her foot and with the other hand reached underneath the hummingbird to quiet its whirring, and then she unscrewed it.

Dixie Clay opened her palm, but the hummer didn't fly away, just sat, stunned, its heartbeat rapid. She lifted her hand close to her face. The hummer's grommet had three or four scarlet flecks, and so she knew it was a young male, just easing into its ruby muffler, one feather at a time. Like Willy's eyes, which she'd studied earlier that day, in the process of turning from blue-gray to brown, not by darkening overall but dot by chocolate dot.

I'll show you hummingbirds, Willy. I'll show you every wondrous thing.

And then the bird lifted and flew like an arrow, westward and gone.

Dixie Clay took Willy inside to the kitchen and laid him on a pallet so she could wash the jelly roll pan. As she began to scrub she remembered how, when she was a girl, she was like a baby hummer, genderless to look at, a quick darting thing, preferring the woods behind her home to the home itself.

Every winter since she was six, her papa had taken her on his weeklong hunting trips, leaving her younger brother, Lucius, home with their mother. Those weeks were better than Christmas, opening the tent flap to the dawning world woozy with hoarfrost, Papa already setting a match to the crackling rosin pine tinder they'd gathered the night before. She'd tote the aluminum kettle to Petty Creek and fill it and set it on the fire for coffee. Papa, checking the guns, whistling, mockingbird answering. Soon, the smell of bacon fluttering its fatty edges in the pan. Blue digging his front paws into the grass and pulling his weight back to stretch in what could only be pleasure. Ahead of her, the synchronicity of her shot hitting, as if all she had to do was aim her eye at her target. A few years prior, government men had put telephone lines between Pine Grove and Birmingham, and though her father explained the science — the voice translated into a wave of sound that was sent down the line — she knew that the real explanation, like how she knew her bullet would hit, owed something to magic.

It was the last trip of her twelfth winter, right before spring planting, the grandpa's greybeard blooming so thickly the tree trunks looked covered in tatting lace, when she'd shot the panther. Papa had taken the long way home, pretending to need horseshoe nails at the mercantile, really wanting to brag on her. But his pride cost them. It was then that some of the women began asking how old she was, and did she not go to school? Soon there was a rare visit to the old home place from the plump red preacher. Dixie Clay, making dinner, had been sent to the kitchen but heard enough. It didn't look right, not with Dixie Clay turning thirteen and becoming a woman. Besides, the younger son was coming up, right? Nearly eight, wasn't that right?

"Nearly nine," answered her father.

"Well, there you have it," and the preacher smacked his palms together, or that's what Dixie Clay imagined from the sound. She pushed through the swinging door into the parlor and found the preacher standing before the mantel, hands clasped behind his back, examining the photograph of her mother, dead from childbirthing, the baby swelling her dress also dead. Would have been her younger sister. Then girls would have outnumbered the boys. The preacher turned and his lips were drawn back as if snagged by fishhooks: a smile. "What's that delicious smell?"

She'd shot two rabbits and fixed stew with sweet potatoes and onions but now wished she hadn't. She glanced at her father, who offered no help. "Please join us, Preacher Nettles, for stew and biscuits." They followed her into the kitchen and, with her back to the table, she covered a nostril with her finger and huffed snot into the preacher's bowl. Yes, she was a good shot all right.

And that was why she was alone when the fur trader drove up. Papa had given Lucius a rifle for Christmas, the Winchester Model 1895 Takedown chambered for the 30-40 Krag cartridge that Dixie Clay had admired in the catalog so often the book fell open to its profile. So far, Lucius had done nothing with it but sit on the gallery and shoot holes through her underwear clothespinned to the laundry line. But now they'd gone into the woods with their rifles, leaving Dixie Clay stuck at home to tend to the turpentine trees, with Bernadette Capes checking on her. They had near five hundred pines, and it was February first, so yesterday she'd swept the pine straw away from the trunks to protect them from fire, and today she slashed the V low on the trunk and attached the drip iron and patent cup to catch the gum. She hoped to get through half the trees before sunset, but heard a wagon, coming fast, its trace chains singing like fiddle strings. She walked back to the house and saw the fur trader's wagon, the same one drawn by the same mules as last year, but a new driver atop the buckboard, not the old man she expected. With the sun behind him, she couldn't see his face, even shielding her eyes.

"Howdy," he said, looking her over. "I'm Jesse Swan Holliver, and I've taken over the trading from Cody Morrison, and I'm here to see to your skins." He cinched his reins and swung off the bench. He wore a fine beaver hat and a red kerchief at his neck. His hair was black and curly, which she saw when he tilted the hat toward her.

Dixie Clay said nothing, and he lifted his gaze from her face to the house. "Your people home?"

"No," she said. "But I'll fetch the skins. Got a mess of 'em."

"Well, that's good to hear, seeing as how I had to fight to reach you. Those roads from Kirby are washed out. My axles were dragging."

She turned toward the house and he strolled alongside her. "Wagon got stuck on Reynders Road. Had to throw down some pine knots to pull out and not fifty feet later move a big tree; took me an hour."

They climbed onto the gallery and Dixie Clay invited him to sit on the rocker as

she'd seen her father do with the fur trader.
She went inside to fetch him a glass of buttermilk and made a second trip to carry the
bundle of skins, which she set on the floor
and inventoried as she cut the strings.
"Three coons, three otter, three mink, two
skunk, one pelt nearly black entire —"

This was a particularly fine fur, and she
flicked her eyes up at the trader's face to
see if it showed interest, which it did —
"one white possum, a civet cat —"

"A civet cat?"

"He was borrowing my eggs, and I got
tired of lending 'em."

He hooted.

She continued, "One civet cat, three deer,
and, oh yes, one large panther."

She rocked back on her heels and watched
as he graded the skins, turning them over.
"Who shot 'em?" Jesse asked.

"I did."

"Who skint 'em?"

"I did."

"And you stretched 'em, too?"

"I shot 'em, skint 'em, stretched 'em,
scraped 'em, cased 'em, and I'm selling 'em.
Ten dollars for the bundle."

At this the man laughed, and his laugh
was boyish. She thought of the root beer
float at the lunch counter at Wiggins', the

ticklefizz in her nose. Maybe he was younger than she'd guessed, seventeen or eighteen.

"Can't see my way clear to paying more than five." He fingered the panther pelt, well shaped and soft.

"The skunk alone is worth a dollar."

"This old black skin?" He dangled it between his fingers. "Ain't hardly got any white on it at all."

"And that's precisely why they want it in New York City." She felt his eyes flick to her face, but she continued smoothing the skins. "Yup, Papa decided not to wait on Morrison this year. Said prices traders pay around these parts weren't hardly worth checking his traps for." She began stacking the skins, all business now. "Said this year we're sending them straight up to Fogarty Brothers of New York City." She squeezed the skins to roll them into a bundle.

Jesse looked at her shrewdly. "Your papa wouldn't go to all that trouble."

"Would too. These skins were wrapped in burlap, all ready to be toted to the post office, before I opened them for you." Dixie Clay wondered if she could support this, but couldn't think of a single piece of burlap in the house. She squeezed the bundle together with one hand and slid the twine beneath it. "Now press your finger, please, sir, so I can tie a knot."

"I'll save you the trip to town. Give you six dollars."

"I fancy a trip to town. Make it ten."

"Seven."

"Ten. Fogarty Brothers're keen on otter right now. Say they're drowning in orders for otter-trimmed opera cloaks with three-quarter bell sleeves and ivory buttons." This came straight from the Sears catalog. When she'd seen that cloak, she'd thought of her mother but didn't know why: she'd never been to an opera, nor worn a cloak for that matter.

Dixie Clay was still cinching the bundle, waiting for his finger so she could knot the twine. But instead he rocked back with a smile and took off his hat and laid it on his knee. Dixie Clay sat on her heels, figuring out what was so funny about his eyes. One was blue, the other green. She wasn't sure which one to look at, both so marble-pretty, and almost like you could choose between two people to talk to. Like a baby doll of Patsy McMorrow's that had a smiling face in the front, and, if you twisted its head around, a crying face on the other side.

Jesse set his hat back on his black curls. She was sad to see them go. He took a long pull of buttermilk, and she had the urge to offer him something more. With her father and brother gone, she hadn't been fixing meals. But if it was a month later, she'd have rhubarb, could offer him a piece of pie.

He leaned forward then, elbows on his knees. "What's your name?"

"Dixie Clay."

"Dixie Clay. And how old are you, Dixie Clay?"

"Thirteen."

"Thirteen. Well, well, well. Miss Dixie Clay, thirteen years old, how about that." He bent down and at last placed his finger on the twine she was still pulling tight. "I suppose I've been outfoxed. And I'm not even sure I mind. Ten dollars it is."

She tied the knot, feeling how close his face was to hers.

"I've traded in five states, Miss Dixie Clay, and if I had a nickel for every time I'd run up on a gal as pretty as you —"

She felt her cheeks warm and worried he'd feel the heat.

Then he stood, lifting the skins. "— I'd have a nickel," he finished.

She stood too and he stuck out his hand to shake. A business deal, she thought, and held out her hand, but he didn't shake it, just stood holding it, and holding it some more. She wasn't sure what to do with her eyes so she trained them on her hand in his, which was white and clean.

"Tell your father," Jesse said at last, "he raised a heck of a deal maker. And a heck of a hunter."

When she looked up, he tilted his head — a flash of green eye beneath hat brim — and then he released her fingers suddenly and turned to walk down the steps.

She followed him to his wagon, where Jesse overhanded the bundle of skins into the bed. With a key he opened the lockbox under the seat and removed ten dollar coins. She'd almost forgotten about the money, somehow. The coins felt cool in her palm where his had been.

Jesse found his seat and his reins. "Give Fogarty Brothers my regards," he said, and winked. Then with a "Git!" he turned the team and set off at a quick trot, the chains singing, a music she listened to until there was no more of it to hear.

The next year he'd come in the same manner. She'd been waiting. Lord, she'd been waiting, impatient when the winter rains kept Papa from the hunting, but at last they'd gone. She had a new dress because, though she was still slight around the rib cage and nimble at the waist, her old dress pulled across the armpits where her breasts had grown to fill her own surprised palms. Papa had given her money at Christmas, the same amount he'd spent on a new hunting coat and ear-flap cap for Lucius. Papa didn't say what he expected her to do with it and seemed surprised when what she did was walk to the mercantile and buy a pattern, McCall's "Misses Empire Dress, Suitable for Small Women," along with five and three-eighths yards of fabric. She'd eyed a bolt of silk georgette crepe but knew it wouldn't last, though the gossip would. Instead she selected cotton voile in "Copenhagen blue," a name she said aloud on the walk home, whirling around after to make sure she was alone.

At her sewing table, she pinned the brown tissue to the fabric and chalked and scissored. Then she pieced it and stitched it and basted it, and she put it on and ran to show her father and then stood embarrassed as he looked up from the account books, embarrassed, and said nothing, and she said nothing, and turned and walked somberly away.

Clad in Copenhagen blue, Dixie Clay stood in the piney woods and heard Jesse's music, almost as if he'd known she was finally alone. She ran to the house but when he crested the drive, she slowed to a stroll, even made herself toss the chickens some scratch. He'd grown a mustache, a fetching, fetching mustache. She'd baked a chess pie and hidden it from her brother under a tea towel in the icebox. She sliced it for Jesse, who ate two pieces, but she was too nervous to eat. When he left after the trading — she only got $3.40 but Lucius had buckshot both deer he'd managed to bring down — Jesse walked her out to the turpentine trees. They stood before a young pine with two V's etched low into the trunk, last year's V scarred over and, below it, the fresh cut she'd made that morning, oozing its honey-brown gum. Silently they watched the sweetness bead and stretch and elongate over the aluminum cup and finally, finally drop. The *plink* seemed loud.

Jesse reached and took her hand. "When there are two more slashes there," he said, nodding to the trunk, "I'll be back for you. I'll take you to Mississippi." And with his other hand he lifted her chin and she looked into those eyes, trees and water coming closer, and her own eyes closed and, yes, he kissed her.

Two more slashes: two more years. She would be sixteen. She loved the smell of pine trees now. She sometimes took her sewing to a stump in the piney woods.

She waited. What did she do while she waited? She went to Pine Grove School to satisfy the nosy neighbors, though she didn't learn as much as she had at home with her papa and his books and maps and telescope. When she wasn't at the schoolhouse, she canned and skinned and looked after the animals and tried out new recipes on her papa, and at the neighbors' turpentine boil she granted each boy one dance and one dance only: she was waiting for Jesse Swan Holliver, because Jesse Swan Holliver was coming for her. And he did, he did come; she was sixteen and Jesse Swan Holliver courted her and married her and took her to Mississippi.

Now, in Mississippi, in Sugar Hill where Jesse had brought her, she'd finished the dishes and it was dark enough to shine. Willy started to rouse and she picked him up and he turned his head from side to side, searching for the smell of milk. She wished she could feed him from her body, as she had Jacob. When he'd fallen asleep while nursing and his lips slackened and fell off her nipple, she could see his tongue flexing a time or two, her creamy hind milk pooling there, or even leaking down his chin.

She carried Willy to the stove and patted

his back, which melded to her body, curving over her chest and shoulder. She fixed the bottle and held it to his mouth and he sucked it with a determined round chewing motion she liked and then she wrapped him in the afghan and took him to the still.

Looking back, it surprised her, it always surprised her, how long it took her to learn she'd married a bootlegger. She'd been a smart girl, first in her class at Pine Grove School with figures and letters both, so all she could reckon was that she didn't *want* to learn. Sometimes she'd imagine explaining it to a girlfriend, if she had one, just like it'd appeared to her as a new bride. The friend would reassure: "Dixie Clay, you couldn't have guessed! No one could have guessed," and the friend would hug her, and they would cry a bit and laugh a bit.

Because, looking back, the signs were everywhere. After the night at the Thomas Jefferson Hotel they'd made slow progress to Hobnob because most every time they met a buggy or motorcar, Jesse knew the driver. He'd pull up on the mules, and she saw how easy he was, telling a joke, asking after one man's sick wife, after another's new boat. It was this friendly manner Dixie Clay's papa had been charmed by when Jesse'd come to ask for her hand. Of course her papa had asked him how he made his living if his part of Mississippi was no good for cotton and Jesse had spoken only of fur trading and shipping the furs south to New Orleans. Lucius had sat by Jesse's feet like a hound treeing a coon. For dinner, Dixie Clay made a roast. Jesse waited until her papa had gone to the parlor before he asked Lucius, "What's the difference between roast beef and pea soup?"

Lucius didn't know.

"Anyone can roast beef."

Lucius laughed so hard he snorted.

Yes, Jesse was charming. She wouldn't have to explain that to her girlfriend. But his charm didn't obscure certain oddities. On her second day as a bride, as they passed the sign saying WELCOME TO HOBNOB, a car pulled alongside them — a Dodge Brothers touring car, said Jesse — and the man in the passenger seat cranked the window down.

"How's business?" he asked.

"Good and fixing to get gooder. Come out to Sugar Hill," Jesse shouted over the motor. "I got what you're looking for."

As they drove on, Dixie Clay wondered — what furs did these men want? Also — why was his house named Sugar Hill? She wondered again when she saw the house, which wasn't on a hill but in a wooded gully, at the end of a drive you'd pass without knowing unless you spied the crescents of wheels etching the turn. And why call it Sugar anything when cane wasn't grown in these parts?

But she was surprised and pleased by the house. It had been built as a dogtrot with the open central hall, and when Jesse bought it he'd enclosed it and added onto the back, so now it had three rooms on either side. To the left, a parlor, dining room, and kitchen, and to the right, three bedrooms. Corner cabinets, a butler's pantry, wainscoting up to the chair rails, an inside bathroom, electric lights that went on when you pushed a little circle in a box on the wall. A back door that headed into the woods, a screened front door that opened onto a deep shady gallery with straight chairs and rockers, bordered by a rail the perfect height, Jesse said, for resting boots. He was almost twenty and had no kin to speak of, so he must have selected the brass chandelier, the mahogany mantel clock, the valance curtains in blue silk trimmed with rose, and the Queen Anne walnut bedroom set for which he was making payments of twenty-two dollars a month. The house matched him, his clean oval nails and waxed mustache.

"How do you like your new house, Mrs. Holliver?" She was standing on the front gallery and looking to the west, and Jesse had come behind her.

"I am well pleased, Mr. Holliver."

He rested his chin on her head and slid his hands around her waist and squeezed to make his fingers touch. He was shorter than average, but she was so slight that their bodies fit like a dovetail joint.

She continued, "Of course — do you think — maybe the drive is a bit overgrown?"

He said, "You let me worry about the outside of the house. No need to go chopping down perfectly good trees when we've no need for lumber. But the inside's yours to fool with." He kissed the crown of her head. "Tell you what — I need some supplies. Let's see if there's anything you want at the Hardware to gussy things up."

At the Hardware, Jesse had an account. "Put it under Mrs. Jesse Swan Holliver," she told the clerk, though he clearly knew Jesse. Dixie Clay was enjoying the song of her new name: "Mrs. Jesse Swan Holliver, with an H." The clerk's fat wife, perhaps jealous that Dixie Clay needed so little fabric for her dress, sullenly pulled out bolts for Dixie Clay to thumb the slub. She charged dot crepe faille in "palmetto green," sixty-eight cents a yard, and yellow paint, and green-checked gingham to make box pleat curtains for the nursery, yellow and green she figured good for either sons or daughters. Who wouldn't be long in coming: every night she woke to Jesse sliding in bed behind her, peeling her nightgown up with his cold fingers — why cold — had he been outside? — a thought that disappeared as his hands slipped between her thighs, his thumbs inching higher, twiddling, the chilled thumbs warming and readying her along with his breath in her ear, then the hands on her breasts, "Sugar Hills" he was whispering, then the hands on her hips, flipping her and tilting her backside up, and then he was fully inside her and it was happening, hugely. After the first time in the Thomas Jefferson, it hadn't hurt at all. *I'm made for this,* she thought, taken deep into the rhythm.

After Jesse had fallen asleep on her, still moored, she would lie, smiling a little, feeling him shrink out of her ever so slowly, his chest rising and falling. He was the boat and she was the sea. His breathing deepened into a snore. Perhaps they'd made themselves a child that very night.

But they hadn't. Nor the next night, nor the next. Spring turned into summer, and she sewed an eyelet ruffle for the wicker bassinet. She made rhubarb preserves. She canned apricots, tomatoes, pears, peaches. Put up watermelon rind pickles, bread and butter pickles. Kumquats, sugared satsumas. Summer turned into autumn, and she put up applesauce, spiced crab apples, figs, wished for lemons to make curd but they were too far north. Autumn turned into winter, and Jesse had business in town a lot, more and more it seemed, or he went hunting in the woods. She would make special meals for him when he returned, but he wasn't a big eater, unlike her father. She didn't even have a dog to feed the scraps to. Jesse didn't like dogs. Why, she asked him once. "Maybe I got bit as a child," he answered.

But Dixie Clay missed the cool button of dog nose in her palm. Missed how Blue would nudge her leg where she sat reading until she scratched his ears, and how his red rubbery eyelids would droop in doggy pleasure. She thought of afternoons with Bernadette Capes in the dark, chilled springhouse, which smelled faintly of sour clabber. They'd take turns holding the churn between their knees and plunging.

After a bit Bernie, like a lucky fisherman, would draw up a net that held a crock of cream, and they'd sit under the cottonwoods and pour the rich yellow cream over berries and biscuits. She missed churning butter while Bernie recited "Lament of the Irish Immigrant," missed playing jacks with Patsy, missed buffing her riding boots alongside her papa while he hummed "Les Huguenots."

One day almost a year after they were married, when Jesse said not to hold supper, that he had business in town, she asked to go along. She asked as if asking were the most casual of whims and kept stirring the junket she was fixing to set.

When she looked up, Jesse was eyeing her, but all he said was "I reckon. If your cooking can keep, come on then."

And they rode into town, Dixie Clay noticing two sets of tracks, the outer tracks for wagon wheels and the inner set for car tires. It was March and the dogwoods, usually lost in the understory, were offering their white teacups. Jesse held the reins loosely in his yellow leather gloves, and Dixie Clay thought, with his black curls against the greenery, he looked like a jungle bird. He was telling her the plot of *Nosferatu,* the last picture show he'd seen. Today he would take her to Valentino's *Blood and Sand,* he said, before conducting business. He said before the picture began, a blond midget named Big Boy Lloyd Adams walked down the aisle in his light blue tuxedo and climbed a riser to the piano bench and flipped out his tails and started to play. The music helped those who couldn't read — the darkies sat up in the balcony, Jesse said — and Big Boy Lloyd could make thunder with his piano, or rain, or locomotives, or autos, or just about anything.

After the movie, they went to McMahon's diner for forty-cent coffee-and-waffles. Jesse didn't eat much but smoked and shook hands with the men who dropped by their booth.

"So this is the missus," one would say, and tip his hat. Another would add, "Well, Jesse, now we know why you've been keeping her all to yourself."

Jesse expanded, arms stretched along the back of the booth, entertaining and entertained. He asked, "Boys, I bet you're all wondering how I keep my youth." He paused, then: "I give her anything she wants!"

The men exploded into laughter. When they slapped Jesse's back in farewell, he invited them to come by the house. "Business is fixing to expand. Grand opening on Tuesday," he would say. "Tuesday, dusk." In the wagon on the way home, she asked him about this, but he said he was tired, too tired to discuss it, and she didn't press. It had been the nicest day she'd had in ages. She laid her head on his shoulder and looked at the falling stars.

"Maybe I'll buy you one of those waffle makers," he told her.

And Tuesday as Dixie Clay washed the dishes she heard wagon wheels, then car wheels, and she dried her hands on her apron and set to tucking her pin curls and just when she had redrawn her red Cupid's bow smile and was ready to go in and offer coffee with it, she heard the front door slam. Jesse clomping down the steps. She walked to the window but it was dark out and she saw not a thing but the lantern's aureole bouncing away into the night, the men's boots muffled by pine needles. Three times this happened, and at last she went to bed with Jesse still out of the house, and hours later when she woke to moonlight and Jesse over her shoulder and the nightgown yanked up, the seam ripping, she named at last what she smelled and had been smelling: whiskey.

Jesse's secrecies and disappearances. Jesse's popularity with the men, all the visits, but all so quick. The ugly look from the clerk's wife at the commissary. How they didn't go to church. How she'd thought to make turpentine like she'd done in Alabama, figuring Jesse would be glad, but what he'd said was, "Don't go beyond the ridge." How often he went hunting, yet how little game he killed. How measly, how unloved the vegetable plot was. How nice their house was, though nearly lost in the pines, and in a gulley, a gulley that everyone called Sugar Hill.

Night visitors for three weeks, and then one day Jesse hitched up Chester and Smokey and stayed away three nights. When he came home, it was behind the wheel of a black Model T, with only Chet hitched behind. The noise brought Dixie Clay outside and she put a hand to her eyes to admire the car against the sun. He laughed to see the wonder on her face. Jesse must have swerved a bit on the road, as a sprig of bridal veil bush was fretted into the grille-work. She squatted to slide it free.

"How does it work?" she asked.

He showed her beneath the car's hood, let her sit in the passenger seat, modeled how to set the throttle — "This controls how much gas goes into the engine" — and adjust the choke. In front of the car, he bent to crank it with his left hand, his turquoise silk four-in-hand flapping over his shoulder.

"What do you think?" he yelled over the noise.

"Can I try it? Please?"

Jesse chuckled. "Maybe not, squirrel. This machine cost two hundred and sixty dollars." He slid into the car and turned it off, pocketing the keys.

Dixie Clay wished she'd had a chance to say good-bye to Smokey, rub his floppy black-edged ears, but mostly she was wondering where Jesse would keep the keys.

What Jesse didn't know was that while he'd been finding his car, she'd been finding his still. She'd followed the path over the ridge, the sweet medicine smell growing, and discovered a low, rusty shed of corrugated metal, slanted like a house of cards. Inside the dust-mote gloom was a chain of fifty-five-gallon steel drums, each attached to a smaller keg with an elbow of pipe that was attached to another steel drum, and so on, for about fifteen feet — field hands lifting heavy pails. Dixie Clay peeked under a lid and the fumes backhanded her and she dropped it. Then, turning her head and taking a deep breath, she lifted the lid again, studying the thick bubbling sludge, a few mosquito hawks dead on the surface. The last drum must have lost its lid, for it was covered only by a sheet of rusty metal. When Dixie Clay lifted that, she saw a dead squirrel in the bubbling mash. She'd scooped it out with the metal sheet, flung it into the woods, and returned to the house to brood.

Now, in the slow of the afternoon with the purple hulled peas coming to a simmer on the stove, she sat at the secretary with a glass of lemonade to write her weekly letter to her father and brother. This time she could tell them about the Model T. Lucius had been so smitten with the first automobile they'd seen that he'd chased it for a mile, and the next day he sketched motorcars in the church hymnal until the choirmaster boxed his ears.

But if she wrote about the Model T, she'd have to explain where the money came from. She laid down her pen. When she picked it up again, it was to write about the weather, and in this way she said good-bye to her home, good-bye to her papa, the man she had yelled for at the age of eleven when they were hunting and she'd looked down and seen blood on her saddle, blood on the pommel, but she hadn't cut herself or her horse — this man whom she could go to even with that, and who turned their horses homeward and went upstairs and fetched his dead wife's elastic sanitary belt and then had stood outside the bathroom door and explained to Dixie Clay how to pin the cotton gauze — to this man, she wrote about the weather. Good-bye, good-bye.

And good-bye to Jesse, too, in a way. Certainly good-bye to the dream of Jesse. For maybe if she'd confronted Jesse the night he'd driven back in the Model T, they might've been able to find a kind of honesty, damp kindling that wouldn't warm much but would be something to stretch their hands toward. But she didn't, wishing him to tell her, so she waited, pretending she didn't know, and went on mending his shirts and frying his eggs. He still came to her cold fingered in the night, but she enjoyed it less. Before, what she took as his hunger for her made her hungry as well. But now she felt she could have been anyone to him. Still, she never refused. *A baby a baby a baby,* she chanted inwardly to the gentle thump of the headboard.

After a year of pretending to be stupid, she was stupid. One evening, she came to, near the henhouse, startled to see a porcupine waddle just a few feet from her toes. Had she been still so long she'd given the impression she was a statue or a tree? The basket of chicken feed balanced on her hip, her fist sunk into it, and she raised and flexed her dusty fingers. She remembered the girl who'd shot the panther and traded its speckled skin to the handsome stranger, and she recognized neither herself nor the stranger. She remembered also how she'd thought his two different eyes made him look like two different people, like that turn-around doll, and understood how right she'd been. He was two people, but she had only married one. And the one she'd married was never facing out.

And so the night of her eighteenth birthday (he gave her a silver brooch and a thimble engraved with her initials; he liked to buy elegant gifts), she made Jesse a business proposition. He'd just returned in the Model T and was tugging his leather driving gloves off as he climbed the gallery steps. From his smile, she guessed he'd made a big sale. She met him at the top. "Teach me how to cook that moonshine," she told him. Jesse finished removing the second glove and paused.

"You can't cook it steady and deliver it, too," she continued.

When he looked up, his eyes were keen, and she realized how long it had been since he'd really bluegreen looked at her. "Well,

well, well," is what he said. Then he slapped the gloves against his palm. "Alrighty then."

So in this manner the Jesse Swan Hollivers entered the business phase of their marriage. The following evening, Jesse showed her the shed where he stored the corn, bran, yeast, and sugar. He taught her to mix the mash and ferment it and cook it off, to heat it just to the point where it would steam but not boil. The risen steam threaded through the arm pipe and into the thumper keg for the double run, filtering out any solids, and, now pure, coiled into the worm pipe and condensed in the worm box of cool water. Jesse filled an aqua Ball "Perfect Mason" fruit jar from the spigot at the barrel's bottom and took a sip and swallowed hard. "Wildcat whiskey," he said, holding it up. "White lightning. Mountain dew." He swooped a thumb under the end of his mustache and flicked it into its curl, then repeated the gesture on the other side. He looked at her, as if considering, and held the jar out, but she shook her head.

The next morning found Dixie Clay hurriedly tossing the chickens their scratch as the sun, like a yolk, slid over the pines. Nor did she spend time on Jesse's breakfast: he could have bread and cheese. When he strolled to the still later, he found her scrubbing the drums with steel wool, wearing an old hat and a pair of his trousers. By midnight she had her first batch bubbling. By the following week, she was experimenting with flavors, adding plums to a specialty batch, adding Dr. Pepper to another. She sampled those early batches to learn from her adjustments but never grew a taste for it. Jesse couldn't deliver it fast enough and ranged farther and farther, to Columbus and to Clarksdale (the cathouse there put in a standing order for her woodchip-flavored whiskey). In a few months, Jesse would ship whole barrels to New Orleans from the Hobnob dock. Even in this, Jesse had style. He loaded them in plain sight but had them painted first with fancy gold cursive: *Mississippi Turpentine.*

Whether people thought Jesse was still cooking the shine, or whether they assumed he'd recruited some knowledgeable distillers, she didn't know and didn't care. For her the pleasure was in the process, in busy hands and rows of jelly jars purring Ball-all-all. After her first twenty-three months of marriage, the paralysis of waiting, the nights with her backside raised, waiting for Jesse to plant the baby who would make her life start, the baby who called for her once in a dream and left her hugging her stomach —

she finally had something she could point to, she could build on. She was patient and she was thrifty, the same girl Bernadette Capes had taught to use egg whites for meringue and egg yolks for mayonnaise, and now when she scraped cobs, she used half the kernels for creamed corn and half for the still. She increased production by applying a bandage of bread dough to the cap arm to prevent escaping steam. She hung the green-checked curtains intended for the nursery on the wall of the still, to pretend she had a window. When she finished a batch, she lined the baseboards and shelves of the storage shed with jelly jars. Before leaving at dawn she'd open the door and look back at the work of her hands, the bottles glowing in the morning sun like the lights on the barges pushing down the Mississippi.

She hardly saw Jesse. Once, a few months into her career as a shiner, he came in as she was pouring sugar into the bowl to start the ferment. He said, "How come you're not measuring?"

Dixie Clay shrugged. "I eyeball."

"How many cups of sugar you reckon you just poured out?"

"Four," she said.

"Exactly?"

"Exactly."

"You're sure?"

"I'm sure."

So Jesse lifted the measuring cup from its nail on the wall and withdrew a knife from his boot and flicked it open. Then he dug the cup into the bowl of sugar and leveled the knife across. "One cup," he counted as he dumped it back into the sack. Dixie Clay was holding her breath. "Two cups . . . three cups . . . four." And the fourth was level too, and not a grain left in the bowl besides, and Jesse had clapped her on the back and said, "You're okay, Dixie Clay."

She grew even more okay. Her whiskey became the best in Washington County. So clear you could read a newspaper through it. About that time, Jesse stopped making the deliveries himself, instead taking on runners who'd motor the *Jeannette* up to their dock. Jesse's specialty became "client consultations." His was the face, his was the voice recognized by the guards through the door gratings of speakeasies. He spoke easy. He spoke highball stingers, Charleston bracers, cholera cocktails, orange whiskey sparkles, locomotives, whiskey smashes. He came home smelling like whorehouse. Strange how little Dixie Clay minded, tossing his clothes in the washing machine.

Jesse'd bought her the washer. He wanted to use her time wisely. She had orders to fill. Sometimes Jesse asked if she didn't want to take on some workers. Skipper Hays and his son Gabe, for instance. But Dixie Clay said no. That's how bootleggers got caught — sooner or later they'd whiskey brag or skim or double-cross or rat or shoot each other's fool heads off.

And then, for no seeming reason, it got harder to stay up all night in the still. And harder to stir the bubbling mash, to let that poison curl into her nostrils. More than once she forgot if she'd already added the yeast. Then one night she fell asleep on a stack of grain sacks in the shed and let the still overheat — not just ruining the batch but coming close to exploding the still. When she was a girl, a still in Chilton County had exploded, killing five brothers. See, she was acting odd, unlike herself. Maybe she was sick. It wasn't the influenza because she had seen it in 1918 and knew it came on faster. But still, Jesse said the next doctor who came to buy hooch would give her an exam. And so one did. She was with child.

"Your brother. He'd have been your older brother," she whispered the strange thought to Willy, who'd been sleeping on the thumper keg. Willy's faint eyebrows twitched, he was waking. Good, she'd missed him. She slid her hands beneath him, warm and soft as dough risen in a bowl. She lifted him onto her shoulder and swayed and sang, *Trouble, trouble, trouble, I've had it all my days:* it was the cowboy's song she crooned in Willy's seashell ear, and together they waltzed around the still.

CHAPTER 7

The morning after drinking with Ham and Jesse, Ingersoll woke late into a helmet of headache. After a minute, he swung his feet to the floor and twisted his shoulders and bowed and arched his back, each movement giving its own pop or snick. The bathroom was down the hall so he gathered his towels, looking forward to the hot water but not to pulling dirty clothes over his clean body. He promised himself a new getup today. When he opened his door, he nearly tripped on a bundle, which turned out to be a new red Henley shirt and stiff dungarees, and balanced on top, a party favor — a small waxed envelope of BC Headache Powder.

Ham could do that. Could surprise you.

After showering and dressing, Ingersoll walked downstairs, and he found Ham standing before the hall tree in clean clothes as well, with a new oyster-colored nutria hat that he blocked in his fingertips and then pressed on his springy red hair. They met eyes in the mirror and Ham grinned.

"I know you're too fond of that old brown derby to part with it," he said.

"Can't say I fancy a new hat, but after bacon and eggs we could buy us some new boots." Ingersoll raised a bare foot. He'd left his wet boots steaming on his radiator, beside the long, limp tongues of socks.

"No bacon and eggs for us, dewdrop." Ham gestured to the door of the dining room where a sign read BREAKFAST 6 A.M. TO 8 A.M., SHARP! and beneath that, in cursive, *Mrs. Stanley Vatterott.*

"Ah, hell."

Ham shrugged. "Banana?" He lifted a large bowl from the sideboard and set it on the coffee table, and Ingersoll snapped a banana from the bunch, peeled it, and ate it in three bites, then another. The boarding-house was quiet, just the ticking of the Mora clock standing in the corner, all the engineers already on the levee.

"Catch me up," said Ingersoll.

Between bites of banana, Ham told him about arriving and taking his supper with the other roomers, eight men around an oblong table, Mrs. Vatterott at the head ordering a poor Irish housegirl thither and yon. A few of the boarders were newspapermen, a few government men, and a pair of Atlanta engineers. It was these on whom Ham eavesdropped discussing the flood level, now a record fifty-three feet. They were overseeing the building of mud boxes — planks nailed together and propped up by sandbags — to fight the wave wash. But they didn't think the levees would hold, despite the fact the levee commission had halted the car ferry. The engineer on the right said his wife had asked him to return home, and he was going. "The flood of 1922 only reached fifty-one feet," he said, "and we saw what happened there."

The engineers were discussing the weakest spots on the levee, and the best location to have dynamited the meander bend, *if* the deal had gone through and the town accepted the bid from New Orleans. Ham saw one of the engineers tip up a battered flask so when the *Times Pic* reporter on the left excused himself, Ham slid into the empty chair. They chatted for a bit about the Braves, and before long the flask was passed his way, just a spit-sip left but delicious. Where can I get more a that, Ham had asked. The one who was heading home said, Try Club 23. Who should I speak with, Ham pressed. "Local man named Jesse is in charge," said the engineer. "But he won't sell it to you directly. Ask for Mo, the manager, an Arab."

So Ham had gone scouting, turning down a brick alley by Freeland's law firm and knowing he was getting closer when he found a red high heel in a puddle. Beside a high stack of wooden crates, a reinforced door opened just enough when he knocked for a password to thread through. In place of a password, Ham found a twenty worked fine.

He didn't have to work to figure out who was Jesse. The whole joint seemed centered around him, the piano player angling his mouth to croon in Jesse's direction, the bartender polishing a glass and holding it to the light, Ham was saying, as if for Jesse to admire his crystal-clear face. "Strange how a small man can command a room," said Ham, peeling another banana.

Ingersoll grunted. He was recalling the restaurant the night before, how Jesse had sent a round of drinks to a table where the police captain's high-crowned navy hat was propped on the corner of the banquette. A single finger was raised in acknowledgment of the whiskey, a single finger raised in acknowledgment of the acknowledgment, like Pat Collins ordering up fastballs from Herb Pennock.

"What happened then?" asked Ingersoll.

Ham said that he started drinking with some engineers and made like he engineered, too, not a difficult bluff after their bridge detail in the war. Jesse made rounds like a politician, and Ham offered him a drink, and Jesse said, "No, I'm buying *you* a drink," and before long they were round for round and agreed to have dinner the next night. Ham didn't get anything much out of him but knew, sure as a cat has a climbing gear, that Jesse was their ticket to the moonshining.

By now Ingersoll had eaten three speckled bananas, and Ham had eaten three speckled bananas, and they'd each eaten a green one and regretted it. The Irish housemaid pushed through the swinging door from the kitchen and saw the men and the peels, like a ball of winter snakes, and gave a squeak and flapped back through the door.

Ham watched the freeze-frames of her skinny backside hurrying away. "I'd like to fatten her up. Feed her a potato."

"Ham, everything you say sounds nasty."

"You arse licker. Not everything." Ham grinned. "Now, to business. Let's hit the town."

"Don't you wanna hear what happened with the baby?"

"You got rid of it, didn't you?"

"Yeah."

"Then what's to hear? Come on."

In Ginsberg & Levine Dry-Goods, they each bought a Coca-Cola and a bag of Planters Peanuts and shook them into the bottles and sipped as they examined the footwear. Ingersoll favored cowboy boots but needed something watertight and lifted a leather lace-up from its display.

"Floodproof?" Ingersoll asked the clerk, who was pulling up a trapezoidal wooden box, a stool he used while fitting the customer.

"Not entirely," said the clerk. "But that one is." He gestured with his chin toward the highest platform of the display, lumberman's boots with vulcanized rubber bottoms. Ingersoll upended the boot and whistled to read $4.25.

"I hope you got some of your Hoover dollars left," Ham said, "and didn't spend 'em all on baby duds."

Ingersoll bought the pair and then returned to where he'd been sitting to pull them on. Ham, having tried and rejected the other three models already, stretched his legs and wiggled his toes in his socks.

"I'll take the same," he said to the clerk.

"And they better be waterproof as a frog's ass. Size 11 right foot, size 12 left."

The clerk, stacking the boxes Ham had heeled away, looked up. "I can't sell them like that, sir," he said. "Unless you wanted to buy both pairs."

"Now, why would I want to do that?"

"But, sir —"

"I got different-size dogs. You gonna discriminate against me? Got different-size balls, too, for that matter. Hey," he called brightly to Ingersoll, "you think that's related?"

Ingersoll, wearing his new boots, walked to the door but not before he heard Ham's next gambit: "Why, sure you can sell the mismatched pair. Bet you have a whole posse of one-legged veterans hopping around. Unless . . . this is a town of dodgers?"

Ingersoll crossed the gallery to the barrel, lifted his old cowboy boots in the air, soles flapping good-bye, and dropped them in. He knew Ham would emerge shod and shit-grinning. Meanwhile, he lit a cigar and leaned against the post and gazed at the sky the color of old dimes sliced by a levee that banked around the river's curve, higher than the two-story buildings the next street over, and he thought of living next to such a structure, a massive mound of earth walling out the mightiest of rivers. Until it couldn't anymore. The river took a turn much like this below New Orleans, at a place called Poydras. In the flood of '22, the levee had collapsed at the Poydras bend and a wall of water 115 feet tall exploded onto the land, flooding Plaquemines and St. Bernard Parishes. It was what saved New Orleans that time around. But what would save New Orleans — what would save any of them — now? The river had already exceeded the '22 record levels, and "water in sight" — the upriver tributaries — showed the crest was still about a week away.

Ham stepped out in his new boots, pants tucked inside, and roostered down the gallery to Ingersoll. They mounted the horses and snugged their hats on, Ham his new and Ingersoll his old. It felt heavy, and he wondered if it would ever dry out. Or if he would. He should have bought another BC Powder.

They rode along Broad Street, past the McLain Hotel, along a row of parked cars, to the bottom of the levee, where two white men in yellow slickers stood beside a third sitting in the cab of his truck, a rifle propped on his knees.

"Who're y'all?" asked the guard with the rifle.

"Engineers," Ham said.

The guard nodded, so they nudged their horses up the incline behind another pair of men who were using a bullwhip to drive a soggy mule, a pallet roped behind it and piled with sandbags.

At the top, Ham pointed. "You head right, and I'll head this way. Make friends and listen sharp." They'd already decided not to search for the still, reckoning it was on Jesse's land, and searching might alert him. Better to see if they could sidle into the operation sideways, probably by befriending some of the distributors. Over the years they'd found this worked best. They'd come to a new town, taste the shine, and say, "Shit, you call this whiskey?" And then, because they knew their stuff, "This run was allowed to boil." Or "Look how fat these bubbles are — might as well be drinking ginger ale for all the alcohol in it." And soon enough, the shiners would approach them.

Ingersoll and Horace picked their way along the muddy road that topped the levee, with its line of poles where lanterns would illuminate the rain come evening. To Ingersoll's right, the commerce of Hobnob, its dock and railroad station and town hall and smokestacks. To his left, kicking up spray, the waves of the Mississippi, looking more like an angry ocean than any river. It was unsettling to have it so close when one got used to seeing the levee slope down at a forty-degree angle to a giant ditch, and beyond the ditch, a flat, cracked, red soil floodplain, an acre or two across, scrub trees wrapped with detritus from last spring's rising, broken bottles and rags of burlap and rotted wooden crates. Now the river actually topped the levee and only the sandbags held it back, and still it was lapping, lapping, lapping in, like the sea at high tide, closer to your feet with each wave. *Sea of Mississippi,* he thought. Was that a song? Should be. He wondered if his guitar was warping, coffined up in that locker in Memphis. He thought of that taterbug mandolin he'd discovered on Dixie Clay's porch while waiting for her to return. He'd tuned it a step and a half below standard so he could play the blues keys.

Ingersoll slid off to take a piss, leaning back on his heels for purchase where the grass was slicked down like the hair of a balding man, and he could feel the levee wavering like a struck tuning fork. Horace felt it too and flicked his ears as a big wave

181

slapped the levee just ahead of them and sent a flange of spray over their legs. Horace danced sideways and nickered. Back in the saddle, Ingersoll laid a palm on the horse's neck where a thick vein pulsed. He allowed Horace to turn them and trot forward, which felt better. Not that they could outrun the river if the levee blew.

He thought of Dixie Clay and the baby. How safe were they? That house was plenty close to the river. Still, he recalled her with that gun braced at her shoulder and figured they'd be okay somehow.

Ham still thought he'd dumped the baby in an orphanage in Greenville and he felt uneasy about that. But Ham didn't seem to want any details.

"Shh, now, it's okay," he said, to himself or Horace he wasn't sure.

He rode along, each post propping up a guard. Often he slid down, especially where men were gathered, discussing the closing of the bridges at Flannery and Wyatt. What he was listening for he didn't exactly know. He perked up when the first guard offered him the same whiskey he'd drunk with Jesse, but later he realized all the guards had that whiskey. And they were all on edge. "Hope one a these foggy nights some Arkansas bastards make it across and try the part

I'm guarding," said Bill Griffith, the former shoeshine, now a sandbagger as the whole town had pretty much decided to hell with shined shoes. Bill rattled the cartridges in his pocket and rocked back on his heels. "Damn right," said another.

"Boil!" came a shout down the levee. "Boil! Boil!"

Ingersoll ran with the others to the geyser, thick as a man's arm, water shooting twenty feet into the air. They grabbed sandbags and heaved them at the base of the boil, stacking them around the bubbling sand to create equilibrium. The water bounced down to head level, then knee level, then fell with a splash. The men stood watching as if it were a tunnel to hell. "A dirty boil," said Bill. "Punched a hole through the levee." The others nodded grimly or dragged sleeves across their faces to wipe the water that had splashed there. After a few more moments, Bill spat on the bubbling mud and turned and they all trudged back to their poles and resumed guarding.

When it was one o'clock, the train station whistle blew for a shift change and the men bandy-legged down the slick levee, converging on the makeshift mess in the train depot. This would be a good time for eavesdropping, so Ingersoll joined them.

About a quarter of them were Negroes, milling about, waiting for the whites to eat first, and they looked and sounded so much like those he'd known in Chicago that he felt oddly homesick. The carbide lamp glazed the broad forehead of a one-armed man he could have sworn used to flip burgers at BBB, and another, whose long face was bisected by a wide mustache, like a barber's comb, could have been the brother of a harmonica player who owed him a fiver. And for all Ingersoll knew, they *were* brothers; many Chicago Negroes started in Mississippi before booking passage on the *City of New Orleans* to the City of Big Shoulders. So as Ingersoll passed the sandbaggers, he kept hearing familiar expressions — not "it's going to rain," but "it's fixing to," not "I can barely lift it," but "I can't hardly" — someone pulling from a lunch pail exactly what he'd expect, a drumstick wrapped in a napkin transparent with grease, someone else with a guitar under the station overhang and strumming what Ingersoll could strum better, Alberta Hunter's "I walk the floor, wring my hands, and cry."

Ingersoll knew enough not to linger. These Negroes didn't meet his eye, stopped playing if he came close. And why shouldn't they? Somewhere just out of sight was a

National Guardsman with a rifle whose sole job was to make sure they didn't join a band in Chicago.

Back when Ingersoll had been in Chicago, there was less division because the Negroes had something the white folks wanted. Music. Ingersoll had wanted it, too. He started sneaking out of St. Mary's Foundling Home for Boys at the age of eleven, hopping the cable car to Indiana Avenue on the South Side, then going round back of a blues club, crouching in the alley beside the kitchen door propped open with a brick. It smelled like piss and stale beer, and once as he sat nibbling an apple with his legs outstretched, a rat darted right over his boots. But with the blues rolling out of the door, Ingersoll didn't care. The joint was called the Lantern, a Negro club, but adventurous whites started showing up in giggling groups, drawn by rumor of this new music. And pretty soon young Ingersoll was such a familiar face in the alley that if the bartender needed a bucket of ice or the cigarette girl ran out of Chesterfields, he'd be sent to fetch and rewarded a penny. And after maybe six months of that, he was in the kitchen sometimes, carrying crates of lettuce from the delivery truck, taking the garbage out. Then six more months and he was busing tables, the house now full of whites. Sometimes he'd be sent to tell a wife to collect the passed-out husband who'd spent her grocery money on Irish whiskey.

Ingersoll liked best the chores that kept him at the front of the house so he could hear the music of Lizzie Looey and the Lo-Downs, five Negroes playing the blues better than anyone'd ever played the blues. In exchange for free drinks, Skinny Nellie, the guitarist, taught Ingersoll blues licks between sets. When Skinny played a solo, Ingersoll became almost hypnotized, sweeping the same emeralds of a smashed bottle back and forth as he aped Skinny's chords on the broom handle. He liked to watch Lizzie, too, stuffed into a blue sequined dress that popped in the spotlight, an ostrich feather headband that vibrated when she hit the worried note, that flattened fifth. The crowd would slap their hands until they stung. When the clapping stopped, she might smile. It was a famously slow smile. It began in the middle like a red curtain drawing back and kept going until two bright rows were displayed, lots of red gums, and then it went in reverse, also slow, the curtains closing. That was the only time Don, the manager at the Lantern, ever got on Ingersoll — sometimes after Lizzie finished a song and the audience hooted and rose to its feet, Lizzie smiled that slow smile and Ingersoll'd forget that he'd been sent to change the toilet paper in the gents', or fetch a box of swizzle sticks from the storeroom. He'd stand there, blocking the view of paying customers.

He was learning more at the Lantern than at school, so he quit. Sister Mary Eunice heard and she found him out back of St. Mary's hanging the nuns' wet habits on the line, giant black ovals, as if they'd peeled away their shadows. Laundry was his favorite chore because he'd lug the old Grafonola outside and wind it up and listen to records of Ma Rainey, only fourteen when she made her debut, one year younger than he. Sister Mary Eunice stood beside him and reached into the basket and they worked together in silence for a while. When all the habits were hung, she turned and put a hand on his shoulder. "Would you pray on it, Teddy?" He loved her too well to lie and lowered his head and pushed his hand into his pocket and withdrew the money he'd made since quitting school. She looked down at his hand, her wimple rippling folds of flesh at her neck, sighed and accepted the money and walked slowly inside.

Monday through Friday he earned $1.50

a day working in the sausage department of Swift's Packing Company. He hated the slaughterhouse reek that wrapped him like a scarf as he stood at the 'L' stop, stamping his feet against the cold. But after work he'd take the Stock Yards 'L' from Packingtown to Indiana Avenue, the club now filled to bursting with rich white customers who thronged to hear Lizzie Looey's ragged, wrenching voice.

And then came the night when Skinny fell off the stage drunk and broke his wrist. The band was about finished with their last set so they wrapped things up but stood arguing at the door as they'd promised to play a rent party at 2 A.M.

"Ain't nothing we can play without a guitar," said the drummer. He took a last drag on his cigarette and then flicked it toward Ingersoll. "Ask the white boy."

No one did exactly, but he got his coat and stepped outside and they were waiting for him by the cable car and he climbed on. They talked and passed a bottle and he listened and drank from the bottle, and then they were at an apartment building in a Negro neighborhood. "He's with Lizzie," the drummer told the doorman collecting dimes. "White boy can play."

Inside the sweat-sharp apartment, furniture stacked against the wall and the rugs rolled up, a buffet of pig's feet and biscuits in the kitchen, Negroes were dancing to the radio. The band set up in the living room and Lizzie began by giving him the notes but soon saw he didn't need them; he could play any song he'd heard them play. He played with his eyes closed and forgot he didn't belong. His fingers belonged. The band passed the hat at break and paid the host's rent and split the rest, and at dawn when the milkman opened the gate of St. Mary's, Ingersoll was right behind him, possessor of four dollars and a note asking him to meet a girl named Denise at a diner on Wabash.

There were eight nights with Skinny gone that Ingersoll played with the band at the Lantern and two more rent parties, as it was the end of the month. While he played he stood beside Lizzie, just out of the spotlight that lit up her dress and the smoke like drifts of Chicago snow. He studied her red lips bending the notes because, he told himself, she *was* the blues, the way she sighed, a bridge of sighing between lines, every line like something she was tearing off and throwing away, almost chewing her words, or moaning them, nothing precious, coming in late, so loose, changing her own lyrics for no other reason than she wished to, so loose, so loose. He was missing that part, the part where you sang like you had nothing better to do. He was precise, nimble, pitch-perfect, maybe too perfect, and sometimes on the 'L' home he'd open his jaw wide and it would pop because he played with clenched teeth.

On the eighth night, after the show, he bent down to pick something up, not a dime, which might be what it looked like from the audience, but one of the beads that had leaped to its death from the blue spangled hips of Lizzie Looey, and when he stood light-headed, he realized he was in love with her. He glanced at the door where her skirt was swishing through and he knew she knew.

On the ninth night, Ingersoll came determined to announce himself. *Lizzie, I love you. You are thirty-two and I am sixteen, but when we're eighty-six and seventy, it won't matter.* He couldn't imagine ever being seventy or Lizzie ever being anything but what she was, soft brown arms with the vaccination scar high on the left shoulder, a divot he wished to stroke with his guitar-callused finger.

But when he reached the Lantern, he heard a bassoon like a man's baritone, though there was no bassoon in Lizzie's band. He pushed inside and the bassoonist was talking to a tall yellow Negro running a brush against the reeds of his harmonica. Ingersoll ran past them and found Don in the storeroom, counting cases of gin.

"Where's Lizzie? Where's the Lo-Downs?" Ingersoll asked, aware his chest was heaving.

Don took a pencil from behind his ear and wrote on one of the cases. "Got a new band now. Skinny's wrist ain't better, and Lizzie and the rest of them lit out for St. Louis on tour."

"No —"

"Yeah. Thanks for helping out. You're bar back again, kiddo. If you could grab a case of —"

But Ingersoll was through the door and leaping onto the steps of the cable car he'd ridden to that last rent party, which he knew was in Lizzie's neighborhood. Off at the stop and running down the street past faces that turned to watch him then turned back to see who was chasing him. He expected to hear her voice coming from a saloon, but instead he glimpsed a flash of her coffee-colored legs crossed in a coffee shop window and skidded and ran back and yanked open the door. Lizzie.

She sat with a friend in a booth and didn't seem surprised to see him. He stood over them panting and finally blurted, "You are thirty-two, and I am sixteen, but when we're eighty-six and seventy, it won't matter."

It sounded all wrong. He was going to lead up to that.

Neither of the women looked up.

The friend snapped a quarter against the Formica beside her cup and peeled her legs off the vinyl and scooted down the bench. "Tell Sam and Jake ten o'clock," she said, and then was gone.

Lizzie lifted her face, the skin beneath her eyes plum colored and tired. She looked different, older, in a tan dress and jacket, wearing a little tan hat. He waited for her to say something, but she just looked down again and tapped her fingernail against the handle of her mug.

Should he sit down? He stayed standing.

Finally she said, "You could live a hundred years and I could freeze at thirty-two and you'd never catch up to the years I done lived."

"I'm a fast learner, you said that yourself. Remember, the Chippie Hill song?"

She didn't answer, so Ingersoll continued. "Take me to St. Louis."

"No."

"Please. I want — I want to play with the band." That seemed the most he should say now.

"It's no offense. But you can't play with the band. You ain't got the right style."

"It's 'cause I'm white."

"Naw. But I noticed that."

"It's 'cause I'm young."

"Naw. But you're pretty young."

"It's 'cause I don't like being looked at."

"Naw. Though that doesn't help."

"What is it, then? What's wrong with me?"

She picked up a crumpled straw wrapper and began straightening it between her fingers, *zzzzzt, zzzzzt, zzzzzt.* Finally she said, "You ain't got the blues."

"Lizzie," he said. She kept drawing the paper between her index and middle finger. "Lizzie," he said more loudly, and now she looked up. "I'm an orphan. I got nobody and nothing that won't fit in a guitar case. If I disappeared, hardly a soul would notice."

"Huh," she said, not unkindly. "And you still ain't got the blues." Then the curtain of that slow, slow smile opened.

"What's it take?" Frustrated now. He caught his reflection in the mirror above the booth, his face red.

"Oh," she said, the curtain closing, slow

slow. "I guess you gotta lose somebody you love. But first, you gotta love."

"Lizzie —"

"Go home, son. Go home now. Just . . . go on home."

When he descended the 'L' stairs by St. Mary's, he faced a door with a poster on it of Uncle Sam jabbing a finger at him, a poster he'd seen and not seen dozens of times. He crossed to the door and pulled it. It opened only a few inches before it got stuck on its doormat. With a mighty yank, Ingersoll wrenched it open and walked inside. He was too young, of course, but being an orphan meant there was no paper-work to prove it. When he walked out, he was Private T. Ingersoll of the United States Army.

And somewhere, probably in a battlefield in Flanders, lay the blue spangled bead wrapped in the handkerchief that he'd carried his first two weeks in the war, the war he'd imagined he'd return from with medals pinned to his broadened chest, a chest he'd clasp a swooning Lizzie Looey to, at which time he'd present her with the bead, holy relic of his holy war.

The bead had fallen on the battlefield. But *he* hadn't fallen. Many of his friends had. Those friends had true sweethearts, some of them, loving mothers, some of them; a few even had children. But it was unloved, orphaned Ingersoll who made it through, losing nothing but the bead.

And his illusions. When he got back from the war, he didn't even try to find Lizzie. Or anyone, really. Sister Mary Eunice had died of a stroke when he was fighting. Even St. Mary's Foundling Home for Boys had shuttered its doors, which he learned only when his letter had been returned, a letter with a five-dollar bill asking the nuns to buy instruments for the boys. He'd moved on, partnered up with Ham, from place to place picking up new assignments and new gear, everything expendable, even themselves.

The train station whistle blew, signaling the end of break. The sandbaggers passed their plates down and the person at the end scraped what few scraps remained, and the men pushed away and muttered to each other as they stood and stretched and huddled back up the levee, leaning into the wind, one man slipping and another grabbing his elbow and righting him.

Ingersoll rode Horace up the levee behind them. At the crest, he peered out at the seething water, which seemed to have risen even since he'd last laid eyes on it. He remembered standing beside Lizzie's booth and telling her that if he disappeared, hardly a soul would notice. And not much had changed. *If I were to fall into this river and be swept away, I don't know who would care.*

Well, Ham would care. He'd have to train a new partner.

The thought of Ham training someone reminded Ingersoll of the missing agents, Little and Wilkinson, and he shook his head as if to fling any distractions out of his ears. He hadn't recalled Lizzie Looey and that foolishness in a coon's age. Why was he thinking of her now? He wished he understood better how the pieces of his life fit together. Would another man with these same pieces see the whole picture? In the army he'd taken the Stanford-Binet exam. His high score, and his marksmanship, had distinguished him somewhat. But having certain kinds of smarts didn't necessarily make him smart, he'd come to figure. He seemed to have blind spots. His heart was one.

"Okay, now, Horace," he said, and turned the horse's nose into the wind to push forward along the levee. "Let's catch this revenuer killer and move on. I'm about ready to get clear of Hobnob, Mississippi."

■ ■ ■ ■

He never heard anything interesting that day, nothing to indicate a large distillery was functioning nearby, no whispers about two missing revenuers, nothing he could report to Ham. He slept for a few hours after dinner and rose at 11 P.M. to the knock that he'd requested, the knock followed by the footsteps of the Irish housemaid fleeing down the hall. He bathed and then rode Horace to the levee for the shift he'd volunteered for, midnight to dawn.

Ham often teased him about being a creature of habit, and it was true that whenever Ingersoll arrived in a new place, he followed a pattern. First he'd get a shave, and he'd stroll around the town. The ritual seemed to make strange places less strange, him less of a stranger.

So when his shift ended at dawn, he rode Horace down the levee to the livery, which now serviced automobiles as well. He tipped the Negro a quarter to be extra nice to the horse and then dragged himself to the barbershop and sat in the last chair along the wall to wait with the other men, the *Democrat-Gazette* spread over his face, resting his tired eyes while the fellows talked of the flood, now at fifty-three feet, six inches, and talked of the failed buyout, sometimes bitterly, and joked about Ingersoll, "the sleeping Yankee," who wasn't sleeping of course but listening. The barber was a big Dutchman named Kamps. He'd been a Flooder and all his customers were, too. One street over, the other barbers, Fisher and Wirth, were Stickers.

With his newly shaved, lime-scented cheeks tingling in the brisk wind, Ingersoll surveyed the town square, centered by a courthouse with a broken clock. A druggist on one corner, a department store on another, a bookstore and a hardware store on the third, and McMahon's diner on the last. The people tried as people do for normalcy, old men still on the benches with canes leaning on their inner thighs, their pipes and applesmoke, and shopkeepers sweeping in front of their stores, trying not to look at the sky again. But the music store advertised a flood sale, and the bowling alley marquee read BOWLED OVER BY LEAKS GALORE. CLOSED UNTIL FURTHER NOTICE. And what else was wrong? No young voices. No boys shooting marbles in a chalk circle on the sidewalk, no mothers pushing prams.

He ate chipped beef at the diner come noon, trying *not* to listen for once. At the table behind his stool, the woman was weeping, about to board the train with her two sons to evacuate to Birmingham, the husband staying behind to see to their farm.

"This might be our last meal together," the woman nearly wailed.

"Shh, Alma, shh, now. We're all gonna be fine," he said. "I'll fetch you soon as I'm able. Corn'll be tasseling out before you know it."

Ingersoll pushed his plate away.

The waitress — not the one from two nights ago, but her older sister, maybe — swooped away his plate and asked him if he was a levee guard. When he nodded, she slid from her apron pocket a flask and quirked an eyebrow. When he nodded again, she poured a splash into his coffee, and he gulped it as he stood and yanked on his coat.

At the livery, freshly curried, Horace turned at the sound of Ingersoll's voice. Ingersoll fastened the cavesson under Horace's chin, thinking whatever, wherever his next assignment was, he'd probably have a car, but he wouldn't mind a horse if it were this agreeable.

He didn't see Ham that afternoon, and that evening when they met up at the Vatterott, they each confessed to learning little. They slept for a few hours and then parted at the levee at midnight with shrugs that were anxious and grim.

Finally, at dawn, Ingersoll did learn something interesting.

The station whistle sang out and the workers began sliding and hopping down the levee, Ingersoll alongside them. They were moving as a herd to the street to cross over to town when a wheeled doughnut cart came careening around the corner and nearly crashed into the lot of them and halted. The man pushing the cart was blocked by doors painted with the slogan DON'T BE MISLED! DEMAND THE ORIGINAL BROWN BOBBY GREASELESS DOUGHNUT! 25 CENTS A DOZEN! The men had begun to sullenly skirt the cart when the doors sprang open and there on the counter sat a case of Black Lightning half-pints. A great cheer went up among the workers. "Sandbaggers' special!" yelled the vendor, and instantly a line formed. One of the lucky first customers walked by, tilting his head to nibble the hot doughnut ringing the neck of his half-pint.

"Capa! John Capa! Gimme a bite a yo doughnut," called someone at the end of the line.

"Shit. Give you a bite a my skinny nigger ass."

The men laughed and Ingersoll laughed with them and reached to his pocket to pull out a cigar when he felt a sudden presence at his elbow.

"Ingersoll," said Jesse with a nod. "I thought you'd still be at the Vatterott, sleeping off our debauch of a few nights ago."

So Jesse had learned where they were staying. "Naw," said Ingersoll, resuming his reach and pulling out a Natchez cigar that betrayed the curve of his chest. At least all the rain kept it from drying out. He found another sad curved cigar and offered it to Jesse, who shook his head.

"What are you about?" Jesse asked.

"Levee engineers should be engineering the levee, don't you think?" Ingersoll put the cigar between his lips and flicked a match and held it to the end. "But I'm surprised to see you out here." He dropped the match into a puddle, small hiss.

"Well," Jesse shrugged, "I got me two bucktoothed sisters from Arkadelphia in the honeymoon suite" — here he thumbed at the McLain Hotel to his right. "Thought I'd give 'em a ten-minute break so they don't get too sore." He lifted a half-pint of Black Lightning from his pocket and took a drag and offered it to Ingersoll.

Ingersoll exhaled and took it, nodding his thanks.

"Want me to see if the sisters can find you a sister?"

"Not while I'm working," said Ingersoll.

"Suit yourself."

They watched another satisfied customer prance by, this one with a bottle in each hand, turning his head to nibble one doughnut, then the other. A sandbagger tried to cut in line and there was a scuffle and he was pushed away, spinning to a stop in front of them.

Ingersoll handed the whiskey back to Jesse. "You don't seem very worried about Prohibition around here," he said, doing some quick math on the profits from this line of a hundred workers.

"Prohibition don't seem very worried about us."

"No revenue agents around these parts?"

"None that stay long."

"How's that?"

"Can't say for sure. Maybe they learn it's all small potatoes around here, no stills worth busting. Or maybe they head on back where they belong because they don't enjoy our company." He took a drink. "But some folks find us good company. You, for example, seem to be fraternizing with the locals."

There was a strange bite to the word *fraternizing*. Ingersoll glanced at Jesse, who was still facing the whiskey line. Then with a pivot, Jesse stood in front of his face. "Like my wife."

Ingersoll lifted his chin to blow a funnel of smoke, considering what Jesse could mean, scanning his recent encounters — he'd been there when Ham had flirted with a gal at the lunch counter and the soda jerk hadn't liked it — but there was nothing to occasion this. Finally he said, "I think you've been misinformed."

"Misinformed?" Jesse's eyes seemed to spark.

"I've been working. I haven't been messing with any women, Jesse."

"Not unless you call riding out to a man's house and giving his wife a baby messing."

There were no words. He felt his throat close as it had when he'd choked on the whiskey. Jesse's eyes danced all over Ingersoll's face, his face round and stupid as a doughnut.

"I took her a baby." He almost croaked it. "It needed a mother. You weren't home to ask."

"And you didn't see fit to tell me this

while you were snorting good whiskey all over the menu?"

"I hadn't put it together yet," said Ingersoll. "Who you were."

"And now you know. Who I am."

"Yeah. Now I know."

"Don't forget it." Jesse turned and walked straight at the whiskey line, which parted to make way for him then closed around him again, blocking him from Ingersoll's view.

CHAPTER 8

"You're my best friend."

It was a strange thing to tell a baby, but that's what Dixie Clay found herself saying. He'd been hers for five days. Willy was lying on his back on the afghan between the wide V of her legs. She would lift her hand high in the air and wiggle her fingers and he would watch, rapt, and then she'd make a clucking sound louder and louder as her fingers crabbed closer to his chins, which she'd tickle. "Gimme your sugar," she'd say. "Such good good sugar." He could barely stand it, pulling his legs into his chest and huffing happy air. After a dozen rounds or maybe more, he looked off to the side instead of at her waggling fingers, which meant he was tired, and she picked him up. Usually when she did this his little back was alert, such effort to lift that big noggin on his stalk of neck, but now he let it thunk onto her shoulder with a little puff ball sigh.

She was learning him so well. He was teaching her so well. Amazing, she thought, they'd never even exchanged a word.

After a while it was time to feed Willy and she did that, too, on the afghan, though it now would need a washing. She'd like to order a high chair from the Sears catalog. There were plenty of layette items she'd like to order from the Sears catalog. She had the money. Well, Jesse had the money, but she had earned it. There were rooms in her head, and one of them was a dangerous room because she was decorating it for Willy. In this room, there was no Jesse.

After Willy ate, she fixed him a bottle of milk and walked him out to the gallery. She began the bouncy walk and didn't look down, didn't need to, to know when she crossed the dime-sized bullet hole in the floorboards after she'd missed that revenuer's pack of Lucky Strikes. *Dear God, let the revenuers turn up somewhere far away and alive.* This was the second thing she'd said this morning that surprised her. She didn't talk to God, hadn't since Jacob died. Because after the funeral, when she'd gone to the kitchen to return the borrowed clothes, she'd overheard Mrs. Vatterott say, "Isn't it a shame that little baby was never baptized, so he can't go to heaven." Dixie Clay was too much outside, or beside, or underneath herself to absorb this statement at the time, but she'd reflected on it plenty in the days to come. *Fine, if my baby can't go to heaven, then I won't go either. If Jacob's not there, it wouldn't even be heaven. I'll stay below with him.*

She'd vowed to stop praying. It had been hard at first because prayer was a habit, but every time she caught herself, she'd made a little tourniquet of her thoughts. But now with Willy here she couldn't quite stanch the flow. And she no longer knew if she should. *Thankyouthankyouthankyouthankyou. God.*

Long shadows of the pines fingered toward the gallery and she walked through them with Willy quiet on her shoulder, avoiding the earthworms that had squirted out of the waterlogged ground. She checked the box but there was no mail. Why would she expect any? She'd gotten her weekly letter from her father just yesterday. The cowboy ghosted through her thoughts, and she flung the mouth of the mailbox closed. She had Willy, she had everything she needed. And she sank onto the gallery rocker to wait for full dark to go to the still, where he was such good company, sleeping or awake.

She'd had company at the still only once

before, and it hadn't worked too well.

This was two years ago, after Jacob's death. She'd grimly resumed shining. One dawn, Jesse yanked open the still door and stood scowling at the harsh smells and bubbling rumbles.

"It's brighter than a bitch outside," he said. He walked to a case, batted open the flaps, withdrew a jar and squinted at the shine, slid it back into its coffin. He was sober, irritable; he made her nervous. He lifted the lid off the heating mash and was smacked with a faceful of steam, and he coughed and clanged the lid down.

He grabbed an empty mason jar and went to the spigot where some hooch was making its final run through the worm coil. He tasted it and then leaned into the barrel of buckwheat bran and levered the scooper full. He was about to toss the bran into the whiskey when Dixie Clay cried, "Wait!"

"What?" he stood with the scoop hovering over the mash.

"I added it already."

"What about the cake of yeast?"

"Yeah, it's in." *Obviously,* she wanted to say. They stared at each other balefully. She remembered Sundays after church when her father would come snooping about the kitchen. "Too many cooks spoil the broth," her mother would say, and wave him away, and likely as not he'd grab a pinch of the tender meat on his way out, or give her a saucy pat on the bottom, or both, and her mother would say "Shoo now," trying to sound annoyed but smiling as she whisked the gravy.

Jesse poured the scoop back in the barrel, then turned and leaned against it. "I'm changing the recipe."

"What? Why?" Dixie Clay pushed the hair that had come loose from her braid out of her eyes. "Have there been complaints?"

"No, nothing like that. Opposite, in fact. I'm busy as a stump-tailed cow in fly time."

"Then what's the problem?"

"Can't keep up. So we're gonna switch from corn to only sugar, double our yield. All over Washington County everyone's already done that."

"But it's as bitter as gar broth."

"Dixie Clay," he said, and let out his breath. "Don't sass me. Can't you see I'm tired?"

He did look tired, actually, despite his new pink suit. His green and blue suits did better to ice down the ruddy in his cheeks as well as bring out one eye or the other, but he liked pink and yellow suits because he'd read that Al Capone favored them. Once he told her admiringly that Capone had the right pocket of his suits reinforced for the weight of a revolver.

Dixie Clay pressed her lips together and kept straining the whiskey.

Jesse continued, "From now on, we use sugar only, we ferment for three days instead of a week, and we stop this overpurifying," he said, gesturing to her sieve.

Dixie Clay kept straining.

"One other thing. I've got you a helper."

Now she looked up. "A helper?"

"I've sent for Uncle Mookey. Should be here tomorrow. That way you'll move faster." Jesse pushed off the barrel he was leaning against and brushed his palms against each other, bran pollen dusting to the floor.

"Uncle Mookey? From Louisiana? But — didn't you say he was touched?"

"Right-ee-o. But he's easy to work with. Does everything I tell him to. Everything." Jesse opened the still door.

"Jesse —" But he was gone, the door slamming so hard that the oak and willow branches she had crisscrossed over the tin roof for aerial camouflage slithered down with the noise of a chain going over a gunwale.

He wasn't really Jesse's uncle. Mookey

and Burl were twins who'd lived next door to Jesse's father, Julius, in Concordia Parish. They'd all gone to school together, then later they left together to serve as dough-boys with the U.S. First, earliest of the American Expeditionary Forces at the western front, and they'd vowed to their mothers that they'd look after one another.

But according to the story Jesse told, back when he told her stories, Julius, Mookey, and Burl made it out of France, but it took just one weekend back in Louisiana to ruin all three. It was spring of 1918, the German troops already faltering. Telegrams found them where they were stationed at Belleau Wood: their fathers had the Spanish influenza. The sons hurried home on leave. By the time they'd arrived in New Orleans, their fathers were dead, and Julius, weak-lunged because he'd been gassed at the front, took the influenza, too. He was sent direct to Camp Beauregard, Louisiana, where they'd been trained, to be looked over by a doctor at the general hospital. As soon as he arrived the whole camp was quarantined. Julius was dead within twenty-four hours of touching American soil. Jesse, a teenager, hadn't seen his father in two years, and now saw him in a coffin spiky with gladiolus.

Neither Mookey nor Burl fell ill. They attended the funerals of their father, and Julius's father, and then Julius's, helping to dig the graves because the gravediggers couldn't keep up with all the corpses. In five days' time they were ready to return to the front. At the train station in New Orleans, Mookey wearing Julius's Sam Browne belt, they hoisted their duffels and kissed their mother, who stood weeping into her handkerchief. The train pulled clanging alongside them and blew its whistle, and Mookey fainted. Out cold, for no seeming reason. When he came to, helped up by Burl, he couldn't talk at all. Damnedest thing, said Jesse. Couldn't even form words with his mouth, the mouth just used now for breathing and eating as if it had lost that other function entire. Also, his brain seemed different. He was, folks whispered, simple. Mookey was evaluated by an army doctor who diagnosed him with the Shell Shock and prescribed six months' rest and physical activity in the woods around the camp.

Burl returned to the Aisne Offensive, but his first night at the mess some of the squaddies were talking, saying Mookey was faking so he wouldn't be sent back to the front.

"The way I heard it?" Jesse said. They

were in sitting in bed, Dixie Clay leaning back on Jesse's chest, the first year of their marriage, must have been one of the first months of the first year. Jesse was rivering his hands through Dixie Clay's sex-snarled curls, and when he found a tangle he'd spread his fingers and work it loose. "Burl leans over their table and says, 'Call my brother a coward again, I'll cut your tongue out for you.' And the guys all look at each other and it gets real quiet and then a big tough from upstate New York, guy named Otis with a good-looking mug, crosses his arms over his chest, looks up and says, 'Coward.' So Burl kept his promise."

Jesse was laughing though Dixie Clay was not. It'd grown cold in the room and she pulled up the sheet. "What happened to Burl?"

Jesse was still smiling. "Bunking in Angola."

"Angola? Landsakes, Jesse."

"Well, there was that tongue incident, which got him discharged, and later he had what you'd call a tough time readjusting to civilian life."

"And Mookey? What happened to Mookey?"

"Uncle Mookey stayed on at Camp Beauregard. Never said another word. The day his R&R ran out, he picked up a broom and began work as a night janitor. Been there ever since."

Until, that is, he'd been summoned by Jesse for another nighttime cleanup.

The next evening when she arrived at the still, Mookey slid out from behind a tree twenty paces off. She recognized him from Jesse's description, "bald, fat, and white, like something you'd see squirming if you lifted up a log in the forest." He wore dungaree overalls that were straining at the sides, revealing a crescent of white flesh between buttons, the chest bib pulled low to tent the giant belly.

"Hello?" she said.

He made no gesture. His head was bowed, and the moon glinted off his shiny pate.

"Um . . . Uncle . . . Mookey?" She waited, then moved to the door, gripping the key in her fist, and she didn't turn her back to him as she unlocked the latch and hurried to light the lantern.

He followed her inside. Jesse must have instructed him, because he set about flipping fifty-pound sacks of sugar over his back, unlike Dixie Clay, who had to wrestle first one corner of a sack onto the hand truck and then the other. The boxes of mason jars he stacked and carried four at a time. When it was time to fill them, he fished one from its cardboard compartment and handed it to her just as the jar she was filling brimmed, which he removed with his other hand, not a drop spilled. Together they worked deftly, but Dixie Clay was anxious. Mookey never met her eyes. When she looked down, she'd feel him studying her, but if she lifted her face, his vacant gaze was on the wall. Near dawn, when a squirrel landed loudly on the tin roof, she jumped and upset an open jar of shine. Before she could grab a rag, Mookey was mopping it with a bandanna pulled from his overalls.

It was a relief when a crack of light caned beneath the door. Dixie Clay stood and stretched. "Well," she said. "Time to hit the hay."

He went to the wall where she'd hung two brooms, the old corn broom and a new plastic one that had a dustpan suctioned to its handle. He lifted down the corn broom and the battered tin pan.

"You don't have to," she said.

He stood, looking down.

"You must be tired."

But he simply set to sweeping. She watched his broom puff its small clouds, and then she turned and walked into the dawn.

That evening, when Dixie Clay was putting up the baked ham studded with apricots, Jesse said, "Fix a plate for your uncle Mookey. He's staying in the still now."

"Jesse," she said, "please let's not. He gives me the heebie-jeebies. I like working alone. Please, Jesse, I —"

"Goddamn it, Dixie Clay. The man's family."

If he is such family, she wanted to say, *why make him sleep in the still?* Instead, she pulled in a breath and said, "I've been thinking of how to make more money for less whiskey. If we —"

"You make more money by cooking more whiskey. Besides, you're the one who said you didn't want a partner because he'd start blabbing. Well, I found you one who can't blab." Jesse plucked an apple out of the bowl and backed through the swinging kitchen door taking a bite and called back from the parlor, "Now fix that man a goddamn plate." She sawed off a hunk of ham and loaded the plate with the apricots on toothpicks and deviled eggs and potato salad.

At the still door, Dixie Clay thrust the laden plate at Mookey, who took it and slid down the wall and squatted on his heels and ate it — like a dog, Dixie Clay was about to

216

think — but in truth he ate delicately, using his bandanna for a napkin, as she'd neglected to provide one. She waited with her arms crossed and when nothing but a picket fence of toothpicks remained she thrust her hand for the plate, but he rose and walked through the blinking fireflies to the stream where he washed and dried it before returning it to Dixie Clay.

That night was the same — no talking, as if muteness were contagious. Of course Dixie Clay normally shined in silence, but with him there the silence felt awkward. If she spoke, how much could he understand? While she pondered, they worked efficiently, shoulder to shoulder, as the corn planting moon rolled over the tin rooftop. Though Mookey was huge and the shack was small, he somehow never got in her way. He moved lightly on his feet, like a boxer, or a dancer.

Jesse made another rare visit to the still around dawn. He'd just gotten home, was Dixie Clay's guess. He opened the door and stood blinking at the lantern-lit, tidy industry. There was nothing of Mookey's in the still except a tight bedroll in the corner and a toothbrush in a mason jar.

"Well, well, well," he said. "Like little shoemakers, you two. I mean, like the elves who made the shoes while the shoemaker slept. Or whatever." Dixie Clay watched him counting the full boxes, two and a half rows stacked to the ceiling. He smiled. "C'mon, Dix," he said. "You can knock off now. I'll walk you in." He angled his elbow out for her to slide her hand in.

The swish of the corn broom began as they walked away. It was a nicer sound than the plastic broom, she thought, the wooden handle comfortably sunken, bearing the indentation of her fingers.

The third night was the same. Shining shining shining in silence.

The fourth — when she opened the door with one hand, Mookey's dinner in the other, the lanterns weren't lit and from the waning moon's low blue light over her shoulder she saw Mookey rise from a squat where he'd been pouring himself a jar. He left the spigot running and stumbled toward her, tears on his face. They surprised her so much that she didn't step back until she realized he was coming for her. She dropped his plate and turned to run but too quickly his hands were about her waist, sliding around her back. He thrust his face into her neck and she felt the wetness from his tears and his hot squeezing breath and he shuddered his thick lips against her skin. She screamed and he lifted his face and she threw her elbow into his jaw. He dropped his arms then, and she whirled and ran to the house.

She arrived panting, and when Jesse asked what happened, she told him.

Now it was Jesse's turn for muteness. He yanked the napkin from his collar and marched to the gun rack and lifted the Winchester and set off down the path. Dixie Clay, suddenly scared, danced about him, begging him to stop, think, be reasonable, the man was family, he was simple, he was drunk. When they were in sight of the still, she pulled on his elbow and he whirled and lifted the Winchester and crashed the butt down on her shoulder. She crumpled backward, landing hard on her tailbone. He yanked open the door and the shack was empty. Mookey had run. Jesse crossed the floor and lifted something off the thumper keg.

"See this?" he asked.

She looked up from where she was crawling to her knees. Jesse held a mason jar crammed with roses, pink-veined damasks from her bushes by the gallery. "This is why we called him Kooky Mookey, back in Concordia Parish," said Jesse. He lifted the jar and then pivoted like a pitcher catching

219

someone stealing home and threw the vase against the wall. It exploded, and the thick glass bottom, like a crazed monocle, came spinning by and he kicked it away. Then he turned and marched past Dixie Clay, who was climbing slowly to her feet, pulling on an ash tree. Jesse's voice scaled the ridge. "Courting a goddamn married woman with her own goddamn roses."

What was there for Dixie Clay to do but lift the corn broom from its nail and sweep the dinner plate and meatloaf and green beans and mason jar and roses into a pile of ruination. Then she wedged the corn broom against the wall and kicked it in the middle, and then she fed both halves to the fire.

She returned to the house and Jesse was gone. She poured herself into bed. She stayed there all the next day, lying on her side, as her tailbone and shoulder purpled. She counted herself lucky that her collarbone didn't appear broken, then smiled grimly at what she counted as luck. Jesse kept away and she hoped Mookey had evaded him, had faded into those woods that Jesse said he'd crawled from or found his way back to Camp Beauregard.

The following day she doubled a blanket on the saddle and gingerly sat down and rode Chester into town, gritting her teeth when he jostled her over the railroad ties. At the stationer's, the clerk tried to talk her into something flashier, but Dixie Clay held firm, much to his displeasure. She rode back on Friday (she still had not seen Jesse) and picked up the labels. They were gray with a black border and, in the center, a small black lightning bolt. She also went to the dry-goods store and picked up the high-shouldered bottles she'd ordered, eight cases. She paid with money from an oatmeal canister filled with tens and twenties she'd found in the pantry. If her plan worked, she'd repay it. If not, well, she'd figure that out later.

She rode home and mixed a paste with flour and water and dredged a label through, like dredging a chicken breast through bread crumbs, and smoothed the label across the bottle, pressing out the air bubbles, until she ran out of bottles. She filled the bottles and stoppered them, and then she waited for a customer. When one came — it was Ron Shap, a state representative — she showed him the bottle and shook it so the bead could prove its strength, the bubbles small in size and slow to disappear. She opened it and poured a fingerful in an etched glass. She watched him toss it back without a grimace and catch the drop running down his gray whiskers and suck that drop off his finger. "I tell you what," he said, and leaned back in his chair to run his thumbs beneath his red suspenders. "Got reelection coming up. I'll take as much as you got."

"You can't afford as much as I've got," she said.

He laughed and looked at her over his spectacles and said, "Try me."

"Four-fifty a bottle."

"Four-fifty!"

"Too low?" She cocked her head and tapped a finger on her cheek. "Should I charge five?"

"Don't you know I can buy it off Skipper Hays down the road for a dollar?"

"I do. And don't you know — Hays uses denatured alcohol, cut with embalming fluid, mixed in a bathtub that hasn't been scrubbed since God invented soap. Could blind you or kill you or both, and all for just a dollar."

"Come now, missy."

Dixie Clay stoppered her lips and the bottle.

He softened his voice. "Did Jesse tell you to charge so much? Surely we can meet in the middle, just you and me? How about I give you two dollars. You can go to the picture show all week on that. Buy yourself a hair bob for those pretty curls."

"Four-fifty a bottle, and if you won't buy it, maybe Wright Thomas" — the other candidate — "will."

Ron Shap hesitated and Dixie Clay popped the bottle back in the box and stood. "Good luck with the reelection."

He snapped his suspenders and stomped to his feet and out to his truck, where his driver was waiting with the tailgate down. From the front window she saw Shap kick his tire and get into the passenger seat and slam the door, and then get out and slam the door and kick the tire again and raise his fists to the sky and bellow, "Wright Fucking Thomas!" Then he marched up the gallery stairs and bought all eight cases.

And was reelected.

From that day forward, Dixie Clay made smaller batches and charged as much as she liked, no amount too much, and Jesse never again badgered her to change her recipe or take a partner, and Black Lightning became so famous that sometimes the very invitation to a wedding or convention or Klan rally would bear a zigzag bolt to brag that no expense had been spared.

As for Uncle Mookey, he was never seen, never mentioned again, though Dixie Clay often thought of him. And over these past three years, she began to view his behavior, her behavior, differently. She wasn't the same proud girl she'd been, prettiest in all the piney woods, or so folks said, engaged to the prettiest fellow. She saw now that she'd married Jesse while knowing only the pretty part of him. She'd read so many books she'd simply filled in the rest.

She'd paid for it, though, would spend the rest of her life paying for it, and her loneliness had schooled her, scored her a little. So now, when she thought of Mookey, she wished she'd found a way to look beyond his oddness and be his friend. Wished she'd been less frightened, wished she'd been older, wiser, kinder. Wished she'd said, Thank you, thank you for the roses.

CHAPTER 9

Waiting for Ham to come out of the shower, Ingersoll was on his knees picking up the dried mud Ham had tracked across Mrs. Vatterott's carpet runner the previous night. When Ingersoll had finally returned after his shift and his run-in with Jesse, Ham hadn't come back yet. A note taped to the door announced: *There will be no bananas whatsoever in tomorrow's fruit salad! Mrs. Stanley R. Vatterott.* If she hadn't guessed who'd eaten the bananas that first morning, and who'd cleaned out the bowl yesterday when again they'd missed breakfast, she'd certainly guess who'd laid the boot prints because they led, the right slightly smaller than the left, to Ham's door.

As Ingersoll gathered the clods, he recalled Jesse beside the doughnut cart saying "my wife." Christ, had he missed it the night at the restaurant, had there actually been a point when Jesse had referred to her by name? No, Ingersoll would have heard those words, *Dixie Clay.* Had Jesse mentioned having a wife at all? Ingersoll couldn't recall. Too goddamn drunk. And he'd gotten too goddamn drunk because he was trying to forget the woman who just happened to share the bed of the man he'd been sitting across from. Christ, he felt sick about it. He did recall that when he'd first come to town with Junior and stopped at the store and asked where he could find a family that might take in a baby, the woman had referred to Dixie Clay as a married woman. That the man she'd married was a lounge beetle and a high-pillow sharper and most likely a bootlegger and perhaps a murderer must have slipped her mind. Christ, Christ, Christ, and Christ.

Ingersoll had done some things he wasn't proud of, but he'd never messed with a man's wife and wasn't about to start.

Ham came down the hallway now with the towel clutched around his waist, his great hogshead chest pink from scrubbing and squiggled with hair. "Good man, Ing," he said, stepping around him. "Saw that mud this morning and thought, Shit, it's about as clear as cat turds on a marble floor." He chuckled and went into his room, calling back, "In a minute let's talk."

Ingersoll wasn't looking forward to telling Ham how little he'd accomplished on levee patrol. He'd learned a new song:

> I works on the levee, Mama, both night and
>   day.
> I works so hard to keep the water away.
> It's a mean old levee, cause me to weep
>   and moan.
> Gonna leave my baby, and my happy
>   home.

He'd sampled a lovely sarsaparilla-flavored whiskey from Jesse's still, and earned a sore tailbone on Horace, and about renewed his acquaintance with trench foot, but that was it.

He could only hope that Ham had proven more effective. Often, when Ingersoll struck out, Ham came through, or vice versa, and that was why they were effective partners. Ham could tease out a man's secret through cunning, buffoonery, or charm. Ingersoll could learn it by disappearing, an oak of a man blending into the forest until you forgot the oak had ears. Together, separately but together, they could always find the rotten apple, the rotten worm in the rotten apple. And then they'd be on to a new job. By the time the newspapermen ran up with their cameras and flash-lamps, they'd be eating miles in a Pullman while some local prohi got his mug in the paper, axe biting into the barrel stave. Ham would grumble about missing the finale, studying his profile ghosting over the corduroy cornfields. "Always hustling me outta town before the reporters come" — and here Ham would take a pouty pull of their souvenir bottle from the smashed still. "Why, they're just jealous, that's all, not only of our bloodhound noses for whiskey, but of my fine coiffure and matching muttonchops, which be the color, says Miss Tulsa, of an August sunrise."

Ingersoll, head back on the doilied seat rest with his hat over his face, would murmur, "Sure, Ham, whatever. Let's get some shut-eye."

"Burns me up, just thinking about all them grateful antisaloon suffragettes dying to rub their emancipations all over me."

"That don't even make sense, Ham. Shut up, now. Okay? Just shut up, and let's sleep."

And on to another place, different but the same. A shame, really, ruining fine whiskey. Just meant someone else needed to cook it up all over again. And revenuers deserved their reputation for being as crooked as the men they jailed. He'd never seen one yet turn down a bribe — except for Ham, that is. Ingersoll knew they were proud of being unbribable. God, they could be rich, had they chosen that route. So what, though; they barely had time to spend the money they did make.

Revenue work seemed about the only thing he was suited for after the war. Armistice came and he was sent home on the RMS *Carpathia,* the ship that had rescued the survivors of the *Titanic.* He spent the passage playing blackjack with the crew, some of whom had been on board in 1912 and told stories of the rescue. Ingersoll wondered where to go after *his* rescue — he'd land in Hoboken in a few days. Back to the orphanage? No can do. Back to school with know-it-all bespectacled milkshake-slurping boys still warm from their mother's laps? Not hardly. Back to the stinking meatpacking factory? No, it smelled almost as bad as the trenches, and besides, newspaper said the meat-packers were talking of striking. Well, what were his skills?

Let's see. He could duplicate any blues song after hearing it but once, don a gas mask in less than five seconds, and score nine bull's-eyes at rapid fire on an eight-inch target at three hundred yards in a minute's time, which included reloading the rifle with its clip of five cartridges. What else? In the trenches, guarding no-man's-land, they'd run out of water, thirsty like they'd guzzled beakers of sand. That was when his mate, Christopher Tuffo, sprinted with the platoon's canteens all the way to the river to fill them. He was sprinting back, the canteens bouncing against his thighs, when one of the canteens, French issued and shiny, caught the sun and therefore a sniper's eye and therefore Chris was shot two hundred yards away, dancing like a scarecrow before snagging on barbed wire and hanging like a scarecrow, and what Ingersoll knew was how to wait until dark, wait through the hours with Chris calling, "Come get me, boys, I got your water, got it right here," and then Ingersoll knew how to dash to him and unhook his skin and lash him to his back with his belt and carry him and the canteens back to the foxhole where Chris could bleed to death on Ingersoll's knees while drinking clean rivers of water. Ingersoll knew that, all right. It was a thing he knew and knew.

So when he landed in New York, he hung around the blues clubs waiting for something to happen, and that's when Ham happened. And somehow they'd been revenuing the better part of a decade. They'd managed to keep themselves out of the newspapers, though they'd risked their identities once last year when they came across the worst criminal yet, Pastor Bobby Gate, a Protestant minister and a Kleagle, and, though the Klan was staunchly Prohibitionist, the biggest bootlegger in Indiana. This trinity was impressive even to Ham and Ingersoll, who figured they'd seen everything. Gate was grooming his two converts, he thought, to his church, and to his Klavern, when he learned about their service in the war. He bragged to them of lynching a colored doughboy, still in his uniform. Can you beat that! the pastor cackled. Still in his uniform! With all his fancy medals! Nigger in the uniform of a U.S. soldier, refused to give up his gun!

Ham and Ingersoll didn't discuss much, but the next day was Sunday and they rose early and found the minister alone in the woods behind his house, standing on a stump, practicing his sermon. He wouldn't give up the names of his still workers, the ones who'd helped with the lynching. Ingersoll and Ham had had to persuade him, with the help of the axe in the chopping block with a few chicken feathers stuck to it.

Before they left town, they stopped by the

Indianapolis Times to drop off a carton that contained photos, and the minister's Kleagle robe, and his Bible with the names of his fellow Klansmen on the flyleaf, as well as the three-volume book the minister had been proofing for the printer, *Inspirational Addresses from the Pulpit and the Second Imperial Klonvocation, Including Burial Rituals for Klansmen, Instructions for Indoor Klavern Crosses, and Klankraft Exams for Those Wishing to Advance in Rank or Degree.* And the minister's pinkie.

They'd gone on a weeklong bender after that and were in South Bend infiltrating the Nanni brothers, who ginned for the big, merry priests of Notre Dame, when they were pulled off duty by the commissioner and loaned to Hoover, sent to the flooded South. Of course, ever since August of last year they'd seen dishrag-colored clouds being wrung and wrung over Nebraska and Kansas, South Dakota and Oklahoma, the nation's breadbasket soggy and disintegrating, Iowa and Illinois, Kentucky and Ohio. By September, the rivers had overbanked Peoria, four dead, then more rain fell, seven dead, washing out bridges from Terre Haute to Jacksonville. The Neosho River hopped its banks and bowled through Kansas. A tree toppled into an oil pipeline, ten more dead, and then the river was a river of fire, and now the damages were in the millions. Fifteen inches of rain fell in three September days in Iowa, flooding fifty thousand acres around Sioux City.

By then it was October, the dry season, and still fell the rains, the Illinois River at its highest in history. The rain turned to snow, thirty inches in Helena in a day. By Christmas, railroad traffic was suspended over the river, and the gauge at Vicksburg read forty feet at a time when it normally read zilch.

And then the snow melted. The Ohio flooded at Cincinnati on January 28. In early February, the White and Little Red Rivers flooded a hundred thousand acres in Arkansas. New Orleans got six inches of rain in twenty-four hours, and local floods in the Mississippi Valley killed thirty-two. In March, more snow fell, from the Rockies to the Ozarks. And between March 17 and March 20, three tornadoes swept through the Mississippi Valley, killing forty-five while the preachers did a record business, what retributions for our sins, O my Lord, O my Lord. Have mercy.

No mercy to be had. All these lands, all these rivers drained into the mighty Mississippi, and it had spread and spread, eaten up its batture, barrow pit, and berm. Although the Mississippi River Commission maintained that the eleven hundred miles of levees, each mile of levee containing 421,100 cubic yards of earth, could withstand the scour and fury, river towns were quaking. They set up guards in tent cities. Where there wasn't enough levee left to hold tents, shock troops were housed on barges, helmed by veterans of the Great War, the American Legion running levee kitchens to feed everyone. Foremen were white, of course, and the blacks were building the levees higher, bricking walls of sandbags or buttressing them with banquette planks, trying not to get shot or get gone, swept away into the river.

Ingersoll stood and moved aside as two men rushed down the boardinghouse hallway — the Atlanta engineers Ham had chatted up, from his description. One man was dressed and hatted and carrying a valise, the other still in his robe. Ingersoll dumped the mud clods into Mrs. Vatterott's potted plant and dusted his hands. From inside Ham's room his gruff humming paused, which Ingersoll knew meant Ham was shaving his throat. One time in Galesburg Ham had gashed his neck while singing and came to breakfast with a white plaster like a priest's collar and growled, "Sliced my Adam's apple so bad I'll be bleeding cider for a week."

The engineers stomped down the steps, and at the bottom of the landing, the dressed engineer opened the door. He turned and said to the other, "You're a fool, Kenneth. A goddamn fool."

He looked up and saw Ingersoll standing by Ham's door and yelled, "All of you! Fools!" and whirled about and slammed the door.

The commotion brought Ham out of his room, dabbing a bit of lather from his neck with a towel, wearing his not-quite-so-new clothes. Kenneth was climbing the steps slowly and looked up at them and shrugged.

"He's probably right. My wife will be furious. But I can't seem to walk away from a job once I've started it."

"Why his problem?" Ham wanted to know.

"I'm married to his sister. He tells me he'll have to take care of her when I'm blown up."

"Blown up?"

"Yeah. Didn't you hear? About the explosives?"

"What the hell?"

"Last night in Greenville, undercover

police had the train station surrounded, because fifty pounds of dynamite were stolen from Camp Beauregard in Louisiana and smuggled on the train to Greenville."

"Jesus. What happened?"

"When they boarded in Greenville, the explosives had already been removed. Snuck off at a prior stop."

All three were quiet as that sank in.

"Who are they saying is responsible?"

"No one knows who stole it. And no one knows who received it. But everyone is panicked about what saboteurs could do to the levee with fifty pounds of dynamite." Kenneth moved on down the hall. "We all better pray for a clear night, so the saboteurs don't have cloud cover." He stopped and shook his head. "You know, I am a goddamn fool," he said, then continued toward his room.

Ham opened his door and Ingersoll followed him in, saying "Jesus."

"I know. We'd better reach Hoover. I was already planning to telephone him to say we can't wrap this up in a week, that we need more time."

Ingersoll nodded.

"He'll be expecting us to check in after this bit of news," Ham continued. "I'm guessing our job description has been revised to include saboteur catchers."

"I wish we had something to give him. About the still, if not Little and Wilkinson."

Ham had been sniffing out the Stickers, knowing that was Jesse's side, but all he found was a bunch of down-on-their-luck farmers who felt they should struggle and die on the same land where their parents had struggled and died. "I talked to about everyone, and I didn't find anyone with enough gumption to be a federal agent killer," Ham said. "What'd you learn, Ing?"

Not much, though he'd been in the barbershop when the police captain drove by in a new Packard, red spokes on the tires and the word POLICE painted on the side. The other men in the shop had snorted at the sight of it.

"Mighty poor town to be setting up the captain in a fancy new car," said Ham.

"Captain's on the take." Ingersoll turned the cane-back chair around and swung a leg over. "But we'd guessed as much."

A pause grew as they worried about Hoover. They wouldn't use the phone downstairs — it was a party line, with three rings to indicate the call was for the rooming house. They'd have to find a private line, maybe at the post office, and wait until Hoover could be reached at whatever train station he'd be visiting.

Ham opened the drawer of his nightstand and removed a leather grooming case that he must have purchased at the dry goods. He set it on a Bible marked "Property of Mrs. S. R. Vatterott — Do Not Steal," and slid out small scissors and a bone comb and angled a round shaving mirror so he could see his face. He swiveled his head from side to side and trimmed a few stray hairs that were coming in white and of a coarser texture than his coarse red muttonchops. Then he set to combing the chops, and Ingersoll knew he was pondering what they should do.

"Okay," Ham said. "We'd better ratchet things up. It's time to confirm that the still's on Jesse's land, and see if we can spot who's working it, and get them to talk. One of us needs to do that, the other phone Hoover."

The cane-back chair was fraying and Ingersoll tried to press an errant straw back into its weave. He didn't want any part of either.

"I'll telephone Hoover," Ham decided. He clicked the scissors closed and slid them into their case.

So Ingersoll had to go to Jesse's house — her house. "No, I'll find a telephone. You go to his house."

"Naw," said Ham. "I'm tired a horses. Hate the way they smoosh my gems." Ham reached a hand into his pants to give them a shake. "I'll be sterile as a mule, and the world devoid of little Hamsters." He removed his hand and lifted up the mirror to admire his grooming. "You ride on out. But be careful. Somebody's out there cooking the shine while Jesse's goosing the coat check girl. And that somebody's probably nervous as a pig at a barbecue."

"Everybody's gonna be nervous, once word of the explosives gets out."

"After I reach Hoover, I'll go to the levee. We better pray that there's no fog until Hoover has time to send in more agents. Jesus, Ing, fifty pounds of dynamite. And army issue, so it's probably old, sawdust soaked in nitroglycerin and then wrapped in wax paper. The sticks weeping all to shit, crystallized, the case never turned over once, is my guess. And now it's here." Ham was sitting on the bed, his gray eyes narrowed, staring at the wall as if a vision of Armageddon were projected on it. They'd seen photos of Dorena, Missouri, after the levee had collapsed. Houses on concrete blocks were simply swatted away. Houses on foundations filled with water. Folks had rushed to their attics and then axed holes through the ceilings to climb out onto their roofs, where they'd been rescued. Or some of them had. And that was Missouri. This far south, river at fifty-four feet and the flood crest bearing down, it would be much, much worse.

"You'll have to figure out where Jesse lives," Ham continued. "I know it's out in the country a far piece, south of town. Place called Sugar Hill. He doesn't sell from his house anymore, but he doesn't know we know that, so if you happen to get caught, say you come to buy hooch."

If Ham had been looking in the mirror instead of slipping the grooming case back into the drawer, he might have seen a struggle on Ingersoll's face. Why he didn't tell Ham he knew the house, knew the wife, he didn't know, but his instinct was to hide the fact that just over a week ago he'd been there, trying not to get shot by a firecracker of a gal who didn't come up to his shoulder. Hell, barely came up to his ribs, he thought, and remembered the two of them standing close and looking down at Junior's face.

For something to do, he brushed Ham's muttonchop trimmings off the bed with the back of his hand, then walked to the window. They were on the second floor with a good view of most of the square, the people below rushing to work. Outside, he saw a newspaper gust by and tent itself against the face of a suited man, who flung it aside, where it landed on the face of the man behind him.

Ingersoll rose. "See you at dinner."

He was a staid horse, Horace, without a levee trembling beneath him. He plodded along under Ingersoll, splashing through gutters that were like small streams, breaking stride only to jump the whirlpool over the sewer grate by City Hall where a turtle circled helplessly. Ingersoll hated to see it and raised his head to the loud crows on the telephone wire, looking like notes on a music score. Christ, he missed his guitar. After a few years as partners, he and Ham had acquired a Ford. They'd confiscated it from bootleggers, who'd installed an extra gas tank to hide whiskey, and Ingersoll reconverted it so they could drive twice as far without gassing up. There'd been nights, plenty of nights, when he and Ham had driven through strange country. Usually Ham rode shotgun but sometimes they'd switch so Ingersoll could reach an arm through the window and pull his guitar from the rope on the roof. He'd taught himself to play left-handed, the neck out the window, belting the blues into the air frisking him at fifty miles an hour. He'd like to be holding it now, that lovely Slingerland May-Bell acoustic, style number 5.

Might as well add it to the list of things he'd like to be holding.

The pavement ended and the telephone line, too, and patches of woods alternated with cornfields where the wind gusted stronger, tugging a tear from Horace's eye. Ingersoll gave up trying to light his dime cigar. This Natchez tobacco wasn't for shit. Best thing about it was the box, which featured Alcazar — now that was a beautiful horse. "Nothing against you, Horace," he said and patted his mount's neck. He should have kept that box and built himself a throwaway guitar.

The rhythm of the horse took him into reverie, and he found himself picturing his return to Dixie Clay's, in his new clothes, riding down the drive and her running with Junior in her arms to thank him. Ingersoll would say —

A horn spooked him, and he shook his head as a Ford swerved around Horace. *Don't matter if you have a new shirt, that gal's married, even if it's to a husband that doesn't deserve her or Junior. Hell, Junior's probably not even Junior anymore.* What would they name him?

Ingersoll himself had once been a celebrated namer of babies. This began when he was about six, and he came upon Sister Mary Eunice doing intake on a newborn. The baby had been left the previous night on the stoop in a black leather doctor's satchel. Beside Mary Eunice was a novitiate she was training. Ingersoll was too short to see what they were doing on the examining table, but he stood beside Sister's elbow.

"Six pounds, six ounces," the head sister told the novitiate, who scratched her pencil in the ledger. He heard, too, the snap of the measuring tape. "Length, twenty inches." More scratches, another snap. "Head, thirteen inches. And as for name . . ."

Now there was a pause as the sister whisked the yellow measuring tape from the table and began to coil it. She leaned farther over the table. "Peter?"

Sister Mary Eunice held the baby up now and faced it toward the nun-in-training, who tapped her pencil on her pooched lips.

"Yes, I think so," said the novitiate.

"Well, then. Peter."

And the pencil scratched again.

The next day at recess Ingersoll was chasing the kickball when he ran smack into the kneecap of Sister Mary Eunice, connecting solidly through her immense black gown and ending once and for all the discussion among the boys about whether she had legs under there or just wheels. She rubbed her knee as he rubbed his and tried not to cry.

"Come sit," she said.

He did. It was brisk, but the slats of the bench were warm on the back of his legs. They watched a few dried leaves crabbing across the asphalt and the sister stopped rubbing and rested her arm on Ingersoll's shoulders.

"Companionable, isn't it?"

But he was thinking about something else. "Sister? Yesterday, with that doctor-bag baby? How did you know its name?"

"Well, I didn't at first. But if I give a quick prayer, it seems the right name comes to me."

"And Peter was the right name?"

"Did you see that baby, Teddy?"

He nodded. He'd seen the baby later in its bed.

"Did he look like a Peter to you?"

"Yes, Sister."

She smiled. They watched the kickball game for a few rounds.

"Sister?"

"What is it, Teddy?"

"Is that how you came up with my name?

How come I'm a Teddy?"

"Yes, that's so."

The rubber ball bounced to his feet and he caught it and threw it back into the game. "Sister, can anyone do that? I mean, could I?"

"Name a baby?"

He nodded.

"Certainly. You'll name the next one."

He waited, but it took almost three weeks before another baby arrived. He'd already been considering names but chased them out as soon as they sidled in, because he knew it was important to match the name to the baby. So when one came, that's what he did. He studied its wrinkly face, one of those babies who looks like an old man, dark downy hair along the edges of his face like sideburns. Ingersoll closed his eyes and said a little prayer that went, "God, please tell me his name."

And God said, "Brendan."

And Ingersoll said, "Brendan."

And Sister Mary Eunice confirmed it. "Brendan," she said with a nod. "It's a powerful name, Teddy. It's a voyager's name. St. Brendan traveled for seven years, don't you know, sailed the seas and discovered North America."

Poor Sister, she didn't know about Columbus. But he was glad she liked the name. And it stuck. Everyone in the orphanage used it and he was proud each time he heard it and the baby was chosen by new parents within three days. Good-bye, Brendan, tiny voyager.

They let him name another. Emboldened, he pronounced the next baby Ivanhoe the Third. The nuns loved it; he heard them saying the name wherever he went. "This boy has a great imagination," one nun said to a couple wearing matching tweed coats who had come for a baby. The nun smoothed his hair with her palm and nudged him toward them. "A bright boy," she continued. "He named our newest baby 'Ivanhoe the Third.' "

"A baby? You have a baby?" said the tweedy woman. The nun sighed and led them down the hallway.

Ingersoll didn't care. He was the namer. It was his responsibility. It was a big job for a big boy. Someone's name mattered in who they grew up to be.

The next baby he named "Felix Xanadu." Sister Mary Eunice paused and looked up over the log to say, "That's a mouthful, Teddy."

"Yes," he said soberly. "It's meant to be. But he also has a nickname. XX."

"XX, that's his nickname, is it? Well, that will be easy to write in his gowns."

And before too long, the nickname had a nickname, for they started calling the baby "Twenty."

Until Monsignor O'Shaughnessy visited and got wind of Baby Twenty and said to Sister Mary Eunice, "Do you really believe it proper to treat these poor abandoned children as jokes?"

It put an end to Ingersoll's name game and stung a bit, too. Naming was no joke, Ingersoll understood that.

He thought on the names as he grew. At eight he realized the names he'd chosen at six were silly, and he felt a bit ashamed, sending out into the world a boy who'd forever be tethered to "Ivanhoe the Third," when "the Third" is supposed to mean your pop had that name, and his pop, too. At ten he realized no one had been tethered to the names he'd chosen; the parents who adopted the babies would rename them, the nuns had known that all along, so his responsibility, his grand task, was nothing that amounted to anything, just a label to call a baby for three days, and a way to distract a small boy from the fact that no one wanted to adopt him, and he felt shame all over again. As a man of twenty-eight he thought of those names still, and the babies he'd hung them on. He wondered where they were and who they'd become and if they knew they'd once worn a different name, a God-given name whispered straight into Ingersoll's unwashed ear. And though he'd never admit it to anyone, certainly not Ham, he still kind of liked the name Felix Xanadu.

Now the road had gotten hilly and he recalled this stretch from when he rode out with Junior, knew he was close. Ingersoll was at the fourth hill when a squat yellow dog with a peg for a tail appeared. It had a long fish, a mullet, looked like, in its jaws. Ingersoll whistled but it veered wide and kept going, purposeful, its coat wet and tail aimed down, the fish like a handlebar mustache.

The much-missed sun came out as they climbed the fifth hill and Ingersoll decided he should take the rest on foot. He gigged Horace into a copse of cottonwoods, tied him to a foxgrape vine, the kind a boy likes to swing on, next to a ditch swarming with crawfish, small clear ones, shrimplike. Ham had jawed to Ingersoll about these creatures, mud-bugs he called them, claiming they ate them in Louisiana, luring them with string and a lump of bacon from the holes where they blew bubbles. Just another story that might be only a story — you never knew with Ham.

Ingersoll looked around to get his bearings and grabbed his Winchester and set off to find that yellow dog's fish market, a stream called the Gou-ga-something, an Indian name. He'd find the dock and see what kind of boat Jesse had, then trace the stream to find the still. He wondered if Dixie Clay had any inkling her husband was a bootlegger. Sometimes the wives truly didn't know.

He didn't fear making noise, the pine needles beneath his feet damp and springy, and soon he could hear the stream and smell it too, fresh-crisp yet woodsy, like the cool dim icehouse with its block of ice packed in sawdust. The sun felt good warming the back of his neck, and it prismed through the beads of water standing up on the green moss.

The stream must usually have banks but was so fat now it just ran up into the marshy grass. He had to step high to make progress, and with this strange thing called a sun shining down, he was getting hot and stopped behind a sweet gum to unbutton his coat, watching a robin tug a long shoelace of a worm from the ground, and that was when he heard her.

Her voice. No words to her song, just her voice sliding through notes, her voice high and clear, harmonizing with the stream almost. Sweet Jesus. Ingersoll pressed himself behind the gum tree. But, as if her voice was chucking him under the chin, he darted forward and crouched behind a closer gum.

And there she was, with Junior, lifting him high over her head in time to a sprightly tune:

> Is your horse a single footer, Uncle Joe,
>> Uncle Joe,
> Is your horse a single footer, Uncle Joe,
> Is your horse a single footer, Uncle Joe,
>> Uncle Joe,
> Don't mind the weather when the wind
>> don't blow.
> Hop up, my baby, three in a row!

She repeated the last line twice, tossing Junior gently in the air. He made a happy *eeeeeee* sound, his wispy hair lifting in the breeze, then she caught him and tossed him again. She was wearing a simple brown dress with an apron and looked like a wood sprite. Ingersoll wouldn't have been half surprised if she turned into a doe and bounded away. Instead what she did was pivot with the baby on her shoulder to point to a yellow butterfly that bobbed past, and she hopped onto a stone with Junior to follow it, then hopped to another.

Dixie Clay and Junior weren't alone in following the butterfly's trajectory. The creek had a logjam, and from his crouch Ingersoll could see a river otter pop up from the logs, then, as if in a barbershop quartet, three other sleek heads popped over the top. Dixie Clay laughed and turned to point them out for the baby, all the otters' long, long noses flicking in unison left then right then left then right to watch the yellow butterfly dip and dance over the water. And then the butterfly lifted away and her glad face turned to watch it waft into the woods and that was when her eyes passed over Ingersoll, Ingersoll stupidly, openly grinning, forgetting that he was no longer crouching. She gave a cry and almost quicker than should be possible her face tightened, the otters leaping sideways as she staggered backward, one foot slipping from her stone with a splash and her free arm flying up to secure the baby.

Ingersoll lifted his palm and called, "Wait. Don't worry."

But she half ran, half stumbled to a wall

of mossy shelving rocks where her rifle stood and she grabbed it with her free hand and tossed it so it landed in her shooting grip, her other arm still holding the baby.

For the second time in seven days they stood faced off and panting.

"Dixie Clay," he yelled, "I . . . I just came to check on the baby."

"With your gun?"

He'd forgotten about the Winchester dangling from his hand.

"No, I . . . Look here," he cried, and tossed the rifle a few feet off and gave an apologetic shrug.

She kept her gun trained, however. "What are you doing here?"

He said it again, this time with more conviction. "I just came to check on the baby."

"Why were you spying?"

"I wasn't. I mean, I didn't mean to. You just looked so happy when you saw the otters —"

"I was happy because I trap otters. Sell their pelts."

"Oh." Her face hadn't softened at all. "Can I see him?"

She paused. "All right," she said. "But stay on that side of the woodpile."

He walked to his side of the logjam and

felt foolish. He said he'd come to check on the baby, and clearly the baby was fine. Better than fine. She wore him slung on the saddle of her hip, one of his legs in front and one in back, like he'd been riding there all his life.

"Why do you want to check on him?" Dixie Clay wasn't smiling.

But the baby was. "What do you know. He recognizes old Ingersoll."

Dixie Clay frowned like she wanted to deny this, but the baby was leaning toward him. Ingersoll skirted the logs to reach for him, but she pivoted her hip. "Well?" She hoisted the baby a little higher. His hair looked fluffy, like she'd just washed it. He was clasping the bib pocket of her apron.

Ingersoll shrugged. He felt his cheeks pinking.

"I know you didn't come to take him." She said it as a statement, but when he shook his head, her shoulders softened a little.

"No, I didn't come to take him."

"I know. I just said that."

Ingersoll wasn't sure how to reply. He wanted to keep her talking. He considered and discarded several observations, and the pause lengthened, and the longer it got, the harder it was to bear.

The baby broke the silence, squealing and then flinging his arm up to Dixie Clay's face. His index finger hooked her lip. She detached his finger and pushed his hand down, but he flung it back up and hooked her lip again for another round.

Ingersoll laughed and the baby turned and again seemed to recognize Ingersoll and lean toward him.

"Hey, sport," he said. Dixie Clay didn't move the baby away this time.

"If you were here to check on the baby," she asked around Junior's finger, her words slurring, "why not come to the house?"

Ingersoll shrugged. He looked at the sky. "It turned out to be a nice day. I hadn't seen the sun since I couldn't tell you when. And when it came out — I was past the cornfields and by your woods, and when it came out —"

"Seeing it made you happy," she said.

He shrugged. All he could do around this girl was lift and lower his shoulders like a stupid wooden puppet.

She removed the baby's finger and bent her head to kiss it.

There were things he could say, if he were the kind who could say things. Dixie Clay, seeing *you* made me happy.

She looked up at him over the baby, who

254

was wriggling in Ingersoll's direction. "Well, since he won't be denied," she said, and didn't give Ingersoll the baby so much as stop fighting him. Then Junior was in his arms, familiar feeling. He laid his face on Ingersoll's chest like he was hugging him, he just didn't know to use his arms to do it.

"He likes you," she said.

"We're old war buddies." His voice was muffled in the baby's neck. He could smell Junior's breath. "What are you calling him?"

"He's Willy."

"Willy Holliver."

"Yeah."

"It's . . . nice."

She turned and started walking and he turned and walked alongside her, matching her pace.

"I'm glad you came back," she said, "because I wanted to know — it all happened so fast — I never asked anything. Like how you found him. And where, exactly?"

Ingersoll bounced the baby, and they walked beside the creek and he told her, him and Ham two engineers, riding along, and he described the store and the bodies on the gallery and the dying clerk inside and how he took the baby to the Greenville sheriff's then the orphanage, but that it wouldn't do.

Ingersoll was aware she was watching him and he glanced to see her face, curious and considering and maybe relieved, he thought, hearing again that no mother out in the world roamed it searching for her baby.

"But . . . why did you help him?"

They walked past a thicket of blackberries that didn't want Dixie Clay to pass, but she tugged her brown skirt free. She seemed to be giving him time to find the words. He looked at Junior, who had gotten quiet, his breathing deeper like he was nearing sleep. Then Ingersoll told her, "I know what it's like, being an orphan. I'm — I was one. I grew up in an orphanage."

They walked on and, without discussing it, angled off from the creek into the woods. They came to a clearing and stopped. With the thick, tranced sunlight, and the mist giving up a few wisps as it steamed, and a dragonfly that zipped beside them, hovered, then zipped on, Ingersoll had the strange feeling that they were underwater. They stood close, the baby between them, all the world leaning in to hear.

"What are you doing out here, really?" she asked.

"I had to see you." He had not known this until he said it.

Neither spoke. Slowly she reached her arms out and, her eyes on Ingersoll, lifted the baby out of his hands. She placed Willy on her shoulder and stepped back, still tethered to Ingersoll's gaze, and took another step back, and then turned and walked rapidly into the woods. Ingersoll couldn't be sure but he thought, just before she disappeared, her small hand had raised, a white flash like a doe's tail, but whether in farewell or warning he couldn't say.

The sting of a blackfly on his neck and the slap he gave it roused him and he turned the way they'd come to retrieve his gun. It was still there, by the logjam. He slung its rawhide lace over his shoulder and decided to find the still quickly before Dixie Clay returned.

He found a barn, well swept and mostly empty, nothing but a milk cow with long green saliva dripping from her cud in a stall beside a swivel-eared mule. A path angled off behind the barn and he followed it and the breeze took on a metallic sweetness, like a spoonful of castor oil. It was easy then, he could just follow the odor. Amazing that he didn't smell it the first time he was here. He'd provide excuses — the wind blowing from the west, say — but he knew his lapse owed more to a baby fussing in his lap, and a pair of speckled blue eyes coming up the gallery stairs, blue eyes with a rifle barrel between them. Of course, if he had known then that Dixie Clay's husband was a bootlegger, he never would have left Willy here.

He spotted the shack over a little ridge and in a hollow, looking more like an elf cottage than a distillery, its slanted roof crosshatched with pine branches and tucked among the pines, the way a clever bird hides her nest.

Ingersoll flicked the safety off his rifle and waited. He heard nothing but a pileated woodpecker's knock-knock joke and saw nothing but the invisible hand of a breeze smoothing the ridge's long grasses. The grasses weren't long by the door, though — feet had beaten a path to what must be the supply shed. Etchings of wheelbarrow tracks filled with water. And another path must go back to the stream, where there'd be a dock. He could imagine Jesse's whole operation now.

After another moment of waiting, he darted to the door, laid his ear against it, and heard no sound. He brought his eye to a crack in the boards and saw no movement. The door was locked. He thought of his old trench knife with its knuckle guard, left beside the German belt buckle embossed *Gott Mitt Uns* in a motel in Jersey City that he and Ham had had to vacate precipitously. Instead of the trench knife he had a utility knife now with several blades, and one did the trick. He swung the door open with the barrel of his rifle and found what he expected to find, the large drums and kegs connected with pipes, funnels, and coiled tubes.

But he found, too, what he did not expect. Even with only the light from the door, he could see the place was tidy, the dirt floor patterned from the drag of a broom's bristles, the kegs gleaming where a shaft of sunlight reached them. A shelf where bottles were lined, several varieties in neat rows, slashes of black lightning aligned. Something was off here. There was a map or canvas on the far wall, must be hiding something. He crossed in the gloom and with his rifle lifted the corner of the cloth but nothing was there but more wall. The cloth floated down and then it occurred to him what it was. Curtains. Green-checked curtains. Beside a table that held a stack of books. He picked up the top one: *The Sonnets of Elizabeth Barrett Browning.* The next: *Best Loved Poems to Memorize and Recite.* Smudge on the wall to show where the kerosene lantern usually sat.

Christ almighty, this was *her* still. It was Dixie Clay, not Jesse, he should be arresting. He reeled toward the door and then saw it. On the thumper keg, one of the nippled baby bottles he'd bought for Junior and left with the girl.

She was running the still with the baby.

He'd done something worse than giving a baby to a bootlegger's wife. He'd given it to the bootlegger.

He flung the door open and it smacked against the wall and rebounded closed. In the harshest light imaginable he stood and realized he'd have to tell Ham. He gave a snort of bitter laughter, recalling the cupped flame of his precious pride, that he hadn't abandoned the baby in the Greenville sheriff's office or the chaotic orphanage. Oh no, not Ingersoll, saint of orphans and outcasts: he'd given the baby to a bootlegger, perhaps a murderer. And now the baby would be orphaned once again, Dixie Clay destined for the prison or the grave.

CHAPTER 10

Dixie Clay was torn from her nightmare by the shovel-in-gravel scrape of thunder. She lay stunned by her visions, for they were of a terrible black steam train. Long windowless cars humpbacked over each hill on Seven Hills and chuffed closer, louder, needing no track at all, coming to cart her away, to take her to the lynching tree. The two missing revenuers were leaning out the windows. So she snatched Willy from his baby bed and took off into the woods and up the ridge, and when she turned, she saw the train slow at her drive then take the sharp right, following her yet. She thought, *I'll lead it to the still, I don't care, and we'll make our escape.* So she ran past the still, but the train kept coming, gaining on her. She broke through the woods to the stream and held Willy aloft while fording, passing the bloated carcasses of a doe and fawn caught in a logjam, the train snorting its smoke at her back. That's when she realized it was coming not for her, or for the still, but for Willy.

She was glad the thunder had woken her, though Lord she hated thunder by now, hated thunderclouds, hated clouds. It stormed so often that storms managed to be both terrifying and tedious. Still, better wake in this storm than sleep in that dream. She lay unmoving in the dark and then heard the shovel-in-gravel again but it was coming not from outside but inside her room. It was coming from Willy.

When they'd returned from the still around 3 A.M., she'd given him his night bottle and he'd coughed then too and she'd thought he'd gobbled too much milk — greedy baby! — and it had choked him. His cough had not been his sweet airball cough, a teacup-sized cough, soft as a match struck to light a lamp. His cough had been a knife scraping a tin plate. Now, shortly before dawn, he gave it again.

She rose and bent over his willow branch baby bed and studied him in the dim light. His color seemed high and fine, pink cheeks and closed eyes. She heaved a breath and made a step back to her bed when he coughed again. She turned and saw his body knock with the force of it, his eyes slitting open and gleaming in the half dark.

Hmmm. Willy has a cold. Naming it made it better: babies got colds, didn't they, poor things. They got colds and you fretted but then they got better.

She'd had Willy for eleven days now and he'd not suffered so much as a sniffle, but this weather could get the best of anyone. Yesterday in the seam where the chimney met the wall, a line of mushrooms had knobbed forth like hat hooks. It was, as Jesse would say, wetter than an otter's pocket. Where was Jesse now? She hadn't seen him since the day Ingersoll had met her at the stream, and that was four days ago.

Well, okay, she wouldn't go shining this evening, not one drop of rain splashing onto Willy as she ran to the still, no toweling off the baby's plump legs as he balanced on the thumper keg. It was a pleasant thought to settle into. She'd baby her baby today.

Dixie Clay lifted Willy to her shoulder and walked to the kitchen to warm his milk and her coffee. It was still dark, so she turned on the electric light. At the sink, filling the kettle, she saw Willy's reflection, the back of his neck looking mottled. She lowered him and found the pink of his cheeks was blotched onto his forehead and neck. She put the back of her hand to his brow and it was warm. Too warm. Fever warm. In fact, she could feel the heat of his body through her nightdress. She carried him to the marble-topped console she'd conscripted for a diaper changer and lined with towels. Usually when she laid him down, he'd ball his legs into his body, sometimes grabbing a foot, but now he lay lankly. He did not cry. The diaper wasn't wet. She pinned it around him again, frowning.

Back in the kitchen she made his bottle and carried him to the rocker. Usually when she held up the bottle he fastened his eyes on it and opened his mouth and sometimes even flapped his arms. He'd suck, gazing at her, perhaps lifting an erratic arm to swat her nose. But now his mouth wasn't even closing around the rubber nipple. Dixie Clay squeezed it, but his tongue was slack and the milk dribbled out. He seemed to be panting. She put the bottle down and lifted him onto her shoulder again. His forehead was sweaty on her neck. An aura of heat emanated from his body, and patting his back was like moving her hand toward and away from a fire. His panting grew a furry quality. He coughed again, and it was terrible. Great wings of panic thrashed in her. *Not again, Lord. Not again. You took my firstborn. You leave us now. You leave me this child. You let him be.*

Behind the thunderheads, the sky had lightened a notch. She rocked Willy and prayed except it wasn't prayers so much as threats, promises and threats, lamentations and threats. His chest spasmed with each raspy-aired bark. And Jesse gone with the car. And Jesse gone every time she needed him.

Lord, if this child dies, I will kill Jesse. And it will be your fault.

The rain fell in gusts, which she watched out the kitchen window over the baby's damp head. Sheets of rain were blown from the left to the right and then passed beyond the window, like panels of rain, like funny papers erased of their pictures and words. She clasped Willy to her and pumped the chair.

That's right, God: give me a son and then set a match to him.

On Dixie Clay's tenth birthday she and Lucius had been playing in the barn's hayloft and started squabbling over a wooden whirligig and she'd hidden his spectacles. When he gave chase, he misjudged the distance to the loft edge and fell over, breaking an ankle. A miracle, said her father, he could have broken his back. "We'll tell your mother it was an accident," he decided. "She's near her time and doesn't need to be ruffled." But Lucius tattled and her mother was indeed ruffled, and three weeks later she was breech-birth dead. Dixie Clay confided in her father that she'd caused them, these deaths her punishment, but her father was emphatic, one hand on each of her cheeks, No, no. It had nothing to do with her. And he made her promise not to think that the world organized itself to spite her or reward her, the world just was, and good could come from praying but not the good she expected when praying for sunny weather for the county fair.

Dixie Clay knew that her father'd been right — she was not so important as to be the focus of God's machinations — but it was hard not to view Willy's illness as retribution for two revenuers who wouldn't be returning to their children.

The day had begun a thousand hours prior, yet the mantel clock read 10 A.M. She rocked her child, waiting for the fever to break, for the rains to stop, for the slam of Jesse's car door. Imagine being able to telephone the doctor from this very room. There'd been talk of installing lines out this far, but of course the city had run out of money after lining Main Street and Old Barn and Broad Street. Broad Street, where the mayor lived. She cursed the mayor. She considered going for help but feared taking Willy out in the storm would make him sicker. Then another cough from Willy like butcher paper torn from its roll. She rose with him and walked to the door. Through the shaking, rain-pebbled window, she couldn't even see the pines beyond the gallery. She turned and went back to the rocker.

Okay, she told herself, *I'll give it till noon, and if Willy isn't improved, we ride for the doctor.* Come hell or high water: she was in both.

The deadline gave her a bitter determination and the rocker clacked like a metronome measuring a song no one wanted to hear. The child's eyes were slits, glittery slits. His pupils seemed small. He would take no milk. He did not cry. She peeled him from her shoulder with a wet sound and checked his diaper and it was wet only from sweat. He'd left a baby-shaped spot on her dress. She gave him a sponge bath with cool water.

Finally the clock struck noon and she sprang like a mousetrap. She suited up like she was going to war, which in a way she was. She bundled the baby inside her apron and yanked on Jesse's old wide-brimmed leather hat as a rain break for Willy's body.

Even through her dress the child felt like a branding iron. Dixie Clay cradled the aproned child as she ran splashing to the stable where she tossed the saddle on the back of sleeping Chester, who brayed and danced sideways. As she tightened the straps she spoke to the mule of what they must do. They set off, through watery mud that completely obscured the road. Only the rows of pines and Old Man Marvin's mailbox told her she hadn't lost it altogether.

She wasn't far down Seven Hills, the rain horizontal, straight at her, when they came upon a brown Chrysler turned sideways in the road, its stuttering engine masked by the storm. Beyond the fogged windows she could see three black hats. The driver's elbow worked to roll down the window.

"Mrs. Holliver!" shouted the driver as she brought Chester closer. "Tell Jesse we come for the delivery but can't get there."

The driver's squashed nose she'd seen before. Where? In the driveway, counting dollars by the light of the Chrysler's head-lamps.

"We're heading back. Tell Jesse —"

"Take us to town. We need the doctor."

"What?"

"Baby's sick. Fever."

"Baby? You got a baby?"

She pulled down the apron bib. Sweat-slick hairs pressed darkly to Willy's skull, eyes closed and too deep in his head, raisins pressed into gingerbread.

"Hellfire." The driver drew his breath. "Get in."

But when the driver turned back to the other two passengers, something was said. He faced her again where she had slid off the mule but didn't meet her eyes.

"I'm sorry, Mrs. Holliver. Can't take no chances on diphtheria. We'll send the doctor out."

"We'll ride in the back," she pleaded. But the driver was already rolling up his window. She shouted, "I'll give you a hundred dollars. Each. A case of whiskey —"

But he had the Chrysler in reverse, its wheels throwing a sheet of water over the mule. "We'll send Dr. Devaney on out," he shouted through the window crack. "You go home now, Missus Holliver. The doc will be there directly and your young'un will be fit as a fiddle by teatime." And with that the car lurched forward and in just a few feet both the sound and sight of it were lost to the everlasting rain.

It was close to 10 P.M., Dixie Clay pacing with the baby held in front of her like a goblet, when there was a banging on her door. She ran to unlock the bolt, already yelling, "Oh, thank God you're here. Thank God —"

But it wasn't Dr. Devaney with his black satchel. It was Ingersoll, shucking off his slicker right there on the gallery, tossing his hat aside. He stepped forward and filled the doorway, rain coursing off the saddlebag that he dropped to take the baby before she could even make sense of things.

"Wait," she said. "No. He's sick, he's burning up. I'm waiting for —"

"Doctor's not coming." Ingersoll wasn't looking at her but walking with the baby to the lamp. He rested the child on one palm and with the other turned its chin from side to side. He parted Willy's eyelids with his thumb and index finger and looked in.

"Not coming? But —"

"Not coming." He thumbed the baby's mottled chin down and peered into his throat. "I need alcohol. Not to drink. For the fever. Alcohol, cold water, towel. Now."

The baby did his cough, one-two-three barks, Dixie Clay with a hand to her mouth while his chest jumped, as if snagged by a fishing line.

"Now!" Ingersoll yelled. And she whirled about and opened the crate by the pantry

270

and lifted a half-pint of whiskey and handed it to him as he strode past into the kitchen. She followed and saw him grab the dish towel off the stove handle, then bite the cork from the bottle and spit it out. At the sink he found a bowl, poured it half full with the whiskey, filled it the rest of the way from the tap.

"Hold him," he said, and then slid one of the baby's arms out of its swaddling and dabbed the dish towel in the bowl and then blotted from Willy's shoulder to his wrist. Then he rolled Willy's limp arm between his large hands, like dough that you elongate for a pretzel. Ingersoll tucked that arm back in and removed the other and did the same, his movements brisk and confident.

"What you're doing — how can I —"

"The alcohol evaporates," he told her, moving to a leg now, "and it cools him, and we rub him down, see, we bring the blood to the surface. We break the fever. It's cooling him. We've gotta break the fever first."

Ingersoll continued with the other leg, the torso, and then took Willy from Dixie Clay and flipped him to do his back. "You got a croup kettle?"

She shook her head.

"Then get your teakettle going."

She ran to the stove while Ingersoll

crossed her kitchen in three long strides and entered the hall and returned with the baby bed. He flung it before the stove and yelled to Dixie Clay, "Get a sheet, a bed-sheet." She flew to yank one from her bed and when she returned he'd laid Willy in his crib. They kneeled on either side and Ingersoll tented the sheet over their heads, holding one end so the kettle's spout was under the sheet.

"What now?" she asked.

"Now," he told her, "now we steam it out."

"Steam it out? Diphtheria?"

"Baby doesn't have diphtheria, least I don't think so. Doesn't have that layer of skin on the back of his throat, where tonsils grow. Baby has pneumonia, which has led to croup."

They bent over the crib in the cloud built by that kettle, Ingersoll massaging the baby's chest or giving him another alcohol rub, Dixie Clay refilling the kettle or tightening the sheet. As the steam grew thicker the baby's brassy cough worsened, his whole body spasming, snatched by some dreadful fist. Dixie Clay rubbed her palm over the baby's slick head, felt that hollow where the halves of the skull met, and the depression seemed deeper, sunken like earth over a coal mine. She tried to make the baby take the

272

bottle, but what got inside was flung back at her with a cough. Each breath seemed to cost him something terrible. She wished she could do the breathing, do the coughing, take the sick into her own lungs. "Please God please God please God," she said silently or maybe aloud. Through the fog of their own making, the man was pressing his ear to the baby's rattling chest, long locks of his brown hair dripping sweat on the baby. She was herself raining, sweat and tears both plopping on the floor or on the baby as she leaned to tuck the sheet around the kettle but keep it from catching afire.

Lord, I beg of you, I've got no reason to live but him.

Lord, you took my mama, you took my Jacob, you spare this child.

More steam, more steam. An hour passed. Two. Was he coughing less? He was. Less of the terrible rattle to it. More like the way a giant bean pod rattles. They attended the lank limbs and above them the storm-tossed pines attended the roof and then there were fewer branches swatting the windows and fewer raindrops falling through the chimney to the hearth and the wind pinched off and they could hear the baby's breath and there was no doubt it was better, a less harsh tearing of his throat. His eyes were closed, but they rolled beneath the lids in an uneasy, restive half sleep.

Dixie Clay and Ingersoll were sitting cross-legged now beside the crib instead of kneeling. It was three thirty in the morning, and from the woods behind the house an owl hooted. Ingersoll spoke for the first time about something other than Willy.

"Ham — he's my partner — hates owls."

"Why?"

"Won't say. Or he'll say, but he changes his story every time, and I reckon I ain't got the real reason yet."

"No need to be scared of an owl, 'less you're a dormouse," she said, and listened as the owl gave again its eight-hooted call. "That's a swamp owl," she said. "Swamp owl asks, 'Who cooks for you? Who cooks for y'all?' "

The owl hooted a third time and Ingersoll tilted his ear and said, "Yeah, I can hear that," looking at her through the clearing gauze of steam.

Dixie Clay looked down at Willy, who was calmer, his chest rising and falling with no tremor, as if it had never been otherwise. "Look how quiet."

Ingersoll nodded and leaned forward to slip his index finger into the boy's hand, which curled around it. "Got a grip to him," he said. "And he doesn't feel hot."

Dixie Clay took the baby's other hand. He felt normal.

The kettle rattled and Dixie Clay rose to turn it off and then dropped two chamomile tea bags inside to steep while Ingersoll excused himself to use the bathroom. They both returned to their spots beside the crib, and as she handed him his tea she asked, "How'd you know he was sick?"

He told her that he was on his way to find Ham and guard the levee because explosives had been stolen and they were worried about saboteurs. He was almost there when the Harper boy ran by calling had anyone seen the doctor or Jesse Holliver. Saying that Jesse's wife had a strange baby at her house who had the diphtheria and wasn't gonna make it. One of the levee workers yelled that Jesse was in Greenville.

"Greenville," Dixie Clay spat. "And the doctor?"

"At the Bradford plantation, easing Mrs. Bradford's ague."

Bradford was about thirty miles south of Hobnob, Barry Bradford the richest landowner in the county. Dr. Devaney was a Dry, his wife, Jenny, head of the Anti-Saloon League. Dixie Clay saw it now, Dr. Devaney earning duck hunting privileges in the Bradford swamp — why would he rush to a bootlegger's house to treat a dying baby that might snatch him into death as well?

But this man came. She studied him as he blew on his tea. His dark hair hung forward in a wedge, blocking his brown eyes. His red shirt was dirty at the cuffs. A large torso, thick shoulders, long legs crossed. A man like that would enjoy a big supper. Who cooks for you?

She asked, "How'd you know how to help?"

"The war." He shrugged. "I was friends with a medic who taught me some, but he was killed in the Meuse-Argonne, in September 1918. Most of our battalion was. Another battalion was skeletonized and more medics were sent, but before they arrived, we all learned a bit of medicine. A bit more than we'd hoped to learn."

He grew quiet and they sipped tea. The baby opened his eyes and gave a little whimper and turned his head, and when he saw Dixie Clay, he gazed at her. She gazed back. She thought, *You have to teach a baby most everything but how to love.* She made the *bbbbb* sound that Willy liked so well. Then she fetched him a fresh bottle and held it to his mouth and his lips closed around it and sucked a bit and swallowed and then slowly his lids drooped and closed in what was sleep, sleep not death, and his lips released the bottle, his tongue still flexing a time or two.

Ingersoll said, "Seems like other than this you two been getting on all right."

She shrugged. "He's perfect." There was another pause. Then, "Amity told you I lost my firstborn." She looked for confirmation and he nodded.

She continued, "He died. Of scarlet fever. Jacob. I was twenty." She paused between sentences because she wasn't used to talking this way, or talking. She laid a hand on Willy's forehead, the hair no longer slick but dried into wisps, longer at the ears.

"Before Jacob died," she said, stroking Willy's head, "I'd sometimes feel a love for him so strong it almost scared me. Like I had to grit my teeth to keep from biting him. And I'd think about women who'd adopted babies. And I'd think that there was no way they could love those babies like I loved my flesh and blood. But now I know better." She'd directed this slow speech to Willy's face but looked up at Ingersoll now, his dimple pulling an asterisk in his scruffy cheek. She wondered how growing up in an orphanage changed a man.

After a few minutes, she went on. "My

mother used to tell me a funny story. She said that when I was four, and she was pregnant with my brother, Lucius, she asked where I thought I came from. And I told her, 'I was a little angel in the sky on a cloud with all the other angel babies and God pointed to you and said, Who wants this lady for a mommy? and I raised my hand.' "

He gave a chuckle, and Dixie Clay smiled and shook her head. It occurred to her that this was not only the first time she'd talked about Jacob but the longest she'd talked to anyone besides Jesse since leaving Alabama. So many words, like a net they were weaving.

The cloudy dawn brightened the room so Dixie Clay rose to turn off the electric light and when she returned to her spot, still warm, it occurred to her that Ingersoll's spot would be cooling soon. She suffered a foretaste of loneliness.

"Ingersoll —" she began, awkwardly, her gaze trained on the baby. "I was thinking, you should take the mandolin. I can't play it, you can play it, you should take it. I wish" — she cast her eyes toward the ceiling — "I wish I could do something to thank you. Without you I don't know what woulda happened. I —" She paused, and drew her breath in, and the sleeping baby broke wind just then, releasing a man-loud whoosh. It startled them both and the air burst from her pressed lips, which made him laugh which made her laugh which made him laugh. Something was punctured in the night and the strain leaked out in laughter, which doubled back and rose again like musical phrases, like singing in the round, like the hoot owl's hooting, Dixie Clay wanting to apologize for laughing but laughing too hard to do so, him laughing deep and loud, the pure musical ha-ha-ha of it — as if he'd read how to laugh in a primer — keeping her laughing. That nothing was funny made her laugh harder, until tears rained from both of them, he was pounding his thigh and she was bent over, stomach-weak, surrendered, resting her forehead at last on the baby bed, wheezy and tapering off into a giggle, then silence, then a giggle.

When she could raise her head, Ingersoll was looking at her and he reached slowly across the baby bed and she felt his fingertip brush her cheek and he lifted a tear and slowly drew his finger back.

"You would have made such a good mother," he said.

"What?" The smile dying from her voice.

"What's going to happen to him? Don't you worry about that?"

"What — what are you . . ."

He was looking down into his mug, his dimple flexing behind his whiskers, like he was biting down on his thoughts. "I wouldn't have given him to you. If I had known."

"Known what?"

"C'mon, Dixie Clay."

"What are you talking about?"

"You're a bootlegger." He seemed to spit the word. "I'm sorry, but it's not fair, it's . . . selfish, taking a baby when you'll have to leave him —"

"Leave him? —"

"You can't keep him in jail, Dixie Clay —"

Her lie sounded desperate, even to her: "You mean — you heard about Jesse, not me, I don't know —"

"I saw it, Dixie Clay. I saw the still, I know what I saw, I know whose handiwork that is —"

"You — you — what business of yours, snooping —"

"I'm a revenuer" — her breath snagged — "so it *is* my business, arresting people like you."

"People like me." She gave a bitter snort. "You don't know a goddamn thing about me."

"I know enough. Know enough to know you shouldn't have taken a baby when you won't be able to keep him."

"What's this about — are you threatening me? Let me guess: Jesse bribed you, but you want even more money?"

He winced.

"You revenue agents are all the same. Trifling, and corrupt."

"I'm leaving."

"Good, get out!"

He tucked his legs, climbed a little stiffly to his feet.

"Get out of my house!"

He moved to the door, bent to pick up his saddlebag where he'd dropped it when he'd first come in those hours, that lifetime ago. She followed, screaming, not caring if she woke Willy: "Get out! Get out! Get out!"

She yanked the door open and he whirled around to exit and instead drew his shoulders up. She wondered if he saw someone — Jesse, home at last? — but behind him she saw not a thing that could make him start so, except for fog swirling over the landscape, draping the hedge like a pall on a casket.

What he did next she didn't understand or expect. Like a bear the big man raised his fists and gave a cry, something wordless and anguished that reverberated in the crystallized air. He turned to face her and his darting eyes were also a wild animal's, trapped, and he reached — she flinched, thinking he was going to grab her wrist, but instead he grabbed the wrist of the mandolin, leaning against the doorjamb, and held it overhead like a woodchopper's axe and crashed it down onto the floor, where it smashed with a great throaty moan. Twice more he smashed it, and fangs of mahogany flew by Dixie Clay's face until he held nothing more than the curled neck with a few limp strings attached to the tailpiece. This he flung against the wall.

Then he crossed the gallery, picking up his hat and his slicker, and ran down the steps toward his horse, lying on its forelegs under the ash tree, wearing its saddle from the night before, nickering in the fog.

CHAPTER 11

"Where the hell were you?" Ham asked. He was sitting on his bed facing the window overlooking the square.

Ingersoll stepped into the room and lowered his pack to the floor and shut the door. Ham still hadn't turned around. His shoulders were rigid, stretching horizontal lines in his undershirt.

Ingersoll tried to think how to answer. "I was . . ." Hopeless. All the interrogations he'd seen Ham conduct, all the men squirming and eventually confessing. Ingersoll just needed to tell it now.

His dread had started the moment he stepped outside Dixie Clay's house. Stepped outside into the drowned cloud, the fog the saboteurs had been waiting for. The hairs on his forearms raised and not just from the chill.

He'd leaped onto Horace and kicked his ribs, the saddle soaked through, water gushing down the horse's ribs as Ingersoll leaned forward to help the horse uphill. They nearly fell more than once as Ingersoll pushed the horse harder and harder on the muddy road, the fog clearing a bit as the sun climbed, but his dread not clearing. He arrived at Hobnob around seven and though the shops should be closed, the square was clustered with black raincoats, like a murder of crows, flapping and gesturing, exclamations, ejaculations: "The sheriff said —" "House shock troops on the barges with the prisoners from Parchman —" "But if we billet the National Guard in boxcars, we —" "Blow a hole clear to China." Ingersoll knew enough to know.

"I was —" he said again.

"You was what?" Ham said.

"I was coming to the levee, coming to find you," said Ingersoll, "when somebody told me the baby was sick."

"What baby?"

Ingersoll didn't say anything. Out Ham's window, the courthouse flag was snapping. The halyard had come loose and the clip was clanging against the pole.

"Oh, Jesus, Ingersoll. That orphan baby? But you dumped it in Greenville."

"No, I tried to, but I couldn't. I gave him to someone in Hobnob, and . . . look, Ham,

I sent a boy to the levee to tell you I wasn't coming."

"What boy? There was no boy."

"The Harper boy. Ham, look, the baby was sick, what was I supposed to do?"

"So you're a doctor, Ing?"

"The doctor wouldn't go."

"What business of that is yours?"

"I felt like I had to, Ham."

"So to save one mutt of an orphan you risk a whole town?" Ham rose now and turned, his face red as his sideburns. He roared, "A whole goddamn town?"

Ingersoll was silent. He could not explain the choice he'd made.

A muffled click came from Ham's giant fist and he opened it and looked. There was the bone grooming comb snapped in two, a sad skeleton on Ham's pink palm. He threw it against the wall where it bounced onto the floor.

"What happened on the levee?"

Ham considered him.

"Ham? Please."

Ham looked to be struggling, but Ingersoll could see he wanted to tell. So Ham began, describing how he'd ridden to the levee as dark fell. The dirt road at the top was about twelve feet wide, a guard stationed every three hundred yards, which seemed plenty close enough in the day but now the aureoles of lantern light seemed distant stars, the men's coughs or calls paltry things compared to the river's roar. Ham rode along the line of volunteers, most from the Elks or the American Legion, some he knew already from Club 23. Each man hunched over his cigarette, collar raised against the spray, nipping occasionally from his flask, stamping his boots. So sharp, the wind. So cold, the foam flicked from the fingertips of waves.

Fog sheeted in about 3 A.M. Ham stayed put, knowing Ingersoll would be on his way, knowing trusty sharpshooter Ingersoll would be on his way all right. So the fog got thicker, and Ham kept riding, wishing he weren't posing as an engineer but was a lieutenant again with soldiers to follow his commands. He was approaching the station guarded by Roberto Guccione, the town's favorite dago, like a pet he was, barely spoke English but let the levee workers eat free spaghetti at his restaurant. Through a portal in the fog, Ham saw the hazy shadows of three forms; three men where there should have been one. As he kicked his horse and reached for his Winchester, he heard a terrible muffled scream, and the smaller form, Roberto, dropped. Thud of his body hitting the ground.

Ham pulled his horse to a stop and lifted his leg over the horse's neck and slid off, edged away so the horse wouldn't kick him. He crouched and aimed at the two fat charcoal profiles.

Even then, said Ham, even then he hesitated, knowing Ingersoll would appear at his elbow and want to get the first shot. But Ingersoll hadn't appeared. So Ham trained his Winchester at the closer of the two profiles and shot and levered and shot again and levered again and shot a third time, and this bullet sent one man lifting onto his toes, and with a strange high gurgle, he crumpled sideways into the shadow. The other man had jumped into the river at the first shot, and as Ham ran forward he heard an outboard motor, spookily close in the magnifying fog, revving and spluttering, and from either side of him and from the Arkansas bank too came the pandemonium of men unloading their rifles in fear and fury, having no target but not stopping until their guns were empty.

Ham lifted Roberto's lantern from its pole and crossed to the man he'd shot, bottom half of his face torn away, revolver still in the straining belt hemisphering his enormous belly. He yanked the gun out and slid it beneath his own belt, the metal warmed from the dead man's flesh. Then he examined Roberto. There was a slit in his neck like a wide red grin, and blood bubbling with a snoring sound that, even as Ham watched, wound down and stopped.

And that's how they found Ham, the men who came running, guns drawn, who might have shot, who might have killed him right then, but didn't because someone yelled, "Don't shoot, he's one of ours."

Beside Ham's size 11 right boot, illuminated by the lantern, four bundles, thirty-two sticks in all, of dynamite. And blasting caps and a spool of wire.

Ingersoll closed his eyes. It was a blow as much as if from Ham's palm. "Wait — four bundles — that means —"

"Let me help you with the subtraction, Ing. Thirty pounds of explosives from the case unaccounted for. So they can try again."

"Oh, Jesus."

"And then Captain Trudo comes huffing up," continued Ham. " 'Who the hell are you?' he's wanting to know."

" 'I'm an engineer,' I say. 'An engineer, sent to evaluate the levee.' And this tall, skinny guy I'd won a poker hand from at Club 23 steps forward and says, 'That's true. He's an engineer, him and his partner both.' And all the fellows are nodding. And you want to know what happens then, you want to know who shows up right about then? My partner of eight-plus years? No, not my partner of eight-plus years. Coming along the road from town and angling up to the levee is a Ford, and Jesse damn Holliver steps out."

Ingersoll's face was bowed into his hands, his fingers grasping the sides of his cheeks.

Ham continued, "Jesse Swan Holliver, that little . . ." — Ham was actually searching for a word, that was how angry he was — "dandy, that fop, that daffodil, in his frock, and Jesse says, 'I'm just now back from Greenville. What's happened here?' and the poker guy tells him how I'm an engineer who'd shot the saboteur. And Jesse says, 'How you know that, Tucker? How you know he's only an engineer? He seems to know a lot about munitions.' And all the men grow quiet and look at me. Jesse asks Tucker, 'How long he been around?' and Tucker gets thoughtful and says, 'Only a few weeks, I reckon.' And Jesse says, 'How well you know him?' and 'I guess I don't,' reckons Tucker. Then Jesse turns to the captain. 'I wonder where this partner of his could be,' says Jesse, and leans over the levee to scan the water, peer off in the direction of the boat."

Ingersoll was shaking his head, still grasped in his hands.

"So the captain turns to me, 'Where is this partner of yours?' Which is a hell of a good question."

From somewhere below them, the kitchen, came a clattering from a dropped tray, something smashing, a sound Ingersoll couldn't help but interpret as angry. Had he left dirt clods? Eaten an accidental banana? Fallen in love?

"And so Captain Trudo says, 'I'm taking you in.' "

Ingersoll looked up from the net of his fingers.

"And he gets out his fucking bracelets."

"No."

"Oh, yes. Oh, yes he does. He cuffs me and shoves me down the levee toward the station when Jesse yells, 'Stop.' "

Ham paused and even as Ingersoll endured the pause, both desperate and dreading to learn what came next, he admired Ham's ability to pace a story.

Ham continued, "So the captain yanks my cuffs to stop me. And Jesse says, 'While you got him so accommodating, I've a hankering to know this fella's real name. Thinks it's cute not to say what Ham stands for.' And the captain says, 'That's easy enough to ascertain,' and reaches into my back pocket and starts pulling out my wallet."

"Oh, Jesus, Ham."

"So I say, 'Okay, Jesse, I'll 'fess, no need to go snooping around a man's wallet, Ham stands for —' "

Ingersoll found himself leaning forward.

"And at that moment, the captain flips open my wallet and says, 'Well, I'll be damned. This fellow's a federal revenue agent.' "

"Oh, Jesus."

"And all the men kinda rear back from me. That guy Tucker is taking a swig of a half-pint and midswallow just drops it to the grass and the whiskey burbles out. And I'm looking around and it's like somebody pulled the curtains over each face. Except Jesse's, of course. That face is always curtained off. And Captain Trudo isn't quite sure what to do, but he knows he can't arrest me now. So he gets out his keys and takes the bracelets off and says, 'You find any stills around these parts? 'Cause we ain't got any. If we did, I'd know about it.' And I say, 'No, ain't found shit and don't expect to.' By now the men are all drifting away, whispering. The captain says, 'I didn't know we had an undercover agent among us. You might have alerted me, I wouldn't have had to blow your cover.' And because there's nothing else I can say, I say, 'You're right about that, sir, and I'm sorry.' And Trudo nods and says, 'I still want to talk to your partner, the other agent. Tell him to come by the station. First thing. I'm sure he has a good alibi.' "

Ham's gray eyes were like ball bearings under his bushy orange eyebrows. "Well, do you?"

Ingersoll took a breath and started at the beginning, telling Ham about giving the baby to Dixie Clay and not knowing she was a bootlegger. Learning that Jesse was her husband. Seeing her by the stream. Finding the still. Figuring out she was operating it.

Ham shook his head. "I'll be damned. Why didn't you tell me?"

"I don't know. I'm sorry. It's just — I hate to think what's gonna happen to that baby when we break this case."

Ham turned back toward the window and pressed his fingertips to the glass. "Jesus, Ing."

Ingersoll picked at the pompoms on the bedspread and thought about meeting Ham nine years ago. When Ingersoll's battalion had been crushed early in the Meuse-Argonne Offensive, and the remnants of another battalion joined his, he had a new lieutenant, and that was Ham Johnson. Ingersoll had made corporal by then, probably could have risen higher, but the fact that he hadn't gone to school past the age of sixteen was sometimes apparent, not because he didn't know troop movement or bullet triangulation or code breaking but because he didn't know the prep schools the officers threw about.

When the new lieutenant arrived, he sent a message to Ingersoll hunkered in the trench, scratching his body lice, demanding he report at Lieutenant Johnson's tent at 0600 hours. Ingersoll did, wondering why he was in trouble, standing at attention while the lieutenant sat in a field chair on a rectangle of Oriental rug, peeling an apple with a knife. When he was done, he dropped the peel to the rug and stuck the knife between two of his brass buttons and scratched a little, appraising Ingersoll. Ingersoll gazed straight, over Johnson's head. Behind the lieutenant, in his tent, a grunt was rolling up mosquito netting.

The lieutenant removed the knife from between his buttons, examined it, then wiped the blade against his trousers and set it down. Finally he spoke. "So, you're ole Dead-Eye Orphan."

"Yes, sir." Sooner or later everyone heard the story. When Ingersoll had arrived for basic at Camp Grant in Illinois along with the other enlisted men, they were introduced to the sergeant-instructor on the parade ground who yelled at them about the working components of their rifles, the bolt, the breech, the upper and lower sling swivels, demonstrated how before resting they'd stack their rifles into a teepee to keep them clean and ready to grab. Then they practiced shooting. When it was Ingersoll's turn, shooting from sandbags at a hundred yards, each of his ten bullets (as well as the three warmers) hit the target, and Sergeant Karkos halted the exercise to yell, "Most of you apes can't even hit the target! This soldier has a six-inch cluster. That's how it's done, boys!"

"Show-off," said his bunk mate, a dairy farmer from Wisconsin, as they walked to the latrines. "Just 'cause you spent your youth hunting coons don't mean you'll have the courage to do it when it's Fritz." He apologized the next day, and later they became friends, and Ingersoll never told him that he'd never been hunting, never held a gun until the government thrust one into his hands. But it felt right there, that bolt-action ten-inch twist star-gauged Springfield, that was what the sergeant had said when handing them out, and Ingersoll liked the description and remembered it. The gun was like his guitar: a thing that had power because of the hole in the middle. Maybe like Ingersoll, too, for that matter.

Basic had lasted six weeks, and in Ingersoll's fifth week he was in the mess tent filling his canteen with weak coffee when he heard the air-raid siren, though there was no drill planned. He ran out of the tent and looked to the sky: no bombers, no shrieking shells, though the officers were huddled, gesticulating, the camp commander at the center.

"What's going on?" a private behind Ingersoll hissed to another who was running from the officers' tent with a spool of telegraph wire. "There!" the private yelled, thrusting his chin at the water tower, which loomed like a giant mushroom. "Someone's climbing it, he's going to poison the water supply!" Ingersoll could see a dark shape, pack on his back, scrambling up the metal rungs, silhouetted against the dusk, and thought of "Itsy Bitsy Spider," which Sister Mary Eunice used to sing to the wee ones, twisting her fingers up an imaginary web.

The camp commander called, "Karkos," and the sergeant hustled over, and a moment later Ingersoll heard his name ring out, as he suddenly knew it would. He stepped forward, already pulling his gun from his shoulder sling and dropping to one knee. Karkos was at his side now. "Steady," he cautioned. "Don't hit the tower." Ingersoll could feel Karkos's hand on his shoulder and hear the men shouting and pointing and a field light behind him threw his shadow to the dirt. He brought his rifle up, flicked the safety off, squeezed his right eye. "Shoot," Karkos ordered. Ingersoll did not shoot. He went into the quiet place. He rolled Sister Mary Eunice out of the way and shoved Karkos's hovering presence farther off and silenced the men and did not hear Karkos order "Shoot!" again more frantically because Ingersoll was calculating wind velocity and the distance of fifteen hundred yards, and when he opened his right eye, it was to watch the spider sail away from his sticky strand of web, far off spider-scream falling as it fell. Ingersoll didn't remember squeezing the trigger, yet the men were shouting his name and clapping him on the shoulder.

The camp commander pushed through the crowd and held up his hand. "Karkos," he ordered. "Have the field telephone brought over. This private is going to telegram his folks and tell them of his status as a sharpshooter in General John J. Pershing's army."

Ingersoll said nothing, even when the phone was put in his hand, the commander squeezing his shoulders, telling him to go ahead son and tell the operator what he wished to say to his folks. He looked at the mouth cup. He felt the men, a silent mass, behind him, and he almost wished he hadn't shot the saboteur just to be spared this scrutiny. The commander's smile left the corners of his lips. "What is it, son, never used a telephone before?"

"It's not that, sir," said Ingersoll, though that was also true.

"Then what?"

"No folks to telegram, sir."

"No folks?"

"Correct, sir."

"You're an — orphan?"

"Yes, sir."

"Well, by God," said the commander. "You're an orphan no longer. You've just been adopted by your Uncle Sam." The commander pounded his back, more cheering behind and laughter, his name a strange chant on the lips of strangers.

As the commander moved away to the officers' tent, he stopped in front of Karkos. "That's exactly what we need to win this war. You come across any more sharpshooter orphans with steady hands and dead eyes, you let me know."

A nickname was born and evidently had made it into his file because Lieutenant Johnson was smiling. He sank his teeth into the apple, which calved like an iceberg on his tongue, and over its crunching he spoke. "I have a French 75 arriving within the week."

It was the most unlikely thing he could have said, but Ingersoll maintained his forward gaze. He heard the snap of the lieutenant's teeth once more cleaving the apple. "Know how to work one?"

"No, sir."

"Can you fake it?"

Ingersoll paused, not sure how to answer. "At ease, Corporal," said Johnson, and Ingersoll widened his stance.

"No, I mean it," said Johnson. "Be at your ease."

Ingersoll looked at him now, the man's jaw working like a circular saw. He swallowed noisily and then yelled over his shoulder, "Malone! Bring him a chair."

A second field chair was produced and

Ingersoll sat.

"Apple?"

"No, thank you, sir." Though he hadn't seen an apple in weeks.

"Listen," said Johnson, leaning forward, one hand on his knee, the other gesturing with the core. "I brought you here because I need your help." Now Johnson brought the core to his mouth and bit the bottom off. "They said I could have one of the French 75s" — another hunk of core was bitten, and he chewed as he spoke — "and the horses to pull it and the melinite high-explosive, *if* I had an officer from among the graduates of the engineering school experienced with its workings." Ingersoll could hear the swallow and thought he should be able to see the lump of core travel down Johnson's throat. "And I need that cannon. We need that cannon."

Ingersoll nodded. He'd made the same argument to his previous lieutenant. They needed a field gun capable of devastating the waves of German infantry attacking in the open, and the French 75 could shoot up to fifteen rounds per minute because its recoil was hydropneumatic and so remained perfectly still on its wheels during firing and didn't need to be re-aimed each time. Ingersoll wondered if this new lieutenant was aware that he'd been making this very argument to his old lieutenant — up to Tuesday of last week, that is, when his old lieutenant got shot while trying to re-aim the cumbersome two-rounds-per-minute field gun that was all they'd had.

"But," continued Johnson, "I don't have any engineering officers." Ham tilted his big head up and dangled the last of the core by its stem over his maw and dropped it. "But you wanna know what I do have?" he gargled over the chunks of core.

"Yes, sir."

"Ole Dead-Eye Orphan. And that has to be just as good, don't you reckon?" Johnson's Southern accent revealed itself in the question.

Ingersoll half shrugged, half nodded. "Yes, sir."

"Good." The final swallow. "Then it's settled." Ham lifted the pocketknife from his thigh and speared it into the snake of peel on the carpet. Then he began nibbling the peel off the knife. "When the 75 arrives, you're in charge. Don't let on that you don't know what the hell you're doing. You'll have four men to assist you and two for the horses, and if you show any doubt, they'll smell it. And we'll both be demoted."

So the 75 arrived, and Ingersoll figured it

out while seeming to inspect it, and he used it, under Johnson's command, to cut corridors across the belts of German barbed wire up to five miles away. By late September, during the final Meuse-Argonne Offensive, they broke the Hindenburg line, one of the four main factors, war analysts would later state, leading to Armistice.

And the two men had become friends, or as much as you can become friends with your superior, fourteen years your senior. It was Ham who'd had Ingersoll tested, ordered up the Stanford-Binet exam on which he'd scored the 112. Others had known Ingersoll was a good shot. Ham was the first to see Ingersoll was smart. Even Ingersoll hadn't known, really, until the results came in. Which was the point, Ingersoll figured later — not for Ham's edification but for his own.

And now he had let Ham down, getting involved with the wrong people, withholding facts from the investigation. He was ashamed.

Ham had also been thinking of the war. He said softly, to the window, "I remember, after — after that day, you know — writing the recommendation for your medal. *For conspicuous gallantry and intrepidity above and beyond the call of duty in action with the* enemy."

Both men were there, in Mrs. Vatterott's Cardinal Suite, but they were in Verdun, too. The yellow-brown mud of the trenches with their battalion of eight hundred, after most of the other eight hundred had died. *Ils ne passeront pas.* Shriek of horses and shellfire and shit and blood and rotting flesh, the corpse bloated in the scum-covered water, the only place that they could drink, the man's belly distended as if he'd drunk his fill. Ham received new orders; someone had to swim the contested St. Quentin canal at night and take out the fortified machine-gun nest, and he'd asked for a volunteer. He'd asked the entire battalion but in a way he was asking only Ingersoll, and Ingersoll had understood and volunteered. He'd done what he'd been asked to do. They'd left Verdun with thirty-seven men. In all these years, they'd never spoken of it.

Ham lifted his fingertips from the window and five clear circles appeared, then ghosted over.

"Eight years of partnering." Ham shook his head. "Eight years of . . . friendship."

"I'm sorry, Ham."

"It's that goddamn baby." Ham turned. "Change your shirt and comb your hair.

You're heading over to the station, tell that captain where you spent the night."

"I can't do that, Ham."

"You sure as hell can, and you sure as hell will."

"I can't say I was there at Holliver's house when he wasn't there. People don't know she has a baby. They'll get the wrong idea."

"And what is the right idea, Ing?"

"Don't do that, Ham."

"Don't do what, Ham?" He took a few steps toward Ingersoll, skirting the bed. "Don't tell my subordinate he's so far over the line he might never find his way back to it?"

Ingersoll's fists tightened at his side.

Ham came to a stop in front of him. "Get out of here," he yelled, flinging his arm at the door. He gained control of his voice as he continued. "Go find whoever zipped off in that boat. I've gotta figure out how to tell Hoover we haven't managed to crack the moonshining operation but we have managed to kill one fat saboteur in front of a whole town while letting his fat friend sail off into the sunrise."

What Ingersoll had wanted to do was rush out of Ham's room and down the steps of the Vatterott and into the woods and bust the still and find the other saboteur, then skate clear of Hobnob altogether and forever. Things had been hinky ever since he arrived at this damn drowning town.

But of the things he wanted, he got not a one.

He turned outcast from Ham's door and heard a crash. Ingersoll leaned over the banister. Mrs. Vatterott and the Irish housemaid were bumping an armoire on the staircase landing.

"Nora Cannon, I ought to ship you right back to your potato farm."

"But, ma'am —"

The housemaid was in front, biting her lips, holding her arms behind her to carry the armoire, and Mrs. Vatterott a few steps below, lifting from beneath. The problem, Ingersoll could see from above, was that they couldn't turn it on the landing without the legs hooking the balusters. They needed to lift it higher but didn't know or couldn't manage. Helping them was the last thing Ingersoll desired and he considered the likelihood of a servants' staircase, though even as he considered he knew he couldn't use it. He sighed, then called out, "Hang on, ladies. I'm on my way."

The piece was heavy — though one of them had lightened it by removing the drawers — and bulky, too, and the women, now below, holding the legs, made its maneuvering more, not less, difficult. Finally Ingersoll croaked, "I got it," and grunted it onto his shoulder and trudged it up the stairs.

"Where to?"

"Third on the right, Mockingbird Suite. We've been advised to get valuables off the ground."

Ingersoll didn't wait for the women to catch up. He rested the armoire against the closed door and then felt beneath for the knob and twisted and momentum staggered him in. He gained his sea legs and bumped the piece down on its claw-feet.

Mrs. Vatterott bustled in after instructing Nora to bring the drawers from below. "Oh, Mr. Ingersoll, you are the Lord's providence, you are."

"Glad to help, ma'am."

"Glad to hear it! Glad, glad, glad. If Mr. Stanley R. Vatterott, God rest his soul, was still man about the house, well, we'd be shipshape. But as it is —" She shook her head. "These are hard times for a widow. A poor defenseless widow. Perhaps you heard there was" — she dropped her voice — "a saboteur last night?"

Ingersoll nodded, taking the drawer from

the housemaid.

"They say he was a revenue agent! Can you imagine?"

He tipped the rectangle of the drawer into its mouth.

"Probably crooked. They all are, you know."

He jammed the drawer in perhaps harder than he needed to, thinking of Dixie Clay accusing him of taking a bribe from Jesse. It rankled. Sometimes at night when he couldn't sleep he'd tot up the bribes he'd been offered and rejected and marvel at the sum. But no one would believe in an honest revenuer. Only Ham, whom he'd abandoned.

"We've been advised to evacuate. River's at fifty-four feet. But I can't see leaving my house. Did you hear how many inches of rain yesterday?"

Ingersoll reached for the other drawer.

"Fifteen! Fifteen inches of rain in eighteen hours! There was a crevasse at Pine Bluff, another hundred fifty thousand acres underwater. Do you think our levee will hold, Mr. Ingersoll? The flood crest is still a few days off, the river still rising. Will our levee hold?"

No, he wanted to say. Run, he wanted to say. When Ham had finally reached Hoover he'd been told to downplay the stolen dynamite, cast doubt if possible. Secretly, he and Ham were now charged with finding the saboteurs, as Ham had predicted, though how they were supposed to accomplish this Hoover didn't say. These people had no idea what danger they were up against. To Mrs. Vatterott he said, "Why not consider evacuating?"

"And leave all my pretty things?" She clucked to dismiss the idea and lifted the corner of her apron and licked it and rubbed it on the carved scrollwork. "This was my mother's mother's. Shipped to New Orleans from Ghent, Belgium."

"You've got it safe now, ma'am, gotten it to higher ground. You might as well do the same thing for yourself. All right, if that's it, I reckon —"

"Oh, do you wish to help with the Mora clock? How lovely of you. It came from Switzerland, you know."

Ingersoll thought of Ham down the hall, who no doubt assumed that Ingersoll was right this minute buttonholing the missing saboteur.

"Please? Mr. Ingersoll?"

There was nothing to be done.

The clock was six feet tall but at least could be moved in two pieces, the glass clock face separating from the painted base.

He lugged it to the Mockingbird, breathing hard, and skinned his knuckles chest-wrestling the fluted column through the door frame, and bit down on the curses knocking the back of his teeth. Downstairs at last he edged for the door, and when Mrs. Vatterott ran her fingers along the piano, the lid headstoned with framed photographs, and gave Ingersoll an imploring look, he just darkly shook his head.

"You're a fine gentleman," she said, and patted his arm. "I wish I had a reward. Care for a banana?"

He couldn't tell if she was joking and was too tired to puzzle it out. "Ma'am," and a tip of his hat, and he strode out the door.

On the street, he found himself wishing he'd changed his shirt, as it was lathed to his back with sweat. But then it wouldn't matter, since it was raining again. He passed the hardware store where a sign warned, WE HAVE NO MORE UMBRELLAS, RAIN PONCHOS, OR GALOSHES. And underneath that, in a different hand: OR CARBIDE LAMPS. OR LANTERN FUEL. And underneath that, in yet a different hand, OR HOPE.

The town was an ant hive, men clustered around the radio at the furniture store, others hustling by with lumber balanced on their shoulders, others blocking the sidewalk while hauling a sideboard to a second-story window — so many men, now, the women mostly evacuated — a few pointing to Ingersoll then turning back to hiss and whisper. A newsboy proclaimed, "Gauge at Cairo reaches fifty-six feet! New record!" Ingersoll needed to find Trudo and clear what he could of his name, but he'd heard from Mrs. Vatterott that the saboteur Ham had shot had been laid out in the window of the funeral parlor. So first he'd look at the body and look at the crowd looking at the body, try to learn something.

The line wrapped around the building and he didn't have time for it so he cut in, ignoring the mutterings. It was a good day to be six foot three: by rising to his boot toes he could see pretty well, and what he saw wasn't pretty or well: Ham had shot the jaw clear off this fat, fat man. The jaw must have been about the smallest part, too: why aim so high when a body shot would have been nearly unavoidable? If Ingersoll had been there, yes, things would have been different. He could have clipped him, injured but not killed him, gotten a confession, gotten the saboteurs arrested. Then he could have busted the moonshiners. So if the levee blew it would be from natural causes, not Ingersoll's problem, and he'd be long gone, laying red clay miles between himself and any trembling levee or finger-grasping baby or very married bootlegger. None of it his concern. Nothing to weigh him down. New job, new town, new faces. He turned from the corpse.

"Anybody you know?"

Leaning against the striped barber's pole was Captain Trudo, constructing a cigarette.

"Nope."

"Nope?"

"Nope. But I'm not from these parts."

"So I hear. Weren't you told to come find me and make a statement first thing?"

"I was."

"This look like first thing to you?"

Ingersoll glanced at the parlor window, the corpse on its tilted slab now eclipsed by someone's dripping umbrella, then he turned to the captain and shrugged.

Trudo licked the paper of his cigarette and tamped it shut and put it in his mouth. He appraised Ingersoll while he reached into his pocket for his match safe and thumbed a match out and struck it and brought it underneath the wide blue brim of his hat.

"Come on," the captain said, pushing off the pole. "I'll take that statement from you in my office."

They walked along the sidewalk, mostly shielded by balconies, then jogged across Main Street in the rain. Ahead of them was the levee, high as a three-story building and buttressed with a wall of sandbags. The river was washing at the top of the bags, which meant it was at least a few feet above the levee. The sandbags were stacked even higher at the elbow of the bend, but still Ingersoll could see waves ricocheting over the top, smashing against the bank, boiling with eddies, and then a tree thrashed around the bend, raking its nails against the sky. Soon New Orleans wouldn't need a saboteur to explode Hobnob. The saboteur must be thinking the same thing. Imagine his rush to beat out Mother Nature so he could get his thirty pieces of silver.

"In here," Trudo said, and gestured to the courthouse steps, which they took two at a time. Inside they hung their coats and Ingersoll lifted his hat and held it out the door to let the rain channel off. When he turned, his boots skidded on the slick tile and he grabbed for the captain's elbow and the captain reached for his gun. Ingersoll scrambled to his feet from splayed legs, thinking, *Man is on edge,* and knew it for a bad sign.

He followed the captain past an intake

desk staffed by two harried-looking officers and down a hallway booby-trapped with buckets to catch roof leaks, and they entered a big room and stopped at the end before some chairs and a desk with a typewriter and telephone and piles of papers. On either side were jail cells, two across from two, each empty except for a cot and a pail and the nostril-hint of urine.

Trudo said, "Sit," and pointed to a worn leather club chair and Ingersoll sat and watched the captain, still standing, flip open a manila folder. He lifted a pair of glasses to his nose by their one arm and studied the folder. Then he slapped it closed and dropped it on the desk.

"Do you know what I have here?" he asked, and stabbed with the broken glasses. "A file on the events of last night. Got to make a report." He swung the glasses by their arm and then let them drop to the folder and walked to the front of the desk and perched on it.

"And maybe I'm not so smart at putting things together," Trudo continued. "Or maybe I'm not so good with words. Unlike a fancy undercover fed, say, used to bending the truth."

So. Whatever happened here would be

tainted by bad blood between local and federal.

"But I'm struggling with some of the details."

Talking wouldn't help, so Ingersoll didn't bother.

"Let's see, for starters, I got me a faux engineer/volunteer/levee-patrolman whom witnesses discover looming over a dead local dago and a shot-dead foreigner fat man. Oh, and let's not forget the quadruple bundles of dynamite. Oh yeah, and another man fleeing in a getaway motorboat. And then — and this is where it gets really good — said faux engineer/patrolman turns out to be a fed, incognito, unbeknownst to any of us, least of all the captain."

Trudo picked up the glasses and gave them another few revolutions.

"And then, what else . . . Oh, I know. Said faux engineer/really disguised prohi says, 'I've got a partner, he can vouch for me.' 'Oh good,' says I. 'Where might bumbling, no-good, kept-in-the-dark local law find this upstanding partner?' And you wanna know what the answer is?" The captain paused, then leaned toward Ingersoll until their faces were just a few inches apart and yelled: " 'I don't know.' "

Ingersoll sat there and took it, and hated

taking it. Like at Camp Grant, getting reamed out by an officer when his bunk mate hadn't cleaned his boots. But at least basic had been in service of the Great War. This was in service of nothing but delaying Ingersoll's capture of the other saboteur before he set more explosives.

Just take it, Ingersoll, take it, and then you can get out of here. His hands were in his lap, knuckles skid-marked from the door-frame gouging, and he tucked them under his thighs, thinking he shouldn't gesture with bloody fists while denying having killed a man.

He took a deep breath to siphon any anger out of his voice. "Captain. What Ham says is true. He's a federal agent, sent here to enforce Volstead, and I'm his partner. Have been for years. He was working on the levee to try to keep it safe. I'd been planning to join him, but I — I got caught up with something."

"With what, exactly?"

Ingersoll lifted his gaze to the rain-curtained window. "A friend needed help."

"What friend?"

"Can't say."

"Can't, or won't?"

Ingersoll shrugged.

"Stand up, Agent Ingersoll."

314

He did.

"Step into that cell there."

"What? Surely you don't mean — with the flood coming, you need my help —"

Exactly the wrong thing to say. Trudo pushed off the desk to a stand. "I don't need your *help*. I don't need shit from you, Agent Ingersoll, but an alibi."

"Captain, you have my word. I was nowhere near the levee. Be reasonable."

"Reason with this." And he drew his pistol and aimed it at Ingersoll's chest.

Ingersoll could have drawn his own pistol and shot before the man cocked his weapon. But that would cause more, not fewer, obstacles. Besides, Trudo didn't really think Ingersoll was a saboteur. He was scared, that's what Trudo was, on the take and not sure whether the agency knew.

But, Jesus, Ingersoll was tired and ready to get on with it.

"Give up your sidearm."

Ingersoll laid it on the desk, but Trudo didn't frisk him or make him take his boots off.

"Now get in there until you're ready to play fill-in-the-blanks."

"I don't have time for this," he said, and blew the air out of his mouth. "My partner, Ham, was at the levee, and I would have

315

been there too, but I rode out to the Holliver property. I heard Mrs. Holliver's baby was sick."

"Mrs. Holliver's baby died a couple years ago."

"She has a new baby."

"And how'd she get that?"

"I brought it to her."

"You brought it to her?"

"Yes, and I went to check on him."

"Mr. Holliver didn't mention anything about that."

"Mr. Holliver wasn't there when I brought the baby."

"So you make it a habit of visiting Mrs. Holliver when her husband isn't home."

"Listen —"

"Oh, shit." Trudo slowly shook his head. "Shit and shinola," he marveled, and leaned back in his chair, holstering his pistol. "Makes sense why you didn't flap your gums. Shit. Messing with the man's wife. Shit," he said again, and chuckled mirthlessly.

"I wasn't —"

"I know, Romeo, I know." Trudo flapped his hand at Ingersoll to stop him. "Bet she's a wildcat."

"You've misunderstood. I —"

"Aw, shut up now," he said, picking up

the handset of the Grabaphone. "I've got nothing to charge you with, long as she backs up your story. I'll just make a call to the county sheriff and I guess I'll be letting you go. But if I were you, I might just stay put. You'll be safer in than out, once Jesse hears." He held his broken glasses close to the number disk and began dialing. "And Jesse always hears."

Ingersoll flopped back into the club chair and waited as Trudo gave the exchange to the operator, then swiveled in his chair so his back was to Ingersoll as he spoke low into the mouth cup. He paused and Ingersoll watched Trudo's back grow more alert, and when he finally replaced the handset on the cradle and swiveled forward, he wore a considering look.

"Sheriff says not to let you go yet. Says a fella with your name made a report at his station not quite two weeks ago, about a dead clerk and a pair of dead gypsies at a crossroads store. Says corpses seem to turn up wherever you do. Says for you to cool your heels while we check with the Bureau of Prohibition."

"Oh, for Christ sake. I've got work to do."

Trudo smirked and gestured to the cell, and with no choice Ingersoll walked in, hearing the door clang behind him.

CHAPTER 12

It was the day after the night Willy didn't die, and Dixie Clay had him tucked inside her apron as she rode Chester to town. When Ingersoll had left, she'd pulled Willy onto her lap and rocked with him, both dozing, but waking often, the baby puny on her chest. She startled upright when he gave a cough, listening to its timbre, and replaying the argument with Ingersoll. Ingersoll the Prohibition agent. Her first thought was that she should warn Jesse. Then it occurred to her that he probably already knew. So her second thought was to warn Ingersoll. In the end she thought to hell with both of them. But she was frightened.

A car passed too close and Chester danced sideways. She found herself tensing at every car, in case one carried police. What would Ingersoll do? He must have found the still the day she met him by the stream — the day she'd wanted to kiss him, the day she felt her body leaning into the patch of sunlight where he stood, her face tilting up to his face. *I had to see you,* he'd said, that's what he'd said, and she'd believed him. What a fool. She was no nickel-novel heroine. Her hair wasn't swept atop her head like a Gibson girl's. It was plaited into a braid thick as Willy's arm, to keep it out of the way of Willy's arms. She wore an apron. Her perfume was moonshine. She was a bootlegger. And Ingersoll was a revenuer. That was the end of it.

Or was it? Why hadn't he arrested her then? Why hadn't he arrested her since?

But — it wasn't just a matter of looking the other way, pretending he hadn't seen the still. There was the matter of the two missing revenuers that Ingersoll and his partner — oh, God — had been sent to replace. Ingersoll would arrest her, he'd have no choice. Or that partner of his would. And didn't she deserve it? She'd spoken to no one about her suspicions, but they'd only grown. Jesse had been erratic, keyed up, leaving suddenly and mysteriously at the oddest hours.

Just a few weeks ago, the thought of going to prison seemed bad, but her life here had been a prison, and she'd faced the thought dully and without trepidation. Now going to prison was inconceivable. Orphan Willy again? No. So a few hours ago, when the rain stopped, she stood up from the rocker with Willy on her shoulder and decided to flee. And that's why she'd bundled Willy, sickweak as he was, into her apron.

It would have been easier to pack up Willy and take one of the barges to Greenville, where there were five Red Cross tent camps — one big cramped camp for Negroes, one small cramped camp for Mexicans, and three better ones with kitchens and hospitals, for whites. Earlier, before the run-in with Ingersoll, she'd considered evacuating alongside the other women, but she'd decided against it, figuring she might be safer riding out a flood in low-lying Sugar Hill than in seething crowded Greenville. The camps were violent. Greenville was cotton country, and Negro sharecroppers still lived on the land where their parents or grandparents had been slaves. And it was like slave times again to hear tell of it: with the cotton drowned, the sharecroppers couldn't repay and so they fled north. But the landowners got worried there would be no one to pick next year's cotton. So now the workers were forced to sandbag for seventy-five cents per day, overseen by National Guardsmen who occasionally, when someone refused to keep sandbagging, shot him and dumped his body into the river. Which would be followed by talk of uprising. If that weren't enough, it was rumored the camps had an outbreak of Yellow Jack.

So Greenville was no solution. Besides, they'd find her there. Her thoughts sailed to Pine Grove, as they often did, but ran aground there, as they always did. Her brother was married now and Blue was dead and her father was suffering from lumbago and hip gout. He hadn't been hunting in years. His last letter included a portrait of a tired, bald man. And of course, Pine Grove would be the first place they'd look. So where? Chester flexed his backside and raised his tail and Dixie Clay lifted off the saddle to make it easier for him to do his business. It didn't matter if she knew exactly where, she decided, as long as they got away. They could camp, if need be. She considered what she'd need to buy, kerosene and candles and food — the last time Jesse brought her supplies he'd brought only ingredients for the shine. She needed Pet milk for Willy. And bullets.

Dixie Clay wondered what the engineers were saying about the levee, and what folks were saying about what the engineers were saying. Yesterday's storm had torn shingles from their roof and most of her pans had been conscripted to catch leaks. A rain gauge that hung from a suction cup on her kitchen window had overflown. At least ten inches in sixteen hours. How could the clouds even hold that much in their jowls?

The road to Hobnob had shrunk, just a tongue of mud between gulleys of rain. Old Man Marvin's land had always been swampy and now water reached his door. Through the lake of his lawn rose rusty farm equipment, abandoned the day he was kicked by his horse and gave up farming for shining. There was no wind, and the tractor and baler met their twinned reflections.

Sleeping in her apron front, Willy had his neck canted at a precarious angle. She lifted his head and pillowed him on her chest. The mule slogged on, and water on either side mirrored the cumulus clouds. Overhead, the pine branches met and meshed like two halves of a zipper. It was the stillness after the storm and in its way beautiful. A chuck-will's-widow announced itself from a pine and then darted a few feet to another, keeping pace. Bernadette Capes had taught her its call — "Chuck Will's widow!" — and taught her also that the mother builds her nest on the ground. Perhaps that explained this mama's frenzy: its young had been drowned by the ten-and-some inches of rain.

Willy gave a little mew and she leaned to kiss his crown. One thing about his sickness: she knew, more than ever, that Willy was hers. These twelve days since he'd come to her, she'd schooled herself in his moods, his looks, his limbs and parts, like a courtship deepening. The smell of his head, and how after she washed it the hairs fluffed like duckling down. The unfolding rose of his bendy ear when she swooped it, whole, into her mouth. The look of concentration, like a tiny judge deliberating, while he soiled his diddie. The tender red spot under his privates where she'd dab petroleum jelly. And his spit-up, pleasantly sour when she'd jimmy the washrag under his chins. And even one day the taste: playing airplane, she lifted him high and then lowered him to her delighted face and he blurped, like a carnival game, right into her mouth. As she powdered her pumice stone to make toothpaste, she'd imagined telling a friend, though she had none: *You wouldn't believe what my baby did today!*

My baby. My baby. She loved to call him Willy, but others could also call him Willy. Only she could say, *My baby.* But as much as he was her baby then, he was more so now, after the vigil on her knees, after the curses and after the prayers, after the weeping and after the begging, after going into the deepest blackest place. Ingersoll had seemed to go there alongside her. But — why ride out to help her, to save Willy, if he planned to arrest her, take Willy away? She simply didn't know how to feel about him. His affection for the baby was genuine, that she knew. In the long night of Willy's illness, their heads tented close in the hot rattling steam, she'd seen that not all the water dripping from his face was sweat.

Chester turned from the mud of Seven Hills onto paved Broad Street. Now his hooves clacked instead of slurped. The pavement made the center more passable but even narrower as the water had nowhere to soak. At the corner of Broad and Old Barn Road was Dr. Devaney's three-story home with its porte cochere. Water had crept past the oak-leaf hydrangeas and the rose arbor and halfway up the croquet court. Cinching the house was a chest-high wall of sandbags. It was almost complete but for a twenty-foot gap, where a few sandbags slumped on their ends like exhausted workers. The house had two grand columned porches. Usually the wicker furniture was filled with the sweet-tea-sipping Anti-Saloon League. Today, each porch held a car, and a newly built boat was tied to a column.

Dixie Clay and Willy turned from Broad Street onto Main, and soon there was a wonderment of traffic — horses and mules and cars all in this center lane, and in the canals, boys in canoes. She halted Chester at Amity's store, but the hitching post was surrounded by water so she reined him to the stair rail and mounted the steps. At the door she saw a sign: GONE TO THE VIEWING, ENJOY A REFRESHING COCA-COLA AT 3 WHEN WE REOPEN. Cupping her hands to the glass, Dixie Clay saw that the display cases had been raised onto sawhorse platforms.

The town had an odd, almost festive air, with the stores closed and people rushing to the square. She left Chester at Amity's and continued on foot. The noise grew as she neared, and turning the corner by the bookstore she saw a mass of people, but not milling about — most facing toward the Confederate soldier statue at the south end of the square, and she realized they were in a line, four people across, moving slowly forward. Skirting along the sides were barkers, a balloon hawker, a preacher standing on an orange crate and quoting Revelation.

Dogs dashed and barked through the crowd. A shoeshine man moved his wooden case down the line. "Show your respect for the deceased!" he sang. "Ten cents a shine! That's a nickel a boot, folks!"

Dixie Clay wove among the people, both arms wrapped around Willy to block a jostling elbow or the ash of a cigar. She was looking for someone she knew so she could learn what was going on. She was too short and all she saw were shoulders and backs. A blue postbox on the corner by the stationer's was the perch for twin boys sucking icepops and Dixie Clay wished propriety didn't forbid her from scaling it too.

"Excuse me, Mrs. Holliver" came the voice above her, for it was Joe Adams, the banker, who'd stepped on her heel.

His wife wasn't with him, which must be why he addressed her. Lauren Adams was a Dry from Little Rock, so biggity she called chicken breasts "bosoms." But Joe had slyly bought three cases of Black Lightning for the bank's fiftieth anniversary in '25.

"What's happening?"

"You haven't heard?"

She shook her head.

"Someone tried to blow the levee." Adams called to the man standing in front of him, "Hey, Ace, give me one of those gaspers," and then reached to accept the cigarette.

"Blow the levee?"

"Yeah, somebody tried to dynamite it." They were jostled by the folks behind.

"When?"

"Last night." The crowd pressed against them. "Come on," he told her. "I don't want to lose my place."

She stepped forward as he patted his pockets and found matches. "Who? Who did it?"

"No one knows," he said, ducking his head to light the cigarette, then raising up on his toes to peer at something she couldn't see. "But we're about to see one," he exhaled.

"See one?" She laid her hand on his elbow to bring his focus back to her. "Where?"

"Hobbs's," he said. "The body's laid out. Shot to death by a revenuer who caught him running away after planting the charge."

"Oh my God," said Dixie Clay.

"Yeah," Adams said, and took another pull from his cigarette. "Except there wasn't nothing of God about it. He sliced the throat of a levee guard. Tried to flood the whole town."

The crowd nudged them around the corner, and suddenly they were before the window of the Hobbs funeral parlor. Adams and the other men closed in, blocking the black-suited corpse. They didn't remove their hats.

"Ugly," said one of them. "Even if he still had a jaw, he'd be ugly."

"Fat, too," said another.

"So fat he'd leave footprints in concrete," said Adams, and the men laughed. He flicked his cigarette away. "Glad I'm not a pallbearer."

"Never seen him before."

"Me neither."

"Me neither," added a third. "But he don't look like he's from around here."

Dixie Clay lifted onto her toes but couldn't see. Over the men's heads in the window were two signs. The first said, THE PREPARATION AND EMBALMING OF THIS BODY COST FOURTEEN DOLLARS, AND IT WAS REALIZED BY THE PROPRIETORS OF HOBBS AND SON UNDERTAKERS FOR THE GOOD PEOPLE OF HOBNOB, SO THAT THEY MAY LOOK ON HIM WHO WOULD DO THEM EVIL. The second sign, in block letters, read, "WHEREFORE SHOULD THE EGYPTIANS SPEAK, AND SAY, 'FOR MISCHIEF DID HE BRING THEM OUT, TO SLAY THEM IN THE MOUNTAINS, AND TO CONSUME THEM FROM THE FACE OF THE EARTH'? TURN

FROM THY FIERCE WRATH, AND REPENT OF THIS EVIL AGAINST THY PEOPLE." EXODUS 32:12.

The crowd was trying to jostle the men along, but they held firm.

"Four bundles of dynamite, they say. Thirty-two sticks." This was the first man speaking.

Another — the one called Ace — whistled. "Blow us all to Kingdom Come."

"Too bad his face's messed up," said the first. "Makes it harder to find out who he is."

"Was," said the third man. "You mean 'was,' Larry."

"Was," said Larry. " 'Course he's just a packhorse. Real question is who he worked for."

The third man spoke again. "They already got a poster out. Got an artist who sketched out a jaw for him."

"I heard a ten grand reward."

"I heard twenty."

They were nudged again by the crowd. "Move along up there!" someone yelled.

Adams made a guttural sound, and from the thrust of his back Dixie Clay knew he'd spat onto the window. "Burn in hell."

The men moved on, but before she was shoved away Dixie Clay darted to the glass.

Behind the window dripping with thick sputum was a face she knew, even without its lower half.

The face of Uncle Mookey.

Did a gasp leak from her mouth? Later she'd wonder. She whirled away, already leaping into flight, when she crashed against the round chest of a man and bounced off, Willy on her shoulder getting mashed between their bodies. Dixie Clay was falling back, about to land hard when the man made a low quick grab, one arm vising each bicep, and he levered her to her feet. She turned to examine Willy, squalling furiously.

"Oh my baby, are you hurt? Are you hurt?"

Willy lifted his two middle fingers into his mouth and began to suck on them, still crying but muffled now. Dixie Clay kissed his brow. "I'm sorry, Willy, I'm so, so sorry."

She nestled the baby onto her shoulder and felt her elbow wrenched sideways. "Hey!" Dixie Clay yelled as the man pulled her around the side of the funeral home into the alley, as if they were dancing a reel. "Hey! Stop!" She came to a halt with her back pressed against the bricks and turned to look over her shoulder: Where was Adams, the others? The crowd was loud and roughhousing and no one noticed her abduction. At the alley's end, a man was pissing beside a trash bin. He gave a quick shake, then ducked around the corner.

Dixie Clay faced the man who'd pulled her here: large, with grizzled orange hair thick as the bristles on a hog, something almost comical about that orange hair over the pink cheeks but between them were eyes discerning and gray.

"I know who you are," he growled.

"I've never seen you before."

"I know what you do." He stepped closer.

"Listen, I don't know what you —"

"Shut up. That man's shot because of you," he said, jerking his thumb in the direction of the funeral home. "I shot him. I killed him, and now we can't question him and find out who he works for. He's shot because of you and because of this baby my partner brought you and forsook his post to dote over."

"Your partner? You mean — your partner is — Ingersoll?"

"Yeah. But he wasn't much of a partner, was he, when he left me on the levee to ride out to your place."

Dixie Clay was struggling to stitch these quilt blocks together. Ingersoll's partner was Ham, who was the revenuer who shot Uncle Mookey. Last night. When Ingersoll was at her house.

"And I watched you just now, missy. Watched you real good. Watched you watch that dead saboteur, and I got a hunch that you know him." Ham's eyes were like pewter nails pinning her to the bricks. "That you got something to tell."

Ham must know she was a bootlegger. Would he arrest her? Willy squirmed, she was holding him too tightly.

The man stepped forward and there were only inches between his face and hers, the baby on her chest. "Tell me," said Ham. "Goddamn it, tell me who he is."

They were just ten yards from the entrance to the alley where the crowd swarmed. Someone would hear her if she screamed. But there was menace in the way he placed his right hand on the wall beside her shoulder, blocking her exit.

"I don't know," she said. "I don't know who he is. I don't know anything."

His eyes rummaged hers. She met them with her chin raised. She was aware of someone at the alley's end, pausing to peer at them, then moving on. The baby gave a cough.

For a long minute, Ham didn't move and she didn't move. A rat scurried down the alley, which smelled like rotten vegetables.

Finally he let his arm drop and stepped back. As she watched, his face seemed to soften into oafishness. His lips poked out and it was the doughy cheeks, not the drill-bit eyes, which gained dominance. It was like watching someone pull on a rubber mask.

"Well then," he said, and lifted his hand to his muttonchops, "that's your story, huh. You don't know nothing."

He scratched his chops and turned toward the front of the alley. Even his frame seemed to diminish, the chest still big but something shambling in his gait, as if he were a man without access to his power. He moved past the painted bricks advertising Pinkham's Medicinal Liquid.

"Who are you, really?" she called. She didn't even mean to ask it.

He paused, his back to her. "Who did Ingersoll say I am?" He turned to see her answer.

"He said nothing."

"Nothing? Not one thing?"

"Well, one thing. We heard an owl hoot. And he said you don't like owls."

"Owls," he said, and snorted. "No, I don't like owls."

"He said you won't say why."

"They're a portent. You hear an owl,

something bad's gonna happen."

"Something bad had *already* happened. My baby had got pneumonia croup and nearly died. And that man" — she thumbed toward the funeral parlor — "had got shot."

He was quiet so long she thought he wasn't going to reply. He turned toward the front of the alley and spoke with his back to her. "You ain't seen the end of bad," is what he told her before ambling away. "You ain't even seen the beginning of the end."

CHAPTER 13

Ingersoll sat on his cot and looked across into the other cell, which was like looking in a mirror and not being there. Captain Trudo at his desk chicken-pecked the typewriter and ignored Ingersoll. The chicken-pecking of rain on the roof stopped and Ingersoll could see through the window an arc of levee, men hunched in raincoats willing the water back. Somebody had the rest of the dynamite. What if the levee blew and he was locked in this cell?

"Can I make a phone call?"

"Not till I hear from the sheriff."

How long until Ham would figure where he was? Ingersoll had to have been moving Vatterottian furniture for thirty minutes at least, then maybe thirty to find and view the body, then another thirty with Trudo. Ham would expect him soon. But then again, maybe Ham wasn't so confident about his expectations anymore.

Trudo withdrew rolling papers from his desk drawer and set one out on the manila folder.

"Can I have a smoke?"

"Not till I hear from the sheriff."

Stupid, stupid, stupid.

The captain's phone rang and when he answered it, he glanced at Ingersoll and swiveled on his chair and hunched his back. "Naw," he said after listening a moment, "I'm tied up here. Start without me." He set the phone down and blew air out of his nostrils. *He doesn't want me here any more than I want to be here,* thought Ingersoll, which gave him an idea.

He reached through the bars and stretched his fingers until they caught a bent straw of a broom leaning against the wall. He tugged it closer and it toppled, loudly smacking the concrete floor, but the captain just glared and turned back to his typewriter. So Ingersoll kept working to tug the broom into the cell. When he had it, he got his utility knife out — using the same blade he'd used to jimmy the lock of Dixie Clay's still — and wedged it beneath the staple that held the coiled steel wire at the neck. He pried the staple off, then unwound the several feet of wire. He could tell the captain was watching but trying not to. Ingersoll tied one end of the wire to a bar and the other beneath the leg of the cot so it stretched in a taut diagonal.

Trudo couldn't stand it anymore and batted down the paper sticking up from his typewriter for an unobstructed view. "If you're aiming to hang yourself, you might could tie that wire higher."

Ingersoll crouched and stuck his arm between the bars to grasp the wooden triangle propping open the hall door. It swung closed as he brought the doorstop through his bars and toed it under the wire by the cot leg, tensioning it.

"Just what the hell do you think you're doing?"

Ingersoll got out the empty half-pint of Black Lightning still in his pocket from Dixie Clay's. He struck the wire with it, and the sound was bright. Then he began to play, sliding the bottle down the string to change the pitch and plucking with his other hand. He sang prison songs, and he sang loudly; he strummed and picked that diddley bow as the captain pretended to type and pretended to read and pretended to think. Ingersoll could play prison songs all day; he'd learned a bunch from the Negro soldiers he'd met in France. He'd had one of the great surprises of his life over there when he and a buddy got a weekend pass and hightailed it to Paris's Le Grand Duc, said to have the best music in Montmartre. Ingersoll had just settled down with a bottle of wine and two squat glasses when he heard a guitar riff and snapped his head around and by God if it wasn't Skinny Nellie, who had taught him guitar in that other life, in the Chicago of Lizzie Looey. On Skinny's break they embraced, more than they'd ever done back at the Lantern. It was easier in France. Skinny said as much, around back behind the club where they walked together. They leaned on the alley bricks and shared a cannabis cigarette, which Skinny referred to as "tea leaves." After a big drag, Skinny blew the smoke out and shrugged. "White folks can like the colored over here. When I do my solo and walk out among the tables," he said, and grinned, "all them white womens slide they skinny asses over to make room in they booths, hoping Ole Skinny'll rest his dogs for a spell."

They'd laughed together and it felt easy. A busted bicycle lay by their feet and Skinny removed its flat tire and as they talked he knifed the wire from it and tied it to a nail stuck in the back door. Ingersoll had played the one-string before he'd gotten his first guitar but hadn't made one in years so watched carefully. Skinny must have known he was giving his last lesson to his old student because his movements were precise, tying the other end and using a snuff can as the wedge. Then he plucked that diddley bow while they traded stories about Paris and the music scene, reminisced about Chicago, but didn't mention Lizzie. Ingersoll didn't ask and didn't want to know. Then it was time for the second set and Skinny offered to roll Ingersoll some more tea leaves but Ingersoll said no thanks, and Skinny socked him lightly in the shoulder and went inside and Ingersoll took just another moment in the alley thinking wasn't the world both so big and so small.

Ingersoll now played one of Skinny's songs, bellowing at the captain, "Set Me Free" —

Well, I was a good man and should be free
State made a prisoner out of me.

The captain took another phone call, shouting to make himself heard. Ingersoll played louder, wishing he had a paint can for a resonator, remembering a diddley bow banjo he'd later made in France from a cookie tin and a bicycle wheel he'd found in the cellar of a bombed-out house. A bo-jo, he'd called it. Loud? Whoooo-eeeeee, that baby was loud. Loud and twangy. He never could decide whether it sounded wonderful or terrible. He played it for the men one night when they were being shelled, he played it and sang hard to muffle the shrieking sky tearing out its hair. *Louder,* one of the men would shout. *Louder,* and he played louder. When dawn arrived at last, it found them alive, alive every one and every one with an earache. He'd lost his voice for two days.

"Whoa, Rosie," he wailed now, rising, almost drunk with exhaustion — how long since he'd slept? the levee, sick baby, the slammer — "Whoa, whoa, Rosie." He repeated twice his favorite verse, facing the captain's back:

Stick to the promise, gal, you made me —
Wasn't gonna marry till I go free — Whoa,
     Rosie —
When she walks she reels and rocks
     behind
Ain't that enough to worry a convict's mind.

Ingersoll started in on the "Whoa, Rosie"s again and noticed the door to the hallway was cracked and the intake policemen bobbing their heads. "Whoa, Rosie, whoa." The captain dropped the phone onto its cradle and yanked out his paper from the typewriter and packed it in his hands. Ingersoll started on "Early in the Morning" and had gotten to the best line, "Eagle on a dollar quarter, gonna rise and fly," when the captain grabbed something from his drawer and ejected from his seat and stomped to Ingersoll's cell. *At last,* thought Ingersoll. But the glinting metal wasn't a key. It was pliers, with which the captain snipped the broom wire, which flung itself like a cottonmouth at Ingersoll's head.

Now he sat sullenly on the cot with his chin in his hands. He felt fatigue squatting on his shoulders like a Vatterott armoire. Not just the fatigue from moving that furniture, or from the sleepless night he'd spent hovering like a dark starless ceiling over that sick baby, or from figuring what he should do about Dixie Clay, or from trying to find the missing revenuers, but also from feeling he needed to hold back the Mississippi, with his own arms, if that's what it called for, and it seemed to. He half remembered a story about a boy pressing his finger to a crack in a dam and Ingersoll was too tired to remember how the story turned out and felt a surge of exhaustion like nausea and thought, *If I close my eyes and lie down, I'll remember it.*

When he woke, it was dark out the window and bright in the room and both dark and bright in Ham's furious gray eyes squinched between his furious red muttonchops. "You've been here? The whole time?"

Ingersoll swung his legs off the cot, and like smoke the strange dream of Dixie Clay evaporated, a dream in which she'd asked him to hold Willy while she magicked the river into moonshine and the townspeople drank it and everyone was safe.

"Ham," Ingersoll croaked. "You're here."

Ham turned to the captain, who was playing solitaire. "How long he been asleep?"

Trudo made a show of considering his cards. "Six, seven hours."

"Let him out so I can murder him. Then you can put me in."

"Pick a different cell," Trudo stated, slapping the card down. "He's locked up till I hear from the sheriff that the Federal Revenue Agency can vouch for him."

"Give me the goddamn phone," Ham said, and when he got it he yelled at the local operator to get him a long-distance operator and even in his cell Ingersoll could hear her chilly "Stand by." While the call was connected, Ingersoll bowed his head, toed the loose pile of broom straw. Somebody should weave it into gold.

The revenue commissioner took the call and just that easily Ingersoll's identity was confirmed and the captain laid his cards down to fish out the key for Ham, who unlocked the door and swung the bars open and Ingersoll stepped out.

"Your sidearm," the captain called after Ingersoll, who was halfway out the door, and he reversed and snatched his gun off the desk and then scooped up two of the captain-rolled cigarettes and handed one to Ham. They'd not even entered the hall when Ingersoll heard the click of Trudo's receiver being lifted off its cradle. Ingersoll could guess who he'd be telephoning. Jesse would be angry at the captain, no doubt, but Trudo had detained Ingersoll as long as he could. Surely even Jesse could see that.

CHAPTER 14

The oatmeal canister slipped from Dixie Clay's trembling hands, and she swiped the air leaning to catch it and nearly fell off the pantry step stool. She grabbed the slick shelf and hung panting and then scrambled to the floor where she grabbed the handfuls of dollar bills and jammed them deep into the cotton gunnysack. She didn't stop to count, but there was a lot of money. She'd need it, wherever they'd run to.

"Willy!" she called. "Just a few more moments, I'm coming!" She heard a tremor in her voice. She'd placed him on her bed and didn't like to be so far away from him, but there was no time to check on him, not now.

Dixie Clay, once freed by Ham, had fled from the alley with Willy and grabbed Chester and didn't wait for Amity's store to open. As she kicked Chester to a faster pace, she started putting together all she'd just learned. In the two years since Uncle

Mookey had run off into the woods after trying to kiss her, she'd never heard mention of him. She'd wondered but hadn't had the courage to ask. She could recall the fury in Jesse's face when he lifted the Winchester off its rack beside the door and set off toward the still.

But Uncle Mookey hadn't been killed by Jesse in the woods; he'd been alive until last night. When he'd been shot while planting dynamite on the levee. She'd never fully understood how much Mookey understood — but she didn't believe for a second that he'd come up with a plan like that.

Jesse had.

She wanted to deny this. Surely Jesse couldn't really mean to blow up the town, his friends, his wife? And Sugar Hill — such a precarious location — surely he didn't want to flood his still, his still that had made him so very rich?

But he looked like he was fixing to get out. He'd often said Prohibition would be ending soon. Of course, it hadn't ended yet — surely there was more money to be made? Yet, she recalled his saying "A last big push." She recalled him saying, "I need someplace more suitable for my ambitions." And: "I could have been a different kind of man, you know."

He meant to flood his house, his still. Go to New Orleans, that was easy enough to see now. The telephone calls and telegrams. The visit to the New Orleans bankers when they'd asked Jesse to bring their offer to the levee board of Hobnob. But even after the levee board turned down the fifty thousand, Jesse'd still gone to see the bankers. And he'd been secretive, hadn't taken any of his whiskey workers; she'd only known herself because of the label in his new hat, "French Quarter Haberdashery," and the cashews wrapped in paper from DeSalvo's Delicatessen, Pirate's Alley.

Oh my God, Jesse cut a deal with the bankers.

That's why he'd been so loud, so public about being a Sticker. It was his cover.

He's flooding the town — he's going to destroy us all — and wash away the still, and the corpses of the revenuers, all evidence of his lawbreaking.

She kicked Chester and he gave a surprised snort and she apologized. She meant to get home, pack the hidden money and the gun. She and Willy could disappear into the woods. She had no tent, but she could find a cave, or some way to keep Willy dry, and avoid the roads. Eventually, find a strange town, take a new name, cut her hair

— dress Willy as a girl — say her husband had drowned, falling into the river while sandbagging. Oh but first, before her escape, she'd call the police, warn the town. But she couldn't call Captain Trudo, he might be in on it —

Thank God, there was the dark house. She'd slid off Chester before he'd fully stopped and didn't even tie him but ran with Willy into the house.

Now she had gotten the money, next the bullets — where were they? Jesse's drawer — and she ran to the bedroom and yanked it out and her shaking fingers couldn't close on the slippery cartridges so she just lifted the drawer and overturned it in her gunnysack.

She lunged to grab her coat and that was when she saw headlights through the rain-blurry window. *Oh my God.* She whirled away from the coat toward Willy on her bed and thrust her arms under him and was running to the back door when the front door slammed open and as it did she flung the gunnysack toward the pantry.

"Whore," Jesse snarled.

She stiffened and turned with Willy's ball of a body on her heaving chest.

Jesse wore his long camel hair coat, its

ends two downspouts of rain, over an oyster-colored suit with a salmon tie. Dangling down and bumping against his chest was, oddly, an opera-length strand of pearls. The hand that had pushed the door open was now leaning there for support and he was panting a bit. Over his shoulder she could see the Ford, its headlights mining diamonds in two cones of rain. Lightning lit the scene like a photographer's flash bar: someone else in the car, too. Jesse took his hand off the door to wipe his mouth and stumbled a few steps into the room. Lord, he was drunk.

"Whore," he said again, moving across the parlor toward her. "Dirty whore. Did you" — the words slurred into a single syllable — "did you think I wouldn't find out? And with a goddamn revenuer, you goddamn idiot?"

"I didn't know —"

His hand snatched the braid running over her shoulder. He twisted his fist to wrap it and yanked her to his chest. She could smell the hooch on his breath.

"Entertaining him in my house? My place of business? Spreading your legs —"

"No —" she cried, Jesse's spittle spackling her face. So he knew Ingersoll had been to the house. She had to get out of here before

Jesse learned that she knew about Mookey, the explosives. Learned she was trying to leave him.

"Shut up, you —"

"Jesse, baby," came a high voice, and they both turned toward the door where a tall blonde twirled an umbrella flipped inside out. Dixie Clay had seen flappers in *McCall's,* and a few in town, but never this close, and not this knife-edged beautiful. She wore a black dress dangling with bugle beads, belted low on her hips.

"Thought I told you to stay in the car."

"I'm bored, Jesse, baby." Her voice pouty and girlish. "Let's get the money and head out. Oh" — pretending to notice Dixie Clay for the first time — "is this the one, whatshername, Dipsie Dirt?" She dropped the umbrella beside the hall tree and pranced over to Dixie Clay, a bit unsteadily. As the woman appraised her, Dixie Clay appraised her right back. The dress stopped above her knees. She wore flesh-colored stockings but she'd rolled them down. Her kneecaps were right there, uncovered. Her feet wore unbuckled galoshes. She had three bangles on each arm and a wrist strap held a beaded purse. On her head a tightly fitting black cloche with a rhinestone clasp, her champagne-colored hair shorn below her ears and curved onto her cheeks like rams' horns. She also wore two strands of pearls that matched Jesse's. She circled the trio — Dixie Clay with her back arched over Jesse's knuckles, Willy on her shoulder sucking his wrist.

The woman stopped and drew her face down to Dixie Clay's upturned one. At the corners of her eyes, face powder had gathered in her starburst wrinkles and Dixie Clay reckoned her not just taller but older than Jesse. She wouldn't see thirty again. She wore red lipstick and her green eyes had tiny irises and she lowered her face until she was just inches away and inhaled. For an instant Dixie Clay thought the woman would kiss her. Then a lightning bolt seared her cheek: a slap.

"You smell like river scum," the woman said. On her shoulder Willy began to cry, startled by the noise or because Dixie Clay had clutched him.

The flapper turned to Jesse. "This little mouse? This country schoolmarm is the one cuckolded you?" She laughed, like a BB gun, and Dixie Clay could see red lipstick on her teeth. The laugh trickled into a cough. The flapper unclasped her purse and brought out a package of Chesterfields and shook one out and one fell to the floor yet she didn't seem to notice. *Drunk, too,* Dixie Clay thought. *Drunk as Jesse.*

Jesse had loosened his grip on her braid, and she craned to see his profile. Beneath his mustache, his lips curved merrily, as did the creases at his watery green eye, in which the pupil looked shrunken, pealike. Maybe he was worse than drunk. "Jeannette," he sighed. "Jeannette."

She swooped the cigarette to her red mouth with red fingernails and directed a look at Jesse. He reached into the pocket of his overcoat and brought out a matchbox but it was soggy. He studied it, befuddled.

"Oh, hell," she said, and reached into her dangling-open purse and pulled out a lighter and flicked the hinge-top — it made a little *ding* — and thumbed the flint wheel and brought it to her Chesterfield. She inhaled deeply, then held the cigarette at arm's length and seemed to address it, exhaling, "I need me more of a man than that."

Willy was still crying, and Dixie Clay held him to her flaming cheek like a poultice. Outside the storm shook the house, and inside another storm shook, crackling with menace. Outside was safer. If she could free herself, she and Willy could dash out the back door and these two would never find

them in the wind-thrashing woods. Jesse
seemed focused on the fact that Ingersoll
had been to the house. Jesse'd always been
jealous but this rage was outsized.

It gives him an excuse to kill me, she
thought.

Jeannette brought the cigarette back to
her lips, sucked, then dropped it burning to
the rug and toed it out with a flick of her
galoshes. She clapped, then held her hands
to Dixie Clay. "Lemme see that baby."

"No." It was as automatic as kicking after
the doctor hits your kneecap. Dixie Clay
hugged Willy tighter.

"What?"

"He's crying," as if the woman couldn't
tell.

"I'd cry too if my mama was a whore."
The woman reached out and waggled her
fingers near Willy's face and he watched the
red nails, rapt, and his mewing slowed.
Then, starting at Willy's left wrist, she began
to walk her fingers up his arm, singing —
"Your mama's a filthy slut, filthy slut, filthy
slut; your mama's a filthy slut who just can't
keep her legs shut!" The red nails were at
the luscious roll of fat that bulged in a V
from his armpit and squeezed it as if testing
dough for doneness. "Mmm," she said.

Jeannette reached to take Willy and Dixie

Clay pivoted her shoulders but her scalp was yanked back by Jesse's hold, which seemed to rouse him. Like a blind donkey set back in a furrow, he continued, snarling, "In my own house!" His face was red. "In my own bed!"

"Jesse," said Jeannette. "Feel how soft."

"Jesse, Willy was sick and needed a doctor —"

"Jesse." The flapper was at Dixie Clay's side, fondling Willy's feet. "Don't these toes look just like little sweet peas?"

"So it's the goddamn baby's fault, is it?" Jesse asked.

"No, nothing's his fault," Dixie Clay said over Willy's cries. "Jesse, please." She tried to angle her face to connect with Jesse's gaze. "When Ingersoll —"

"You speak his goddamn name?"

"Jesse," Dixie Clay said, willing him to look at her. Could those two-tone eyes no longer see Dixie Clay Murchinson of Pine Grove, Alabama?

But the woman was dropping to her bare knees on the carpet. He looked down at her and purred, "Jeannette, Jeannette, Jeannette." He took a flask from his pocket with his free hand and stuck it in his mouth and rotated it to untwist the cap, and the flask fell free, splashing down his tie and on Jeannette's shoulders, though she didn't seem to notice. He spit the cap out. "Goddamn it," he said, and lifted the tie to wipe his dripping mustache and chin.

His face looked rubbery, his hand going to the long strand of pearls on his chest, which he lifted and let fall. Dixie Clay felt she'd never seen him before. And she hadn't, exactly, because while she knew he'd done bad things, maybe even killed those two revenuers, she'd never dreamed him capable of flooding his town. No, she did not know this man.

Jeannette had taken hold of Willy's big toe. "This little piggy goes to market," she sang, and giggled, and then, "This little piggy stays home, this little piggy likes roast beef." Dixie Clay felt Jesse's fist drop from her braid and in that instant she twisted away, her body leaping into what would have been escape if Jeannette hadn't squeezed Willy's pinkie toe. Dixie Clay reversed direction, off balance, and her back leg buckled under her and she landed hard on her backside and bounced but managed to keep Willy on her chest.

Jeannette said, "That was the one that goes wee wee wee all the way home!" and shrieked with laughter. Willy was shrieking, too, a sound she'd never heard him make, a sound no baby should make, and Dixie Clay lifted his foot to find Jeannette's nails had left blue punctures, like staples, above the ball of toe. His eyes were shooting tears and he seemed to regard her with shock: *Could this happen in your arms?*

"You're crazy!" she screamed at Jeannette. "Get out! Leave him alone!"

Jeannette suddenly stopped laughing, sat back on her heels. "Jesse baby," she said, and cocked her head in its cloche. "Didja hear what she called me? Your whore of a wife. Called me crazy. Jesse, you know how that makes me feel."

Dixie Clay twisted and tried to scramble to her feet holding Willy. Jesse caught her around the waist and brought her down hard on her knees, and she broke her fall with her left hand so as not to land on Willy but felt something explode.

"You're gonna hurt that baby," said Jeannette. She sniffed. "You don't even deserve a baby."

Dixie Clay remembered the knife in the kitchen, the Winchester on the gun rack by the door. Ingersoll.

"Let me have that baby," Jeannette said. "Jesse, baby, I want that baby." She leaned a clumsy arm on the coffee table to hoist to her feet.

"Whore of a wife," Jesse said, and his elbow thwacked between her shoulders and pain spiked from her left wrist up her arm. She fell on her side still clutching Willy with her right hand. Jesse reached up to yank her fingers back and Dixie Clay thought they might snap, and then Jeannette was around front, tussling Willy away, and Jesse lunged forward to hold her arms down and that's when he saw the pantry door open, the lumpy gunnysack lying across the threshold. Empty mouth of the oatmeal canister.

"What's that? What have you done, you little —" Jesse stumbled to the pantry, catching his shoulder on the door frame, and bent to pick up a corner of the gunnysack. He shook it and the bullets clacked.

Please God let him just drop the sack. Dixie Clay tried to distract him, pressing to her hands, "Jesse, I'm glad you came home, I —"

But Jesse lifted a corner of the bag and the bullets and crumpled dollars and other items from his desk drawer — a pen and red poker chips and a tire gauge — fell clattering to the floor. He stood, the deflated question of the sack in his hand, and then he whirled toward Dixie Clay and reared his leg behind him and with all his force kicked her. She felt her ribs crunch and the air snatched out and her face smacked against the floor.

"Poor baby feels cold!" said Jeannette, bringing Willy, still squalling, close to her face, wrinkling her nose at him. "Jesse, didn't you tell me this was an orphan child?"

Jesse gave Dixie Clay another kick. She tried to press herself farther away.

"Whore!" Jesse yelled. "Traitor!" He kicked her again, his boot catching her in the shoulder, her arms collapsing.

"Maybe I can be your new mama," Jeannette told Willy.

Now Jesse was yanking Dixie Clay to her feet by her braid. "Trying to run out on me. Trying to steal from me."

"Would you like that?" Jeannette continued. "Huh?"

Jesse dragged Dixie Clay to the kitchen and thrust her in the cane-back chair and jammed his boot into her stomach and then reached for the laundry line she'd strung by the sink. As he reached, his necklace caught on the chair stile and grew taut and exploded in a shower of bouncing pearls.

Jeannette had followed them with Willy. "Oh goody. That was Mama's! Jesse, now you have to buy me another!"

Jesse didn't answer, wrestling Dixie Clay's hands behind the chair. She cried out when he grabbed her left wrist and twisted it and began to lasso her hands with the laundry line.

"Think you can just up and leave me! Ungrateful bitch!"

Lightning flashed outside and Dixie Clay felt she was in the moving pictures. A horror show. Somebody start playing the piano, somebody turn on the lights, somebody wind the film into its reel.

The woman set Willy on the counter and was clapping his hands and chanting, "A-noth-er! A-noth-er! A-noth-er!" Willy was snuffling, calming down from his huge squalling to a whimper, interested in the clapping. Jeannette dropped his hands and left him perched on the edge as she flung her leg up onto the counter. From a garter halfway up her thigh she slipped a silver flask and unscrewed it and tilted her head back to drink.

Willy could sit up only for a few moments. He could fall, hit his head. Dixie Clay turned over her shoulder: "Jesse, please, please come to your senses." Behind her, he was breathing hard as he knotted the cord, then straightened. He'd been the one hand-cuffed to a chair a month ago by the revenuers. If only they'd shot him. If only she'd let them.

"Jeannette," Jesse said. "Get the money."

Dixie Clay felt his foot catch the chair leg and he tripped and skidded on the rainwater and pearls but righted himself. "Jesse," she said again, but he didn't turn. *Something's wrong with him. Something's gone wrong.*

Jeannette came back into the kitchen from the bedroom cramming rolls of dollars into her purse. It was more money than Dixie Clay had ever seen, and she couldn't imagine where it had been stashed. The wads were rubber-banded and several thunked to the floor and when Jeannette bent to get them, the rolls in her open purse fell out. "Gimme," Jesse said, and bent to scoop up the rolls, thrusting them into his pockets. Jeannette turned to Willy on the counter and set the flask down and gathered him in her arms. "This baby's cold!" Jeannette exclaimed. "I guess Dipsie Dirt lacks that maternal instinct."

Jesse straightened with effort, pockets bulging, and walked to the butler's pantry, pausing at the nook where her ironing board hung. He lifted the board and let it fall with a clatter.

Jeannette brought the baby close to her face and kissed his neck. "You taste good. Like a baby should!"

Jesse had his back to them and was fiddling with the panel that controlled their electric lights. In front of Dixie Clay, Jeannette swung Willy toward the ceiling and then hugged him close. Willy was gazing at her red painted lips and he floated his arm up to pat them. "Blow kiss," she said, and she blew a whooozz of air while shaking her head rapidly, nuzzling the tender center of his palm. When she lifted her head, he took his hand away, and then slapped it back to her mouth for another nuzzle, and gave a hiccupy laugh.

"Look," she said. "He loves me!" She nuzzled his hand again, and again he made a noise, a two-syllable happy hiccup. "Jesse, he loves me."

Jesse gave a cry of triumph and the metal panel door swung open.

"Jesse, you said that later on we could have a baby."

"Sure thing, baby. But not now." He reached his arm in, then farther in.

"But I may not be able to have one natural after — after the operation. You remember what the doc said. Let me keep this one. He likes me. See?" Again she nuzzled and again the baby gurgled.

Jesse was pressing his shoulder and cheek against the wall. "We can't. You know where we're going when we leave here. Oh — I think I feel it."

"We'll bring him with us!"

"Babycakes, we can't. Now that Mookey's dead I gotta do setup. Wait — got it!" Jesse yelled, and there was a long wet sucking sound and when he pulled his arm back into the room, it held what looked like a bundle of books, a long tail of tape dangling from it.

"Well, he's so sweet, it's a shame he has to die."

Dixie Clay made a noise, a wail, and it must have reminded Jesse she was there. "Shut up!" he yelled, and then he turned and yelled it at Jeannette, too. "You were supposed to wait in the goddamn car!"

"It doesn't matter what she knows. What do we care. She'll be dead by sunrise."

Jesse brought the package to his mouth and bit down and tore off the tape and stacks of bills fell out. He laughed to see it all.

Jeannette set Willy on the floor and lifted Dixie Clay's wicker laundry basket off the counter and took it to Jesse, who was kneeling now before the money. He began to rake the stacks of bills together and dump them into the basket. "Let's take him," Jeannette said. "When we get to New Orleans, we can say we rescued him from the flood. Think how good that will sound in your stump speech. You'll be a hero. Rescuing a baby from a flood! And when we get married, we can adopt him proper."

He paused and smiled with the side of his face but then shook his head. "No baby. Too complicated."

"Well, I could take him and go on to Greenville. Daddy bought me all those driving lessons, might as well see what I learned, huh? You can meet us there. You'll have Burl's car."

Jesse just shook his head again and reached for a stack of bills.

Jeannette walked to Jesse's back and leaned against him, threading her arms around his neck. "Pwease? Pretty pwease?" She crooned into his ear. "I'll be berry berry gwateful."

Jesse let his head fall back onto her shoulder.

"You know you can't say no to babycakes," she taunted and nuzzled his neck.

He lifted his dazed face and smiled and raised an imprecise hand to flick the ends of his rumpled mustache. "Naw, I can't say no to babycakes."

Jeannette jumped to her feet, clapping, and spun and lunged for Willy.

Dixie Clay yelled, "You can't have him!

He's mine — You're crazy — you —"

They both spun on her, galvanized and terrible.

"I'm *saving* this baby," shrilled Jeannette. "If not for me, he'd die alongside you —"

Jesse stepped in front, blocking the view of Willy. "You don't even know what I have to do now. What I have to do to get out of this. Fucking a goddamn revenuer at my goddamn still!" He picked up the iron frying pan from the sink and hissed, "You don't even know." And smashed the pan against her skull. The chair crashed to the floor and the last thing she saw was a pearl scoot away into the darkness.

CHAPTER 15

There was no singing that night on the levee, no guitar playing, no men stopping to bum a light from Ingersoll and staying to chat. It occurred to him that night patrol on the sandbagged levee was like night patrol in the sandbagged trenches, but the difference was now he was an outsider. As he rode Horace along the crest past the volunteer watchmen, he felt their guns trained at his back, as if he wore a target there. *I'm fixing to get myself shot,* he thought, noting the Southern expression sliding in. *Fixing to. Huh.*

The sky was just beginning to lighten, the blueblack before dawn. He could make out shapes, and he shined his lantern down the town side, checking the matted grass for boils or men slithering up, then played the light along the river side, looking for men crouched in boats.

After springing Ingersoll from jail, Ham

had stomped back to the Vatterott, Ingersoll following a few paces behind and wearing the mud splatters to prove it. It was dinner so they'd joined the table, might as well because saboteurs wouldn't attempt anything before dark. They fed themselves, then the horses, and cleaned their rifles and revolvers. They probably hadn't said a dozen words in all that time. *This must be what it would feel like to disappoint a father,* Ingersoll thought. He wanted to make things up to Ham, yet there was a part, a big part, even now that thought that, despite what Dixie Clay had done, he should be flinging open her door: "Get Willy, get your things. It's time." He couldn't remember ever feeling so conflicted or uncertain in his life.

He'd ridden along the levee for the last four or five hours, rifle across his lap, Horace lifting his hooves and placing them down gingerly as if the levee were a rope bridge. Ham had told Ingersoll to patrol the levee no matter what happened and had said he was heading to the post office to try to telephone Hoover about the dead saboteur. He'd already tried but couldn't get through because of the storm. If he failed this time, said Ham, he'd give up trying and just telegram. Which gave Ingersoll at most a few hours to fix things. But you couldn't fix dead. Nor could the fact of Dixie Clay be fixed. It would require broken vows and broken laws, blood, desertion, and money.

Now, oddly, as Jesse Swan Holliver materialized in his thoughts, that very man materialized on the levee, his camel hair coat bending over a two-wheeled cart, at the spot Dick Worth normally guarded. He looked to be gingerly lifting a sandbag. As Ingersoll rode up he peered over Jesse's beaver hat into the cart — a half dozen sodden sandbags and a carton of Black Lightning.

"Helping the effort?" asked Ingersoll.

Jesse sprang up, clutching at his chest, and whirled around. "Jesus!" he yelled. "For Christ sake, what are you doing, sneaking up, trying to give someone apoplexy?"

Everyone was jumpy, especially after the previous day's attack, but Ingersoll had never seen Jesse like this, heaving a little, eyes wild. "Hardly sneaking up," said Ingersoll, after a pause, crossing his hands over the pommel. "Came to check on Worth."

Jesse scanned the levee, then swung his head back to Ingersoll and it seemed a heavy thing. "I spelled him."

There was mud splattered on Jesse's pink tie. Why was he working the graveyard shift? Or working at all? "You delivering whiskey?"

"Maybe. You gonna arrest me?"

Ingersoll didn't answer, turning over his shoulder to see if he could spot Ham. The weak sun was struggling to do a chin-up, its hairline appearing over the edge of the earth. They were near the elbow of the bend where the river was most furious, and it smashed against the sandbags, and lassos of spray looped for Horace's legs.

Jesse leaned and spat into the clashing river. The air was lightening and Jesse's features growing distinct, his mustache loose at the ends. Ingersoll could smell the booze on him despite the wind. Jesse gazed downhill toward town, the levee ending at the street, across it the shops and buildings, the implacable red-faced McLain Hotel. Beside the courthouse, someone with a wagon was handing coffee to the workers. The blue shadow of the levee melted down the buildings with the sun's climb. "It was a pretty town, Hobnob Landing, wasn't it?"

Ingersoll said nothing.

"Well," Jesse said, "it won't matter no how, I guess."

"What's that mean?"

But Jesse turned, abandoning his post and the cart and the rest of the whiskey, and began to stride away.

"Hey," Ingersoll called, "what about

Worth's spot?"

"You cover it, Ing," Jesse said over his shoulder, flapping a hand. "I got somewhere to go."

Then he took off his hat and swung it, a grandiose farewell that Ingersoll puzzled over as he waited for Worth, who was sloshing his way back along the levee, pulling on a bottle of Black Lightning. Ingersoll studied Jesse's slick-soled dress-shoed descent. Halfway down, he skidded to his backside, but he was quick to his feet and finished with a kind of high-kneed sideways hop. At the street, he glanced around, then opened the door of a dark green Model T, not the black one he usually drove.

There was the *whooo, whooo* of an owl, and Ingersoll turned to see about two hundred yards away the sunrise highlighting Ham's sunrise-colored muttonchops. Ham jerked his thumb toward Jesse, so Ingersoll turned Horace's nose downhill and rode him past the guards, dismounting and tying the horse to a lantern pole.

He and Ham reached the street at different blocks and crossed and met in the shadow of an alley beside the hotel. They leaned around the corner to see Jesse as he hunched over the steering wheel and unset the parking brake and turned the key and adjusted the throttle. The engine ground, refusing to catch.

"He'll flood it," Ingersoll said.

"No, he won't." Ham raised his hand, which held a gnarl of wires and the distributor cap.

Ingersoll smiled grimly. "Ham, what the devil is he up to?"

"I don't know," said Ham, "but I'll find out or die trying."

Jesse gave up and waited a moment and tried again. It ground again.

"Have you been on him the whole time?" asked Ingersoll.

"Pretty much." They watched him pound the steering wheel and throw his head back in what was probably a curse. "I was looking for him earlier, and I saw that car —" Ham paused as Jesse ground the engine, a terrible sound. "Saw it going by slow with a tarped boat on a trailer. I'd just stepped out of the lobby of the hotel. Been jawing with the clerk, trying to see if anything was amiss, any strange guests checked in. 'A few,' says he, 'got one fella, I asked him his name and he had to pause to think on it.' "

The men pulled back against the brick wall as Jesse got out of the car and slammed the door and jogged to the front grille. He was trying to crank it by hand and seemed panicked.

Ham continued, "So I'm taking a smoke in this alley and that Ford tries to back in the boat trailer but the driver doesn't cut the wheel enough and the boat runs up on the curb and into some trash cans, scattering a whole passel of alley cats. Well, I'm heading over to see if I can't help and notice our pal here in the driver seat."

"You don't say."

"I do. So I just duck away and watch, and he finally backs down into the alley and when he comes around the other side ten minutes later, he's got no trailer, no boat at all."

"What did he do with it?"

"Don't know. I decide to stick with him instead of looking for the boat. He parks the Ford and opens the trunk —"

Jesse gave an anguished gargle and left the grille to enter the car again.

"— and nabs a wagon and unloads into it a case of whiskey and a few sandbags. And he pulls that wagon slow as Methuselah all the way to the top, wearing his Sunday-go-to-meeting clothes. So I give the Ford a tune-up and then sneak down a piece and watch him handing whiskey to the guards, sandbag a little. That's when you ride up."

They watched now as Jesse reslammed his

fists against the steering wheel. He flung open the door and whirled toward the hotel, and Ingersoll and Ham drew deeper into the alley but Jesse dashed toward the front grille again.

Ingersoll shook his head. "Peculiar . . ."

"But not illegal," finished Ham.

"No, not illegal. But something here is."

Jesse'd bent again, turning the crank, too violently as it snapped back and he had to flinch out of the way. Finally he whirled from the car and sprinted halfway up the levee and turned toward the hotel waving his hat. "Wait!" he screamed, hand to his mouth as a megaphone. "Don't! I can't —"

"What the — ?" Ham was asking.

The first shot came. Louder than the river, and Ingersoll knew it was a rifle from its timbre.

With the second shot, the sandbaggers broke from their puzzled trances and ran in both directions, diving for cover and yelling. Ingersoll couldn't tell who was being shot at. He'd flicked the safety off his rifle, as had Ham, and they heard another shot and expected to see men toppling dead into the river, but they saw none. Most had scrambled for cover, so the levee was clear of guards. Was that the point — to have a sniper lay down covering fire while a saboteur unspooled wire and set down connecting caps and hurried away, fingers in ears? It made no sense. Another shot, coming from above — Ingersoll and Ham jumped from the alley where they'd been pressed against the bricks and looked to find Jesse and what they saw was the only man on the levee not cowering for cover — he was sprinting down the street leading away, the tails of his coat flapping.

"Ham —"

"Got him. You get the sniper."

Two more shots now and Ingersoll was around the corner, closing in on the hotel door and nearly smashing into a large potted tree. The clerk was on his knees behind the desk and as Ingersoll skidded around the corner and yelled "What room?" the clerk understood and yelled "Three sixteen!" And then Ingersoll was through the lobby and scrambling up the stairs three at a time, grabbing the rail to propel his body around the corner.

On the third floor he pushed open the door into a long hallway, navy carpet with red geraniums. He glided forward, more quietly, glad for the carpet, and heard another shot and slowed outside the room and set his rifle aside as he withdrew his sidearm from his shoulder holster. He placed his fingers on the knob and twisted it and as the door swung open he pivoted through. Before him was the back of a hugely fat man, kneeling at the window, his rifle resting on the sill, a big target who kept firing even as Ingersoll aimed and fired, and then the man slumped as Ingersoll's bullet bit his skull.

In that same moment there came a God-almighty, blaring explosion and the whole world went white. Ingersoll was thrown against the shaking wall, and a billow of scorched papery sparks blasted by him like he was being flung through the membrane of hell, the floor atremble and the lights sparking into roiling darkness, the bottom of the world falling out.

Ingersoll sat singed and stunned, a table lamp crashing to the floor beside him, a mirror, and across the room, outside the window where the fat man's lower half dangled, the river was a volcano of fire. Beneath Ingersoll's legs the floor was galloping and he scrabbled to his feet and through the door, which hung oddly, and smashed against the wall opposite, which also hung oddly, and he went careening down the hall through a noise that was roaring, every creature on earth roaring, and up the fun house stairs and through the fire door onto the roof, where the pea gravel was jumping on the tar paper. It was the end, the beginning of the end, the end of the end, it was the flood that they had feared and expected all these days and nights.

He ran stumbling to the shaking terracotta knee wall that scalloped the edge of the roof. Across from him, the theater curtain of water was pouring through the exploded levee like Niagara. It had already eaten a hundred yards from the center, and on either side the earthen wall continued to crumble as if unzipping before the dirty brown torrent that seemed nearly a solid thing. Below, the water was smashing against the buildings and climbing the walls. The hardware store began to buckle, to kneel, a strange high groaning like a great beast being shot. It toppled and there was a flash of light as a wire snapped loose from a pole, which flamed like a torch and fell.

Ham, he thought.

Dixie Clay. Willy.

Now the hardware store collapsed in a vacuum of bubbles and sloshing waves. Ingersoll pictured the clusters of men he'd seen yesterday in the square — how many of them had been in the store? As if in answer he saw the terrified white face of a man bobbing by clinging to a wooden door, which rose up on its end as if trying to flap him free. Another swell and he was gone and then the door was ejected, spinning, boasting of its success, the unhinged man stripped from its hinges.

He watched from the roof as the torrent climbed and overwhelmed the buildings on Broad Street, edifices moving along in an orderly line, slowly sinking, as if descending stairs. A truck, or half of it, tore by, an A-frame ladder, a garden trellis, some barrels — innards of the hardware store, he realized — then from a wave, an arm emerged, still clasping the brim of a fedora, and sank from sight. Trees, uprooted, thrashing their arms, too, a tamale vendor's cart, a brace of donkeys.

To the north, a small house like some doll's toy was flipping end over end and a strapping teenage boy was running across the face of it, jumping as it turned like a barrel racer, running and running and leaping the corners, and Ingersoll watched him running for his life nimble and swift and then watched his leg plummet through a window and the flipping house rolled him into the deep.

Another section of levee collapsed and a wave hit the building, throwing Ingersoll off his feet. He rolled to his knees and clung to the wall, pulling himself to standing and brushing the bloody gravel from his palms, and looked up in time to see a barking black dog sweep past, then a man spinning on a mattress like a magic carpet, calmly bringing a cigarette to his lips. The siren from the firehouse began shrieking over the water's shrieking — the alarm to send folks to higher ground — but who could be further alarmed?

How long he stood watching the lashing angry surges of dark water filled with boards and planks and poles he didn't know, but at some point a raft came within ten feet, swinging around the corner. It carried three men and a dog, and Ingersoll yelled and ran to the edge of the roof. One of the men reached an oar to the building but it didn't touch, so Ingersoll tied a rope that was on the roof to the chimney and flung the rope and it was caught and fist over burning fist he yanked that heavy load to the roof and pulled the men over the wall and they lay stunned and heaving and then Ingersoll got them to their feet to haul the raft over, too. With the same rope they reeled in a canoe that held three Negroes, one a pregnant woman. There were six of them now rescued from the water and a dozen more had come up from the hotel and they ran across the roof in a confusion of terror, the dog barking and leaping alongside them. One of the Negroes spotted a boy riding a bucking hogshead barrel, and they threw him the rope and he caught it but someone yanked it too hard and the boy was spun off and Ingersoll leaped to the top of the wall, about to dive in, when they saw the boy's fist rising from the water, the rope in his hand, and they pulled him too onto the roof, where he spewed water. "My daddy!" he coughed out and pointed and they all looked and there was nothing in the direction of his finger and the boy let it fall to his side.

Ingersoll scanned the churning ocean pocked with fire. Only a few buildings, like dark ships, crested the water, but City Hall's roof was filled with two dozen folks at least and someone was waving a towel or blanket and Ingersoll realized they must see a plane. Yes, the planes would be coming soon. Those in the treetops — for they could see what looked to be a few forms in the high oaks that lined Broad Street — and those on the roofs would be saved. But the others —

Another moan wrenched from the levee and chunks of earth spewed as the river burst through. The roof shook and men ducked or were jostled to their knees, but the shock wasn't as severe as the last time — some of the power of the avalanche was siphoning off as the crevasse grew. Crouched behind the wall, two men shouted to each other — Did you hear the shots? The explosion? At his elbow, a man sheltered the whimpering dog and wept into his fur.

Strange, but the place the levee had burst wasn't the weakest spot of the bend but the part right in front of the hotel, this front-row seat of a hotel that had withstood the flood.

Ingersoll walked behind the chimney and lifted a dark tarp he'd seen earlier and there was a wooden boat, about ten feet, with two benches and an outboard motor. The kind of boat you built from a lumberyard kit. There were oars crossed on the floorboards over coils of rope, a jug of gasoline, cans of food, a canteen. He let the tarp drop, then walked back to the roof wall. Gazing at the frothing water he was putting together how Jesse put it together, this plan. The saboteur hadn't been a bad shot — he hadn't been aiming at people. He'd been aiming at a sandbag. The sandbag that Jesse had placed there as he, Ingersoll, had ridden up. A sandbag full of dynamite. The gunman had detonated it with ammunition. My God. He could almost admire it. Again Ingersoll saw Jesse's back, walking away, the grandiose hat waving, and understood it for what it was: the signal.

"Look," somebody yelled, and pointed, and they couldn't hear the buzz over the water but they could see the wings of a small biplane, the kind Ingersoll had seen on aircraft carriers. It circled the courthouse where people were waving and leaping. Another plane appeared on the horizon like a fly.

Ingersoll heard the crack of a tree and turned to see it crash into the water and hoped no one had clung in its canopy, waiting for rescue. He counted six buildings and two distant church steeples where people were scrambling to attract the planes or merely holding on.

Ham and Jesse? There was no telling. He yearned to tell Ham about the dynamite-stuffed sandbag, recalled him saying about Jesse's antics, "I'll figure it out or die trying." There was a chance of that. But if anyone made it out of this flood alive, it would be Ham. That had always been the case.

Dixie Clay and Willy. Were they at Sugar Hill, low-lying Sugar Hill, cornered between the river and the stream? Ingersoll faced south and saw no end to the water. He strode across the roof to the boat and ripped the tarp away.

CHAPTER 16

Dixie Clay was lifted toward the waking world on a surge of pain. She would have ridden it down again into the black oozing warmth but some idea of an idea, some thought she had to think, wrenched her, torqued her out, she was gasping like a crappie thrown up on the levee and left to die.

Her mind wasn't right. Cloudy, pierced with lightning bolts of moving pictures. Red lipstick on white teeth. A roll of dirty dollars thudding to the floor. She tried to open her eyes. Her lashes stuck together, then tore apart. She was looking through a blurry window — no, it was just her eyes. She was lying on her side, she knew that now, she was on the floor. She tried to lift her head, Oh God her head was a drawer yanked forward sloshing with knives. And then: Willy, where was Willy?

Her body didn't receive the telegram to move. Why. She couldn't move. Why. She was bound. *Willy.* She said this out loud but couldn't speak or couldn't hear, there was no noise at all. *Willy,* she said again. She looked through her eyes until they stopped bobbing and she was looking at a fruit basket, which was the wallpaper in the kitchen. *Willy Willy Willy Willy;* she scrabbled her legs, she threw her shoulders forward, her sides were branded with fire, she bumped the wooden chair against the floor, she thought she could turn it, she turned it.

Yes, the clothesline. Yes, Jesse had bound her wrists. She twisted her hands back and felt the thick rope, too fat for tight knots, and she grabbed the ends, she folded her right hand and yanked against the knot, with her left held she held the rope, she worked and tugged and yanked the right hand out. It slipped a finger in the knot and loosened it and her hands were free, numb, they felt not a thing and then they did feel, they wore gloves of hot tar, they wore gloves pierced with a thousand needles. Dixie Clay pushed them into the floor heaving and her left arm gave, collapsed. She rolled to her knees and unfolded the legs and pulled against the stove to stagger to her feet. She put a hand to her head and felt gummy oozing that she knew was blood.

Willy. She pushed herself away from the

stove and spun toward the parlor, no Willy, her afghan was bunched on the sofa and she yanked it up, no Willy. The wicker laundry basket, no Willy, the peach basket, no Willy, no Willy on her bed, she dropped to her knees with a thud and peered under the bed no Willy, no Willy in the room she thought of as the baby's though the baby slept with her. Back in the parlor she yanked open the small drawer of the secretary and knew she was hysterical, the baby couldn't fit in there. Gallery, Willy was on the gallery, she crashed against the doorjamb and almost tripped on an inside-out umbrella — the gallery was empty, the rocking chair ghost-rocking in the wind. Beyond it was an eerie yellow-green sky, color of a luna moth. A cackle of rain crashed against her house, loud as a busted strand of pearls.

Then she knew because she heard herself screaming. They'd taken him. Jesse and that woman had taken Willy.

On the gravel driveway there was no car, just slashes where water had filled the Ford's tracks. She remembered its headlights coning through the rain last night, if last night had been last night, now it was day though the sky was dark. Jesse was going to Hobnob, that was what he'd said last night, Jesse was going to Hobnob and that woman was taking Willy to Greenville.

Dixie Clay started to run toward the barn, tearing up the path and down the ridge, knocked back by a tree limb and falling and then scrambling in the mud and running again, her voice a long howl the shape of her son. Rushing past her on the footpath was a string of jackrabbits and then a white-tailed deer was leaping over them and changing direction midflight to avoid crashing into her. Dixie Clay didn't even break stride. *I'll get Chester and ride to town —*

She yanked open the barn door. The wind wrestled her for it. A coil of leaves whirled up and hissed at her knees and then a real snake, a black racer, zipped between her ankles into the darkness. The ground seemed to be trembling, so she must be woozy from her head wound. The trees beside the barn were jittery and dropping their leaves. Inside, Chester was rearing onto his hind legs, galloping through the air, then throwing his hooves against the door of his stall, and the cow was moaning.

Maybe the police were coming. She could hear a terrible rumbling, like a hundred Indian motorcycles racing on a wooden board track. She shut the barn door and ran out to meet them and she was nearly trampled by the panicked animals darting from the woods, deer and muskrats and beavers and mice and raccoons, wings flapping over her head, water shaking from the trees, and everything ashudder. The noise deepened into a roar like a locomotive bearing down on her, the terrible black locomotive of her nightmare, and then she knew. Oh God she knew. She had been told of a thing that sounded like a locomotive. And that thing was a flood.

She screamed and the wind snatched her sound. She changed direction and was running up the hill behind her house now and when she crested the ridge, she threw herself against a trembling slick ash tree. The noise was coming from the left, a wall of sound, and she looked down at her house and looked toward the noise and saw the trees, which appeared to be marching toward her because they were being lifted up and then laid flat and she saw what was mowing them down, a hill tumbling over itself. But it was not a hill, it was the brown water seething with lumber and a chicken coop, and a cow, a bale of barbed wire, a section of fence, all of it tumbling and crashing, a thing malevolent and alive churning through the hollow where her house stood and then where her house had stood. Yes, had stood: as she clung to the tree she saw the water explode against the house and the house exploded, wrenched and splintered, consumed by those living waters, which rushed on.

Dixie Clay left the quaking ash and ran for the biggest tree on the ridge, the oak must be a hundred years, a hundred feet. She had to jump to reach the lowest branch and she did and hung there and her left arm was a fury of searing and she released the branch and dropped. She lay stunned and rib-burst on the rumbling earth and turned to prop on an elbow and peer down, and the hill of water in the hollow where her house had been was surging and screaming higher, rushing on through the hollow but also rising up the ridge toward her. She clawed to her feet and jumped for the branch again and cried out to feel her weight jar and tear on the arm, but she held fast as she swung her right leg and wedged her foot into the branch's crotch and then heaved her body up and pulled her broken wing into her chest and bellowed at the sky. Whether she called for God or Willy she didn't know, it was all the same now and dependent on her climbing higher and she did, leaping to the next branch like a squirrel and clinging there and rocking her body to swing herself up, grit of wet bark in her teeth, sleeve gashing open. She leaped again, to the next branch, and scrambled her feet up the trunk until she could hook them around the limb and swing herself over.

Then she was in the thicker canopy, climbing one-handed and with fingers digging into the bark. She came to a rest at the top where three branches flared, two to couch her back and the lower one to rest her feet upon. These boughs were swaying in the gusts, and she had broken glimpses of surging chocolate water and she craned her head but couldn't see the barn or the still, though she should have been able to, and she had a terrible vision of Chester galloping into the frothy waves. She shouldn't have been able to see the Gawiwatchee behind her but there it was, boiling and odd, and then she realized it was flowing the wrong direction, not into but away from the Mississippi, not flowing but windmilling, a stream become a river filled with things that were not water. A church steeple. A brace of mules. A mailbox. A tree, a tree, a tree, lifted and thrown, then a tree shooting out of the water like a rocket. Between her and the Gawiwatchee was another ridge poking out of the water and as she watched, a coyote swam to it behind a deer, and they scrabbled up and then turned and looked at each other. It was shrinking their ridge to an island.

It was also climbing the base of Dixie Clay's tree. The root ball was submerged and then the wide trunk and as she watched, the lowest branch, the one she'd grabbed and then fallen from, began to go under. A cottonmouth was curled there and lifted the fist of its head and S-curved up the trunk. She didn't even care. A wooden placard shot from the current: GOOD OLD LICORICE FLAVOR! BLACK JACK GUM!

Dixie Clay looked down — she was about twenty feet above the water — and looked up — she had about twenty more feet in the tree. She heaved from her perch to climb. The branches were thrashing and when she reached the highest one that would hold her, about as thick as a man's thigh, she clung, panting, wrapping both arms and legs around it. The tree swayed under her like a ship, and she the masthead, facing into the storm. She heard a noise over the shrieking water, which she realized was her teeth chattering, the rain a cold rain and her blouse a slick wet plaster, her wool skirt and apron a hundred pounds each.

A tree to her left boomed like a cannon and thundered into the water, and a huge wave soared over her and her branch dipped crazily and she vised her thighs around the rough bark and squeezed her eyes, and when she opened them, the water had risen. What may have been the smokestack from the lumber mill shot by, was caught in a vortex, swung like a propeller. How much water was in the Mississippi anyway, yet it kept coming. It approached the three-limb platform where she'd just been resting. A fox in a nearby branch gave a strange, almost chipper bark and leaped into the water and paddled away with its neat black gloves, tail rising from the water like a question mark. Maybe it could make it to the island where the deer and coyote were. Dixie Clay turned to see them but they were gone, no sign of the island at all.

Dear Lord, I need to live, I need to live to find my baby.

The water wasn't rising up the tree anymore, but it wasn't falling either. She peered between the branches at a landscape wholly alien. No, not a landscape, a seascape. She was on an ark, but there was no dove with an olive branch, and no two of anything, just her, alone.

Rescue yourself, girl. But how? She could swim. The water seemed calmer, no big swells, surface plucked by raindrops. Perhaps she should try. But even as she considered this, a surge of brown froth from the left butted her tree — maybe another chunk of levee or a road giving in, giving up — and her branch dipped as if to shake her loose. She clung with her whole body as beneath her a Brahma bull swept by sideways, eyes bulging and tendons in its hump neck cording as it brayed. It was show cattle belonging to Joe York, this she knew even before it barreled flank side up, showing its Y brand. She'd passed this cow dozens of times on Seven Hills, watched it tonguing long grasses into its mouth. Joe York's bull, but where was Joe? And then: Where was the bull?

No, she would not leave the tree to swim.

A navy seaplane with those curved, canoe-like rails flew above her, the kind of plane Dixie Clay avoided while shining, and now she clung with her bad arm and flung her other overhead, screaming, but the tree that protected her also obscured her, and the plane was too high and passed on. Without the house here, how would they know to look for a body clinging like a lichen? Would the Red Cross even search this far out, land of hardscrabble shiners, no telephone wire to lead them?

She put her forehead down on the wet bark and closed her eyes, the chilled rain sluicing the nape of her neck where her braid swung over her shoulder. She thought she heard another plane and lifted her head, but this one was even higher in the porous sky. Above her in the top branches was a clump of mistletoe. As a girl she'd shot mistletoe from the treetops, and once at a Christmas party, Ruben Lippens had complained: "Dixie Clay would rather shoot mistletoe than be kissed under it." Why remember that now? She needed to calm herself. Her head throbbed in the hurt place and she brought her fingers to the blood-gummy gash.

"Yoo-hoo!"

Dixie Clay snapped her head — the wind, or a man? "Here! I'm here!"

"Whose leg is that?"

"Dixie Clay Holliver!"

"So you are." The boat nosed under the branches that were nearly resting on the water, and the ducking figure lifted and beneath the hat brim was Old Man Marvin.

"Marvin, thank God."

His boat was sitting low in the water, filled with cases of whiskey. Marvin wore a yellow slicker and matching hat and bit down on an unlit pipe, dripping rain. He paddled closer, pulled himself in, hugged the tree with one arm. Dixie Clay shifted her legs so he couldn't see up her skirt, even as she was aware that it was a stupid concern.

Marvin took the pipe out of his mouth. "Dixie Clay! Looks like those levee inspectors were a bunch a liars."

"Marvin, help me. Please."

"Why, I reckon I might could. 'Course I'll lose some profit, making room for you in my boat. I was loading it when the flood came. Lifted my house right offen its slab and brung it away. If I hadn't been loading whiskey, I'd a been in that house. Whiskey saved my life! But I'm up a creek without a paddle. See?" He lifted the shovel he'd been navigating with and grinned, even from this distance his teeth the color of tea.

She couldn't grin back. She just needed to get out of the tree and into his boat.

"I'm getting to Greenville," he said. "Red Cross is evacuating us there."

"Greenville's not flooded?"

"Hell, yeah, it's flooded. Everything's flooded. But not near so bad as here, from what I heard. Ran up on a rescue boat, a twenty-two-footer, rigged out with a Model T engine, can you beat that? And with a mailman sitting stern, telling the driver where the houses along his route was, so they could peel folks outta trees —"

"Greenville," she interrupted. "That's where people are going?"

"Yup. Greenville got water, but it's got tents on the levee, supplies and the like, headquarters of flood relief. This here's the worse spot, girl. Triangle-lated between the Mississip and the Gawiwatchee —"

"Take me to Greenville. I'll pay you."

"Girl, you ain't got a thing left in this world. Me neither, 'cepting this whiskey. But it don't matter. I'll take you. Maybe you can make it worth my while," he said, and raised his eyebrows and grinned, and let go of the trunk with one hand to reach up to her.

When Dixie Clay pressed off the limb, smear of blood on the bark, her arms like punctured tires, they heard a rushing moan. A boiling new current swung itself from the north and shot an oak past them, its branches nipping the nose of Marvin's boat. "Damn it all," he yelled as he was spun around the trunk. "Damn it all to hell." She saw his pipe fly from his surprised mouth and he was torn from the tree and grabbed his shoulder as his boat went shooting away. She couldn't see him but heard a metal thunking, and when she next spotted his boat, it had passed beyond the canopy of her tree and was bucking, turned sideways in the current, and he was paddling hard with the shovel first on the right side then on the left. He was only forty yards off but already the scrim of rain turned him blue and featureless.

The boat swung around and he was facing her and she yelled to warn him of the next tree, but it was too late and he was knocked to the floor.

"Marvin!" she yelled — she could see only the smear of his back — "Marvin!"

"I lost my goddamn shovel!" he yelled. "But I'll come back for you!"

"Wait, please, don't leave me!"

"I'll come back. Or send someone else."

"Marvin, please —"

"I'll come back! I always was sweet on you, Dixie Clay!"

There was a giant crack and a tree fifty yards away groaned terribly and toppled. Dixie Clay clung to her shaking branch and turned her face from the spray and when she turned back, she was alone.

She was tired now. A few more planes had passed, and she didn't even wave. Part of her wanted to sleep, but to sleep, she knew, meant death. She picked her head up every few minutes, hoping that a raft or boat would come floating by that she could drop into and paddle to Willy.

Sometime that afternoon the rain stopped, the sun nothing but a lighter gray circle in dark gray sky, and she saw something detach itself from a tree. She squinted in the rain to see if it was a doghouse or a garden shed. Maybe it was a steel drum, and if it was, maybe she should forsake the tree and swim to it, use it as ballast. It came closer. It was a boat.

She was screaming now and grasping the branch with one arm to wave with the other, the boat moving slowly and dodging obstacles; if it had or hadn't seen her she couldn't tell. She thought she saw a man in the boat. She reached behind her and untied her sodden apron and lifted a hip to slip it free and then began waving it, thwacking it overhead on the branches, all while screaming and screaming, until her body started to list on the branch and suddenly she'd swung beneath it and she dropped the apron to grasp with both hands. She turned her head and glimpsed for a second the boat and the figure was maybe waving but then she lost it. She held on but it hurt. She couldn't see the boat and felt the bark shredding her forearms and realized they were letting go and she clung tighter and pressed her face to the limb. Finally the tree's wide canopy, which made a cave on the water, trapped the chugging of a motor.

"Dixie Clay!" Ingersoll. A flash of his red shirt over her shoulder. The boat was below her.

"I've got you," he yelled, and he held out his arms, and she let go.

Five hours later, an hour after dark, Ingersoll pulled the boat over to a conical Indian mound rising fifteen feet out of the water. It had a grassy platform top and Ingersoll dragged the boat up, scattering snakes and a hatchling alligator about a foot long who bellied into the river. They'd already fought upstream along the Gawiwatchee, shooting rapids in phalanges of spray, Dixie Clay grasping the bench seat with one hand and Ingersoll's belt with the other and feeling her body fly up and then the jolt of pain in her hips and ribs as her rump smacked the bench. They'd found the bed of the Mississippi and had fought a good ways toward Greenville.

There was no Hobnob to head to. Dixie Clay kept asking, incredulous. "The diner?"

Ingersoll said, "Gone."

"The library?"

"Gone."

Dixie Clay had checked out a book of Lincoln's speeches, also gone. "The beauty shop? Hobnob Grammar?"

"Gone, too, I think," Ingersoll said.

Thank God they'd closed the school a few weeks back, all the children sent home. Home to houses that were now underwater. But maybe they'd evacuated. "The store — Amity's store?"

"I'm sorry, Dixie Clay."

"But surely Amity —" She turned in the boat and when she saw his grim face, she asked no further.

She turned back and realized — Jacob's grave. Jacob's grave, gone.

They'd seen maybe a dozen other boats, all headed toward Greenville. Going was slow because the Mississippi was pouring through the crevasse in unpredictable rapids and causing other breaks along the way. Eventually, they could tell where the river had lain because a crest of levee poked through, first a stuttering archipelago of levee islands, each clustered with animals, and then later a strip of levee a few feet across on either side of them. Ingersoll steered the boat between these lines of land, knowing the channel was deepest in the middle, but even so they'd gotten stuck in a red mulberry tree, strange to look down into the canopy of heart-shaped leaves. The tree had nearly torn a hole in the boat, and Ingersoll had worked the rudder and finally jumped overboard and swam beneath the boat to free it. While he struggled, Dixie Clay leaned out to pick the bitter unripe berries, all they'd eat that day. Ingersoll told her that when he'd found the boat, it had been stocked, but on the way to her a current had swung it around and an uprooted tree had come shooting toward him. He ducked in time, but when it landed on the far side of the boat, a big paw of a wave swiped the supplies.

"How did you even know where I was? How did you find me without roads?"

"I ran across a rescue boat and there was an old man in it whose fingers were crushed. They were going to get him help somehow. He saw what direction I was headed. Said to rescue a girl named Dixie Clay and told me where to find your oak tree."

They reached what had been the town of Flannery, the levee thicker here because it had supported the bridge, now swept clear away. At the crest was a boxcar and from it poked a waving white handkerchief and Dixie Clay didn't want to stop and luckily they didn't have to because a rescue boat was chugging toward the boxcar.

"Do you have any food, any gasoline?" Ingersoll called over the rescue boat's high motor. The thought of boat fuel hadn't occurred to Dixie Clay.

"None to spare," yelled the captain. "We're going in once the boat is full. Folks in this boxcar, and supposed to be six people in the upper story of an oil mill, have you seen 'em?"

"No," said Ingersoll. "Good luck. We'll press on."

When dusk fell, Ingersoll said they needed to stop, but Dixie Clay begged, she wanted to keep heading toward Greenville where Jeannette had Willy. But then they'd gotten stuck again, this time on a barn roof. Ingersoll had to jump overboard and when he couldn't dislodge the boat's propeller from the gouged metal, he dove down to enter the barn and free it from beneath. He took a long, long time to reappear. She rocked in the listing boat and grew frightened. At last he shot up and threw his arms over the side and hung panting and with a great effort swung a leg over and hoisted his body in, wet red shirt outlining the bars of muscle in his back. He collapsed onto the boat's bottom, which was sloshing with brackish water.

She bent over his face. His lips looked bluish and his eyes were closed. His chest was heaving. "Ingersoll? Are you all right?"

He opened his eyes. "We're gonna die if we keep this up. We're gonna capsize, Dixie Clay, and we're gonna drown in the dark, and we'll never get Willy back. Next place we can, we stop."

She didn't argue. And they'd seen the Indian mound around the next bend.

Now they sat side by side on the only landmass they could see, jutting itself up toward the heavens, like a stage, she thought. Or an operating table. Or an altar. The rain had stopped, and at first the mud was chilled beneath them but it felt good to be out of the boat, and their bodies untensed as the mud warmed. They listened to the river slashing by, tripled in speed.

Creaking, whinnying, the snapping of trees like artillery fire, other sounds unidentifiable and unworldly.

"Dixie Clay," he said. "In the morning, I need to set your arm."

"It's okay," she said.

"No, it's not. It's broke."

He put his fingers on her wrist, his thumb closing the circle, and he began to slowly, slowly ease the circle of fingers-thumb along her blouse sleeve toward her swollen elbow. She gasped and his hand opened.

"That big lump just before your elbow, that's the break. It's clean, I think," he said. "That's good. In the morning, when I can see, we got to set it so it doesn't start healing back crooked."

"Set it?"

"Yeah. I've done it before. Set Ham's once. Only difference is, he was drunk."

"He got drunk to deaden the pain?"

"No, he got drunk because he's Ham."

"Was this in the war?"

"Nope, this was in a Chrysler. We were chasing a bootlegger in a cotton field in Alabama. I spun around the turnrow and Ham was thrown against the unlocked door and just kept going for a spell."

"Did it turn out okay?"

"Yeah, we got the guy."

"No, I mean Ham's arm."

"Sure. But ever since, Ham claims he can't win a hand of Texas Hold'em."

"Hmm. Were you drunk too?"

"I'd been driving."

"That's no answer."

"Yeah, I was drunk. But not as bad as Ham."

"Oh."

"We'll worry about it in the morning. For now, I'm just going to splint it."

He crisscrossed the Indian mound, picking up and discarding sticks, finally deciding on two long enough, though they were damp. Then he sat beside her again and tried to roll her sleeve up but it got stuck and she gave a yelp.

"I'm just gonna tear it off, okay?"

She nodded, so Ingersoll leaned forward and lifted the shoulder seam to his teeth and, biting down, ripped the fabric, a strange loud cry among the other strange loud cries. Then he yanked his own shirt overhead with his right hand, and beneath it he wore an undershirt which he yanked off with his left. "Feels good to get that damp thing off," he murmured as he tied the ends of her sleeve to his undershirt. He set the sling over her bowed head like a beauty queen's sash and tucked a long stick on either side of her arm to splint it, saying, "This will keep it steady for now. In Greenville, we'll get a plaster."

"Thank you."

He shrugged her thanks away, and they sat, facing the river. The rain had stopped and Ingersoll planted a Y-shaped stick in the ground and hung his shirt to dry. Dixie Clay wished she could do the same. In a few more moments it was too dark to see, clouds erasing the stories told by the constellations, just a few scattered points of light, below them the currents sometimes glinting where they knifed open the reflection of a star.

"Might as well stretch out," said Ingersoll. She heard him settle back, and after a moment she lay back, too. She felt the hurt slip in part by part, starting with her head, first inside, then out, then her left arm, her right ribs, her stomach, her legs, her heart, her heart, her heart. Willy.

"Go to sleep, if you can," said Ingersoll.

She shook her head, which he couldn't see in the dark. So she said, "You sleep. It's okay. I won't be able to."

"Me neither." They listened to a sound they couldn't place, metal on metal, something wrenched apart somewhere. Ingersoll continued after a pause. "Never been much of one for sleeping. Lost the habit, if I ever had it, keeping a musician's hours."

"And I lost the habit keeping a bootlegger's."

A silence grew, a cloister of silence surrounded by rushing water. It was so dark. Dark as a stack of black cats — that's what Jesse would have said. How strange to know he could be dead, probably was, according to what Ingersoll had told her earlier, describing the shooting of the saboteur and how Jesse'd been on the levee moments prior lifting a sandbag into place. "So Jesse put the dynamite there," she'd concluded, and Ingersoll hadn't denied it.

"Where did the dynamite come from?" Dixie Clay had asked, and Ingersoll told her.

"An army camp," she repeated. "Camp Beauregard?"

"How did you know?"

And she told him then about Uncle Mookey and his night janitor job.

"I'll be damned," he'd murmured. "Uncle Mookey."

She probed the idea of Jesse's death, waiting for sorrow to descend, but none did. She probed the idea of Ingersoll's proximity, his smooth, deep voice just a few dark inches away, waiting for guilt to descend, but none did.

As the pain slipped back into her body, the thoughts did too, all she hadn't been able to ponder on the river while she was yelling for Ingersoll to steer starboard to avoid a submerged automobile, or leeward to dodge the cottonmouth coiled on a branch. They'd already shouted to each other the facts, but they hadn't had time to press the hurt spots.

"I keep wondering what happened to Jesse and Ham," she said.

"Me too."

"I'm scared," she said. She felt Ingersoll's hand grasp her own where it lay by her side.

"Me, too." And then he let her hand go.

After a while, he said, "Wish I had me a cigar."

After a while, she said, "Wish you had your mandolin."

She listened to his stomach announce itself as empty.

Neither one said anything for a minute. Over the sluice of the currents, a cat's scream, maybe a panther's. Ingersoll's hand had been large and warm. An anchor.

"Ingersoll?"

"Yes?"

"What are we going to do?"

"We're going to find Willy."

"We are?"

"We are. We're going to find Jeannette and get Willy back."

"In Greenville, in the morning."

"Yes, we're going to Greenville, and if Jeannette's already gone —"

"What do you mean, gone?" She was struggling to sit up, pressing her good arm into the soft ground — "They're evacuating to Greenville, all of Hobnob is evacuating to Greenville, you said so —"

"Yes, for starters. But from there, river

steamers take folks to Memphis or Natchez. And if Jeannette has already boarded one" — Ingersoll was sitting up now too, facing her, hand on her elbow — "we'll find out where she went —"

But Dixie Clay was scrambling, a boot caught in her skirt, and lunging to her feet. "Oh my God, get in the boat, we have to go, we have to —"

"Dixie Clay, we can't, we'll die, we'll die and that won't help the baby. At first light —"

But she ran to the boat and grabbed the rope with her good hand and was yanking the boat down the side of the mound. Ingersoll intercepted her and jerked the rope away and gripped her burning hand in front of her chest and shook it for emphasis, "We can't, we can't, calm down." He released her arm, which flew up to slap him. It connected solidly with his cheek, the first solid thing in her day, all her fierceness coiled behind it, and then she whirled toward the boat again, but Ingersoll had already sprung to clamp her shoulders and wrestle her up the mound. She thrashed, twisting her shoulders, her arm sparking with pain, and he lost his footing in the mud and fell back and pulled her with him, her back on his chest.

"Stop it," he yelled. "Stop it," and he hugged her and she couldn't free herself and she couldn't twist loose. She flung herself from side to side and then she suddenly and simply let her head fall back on his shoulder and began to sob.

This whole long day since waking to find Willy missing she hadn't had time to feel anything slowly and now she did and felt nothing but fear. He still held her shoulders but not rigidly and she heaved with sobs and his mouth pressed into her hair as he murmured, "I'm sorry, I'm so sorry." He stopped talking but his lips remained pressed to her nape. They moved to her cheeks and he was kissing up her tears. "We'll find Willy," he told her. "I promise you, we'll find him." She turned her face to tell him something and then his lips weren't on her cheeks but on her mouth. She was kissing him back, his mouth salty from the tears still pressing from her eyes.

She angled her shoulders now and rolled over with her splinted arm tucked to her chest. It hurt and she welcomed the hurt. His arms cinched her waist and pulled her close. His kisses were warm and his arms and slab of chest were warm, and she needed what he was making her forget and what he was making her believe. Kisses on the underside of her jaw and then on her neck, kisses like the paw prints of a fox, some sap in her rising and ambering in the hollows where her clavicles flared like wings as he pressed his lips there. Oh God. The fingers of her right hand tripping down his neck, then her palm on his chest, her fingers sliding through the springy hair and grasping the solidity beneath. Kissing still and his large hands sliding from her waist up her ribs and then his hands on her breasts. She brought her good hand to her blouse to twist open the small buttons but she struggled, and then his fingers met hers and like picking the mandolin he had the blouse open and she shimmied it down her good arm and the fabric bunched around the sling on the other side but it didn't matter. There were kisses on her breasts and on her mulberry nipples, and she reached back to pull her long braid over her shoulder and tugged the band and shook her head and her wet damp waves fell about them as she leaned over him, bracing with her good arm, and he was sliding her skirt up and she was one-handedly tugging loose the trousers and the mud squelched as he lifted his hips to help her pull them free.

They were two small humans on a mound of ancient earth banked by rushing waters and her tears were falling on his chest and their faces curtained by locks of her hair like the branches of the weeping willow where she used to pump her swing in Pine Grove, Alabama, and their eyes were corded and she who had never quite done this now reached below to grasp him and fit him into her. She'd never been filled this way before, cored. They were rocking together, a rescue boat, and then words and ideas of words fell away and they were thrust into the golden light that bodies can climb to. They were there and there and there. Stillness at the height.

And then the slow sliding and somehow Dixie Clay back in her body again, which had again its various pains but was also redeemed. Was nestling on his chest, which was rising and falling, as was her own. Song of his blood filling the cup of her ear.

"I love you, Dixie Clay."

"I know."

CHAPTER 17

They woke before dawn to the lowing of a
cow being washed past the Indian mound.
They unwound themselves from each other's warm limbs and sat up, sheeted by fog.
Ingersoll rose to gather Dixie Clay's damp
clothes and turned his back so she could
dress but spun when he heard a small cry.
Her face was white, wreathed in white fog,
and she was trying to screw her splinted
arm through the opening of her blouse.
Ingersoll bent over her blue fingers, but she
took a step back. "It's not that bad," she
said.

"Liar. It hurts like hell."

"It can wait. Let's go."

He knew she was afraid of him setting the
break, but it had to be done. He slipped his
hands into the splint and closed his fingers
over her forearm and felt the sick place, the
swollen lump of skewed bone, and flicked
his eyes to her unsuspecting face and with a

wrenching jerk he snapped it into align-
ment. He'd forgotten how terrible the noise
was, the grinding of bone against bone,
more terrible even than her cry. Dixie Clay
slumped into his arms, which he'd been
prepared for, but she didn't faint. She rested
against him for a second and then leaned
forward to place her weight on her feet
again and he steadied her good arm and
then she was upright, though her eyes
remained closed.

"You didn't warn me. At all."

"I know," he said. "I'm sorry."

She opened her eyes at last. "No, it was a
good idea. But if you ever try that again,"
she said, smiling up at him, "I'll kill you."

"Gotcha. How does it feel?"

She gave her fingers a tentative wiggle.
"Better, actually. Better."

Ingersoll dragged the boat down the slope
and into the water swirling with scarves of
cloud and held it for Dixie Clay. Then he
shoved off, his boot sinking shin deep into
the mud, and clambered in and sat on the
stern thwart and reached over the transom
to pull the rip cord but there was no growl
from the motor. He tried again: nothing.
He felt Dixie Clay's eyes as he reached to
yank the cord a third time. Oh, for Christ
sake. It stammered and then caught.

411

"What's wrong?" she asked.

"Low on fuel."

They began to needle through the choppy water toward Greenville, and as they rounded the bend Ingersoll had the urge to see the Indian mound one last time so he swiveled his head to view the prehistoric loaf of earth where they had made their love. He remembered pulsing into her, her small fist thwacking his chest three times in an agony of release. Her face above him, the only sky he'd ever want now. As the mound passed from sight he faced forward and met Dixie Clay's eyes — she'd turned around to see it, too. She smiled shyly and he smiled a bit bigger and then she grinned, she flat-out grinned. Dixie Clay. What a woman.

Then they had no eyes for anything but the tree-stabbed rapids and churning trappings of washed-out river towns, all shrouded by dangerous fog. The motor was fifteen horsepower and would make ten miles an hour, but Ingersoll kept it to about half that. "We could walk faster," he growled, though that wasn't exactly true. Dixie Clay, lookout, scanned the water for logjams and whirlpools and submerged sharecropper shacks and alligators — this last probably the least dangerous. When she pointed she did so gingerly, and he'd seen her fingers snake up her side, and he figured on some broken ribs. He wished he could tape them for her. Before they went to sleep, when they were lying quietly and talking quietly, she'd sneezed and squeezed his fingers, as if the sneezing hurt.

They'd gone about a mile when they saw another boat heading toward Greenville, a man paddling his wife and two kids. The man raised his oar, perhaps wanting to exchange news, but Ingersoll merely nodded and touched a finger to where the brim of his hat should have been — they had no news, no food, nothing but a terrible need to press on. In the next mile they passed two more rowboats, both low lying with trunks and valises, folks who lived close enough to the fire station to hear the siren and know the levee had burst. Just once they crossed a boat heading in the opposite direction, a twenty-foot steel motorboat, which pulled starboard. It was loaded with supplies. Ingersoll hailed the driver, a preacher, and they cut their motors. The preacher said that he'd gone to Greenville to set up a church in the tent city.

"White folk that cared to leave done left. Niggers ain't got the option, they's in tents unloading the Red Cross supplies. Plenty of nigger preachers setting up hullabaloo on both banks," he said and spit brown tobacco into the tobacco-brown water. "They don't need me, so I'm taking supplies back to my people, my congregation, in Semmesville."

Ingersoll eyed the preacher's boat, the tarp outlining boxes and parcels. "Red Cross handing out supplies? Thank God," he said. "We need gasoline for this boat. Won't make it to Greenville on what we got. Can you spare some?"

The preacher said, "Gasoline is sparse and fixing to become sparser."

"I bet," said Ingersoll. "That's why we're glad to run up on you. Could you spare, say, ten gallons out of that container there?" He gestured with his chin toward the red gas nozzle poking from the tarp.

The preacher said nothing, gazing at the canopy of an elm resting on the water, thick with meadowlarks wearing their black bibs and warbling worriedly. "Lookit them robins," he said. "All shouting, 'Where's the dang worms?' " He chuckled.

"Seeing how you got the gas free and all? And can go back and get some more?"

The preacher turned from the tree still smiling and brought his fingers to his collar and hooked it from his jowls. Ingersoll saw the skin was pinched and red. This was no

414

man of God. He glanced at Dixie Clay and knew that she knew.

"What'll it take?" asked Ingersoll, a bit of a growl in his voice.

"Ten gallons is a lot, in a hat or a tank."

"We don't have time for this." Ingersoll rose to his full height, which sometimes changed the tenor of a conversation. "What'll it take?"

"What you got?"

Very little, as it turned out. Dixie Clay had nothing in her pockets but a slim waterlogged volume of Longfellow. Ingersoll's wallet held eight dollars. At which the preacher laughed.

Ingersoll stepped to the side of the boat and the preacher choked off his guffaw and threw his boat into gear.

How Ingersoll hated to do it. He yelled to the preacher's back, "Wait."

The preacher looked over his shoulder but didn't slow.

"I got something," Ingersoll yelled.

The preacher was about forty feet away now and killed his motor. "This better be good."

"Federal revenuer badge."

"Lemme see."

Ingersoll reached into his pocket and pulled the white lining out. He propped his foot up on the bench and bent his head and pinched the clasp and then pushed his pocket back into his trousers and kicked and from inside his pants the badge fell out, landing with a splash on the burden boards. He picked up the silver crest and held it dripping toward the preacher, who was motoring closer.

"Toss it here," said the preacher.

"Where's the gasoline?"

The preacher let up on the throttle and moved his foot to loosen the tarp and there were many jugs and cans there. He picked up a small jug and held it toward Ingersoll. "Toss me that badge."

"You first."

"Same time."

Ingersoll nodded.

"One, two, three!"

Ingersoll tossed the badge and in the same gesture hooked the jug. Meanwhile, the badge bounced off the preacher's hand and clattered into the bottom of his boat. He squatted and, smiling, turned it over in his hand.

"We also need food."

The preacher pocketed the badge and stood. "We done transacted our transaction," he said, flipping his tarp down, "so, um, God bless you." His hand went to the boat's tiller.

"Wait."

The preacher's eyes were shrewd, and he drew his lips into his mouth and watched as Ingersoll pulled out his other pocket and fiddled again and kicked again and again bent down. He held up a dripping bronze disk.

"What is it?"

"Valor. Verdun."

"Lemme see."

"Food first."

The preacher kicked the tarp up again and began rummaging and pulling out packages and stacking them on his seat, "Saltines . . . potted meat . . . tin of peaches . . . shredded wheat." He stood. "Now gimme the medal."

Ingersoll shook his head. "Food first."

The preacher lobbed the food, which Ingersoll caught and passed to Dixie Clay. When she'd set down the last box, she looked up at Ingersoll, who was rolling the medal in his hand. He gripped it and then levered it onto his thumbnail and he flipped it. It rose and rose, turning over itself, all three lifting their faces to watch its arc, glint of bronze at the zenith despite the clouds, and then it descended and landed with a smack in the palm of the preacher, who clenched it and gave a hoot.

Ingersoll was already setting their boat toward Greenville, but the motor didn't quite drown the preacher's awkward pronunciation, "A La Gloire des Heros de Verdun," and then some other words, and finally they chugged around a logjam island out of earshot.

"Ingersoll?" Dixie Clay twisted on the bench but he kept his eyes over her head, on the river and its eddies.

"Doesn't matter," he said gruffly. "Don't need a medal to remember it."

"And the badge?"

He gave a small shrug. "I'm done with that life now." Then he dropped his gaze to her upturned, guileless, pale face, freckles standing out. Crust of blood along her hairline. He said it again, and this time softer, "I'm done with that life now."

There was a rhythm to the way they worked, her telling him when to steer starboard or duck or to *Slow down, Ingersoll, I don't like the look of these currents.* Once he saw a floating mass and steered closer for a look and was about to point it out to Dixie Clay when he realized it was a corpse, a man's back in a plaid shirt, mired in the reeds. He tried to point out something on the opposite bank but it was too late, she'd already seen it.

"Should we . . . ?" she asked, and answered her own question, "No." And they passed four more corpses there and a smashed dugout canoe circling in an eddy.

They weren't able to converse much, but he sensed she felt as connected as he did. He liked to let his eyes include her alert frame as he scanned the water. The curls erupting from the tail of the braid that she'd plaited one-handedly, plaited loosely around the gash in her head — he felt so protective of that club of a braid, the shoulder blades it rested between.

How strange to be a twenty-eight-year-old man who had crossed an ocean to fight a war, and to have been shot at, and to have shot, and to recross the ocean to fight another war, and to continue to be shot at, and to continue to shoot, to many times have eked out of death's lunge with a nimble last-minute feint — and yet feel he had something at stake at last. Yes, he was — stupid, but wasn't it true, stupid didn't make it any less true — a new man.

If only he could have met her earlier. What if he hadn't met her at twenty-eight, what if he'd met her when he was sixteen. She would have been, hm, ten. Well, maybe not sixteen then, maybe later, but to have had her in his life earlier, to feel this grounded, this permanent, a thing he'd never felt before. He'd have been able to spare her the things that she would suffer, to have married her before she'd ever laid eyes on Jesse's two-tone eyes, ever become a bootlegger, to have Willy be their own blood baby.

Ridiculous. Not just the part about Willy, but all of it. Because even if their ages had meshed, and even if they had met, Dixie Clay wouldn't have liked him. No way, no sir. A gal that pretty, and that smart — she'd have to choose the Jesses of the world. The handsomest, most charming, most eloquent. Maybe she'd needed her dream to come true to realize it was the wrong dream. Maybe only then could a man like Ingersoll make sense. He realized with a start that his fingers had risen, were stroking the place under his eye where the lumpybumpy — the hemangioma — had been. He dropped his hand to his leg. The strawberry mark was long gone but he still thought of himself as ugly. Didn't give a thought to clothes. And he was awkward; without a gun or a guitar he hardly knew what to do with his hands. The beads of his words strung with too much silence between them.

And that wasn't all. He had some kind of remove. He'd felt, he'd always felt, that he was passing through. Passing over, passing under, passing through. Sometimes he wondered — did everyone feel this way? But they must not. Look at all of them *caring.* He hadn't disdained it, he just couldn't participate. Why had he never felt attached to people? Could he have chosen differently, better? Hard to say. He grew up with nuns who thought he could be adopted at any moment. Then he fought alongside men who thought he could be killed at any moment. Then he took a job that required he move constantly, two-week engagements, two-week acquaintances. In these jobs, he had done what others considered brave deeds, but they never seemed brave to him because he valued his own existence so lightly. He was temporary. Even his name. Teddy, the nuns had written on his intake form. Not even Theodore, because it was just a three-day name, something to call him until he was adopted.

And into this life came a baby, and a mother for that baby. Between them they probably couldn't weigh a buck and a quarter. But now *his* life had weight. He remembered again the jail cell in Hobnob, how it faced an identical cell, like looking into a mirror and being invisible. Until he found Willy and Dixie Clay, he realized, that's all his whole life had been.

A calm swath of river, rivulets flowing in the same direction like a horse's mane curried with a comb. It was a good time to stop but there was no place to bank. Still, the body has needs. Ingersoll cut the motor and Dixie Clay scooted to the bow and turned around and stepped up on either side of the gunwale and squatted, but with only one arm to hold her skirts and also the breast-hook of the bobbing vessel, she was precarious. So Ingersoll climbed over the forward thwart and slid his arm around her back and listened as she made water, gazing over her head at a small house bobbing along, a chicken on the roof.

He lifted Dixie Clay back onto the burden boards and climbed back to his stern thwart, pausing to duck a tree limb that rose from a logjam.

"Ingersoll?"

"Yeah?"

"I'm sorry about that thing I said, about you being crooked and taking bribes."

"Aw, that's all right."

"No, it's not, and I'm sorry I said it."

"Let's not worry about it anymore, okay?"

She nodded.

Closer yet to Greenville, more boats. What looked like steppingstones across the river: the dun breasts of drowned geese. Then the pilings of a dislocated dock, Ingersoll slowing, steering wide.

"Look there," she said.

He raised his eyes: the Wyatt Bridge, low over the water, with a sign, GREENVILLE, 10 MILES.

They would make it.

He began to hum, and then the hum grew corners and became words:

Let me in, please, Charlie: no one here but
    me;
I'm speaking easy: give me a pint of
    stingaree.

He broke off the throaty baritone to ask: "You know that one, Dixie Clay?"

She shook her head.

"You should. 'Blind Pig Blues,' by Barbecue Bob."

"Ream me out some more."

Blind pig, blind pig, sure glad you can't see
    me

For if you could, it would be too tight for
   me.

"You like it?"
"I like it."

I'm slipping slipping slipping, trying to
   dodge United States law
I'm loaded down with bootleg, like to make
   them yammies bawl.

He stopped singing to plunge his hand
over the gunwale and shove them off a
treetop, and then he settled again.

Dixie Clay turned around in the boat.
"You know what?"

"What?"

"I knew you'd come. I can't understand
how I knew, but I did. When I was in that
tree, and I thought I couldn't hold on much
longer, I told myself, 'Hold on. He's going
to find you.' "

"And now we're going to find Willy. We're
not far."

She nodded, then turned back to the
water. "Hand me a sleeve of those crackers,
Ingersoll. We're going to find our Willy."

CHAPTER 18

As they got closer to Greenville and the sun ginned the cottony fog, they spotted more navy seaplanes and rescue boats and a molasses tanker filled with refugees. Still the only land was the levees, which dropped off to water on either side, and they could barely see the levees at all because they were dense with people and livestock. Dixie Clay and Ingersoll were still seven miles out when the *Delta Belle* appeared, ancient sidewheel transient pressed back into service, tornadoing black smoke. She was heading south, Vicksburg, said Ingersoll, who motored their boat closer to the dangerous trunk-clotted bank so it wouldn't be crushed by debris the *Belle* churned up. They bobbed there and Ingersoll cut the motor to save gas and stretched, twisting his torso, and she heard his spine crack. A few wild swans squabbled among the reeds and Dixie Clay tossed them the last saltine, then turned back to watch the riverboat's progress.

"When I was a girl," she said, holding the rocking gunwale with her good hand, "my father used to tell me about going to see a showboat, the *Floating Palace,* how thrilling it was coming around the bend, blasting the calliope, with white plumes of steam." She turned on the bench and picked up the empty potted meat can and bailed some water overboard. "The show started at dark, they could hardly stand the wait. He said they ate pink popcorn." She could still hear the way her father said POP-corn. It was strange to think about him now. She existed in a realm his imagination could not pierce.

Ingersoll must have heard homethoughts in her voice, for when she looked up, he was studying her. She shrugged a shoulder. He pivoted the outboard motor up and pulled leaves and vines from the propeller. Her father would like this man, if he ever met him. Though she'd have a lot of explaining to do. She looked at Ingersoll's profile, slab of hair hanging over his eyes, bump in his nose where it'd been broken, strong jaw with stubble that didn't quite hide the dimple he must not have liked. He was the kind of man who grew better looking the longer you knew him. Whereas Jesse began to tarnish the moment you took him off the shelf.

Jesse wasn't the only person she'd misjudged because of his looks. There was Uncle Mookey, too. She remembered standing before the still with her arms crossed while Mookey hunkered on his heels to eat his dinner. Had she tapped her foot? No, not that bad. But she'd disdained his company. Filling jars with whiskey, she'd shrunk back to avoid brushing his fat, hairless white arms. What had happened in Hobnob, what Mookey had done to blow the levee — in some ways, she was to blame.

The *Delta Belle* gave a moan as it drew abreast, burdened with white women and children, filthy and despondent and laden with parcels, every surface covered. Children stood on top of an improbable piano and others balanced on the boiler and the pilothouse; others clung to the king posts like monkeys. They were the ones who weren't evacuated until the day after the levee break — the poorest ones. Jeannette wouldn't be on this boat, that much was clear.

In front of the steamer floated a fat stump, which Dixie Clay realized was no stump, but a black bear cub. It was paddling from one levee to the other. Where was its mother? Dixie Clay sprang off the bench and yelled "Watch out" toward the steamer, foolishly — the captain couldn't hear her, and even if he could, he wouldn't change course. The cub roundly, earnestly paddled with high paws and a black nose lifted from the water. It crossed in front of the steamer and Dixie Clay couldn't be sure as the cub was blocked from sight but she thought he'd made it. Some of the passengers on the Texas deck were gazing down and must be watching the bear, though none had a reaction that indicated its fate. They seemed dazed, deadened, even the children. Finally the steamer was past. Ingersoll pulled the rip cord and they slapped into the wake, spray hitting their faces.

In another mile, the levees were even more crowded, every inch crammed with cattle and squatting Negroes and shoulder-to-shoulder tents constructed of old quilts or cotton sacks. She turned her head, scanning, as if Willy would be held aloft, waiting for her to claim him. What she saw instead was miserable humanity, lumps of people as if dipped in a slurry of wet clay, shapeless as crawfish mounds. A braying mule scrambled in the mud to climb back on the levee, failing, flailing, sliding deeper into the river. No one helped it.

They motored by these strange bitter tableaux and Dixie Clay recalled the famous Mississippi River panorama that toured through Birmingham, the "three-mile painting" that had to be unscrolled before the audience. But this unscrolling was the painting's opposite — no ragtime-romantic scenes of heroic battles against Indians but a sullen seethe broken occasionally by a brown arm tossing a playing card onto the pile, another flashing a pink palm before swinging against a child's bottom.

Ingersoll steered nearer the levee to avoid another steamer, which gave a blast of its horn, but Dixie Clay didn't watch it pass. Instead, she watched a shrunken woman, dark as a chestnut, sitting on an upended bait bucket, leaning over a cane. Her eyes latched on Dixie Clay's and she pushed heavily on her cane with her elbows jutted out like vulture's wings to rise and then, still glaring, she lifted her cane into the air and shook it at Dixie Clay. She kept shaking it until Ingersoll motored them around the bend. Dixie Clay's forearms prickled with gooseflesh, someone walking on her grave.

She was ill. She knew that. She'd been bonechilled for a day and a night and a day, but she felt hot. Her arm throbbed, her

429

elbow cannibalized in the puffy flesh, her breathing painful. And now her vision bleared. She was a girl on Independence Day with a fever, watching from her bedroom as Lucius and his friends crushed lightning bugs and smeared the phosphorescent paint across their cheeks. She was swooning at that upstairs window. *Come down, Dixie Clay, come down.* She was swooning at the top of a flight of stairs. *Come play.* She felt herself listing and only when her fingers touched the water did she snap to.

Maybe she was going mad.

No. Focus on Willy.

She went to picture his face and nothing was there.

She couldn't remember what he looked like.

"What? What is it, Dixie Clay?"

She didn't know her shoulders were quaking until he asked.

"I can't picture him."

"What?"

"I can't picture Willy! I can't see his face!"

She whirled around in the boat. Ingersoll was scanning the levee as if looking for a place to dock, though there was none. He faced her and leaned forward. "Listen," he said. "Close your eyes."

430

"Oh my God! I can't picture him! I can't
—"

"Damn it, close your eyes!"

She closed them.

"Do this for me. Will you do this for me?
I want you to take a deep breath."

She did, or thought she did.

"No, slower. I'll count to five, and you
breathe in through your nose, and then I'll
count to five, and you breathe out through
your mouth."

He counted. She breathed.

"Now, I need you to do something else. I
need you to think about Willy sneezing.
Okay? No, keep your eyes closed. Good.
Okay, remember how every time he sneezes,
he does it twice, real fast? One sneeze, and
the other right on the heels of it? And after,
he gives a little noise, like a sigh. Can you
hear it?"

She could. She remembered how he
sneezed. Twice, one sneeze following another. She could hear the high sweet register
of his "Choot! Choot!" She could see his
neck snapping forward. She had the sneeze
back. She heard the breathy sigh he always
gave after. She had the sigh back, too. He
always looked a little stunned after sneezing, not sure what had happened or if it
would happen again.

"Do you remember," Ingersoll continued, "his funny squinched-up face when he soils his diddie?"

She did. She could see it and she could smell it. Washrag of warm water, get it up in there. Suds on those little round sugar-lump buns.

"I remember," she told him. Her eyes were still closed.

Fresh diddie, smelling of the breeze on the laundry line. Metal chill of the pin between her lips.

"What else do you remember? You tell me, now. What else, Dixie Clay?"

She started with the smallest thing: his knee. She pictured how it looked when he flexed his leg and the roll of fat puffed on top, kneecap practically without function as he hadn't even tried to crawl, skin still so soft. The knee came back, and the thigh creased twice with rolls of fat, like someone had snapped rubber bands there. Another crease at the ankle, like someone had screwed the foot on. She described it to Ingersoll.

"What else?"

Willy's chin — chins, really. When he smiled his neck looked like a stack of pancakes. She retrieved the chins and the yogurt smell when she'd press her upturned freckled nose in the creases. She described it.

"What else?"

His "b" sound, and his exploratory "ah-ah-aaaaaah," and his "eeeee" when she'd draw his foot sole along her bottom teeth, like the squeal of curling ribbon against the scissor blade.

"What else?"

Her sharp chin playing the xylophone of Willy's rib cage.

Tiny pinprick chill bumps on his legs when she took him from his sink bath. How fast his hair dried as she toweled it, springing into wisps.

Crease of lint between his first and second toes, how'd you get there, lint?

His fist gripping the teething biscuit, how he'd gnaw one end and then flip his fist to gnaw the other but never loosened his grip to gnaw the middle. The sodden biscuit bearing the impression of his knuckles when she'd pry it out at last.

In this manner, bit by bit, she sculpted him aloud while Ingersoll fought the river and prodded her, until she had her baby whole. Her arm was still aching but also now aching to hold his body, body that she knew, that no one alive knew like she knew.

Dixie Clay opened her eyes then and

turned back around in time to see a jewel-wing damselfly, wings like stained glass, alight on the prow and hitch a ride. Her vision wasn't blurry anymore and she was breathing fine.

This was Ingersoll's doing.

He's helping me. He's helping me, and I'm allowing him to.

For so long she'd relied only on herself. She'd needed to. She'd sandbagged her heart. It had felt like strength and she'd had no choice, she'd had no choice but to be strong, so she was strong. But now she'd let someone in. It should have felt like weakness, but it didn't.

She did another of the count-to-five breaths.

Then: "I love you, Ingersoll."

"I know."

She turned and he was smiling.

As they neared the wharf, Ingersoll swerved to avoid a Standard Oil barge pulling out and belatedly blasting its horn. Corrected, then swerved back to avoid a rusty tanker. Finally he gave up on wedging into the sloping concrete wharf and instead brought them close beside the retaining wall at the end of Washington Avenue, topped with sandbags. He yelled to a Negro sitting on top to catch his rope and secure them, and the Negro did and then removed sandbags so they had a kind of passageway. The Negro called that he'd fetch a board to be laid as a gangplank but Dixie Clay shook her head, no time. Instead, Ingersoll grasped her around the waist and lifted her toward the levee and she stretched her leg but fell short of toeing the sandbag and there was a moment when her boot hung in space. Then a pair of brown hands reached to steady her foot. She still wore the sling, but from the sandbags a palm reached out and she grasped it with her good hand and heaved herself through.

Ingersoll propelled himself with the same grasped hand. "Obliged," he said.

"Sho now. But you done gone the wrong way. White folks E-vacuating, not IN-vacuating."

"Yeah. But we're searching for somebody."

"Everybody hereabout searching for somebody." The Negro gestured and Dixie Clay followed with her gaze. Some Negroes were sitting on blankets, some on boxes or valises, some clutched chickens, and one family with eight children sat in cane-back chairs of descending size around a table centered on a rug, like they'd simply moved their parlor outdoors. She looked at the Negro, who still held his arm out, the skin beneath his eyes purple, and she thought, for the first time, that she was not alone in the enactment of a great drama, a great tragedy, that all these people, and there were thousands, all were suffering and seeking, her story merely one story, her despair merely one despair.

The Negro met her gaze and dropped it. "Red Cross lady yonder," he said, and thumbed over his shoulder.

Dixie Clay viewed the city below them, water lapping the buildings halfway up the bottom floors, boats paddling through streets like Venice, rowboats in the middle and motorboats nearer the curb where the water was deeper. All along the levee near the wharf, men were banging hammers into lumber. A milk wagon pulled alongside them.

Ingersoll turned to the driver. "What are they building?"

"Scaffolding," answered the driver. "Right now you can walk above the water from the levee to the Red Cross HQ, to the second floor of the American Legion, to the Opera House, to the Cowan Hotel."

"Who's in Greenville? In charge, I mean. Has President Coolidge come?"

"Nope."

"Does he plan to?"

"Doesn't look like it. But he telegrammed his support." The driver snorted. "Them builders don't leave a body much room to get on by, do they?" He clucked at his horses, who began to skirt the workers, hoofing down the slick levee incline, and momentum started pulling them toward the water, first the horse's fetlocks, then water up to the wagon axles, the horses straining and white-eyed, and then the wagon began to float and the driver uttered a curse and dropped the reins to clasp his cap and the whole floating wagon flipped over, milk cans clattering into the water and bobbing.

"Come on," Ingersoll said, and took her by the hand and they too skirted the workers and darted along the sandbags toward the wharf, through Negroes unloading crates stenciled EMERGENCY SUPPLIES, National Guardsmen aback horses, piles of bricks and rubble, workers building latrines from scrap lumber, a cluster of invalids on cots, three men dragging a dead heifer onto a tarp. The stench was terrible. She was glad for the trotline of Ingersoll's hand. Finally, they were at the bottleneck opening of the sandbags, and an administrator, a man with glasses and a clipboard and a Red Cross armband, was registering female passengers

437

and also arguing with a man in a tweed suit who was clutching an enormous silver tea urn by its double handles.

Ingersoll stepped in front. "We need the police."

The administrator didn't even look up from his clipboard. "You'll have to wait in line. Fill out a request. You'll be given a number, and when it's called —"

"No. You don't understand. This woman is hurt, and her baby's been kidnapped."

The administrator looked up at Dixie Clay. "Kidnapped?"

She sucked in sharply. The word was terrible. Hearing it made it true.

"Your baby was kidnapped?"

She nodded.

"My God." The administrator eyed Dixie Clay's scalp, the dark blood matting her hair.

"We boated here from Hobnob," continued Ingersoll. "That's where it happened. We can describe the kidnapper, and the car she was in. We need access to a radio, the ships' manifests. Are the trains still running?"

The administrator shook his head. "Railroad embankment washed away. Rails are stuck upright, looks like a picket fence."

Ingersoll nodded. "Also — I'm a revenue

agent. I'll need to locate my partner, Ham Johnson. Has he been here?"

"Couldn't say. Greenville's normally fifteen thousand, and there's over twenty-five thousand here today."

"Right. Are the phone lines down?"

"Mostly. They're keeping a few open for emergencies, but they come and go. Try the relief headquarters, the poker rooms of the Knights of Columbus."

"What about the police station?"

He shook his head. "You can try. Police want to stop the looting, but they got no boats. Trying to borrow them from moon-shiners. Anyway, you need more than the police." He paused. His eyes went to Dixie Clay's arm in the sling, and he seemed to decide something. "You need Percy."

"Percy? Leroy Percy, the senator?"

"Yep. Go to his house. The levee board is there. They'll want you to meet with Will, the son, he's the chairman of flood relief. Tell him — No, what you do is" — the administrator stepped closer to Ingersoll's ear — "go around back, to the servants' entrance. Look for the Negro chauffeur, and when you see him, say you need Mrs. Percy, immediately. Go around to the front door, and tell her about the kidnapped child. She'll fetch her husband."

Ingersoll nodded. "How do I get there?"

"Down Percy Street." The administrator pointed with his pen. "He has a phone. Can't miss the house. It's on a hill. He has the only tennis court in town. Look for the top of the net poking out of the water."

Ingersoll stuck out his hand and the men shook. Then he turned and took Dixie Clay's elbow and led her down the sloping levee to the ramp that angled to a boardwalk made of lumber laid across metal risers. They climbed it and walked above the flooded streets, beside the second-story windows. Below them, two boys in dugout canoes paddled furiously. Dixie Clay knew them; they were Hobnob boys, Joe Joe Majure and Jack Wheeler. So not everyone from Hobnob was washed away. Who else had made it out? The iron sign, GREENVILLE: QUEEN CITY OF THE DELTA, usually arced high above the street, but now Joe Joe lifted his paddle and smacked it a few seconds before Jack did, winner of the race, the metal tolling like a church bell.

Dixie Clay and Ingersoll were hurrying along the scaffolding, single file and often pressed against the buildings as others rushed the opposite way. They peered through windows as they passed, rooms crammed with rugs and furniture hoisted up from the ground-floor stores. Dixie Clay scanned rooftops for Jeannette and Willy, then scanned the canal traffic below. At the corner, a boy in rubber waders was yelling, but his words made no sense. "The Sultan of Swat blasts third long ball of the season!" he repeated. Ingersoll saw the puzzlement on her face. "Baseball," he said. "Babe Ruth." Dixie Clay saw now that the boy wore a satchel honeycombed with rolled newspapers. The world was still going on, was it.

She was rehearsing what she'd tell Mrs. Percy. Dixie Clay drew to a stop, and Ingersoll nearly ran into her.

"My God." She turned to him. "I don't even know Jeannette's last name."

She'd been so focused on getting to Greenville, and now that she had she saw that it mightn't solve anything. The city was chaos, refugees pouring in and being shipped out, a man leaning out of a third-story window in his shirtsleeves calling "Jeremy! Eli! Jeremy! Eli!," his voice hoarse and incessant, interspersed with the call of a peddler hawking peanuts, posters plastered to the wall at intervals, NEGRO CURFEW 8 P.M.! and down below, a canoe upsetting, cries of alarm. How would they find one woman and one infant? She brought her hand to her head, which was throbbing like a kicked pumpkin.

"We'll find him, Dixie Clay. I promise you. We'll find him."

A dog brushed her knees, and she nearly lost her balance. The smell of rotting fish — rotting everything — was too much. Ingersoll slipped an arm behind her and led her along the boardwalk. He continued, "There's more to my job than you know. We're prohis, yes, but" — he helped her climb over some pipes — "we're also on assignment for Hoover. Ham and me. And we'll use all the pull we have. Percy can contact Hoover for us. Ham, he'll be hereabouts, he'll have been ordered here to stop the looting — he'll help. You said Jeannette was from New Orleans?"

Dixie Clay nodded.

"Then she probably was evacuated to Natchez. Ham can contact the agency down there. We'll learn all about Jeannette, we'll get a photograph in the papers, we'll wire police stations, we'll telegram Coolidge if we need to."

Ingersoll pulled Dixie Clay against the brick wall of the drugstore as a printer barreled through with a stack of paper in his arms. He was followed by an apprentice, ink on his apron.

Dixie Clay was looking at the fingers on her left hand, so swollen it seemed they'd burst. She realized there was no wedding band. Scraped off on the tree, yanked off by a wave, who knew.

"Listen," she said. "Contacting the newspapers, the police . . . it's complicated . . . you see, it's not just that I've violated Volstead. It's" — she took a breath and pushed the rest of the sentence out in her exhalation — "the two revenuers you've been looking for, I think Jesse killed them."

Dixie Clay turned from him, aswirl with fear and guilt, and stepped into the path of a boy on a bicycle. The wheel rammed her leg, knocking her off balance. Her sling flapped up and she was one-leggedly about to topple over into the water when Ingersoll threw his arms around her. Her ribs, her broken kindling ribs, were lassoed in fire and she screamed.

"Dixie Clay? Are you okay?"

She opened her eyes. Ingersoll was holding her up and his colors were off, the brick wall behind him seeming to pulse. She clenched her teeth and nodded.

"We've gotta get you to the hospital."

"No. Find Willy. Percy. Police." Each word took a breath and each breath was a blade. Her ribs might saw open her skin. Might pop her lungs like balloons. She'd never bought Willy a balloon, though she'd dog-eared that page of the Sears catalog, thinking ahead to his birthday.

Ingersoll took her right arm and gently steadied her, but she couldn't stanch the moan.

"Damn it, Dixie Clay. We need to get you looked at, and then we'll find Percy."

She wanted to argue, but he'd already turned away to halt a carpenter with a pencil behind his ear. "This woman's sick. Where's the Red Cross medic tent? By the wharf?"

"That one's for darkies, and mostly vaccinations. Typhoid and the like. You'll want the tent by the park. Or the hospital, if it's serious."

"Hospital's still open?"

"Bottom floor flooded, but two through four are fine. King's Daughters hospital." The man turned Ingersoll by the shoulder to point to a red-tiled Spanish roof visible a few blocks away.

"You got a boat?" the carpenter asked.

Ingersoll nodded.

"Well, get on then." He was looking at Dixie Clay, leaning against the brick facade.

Ingersoll swooped an arm behind her and carried her, retracing their steps to the wharf, and then he boated her over the streets of Greenville to King's Daughters.

The entrance to the hospital was crowded with boats of every size and function, all nosed toward the door. Some were empty, and a few seemed empty but were lined with napping Negro servants; one held an obese man who clutched his side and alternated groaning with shouting, "I won't go in." His skinny wife looked about wrung out and addressed Ingersoll, who was hitching the boat to a street sign. "Don't matter. Even if he could get in, they won't see him."

"Why not?" Ingersoll asked.

She shrugged. "This is the only hospital open for a hundred fifty miles. They ain't got the time." She looked over Dixie Clay, whose face was pale. "She won't stand a chance, not without buckets of blood."

Ingersoll nodded at the woman and climbed over the boat. The cold water came up to his waist, and he moved through it to the prow and lifted Dixie Clay again, her skirt dragging in the water, and wove between the boats to reach the door of the hospital, propped open by the white-clothed backside of a nurse bailing water with a coffee can. She stood to hold the door for Ingersoll, who entered sideways with Dixie Clay in his arms. "Intake's been moved to the third floor," she said. "But the elevator's out. You need to take the stairs. But only when your number is called. You're 409."

"What number are you on?"

She shrugged. "You'll have to ask her," she said and gestured to a nurse wearing waders in the back of the dim lobby. Ingersoll splashed over, still carrying Dixie Clay, a wailing child to the right, a moaning man to the left.

"Ma'am," said Ingersoll, standing before the nurse.

"So you're 118? I called you twice."

The smallest of hesitations. "Yup. 118, that's us."

"That way then. Third floor."

Ingersoll backed through the door to the metal stairwell and began to trudge up, trying not to jostle Dixie Clay. "You doing okay?"

She squeezed his arm.

"Almost there. Maybe they'll have the elevator fixed" — he was breathing hard — "by the time we leave."

"I've never ridden one before."

"You'll get the hang of it." When he reached the first landing, he paused.

And that's when they heard it. Echoing through the metal door came the unforgettable rip-cord cackle that passed as laughter.

Dixie Clay whipped her head toward the sound and held up her palm. "She's here," Dixie Clay whispered, though she didn't need to. The sound again, a child's bicycle with baseball cards clothespinned to the spokes. "That's her. Jeannette." They were motionless. And then — "Through there," said Dixie Clay, raising her chin at the door stenciled DELIVERY, NURSERY, DIETETIC DEPARTMENTS.

Ingersoll asked, "What are you going to do?"

"I don't know."

Ingersoll couldn't pull the fire door open with Dixie Clay in his arms. He set her gently on her feet, and she worked not to wince.

He yanked the door open. Behind it was a tiled hallway with a lumpy row of classroom desks, most filled with women sitting sideways because the attached chairs didn't allow room for their pregnant bellies. The woman nearest them lifted her head, saw they were not whom she hoped for, and let her head thunk back down. A scream came from somewhere, followed by a call, "Ice, ice, she needs ice!" A few steps away they saw a nurses' station, and behind the desk, barely clearing the top, was a white cap. The short nurse stood abruptly. "Well?"

Neither spoke for a moment. Then Ingersoll stepped forward. "We're looking for someone . . . a flapper named Jeannette —"

"I have patients who are truly sick," began the nurse, scurrying out from behind the desk. She had fluffy red hair beneath her cap and came up to Ingersoll's elbow. "This is an emergency ward, understand? For E-MER-GEN-CIES. I have patients who were pinned beneath joists."

Some response seemed to be expected. "Yes, ma'am," said Ingersoll.

"I have patients who were pulled from flooding cars."

"Yes, ma'am," said Ingersoll.

"Who were on the train when it was washed off its tracks."

"Yes, ma'am."

"I have patients who need morphine because their legs are crushed. Crushed! Not because they got addicted after botched abortions."

"Yes, ma'am," Ingersoll said again.

Now the nurse turned to Dixie Clay and shook her finger so hard that her whole body shook. "Did you know my assistant saw her take a syringe from her pocketbook and fill it from the medicine cabinet and inject herself, pretty as you please?"

"No, ma'am."

"So now, in addition to everything else, I need to keep the medicine under lock and key."

"Yes, ma'am."

"So do me a favor, y'all. Get her gone. I don't care that she's rich or the niece of some New Orleans politician. I need that bed. For truly sick folk."

"Yes, ma'am."

The nurse turned and began to stomp down the gray tiles.

They exchanged a look of wonder and followed the white uniform, but it halted. She turned around and yelled, " 'Bout near as naked as a boiled chicken!"

"Yes, ma'am," said Dixie Clay.

But something more was needed.

"We're sorry, ma'am," added Ingersoll.

The nurse resumed the march. But she wasn't done yet. She paused in front of double doors. "I didn't become a nurse for this," she said, and pushed through.

Inside the ward it was dim and cool. There was a narrow aisle and about a dozen metal cots on each side, all filled, and a few makeshift pallets on the floor. Some of the women were bandaged, one whimpering, most appearing to sleep.

"Nurse Strom," called a woman from the first cot. "It's my time!"

"It's nowhere near your time, Laura," the nurse said, stepping to the supply cabinet and climbing a stepladder to tussle a carton into her arms. She descended and picked up a knife to stab the carton and began sawing noisily. "Go back to sleep." And then, under her breath, "You ninny."

Dixie Clay and Ingersoll walked the aisle. Each cot had a crucifix hanging over it and a face they didn't recognize. At the last cot on the left, a woman curled on her side with her back to them. At first Dixie Clay thought she saw red hair but then realized she saw a blonde wearing a red fur stole. Her bare feet were tucked, toenails crimson. Dixie Clay looked at Ingersoll, who gestured with his shoulder, and they walked around the cot to face her. To face Jeannette. Her eyes were dreamy slits and she was picking at the sheet corner. She was wearing a silk slip with lace trim and the fox stole. The fox clasped its tail in its mouth, and the legs dangled down her chest.

"Jeannette. I need to know where Willy is."

Jeannette didn't startle. She merely looked up and gave an indolent stretch of an arm, bangles clacking. "Why, whadd'ya know, if it isn't Dipsie Dirt, darling little Dipsie Dirt." Jeannette spoke slowly, long pauses between her words. She let her arm fall heavily on the mattress and turned her head to Ingersoll. Her movements seemed underwatery. "And what do we have here? My my, the back door man? The one who cuckolded Jesse?" She appraised him and stage-whispered, "Nice work, Dipsie. Didn't know you had it in you." She made a show of running her tongue across her teeth. "Looks like he's running on all sixes."

"Jeannette," said Dixie Clay. "Where's Willy?"

Jeannette patted the mattress by her hip and said to Ingersoll, "C'mere and give me a taste."

Dixie Clay leaned over the cot. "Where's Willy?"

"A wittle bitty taste." Jeannette plucked a strand of hair from her cot and dropped it over the edge. "Don't suppose you have any hooch on you, huh?"

"Where's Willy?"

"Or some morphy? Some Uncle Morphy? Maybe we could make a trade."

"Jeannette," she said again, moving into her vision, bringing her face close. "Tell me where Willy is and I'll get you anything you want."

"I don't need him anymore, you know. I'm going to have my own baby. A real baby, not some hand-me-down."

"Okay. Where's Willy?"

"Feel," she said. She grabbed Dixie Clay's hand from the cot and flattened her fingers against the cool silk slip. "Did you feel that? Did you feel it kick?"

Dixie Clay shot Ingersoll a look and Jeannette saw it and flung the hand away and pounded the mattress with a fist. Then she seemed to go in reverse. She smiled and whispered, "Wait," and reached for the hem of her slip and drew it up her thighs, up her belly, to her breasts. She had on black lace panties with garter clips that dangled, no stockings. Her body was skinny, sallow, two greenish half-dollar bruises on her hip.

"Feel again," she said. Dixie Clay didn't move and Jeannette reached forward to grab her hand and flatten it on her belly, which was sunken and damp and prickled with gooseflesh.

"Do you feel?" demanded Jeannette. "Do you feel the life inside of me?"

"Yes, yes, I feel it," said Dixie Clay.

Jeannette grinned and closed her eyes and yanked her slip back down. "Told cha. Told cha I was gonna have a real one. A boy." She laughed and said "Told cha" again and turned her head into the pillow and repeated "Told cha, told cha, told cha," the sound muffled. Then she rolled back, a childish cunning in her eyes. "You know, Jesse only married you because you're shorter than he is."

The woman was actually trying to wound her with this. "Where's Willy?"

"Maybe I'll name my baby Jesse. After his father." With that Jeannette rolled her face back into the pillow and they could hear her laugh, muffled but still terrible.

From the front came the nurse's command: "You two! You'll have to leave now. Go to the third floor to fill out her release papers."

Dixie Clay looked at Ingersoll, who put his hand on her back and seemed to transfer strength through it. *Okay,* she thought, *what else can I try?* She lifted a hip to perch lightly on Jeannette's cot and slowly reached out to stroke the blond hair. She almost crooned in Jeannette's ear, stroking the stiff locks, "Jeannette, Jeannette, that's a good girl."

Jeannette turned her face toward Dixie Clay and gave a small humming sigh.

"That's a good girl." Dixie Clay kept stroking. "You're a good girl, Jeannette. And you're having your own baby. Congratulations, Jeannette!"

Jeannette smiled, her eyes closed.

"You don't need Willy. A castoff. An orphan."

"That old thing?" Jeannette blew the air from her mouth, which fluffed her blond bangs. "That old thing. Cries all the time. Boo hoo hoo! What a crybaby. Mine's not gonna cry."

Again the nurse yelled from the front. "Folks! These are not visiting hours! Proceed to the third floor."

Dixie Clay kept stroking, speaking into Jeannette's ear. "That's right, Jeannette, that's right. Willy cries too much. Where is he? Is he in Greenville? Is he with somebody?"

"Mine's gonna gimme sugar. All the time, sugar."

"That's right, Jeannette. You deserve a good baby. Where'd you put that bad old baby? Jeannette?"

Jeannette rolled onto her back and stiffened on the cot and drew a hand to her brow and gave a mock salute to Ingersoll. Then she launched into the soldier's song, in a voice high but surprisingly clear: "Over there!" she sang and jerked her thumb to the side, the fox head on her chest bouncing. "Over there!" She kept singing, again with the thumb. "Send the word, send the word, over there . . . That the Yanks are coming, the Yanks are coming . . . The drums rum-tumming, ev'rywhere!"

Dixie Clay met Ingersoll's eyes and he half shrugged, half motioned to the door. She followed him, hoping he'd have a strategy, down the row of cots as Jeannette's voice sailed after them, "So prepare! Say a prayer! Send the word, send the word, to beware!"

"Can't you shut her up?" called the patient named Laura as they hustled past. "I'd like to slap her six ways to Sunday."

They skirted the nurse, who was looking down, taking a pulse, and Ingersoll pushed open the doors and when he did, she saw the sign PEDIATRIC WARD, with an arrow to the right, where Jeannette's thumb had gestured.

Now Dixie Clay was running down the hallway and around the corner and bouncing off a rolling cart that clanged with metal instruments and then she was pushing wild-eyed through swinging doors, calling "Willy!"

It was a ward like the one Jeannette had been in, but louder, layers of wailing strafing the air, with a low row of children's cots to the left and baby beds to the right. Through the slats of the nearest one she could see a blanket and a foot and she knew Willy's foot and she flew to the crate and looked down.

Willy. Willy! Oh my God. Willy. He looked the same, he looked fine, he was hers. He was sleeping and she reached in and slipped her trembling hands behind his back and lifted him and his weight was so familiar, the good thunk of his heavy head on her chest. The smell of him, she could have scouted him in the dark.

"Ma'am?" A nurse appeared beside them.

Willy opened his eyes and saw Dixie Clay and seemed neither surprised nor pleased. His eyes closed again. Sleepy baby. Sleepy baby doesn't even know what he's been through.

"Ma'am?"

Dixie Clay smiled and inhaled his head, dizzy from it.

"Ma'am? Can I help you?"

Dixie Clay with the baby clasped under her chin turned to face the nurse.

"Who are you?" the nurse asked.

"This is my baby. I've been searching and fearing I wouldn't find him but I found him." She pulled Willy away from her chest so she could look at him. He was even more beautiful. He seemed bigger, which was crazy. How could he look bigger in just two days? She smiled and looked up, but the nurse had squinchy eyes behind her glasses.

She thinks I'm crazy, realized Dixie Clay.

She felt Ingersoll's arm slide around her to support her bad arm, which she couldn't remove from the baby's neck, though holding him hurt.

"It's real," she told Willy. "It's really real. I found you." She hugged Willy close and then pulled him away again to look at his face, but her hands were shaking so that the skin underneath his chin was vibrating. Then she needed his skin on hers again and hugged him to her chest. She smiled at Ingersoll through her tears.

The nurse stood looking from Dixie Clay to Ingersoll to the baby. "But . . . this baby's mother is in the infirmary. She's a . . . she's unwell. Her name is Jeannette Lovelady. Look, it says so here." The nurse pointed to a square of cardboard in a plastic sleeve attached to the front of the baby bed. She tapped it twice with her fingernail, as if that would clarify all.

Ingersoll said, "That woman is not the baby's mother. This here is his mother."

Dixie Clay was pressing kisses all over the baby's head. Her hand cupped his skull. Her hand was a ragged dirty dried-bloody raccoon paw on the perfect baby's perfect downy head.

"I don't know," said the nurse. "I don't

know about that. I — I need Nurse Strom. Y'all stay here, I'll be right back."

Ingersoll nodded and watched the nurse scurry out of the ward, looking back at them as she pushed through the swinging doors.

"What do we do now?" asked Dixie Clay.

"Now," said Ingersoll, "we run."

CHAPTER 19

They ran. Ingersoll with Willy on his shoulder and Dixie Clay's hand in his. They ran through the Pediatric Ward and along the crowded hallway and over the legs of patients sitting against the plaster wall and past the crowded nurses' station and a medicine locker where Ingersoll doubled back to snatch some medical tape and aspirin while Dixie Clay kept a lookout for Nurse Strom. They ran around buckets catching leaks and then around the janitor pushing a few inches of water across the floor with a long broom like a mustache and down the stairs into the lobby still flooded knee-high and seething with the injured then past the nurse in the waders who was lifting a bloody towel off the face of a man on a stretcher and to the door where they saw the same receptionist, still holding the front door open with her backside and still bailing. Ingersoll tugged Dixie Clay to a splashless stroll. When the nurse managed to straighten up, Dixie Clay was walking stiffly past, close to Ingersoll to block the baby that he held against his stomach.

"Well, that was quick!" chirped the nurse. "All better, are we?"

"Oh, yes, ma'am, all better now," Dixie Clay sang back.

They waded to their boat, which was blocked in, and Ingersoll settled Dixie Clay and Willy and then grabbed the line and pulled the boat clear, past the grizzled woman fanning her fat husband who was still swearing he wouldn't go in. At the end of the flooded lawn Ingersoll hauled himself into the boat and pulled the cord and the motor caught and then they were chugging away from King's Daughters, Dixie Clay resolutely, rigidly forward like a carved Egyptian idol though she confessed when they were around the corner and onto Arnold Avenue that she had been expecting Nurse Strom to throw open the window of King's Daughters and order all the king's men to seize them.

By the time they hit Main Street, one side lined with the scaffolding boardwalk, they'd slowed because of the boat traffic. No one seemed to be following them — Dixie Clay whipped her head around to check. Her pain, which had receded in the rush of finding Willy, now seemed to be reclaiming her. In a store window, Ingersoll caught her wan reflection, eyes like two chestnuts in a pail of buttermilk.

"Dixie Clay, we should take a break."

"Don't you think we should get clear of Greenville first?"

"I do not. We need to rest, and eat, and get supplies. And I gotta find Ham. But first things first. And — look here."

It was a store, Neilson's Apparel for Men, Women, and Children. The water came up to the fourth of the five steps, so it was open. They tied the boat to the scaffolding and hopped from the boardwalk onto the top step and walked to the racks and quickly selected some basics, which were totaled up and wrapped in paper, and Ingersoll paid with four of the eight wet dollars that the fake preacher had scoffed at. They asked for dressing rooms and a clerk with pince-nez dangling on a chain led them back and showed Dixie Clay the women's and walked Ingersoll to the men's. As soon as Ingersoll saw, beneath the saloon door of his stall, the loafers of the clerk walk away, he scooted across the hall to the women's side.

"Hey," he said, and knuckle-knocked. "Can I come in?"

"I reckon so," said Dixie Clay. "Can't get this blouse off anyway."

Ingersoll hooked an arm over the door and unlatched it. She'd nestled Willy, asleep, in a terrycloth robe on the settee. Ingersoll tried to help her with the buttons but the torn shirt caught on her splint so in the end he ripped it off, Dixie Clay giggling when it summoned the clerk, who then hurried away, muttering, "Oh my stars, oh my stars."

When she turned, he saw the bruise on her chest in the shape of a boot. He could barely stand to look, but he had to, gently prodded and verified it was just a bruise. Her arm was still purple and puffy but seemed to be setting fine.

Now for the ribs. He asked her to breathe in and out and the uneven rippling of her chest confirmed it, two broken ribs. He took from his pocket the packet of aspirin he'd lifted from the hospital, a paltry thing but better than nothing, and tore it open into her palm and watched her swallow, then yanked out an arm's length of medical tape — another sharp sound to entertain the clerk — and ripped it off with his teeth.

"Is this going to hurt?" she asked.

He hesitated. "Yes."

"Okay."

"Hold here," he ordered, tapping the top

of the stall. When she did, he said, "Exhale all the air from your lungs." Then he pressed the tape on her sternum and wrapped it around her ribs all the way to her spine, Dixie Clay not making a sound but her knuckles like white marbles under her skin. Another strip of tape laid parallel, then two more and it was done. She let her breath out shakily.

He lifted her stiff new brassiere while she guided her arms in and then he went behind to fasten the difficult contraption. Their eyes met in the mirror and he thought, *What a range, what a fullness, she brings out of me. She could be a sister for all the passion in this gesture yet that is a nice thing, too; I wouldn't have guessed it, never having had a sister, but it is.*

By now Willy had woken so they shucked his gray hospital gown in favor of his new blue-checked creeper over a poplin shirt. They agreed there had never been a prettier babe on God's green earth and that the creeper was worth every cent of the eighty-five they'd paid for it. Then Ingersoll dressed in a red Henley and dungarees identical to the ones he took off and left in the dressing room save for the fact they weren't wet and shredded, and he placed on his head a new hat, exactly like the one he'd lost in the flood, and yanked on some stiff new cowboy boots, exactly like the ones he'd tumped into the barrel in Hobnob. He swung open the door and the three of them sashayed past the clerk without looking his way, Dixie Clay turning into Ingersoll's shoulder to muffle a giggle.

Outside they crossed onto the scaffolding and this time when Ingersoll caught their reflection in the storefront glass, he thought — *We look almost respectable,* followed by, *We look like a family.*

The reflection also showed a hanging sign with an arrow, four letters naming no less of a miracle than the burning bush: RIBS. It hung beside another taped to the window, 2ND FLOOR OPEN!!!

He took Dixie Clay by the shoulders and steered her to a door propped ajar with a plank that led from the boardwalk onto a set of rickety pull-down stairs. They crossed the plank and ascended, the noise and heat growing as they reached the top, and then they popped through the opening, at the same level of the ankles of dozens of diners, and the smell of, God let it be so, charred pig. They emerged into what had probably been the attic of the restaurant, now jammed with mismatched tables and chairs of different heights and waitresses with large oval platters on their shoulders, each platter holding five racks of ribs. Ingersoll would eat the five racks of ribs and have the platter for dessert.

A waitress swiveled by and addressed him over the tray on her shoulder. "Y'all look like you been rode hard and put up wet."

Even with the new clothes. "That's about the truth," he conceded.

"Got a table just about to finish up. Gimme a sec and I'll bus it."

When it was ready, he led Dixie Clay there and they saw where the ribs were coming from — a busboy was leaning out the window, pulling the racks of ribs off meat hooks attached to a pulley. Ingersoll waited until the boy left and stuck his head out and by God if the barbecue pit wasn't an old train engine. "You gotta see this," he told Dixie Clay, and she and Willy joined him at the window and they marveled at the red wheels and cowcatcher and brass bell, the grillers shoveling wood into the engine, all wearing waders because they were up to their thighs in water. Ingersoll got Dixie Clay seated again and thought how this was a thing he loved about people — trouble brought out their grit, their creativity. Ribs on pulleys in Greenville, Mississippi; music from a wire in Paris,

France; the world held wonders. And now he had these two to share wonders with, he thought, watching Dixie Clay lick her napkin to wipe Willy's face.

The waitress brought them coffee. "We got ribs," she said, "or we got ribs."

Ingersoll nodded and after she admired Willy with a "Well, couldn't you just sop him up with a biscuit," she was off, and Ingersoll told Dixie Clay he had to do the same. He'd hurry but he had to go to the sheriff's to ask after Ham. He wanted her and the baby to stay and rest and eat.

She nodded but looked worried.

"It's not far," he told her.

"How do you know?"

"That's where I took Willy after his parents were shot. I was looking for someone to take him. I tried to give him away there." He shook his head. "What's strange? Seems like forever ago. But it was just two weeks."

"Two weeks," she said, her turn to shake her head. "Who was I then?" She answered her question quietly. "Just a girl whose life was about to begin."

He stood and put his hand on her shoulder. "I'll be back directly. You can report whether Willy likes sucking on a rib bone. Whether he favors hot or mild."

She laid her hand atop his hand, and then

466

he slid his away and walked down the stairs.

Ingersoll dreaded going to the sheriff's, and as he boated there he played out what would transpire. Reporting at the desk, announcing his name — he didn't even want to do that — and explaining who he was, how there'd be phone calls to Hoover and the Prohibition commissioner and the Revenue Agency, how he'd answer questions and then more questions. How very very much he'd have to answer for, how very very few answers he possessed. Usually, Ham did the talking. And now Ham could be dead. Ingersoll didn't think so, he thought he'd be able to *feel* it, if that were the case — surely a world would feel different, impoverished, without Ham Johnson in it — but he wouldn't leave this place without knowing.

He arrived at the steps too soon and tied the boat and climbed slowly as men rushed up and down. Inside, the same pretty dark-haired receptionist, on the phone, waved and then held up a finger to him. "Uh-huh," she said into the receiver. "Uh-huh." She rolled her eyes for his benefit and tucked her fingers into her cleavage to tug out a lace handkerchief, which she used to cover the mouthpiece. Leaning forward, she whispered to Ingersoll, "Says there's five hundred darkies in the courthouse that can't be fed and the place smells like a slaughter pen." She removed the handkerchief and enunciated into the receiver, "Get them to the levee how, sir?" Ingersoll removed his hat and crossed his arms to wait but was too impatient to sit in the chair she gestured to. The receptionist was enjoying the drama. In fact, the whole station buzzed with importance, men rushing by, shouting. The receptionist lifted her hankie to the mouthpiece again and whispered to Ingersoll, "Someone came looking for you." Then she directed her attention back to the phone call again. "Well, how deep is the water between the courthouse and the levee?"

Meanwhile Ingersoll had started at her words and leaned on her desk, willing her to tell him, let it be Ham.

"That deep, huh? Well, can they swim?" she shrugged for Ingersoll's benefit. She held up her index finger again, but he couldn't wait.

"Who? Who came looking?"

Again with the index finger.

"Ma'am? Please?"

Not bothering with the handkerchief, she lifted her mouth away from the receiver to whisper, "He said you'd come. I remembered you 'cause of the baby."

"Who? What was his name?"

Into the receiver she said, "There's not room on the levee for five hundred more darkies."

"Please —"

The index finger. He'd snap it off if she stuck it in the air one more time. Then the finger was lowered to the underside of her desk drawer, which she slid forward. "He left this," she said.

It was a piece of lined notebook paper folded into a fat rectangle. There was no name on the outside. He unfolded it. Ham's blocky handwriting:

MEET ME IN THE JOINT SELL-ING RIBS, YOU PECKERWOOD.

Ingersoll crushed the paper to his chest and was out of the office and down the steps three at a time and into the boat and through the water and across the boardwalk and up the restaurant stairs three at a time and poking his head into the room and turning past the legs of diners and there they were, beside Dixie Clay's, Ham's irrepressible size 11 and 12 boots.

And then he and Ham were embracing, a thing he'd think about later and realize it was the first time they'd done that, they'd never done that in all those years. Slapping each other's backs, they were, and then hugging again, Ham's huge laugh and the diners nearby not even glancing up, too jaded by the sights and shouts of the last few days to be flummoxed.

An hour later the pile of bleached bones in the center of the table was as clean as fossils a paleontologist would assemble. Ham was red and sweating and fanning himself with his new high-domed white cowboy hat, which he had blocked porkpie style. Dixie Clay had been a little hesitant with Ham at first, which was natural, Ingersoll figured, given what happened when they met outside the funeral home, but by and by she seemed to be warming.

Now Dixie Clay had Willy faceup, on her gently swaying knees. He'd been fussy and she hadn't had a bottle for him but the waitress had brought her some milk in a glass with a paper straw and Dixie Clay had held the strange instrument to his mouth and at first he'd gummed it but then he'd sucked and they'd all leaned forward to watch the liquid being drawn up and when it was almost at his lips he quit sucking and dismayed they watched it fall like mercury. She'd held the straw to his lips once more and Willy had sucked again and the cold milk had hit his tongue and his eyes widened and all three cheered and Willy'd drunk until he was sated and calm. Ingersoll had knifed apart some of the ribs for Dixie Clay so she could eat one-handed, and she'd nibbled her fill, and the men, too, were full as ticks on a fat dog, and now had toothpicks, Ham narrating his quest to dislodge a meaty morsel — "Almost got you, you son of a bitch" — looking up and grinning, "Sorry, ma'am," to Dixie Clay — and then, "Ahh," and smacking his lips, "Tastes even better after marinating between my chompers for a while."

They'd just finished trading stories. Ingersoll had gone first because the ribs hadn't arrived yet and he knew when they did his mouth would be otherwise occupied. He picked up with splitting off from Ham and finding the sniper. Dixie Clay piped in to explain why the fat man Ingersoll had shot in the hotel had looked like the twin of the fat man Ham had shot on the levee — because they *were* twins, Burl and Mookey, Jesse's childhood uncles. Ingersoll continued with the explosion — both men shaking their heads at the ingenuity of dynamite in the sandbags — and then the rescue of Dixie Clay and the boat journey to Greenville and the discovery of Jeannette and then of Willy.

The ribs arrived and Ingersoll and Dixie Clay ate while Ham told his tale, which took four times as long, no need for him to rush as this was his second rack of the day, he said, mouth bracketed by grease-glistening muttonchops.

"Well, I've told some wild ones," he began, snapping the napkin from his collar and wiping it over his mouth, "some that even I didn't believe," and Ingersoll settled into his chair in a satisfied way, his leg electric against Dixie Clay's, touching hip to ankle. Willy was asleep across her lap and her sling arm rested over his rib cage, rising and falling with his breath.

"Yes, sir," Ham said, now wiping his forehead with the napkin. "Talk about your yarns —"

"Is Jesse dead?" Dixie Clay interrupted.

Ham looked up surprised, and his big jaw seemed to reattach itself to his cranium and he reddened a little, not an easy feat; he'd obviously forgotten that Jesse was more than just the bad guy who had it coming.

She sat rigid, her eyes intense.

"I'm sorry. He is. Jesse's dead."

She'd been clenching Ingersoll's hand and now let go, brought her fingers to her forehead. Ingersoll suddenly worried that she might have been hoping for other news. Dixie Clay said nothing. When at last she tilted her face up from the basket of her fingers, there were no tears on her freckled cheeks.

"Are you okay?" he asked.

"I think so. I think so. It's strange. I mean — I'm sure I'll be sad at some point, but right now, I feel . . . I mostly feel . . . relief."

Ingersoll wasn't sure what to do but the answer came when she reached beneath the table and grabbed his hand again. That was a thing he could do.

Ham had looked off, as if trying to allow some privacy. But it was Ham that Dixie Clay addressed.

"He wasn't always a bad fellow," she said.

Ham nodded.

"He used to be different. When I met him . . ." she said, trailing off. Some diner from a back table touched her shoulder to get by and she scooted her chair in. Then she sighed. "But who he became. At the end. I'm glad that person is dead. I" — she lifted her eyes to the window — "I might have killed him myself, given the chance."

The men nodded. If she had more to say, they would listen. But she did not. "Tell it," she said to Ham. "Tell the story."

He looked at her and she inclined her head. "What happened is this," he began, leaning forward. "When the shooting starts, Ingersoll goes for the sniper, him being the better shot, or at least that was his reputation, though in this case his reputation seems a bit unfounded. But me, I'm chasing after Jesse, who I outstrip by a foot in height but he's running faster than a scalded dog.

"When we hear the explosion we both turn. Jesse says, 'Oh shit,' pardon me, miss, but oh shit is right. For here comes the river where the street used to be. It kind of starts at the top of the levee, and like a big paw, it just scoops out the town. By then Jesse and I have forgotten who's chasing who and we're just sprinting balls out and ahead of us the road curves up a bit and there's a church, so we run in there, of all things. Inside the doors, Jesse makes a sharp turn toward the bell tower — we'd both eyed it as we'd run up — and I follow him up those dinky wooden stairs, turning and turning, and when I'm about halfway up I hear the flood coming down on the church and then I'm feeling it, the wall of water crashes against the church doors. I'm knocked to the floor, and the whole belfry sways like a tower made of blocks. I scramble my way to the top just a few steps behind Jesse and then push through to the landing and we look out toward the river and it's all river, there's no place that ain't river. I can't even get my bearings for a second, I mean there's hardly any landmarks left. Jesse's ducked beneath one bell to watch and me beneath the other — the bells were bonging by themselves — and we lean out the case-ments heaving and watch the whole town break into pieces, houses and people screaming by. And then another section of the levee goes and water topples towards us and we can feel it rush into the church like the Holy Spirit himself and it hits the far wall and the tower gives a spasm and with a roar the huge slab of wall behind the crucifix just falls flat out like a child's gingerbread house, sending up a giant wave in all direc-tions, and we see the pews backhanded through the opening, and I think we're gon-ers.

"We hang on, though. Jesse hangs on to his bellpull, and I hang on to mine. Neither one of us has a gun anymore. I think we weren't even worried about each other, we had a bigger enemy, if you know what I mean. We keep feeling the church . . . adjust . . . below us. The whole tower would shiver and dust come down."

Ham covered a belch with the back of his hand. "And after a while we realize that if the church was going to fall, it would have fallen. There are a couple other buildings — the police station, the city hall, the McLain — that haven't fallen either. Jesse gets all shrewdlike and says, 'Ham, since the moment's got so quiet here, and a fellow can take stock, I expect that means we're to survive.'

"I let on how I expect the same thing.

"He says, 'In that case, it seems to me that you are the only person standing between me and my escape.'

"I let on how that was the case."

Ham creaked in his chair, crossing his legs. "Then Jesse reaches into his pocket and I think he's got some kind of pistol but what he draws out is a half-pint of Black Lightning. So what do I do, Ing?"

"Bottoms up," Ingersoll said.

"Indeedy-o. Bottoms up. Finest whiskey known to man," he said, with a wink for Dixie Clay. "So, we drink a spell, passing the bottle back and forth like we're on holiday, like our belfry don't resemble the mast of the *Titanic*. And finally, Jesse says, 'Ham, I wish to offer you a bribe.' "

The waitress came over with coffee and said, "Let me top you off, Ham," and he thanked her with barely a hitch in his story.

" 'If I make it out of here,' Jesse says, 'I'm to be staked by New Orleans bankers in a run for governor, and I expect their confidence in me will be rewarded. Governor Holliver. Has a ring to it, don't it,' he says, and does that little finger flick on his mustache tips." Ham's fingers had risen to scratch his sideburns meditatively, as if he were considering the value of adding a mustache to his arsenal. "I let on that it makes a pretty epithet, and Jesse takes the bottle from me and toasts himself, 'Governor Holliver,' he says, and drains it. Then he throws the bottle overboard and we watch it splash about where the cemetery used to be. He continues, 'And when I'm governor, I'll need me some good men. I had an uncle who was gonna be my second in command. But now I have a suspicion the position has reopened.' "

"Shit," said Ingersoll.

Ham went on. "And before I can say no, Jesse doubles down. Brings out this giant roll of rubber-banded hundred-dollar bills. 'That,' he says, handing it to me, 'is a token of my good faith.'

" 'Holy Mother of God,' I say.

" 'Then we have a deal?' Jesse asks, and slings an arm over my shoulders.

"I look at him sideways and I say, 'You blew up your town, your family, maybe my partner. Our deal is this, Governor: if I live, I'll spend the rest of my days hunting you down. You will die screaming like a stuck pig. I'll see to it.' "

Dixie Clay squeezed Ingersoll's fingers.

"So about then the church gives a great moan. I shake off his arm to lean out the casement and look. And that's when he sticks me. Sticks me with some little knife he's got squirreled away, and as he does I feel his hand yanking on my calf, and he's trying to tump me overboard, but I got a hundred pounds on him easy. He stuck me good in the side but didn't get nothing but fat." Here Ham swiveled his back to them and grabbed his shirt at the shoulder seam and gathered the fabric until it revealed a bandage the size of a dollar bill between thick tufts of orange hair. "So I turn around and we stare at each other. Both of us know it's over. He looks at me kind of sad with those funny-colored eyes, then here he comes one last time, with that bitty knife, and I just let him run himself right out the opening and he bounces once on the roof of the church and sails into the river and I watch him go down beneath the surface and he doesn't come up."

Dixie Clay sucked in her breath and gave a little shiver. No one said anything then. The waitress cleared the table and that was when the men reached for the toothpicks while Dixie Clay adjusted Willy on her knees.

"Anyway," Ham continued after a while, "I spent the night curled up in the bell tower, and the next morning hitched a canoe ride with some coloreds and a truculent hog to a tug that took us all to Greenville."

"Where you been staying?" Ingersoll wanted to know.

"At — at a house on Blanton Street."

"I hope you gave Madame LeLoup my regards," said Dixie Clay with a raised eyebrow.

Ham grinned. "Didn't know you were familiar with the cathouse."

"She serves the best whiskey known to man."

"Thought it tasted familiar." The waitress appeared with her coffeepot half tilted, circling for an empty mug, but they were truly done. "You can just put it on my tab," Ham told her.

As she walked away, Ingersoll asked, "You got a tab?"

"Sure do, sunshine. They've got too much

livestock on the levee, been butchering five hogs a day at the levee kitchen. Ate me several hogs' worth of ribs the last two days, waiting for you to turn your sorry ass up. If I didn't know you so well, I'd a started worrying." He said it with that humorous thrust of his jaw, but his eyes betrayed that he'd been worried.

Ingersoll slung out his arm and lightly punched Ham's bicep, then tossed his toothpick into the ashtray. "What now?" he asked. He truly hadn't thought beyond this point and felt weary about having to.

"Been thinking on that. Turned it over, once or twice, during my night in the bell tower. You know," Ham said, weaving his toothpick between his knuckles, "I just might be getting a little old to go chasing bootleggers."

Ingersoll sat straighter. Ham looked the same as when they'd fought in the trenches nine years ago, his hair not thinning. In fact, his new hat looked like a champagne cork about to blow.

"Prohibition is about tuckered out, don't you reckon?" Ham turned to Dixie Clay and she nodded. "Besides" — he turned back to Ingersoll — "it won't be any fun without you to boss around."

There was silence then for a moment.

Ingersoll asked, "So, New Orleans?"

"Naw, I ain't going to New Orleans. Figure I've seen enough of the Mississip to last me a lifetime. Several lifetimes."

"What then?"

"Fixing to head home for a spell," Ham said, and then "Kentucky," for Dixie Clay's benefit. "Used to be a redheaded arithmetic teacher there, always threatened to civilize me. Prettier than a glob of butter melting on a stack of wheat cakes. I wonder if I shouldn't give her a chance."

"Worth a shot," Ingersoll offered.

"And if that don't work out, I might could mosey over to D.C., that's the District of Columbia for you unsophisticates, see about some cushy government job, you know, get soft riding my keister around in a Packard. Yep, it's horsepower, not horses, from here on out for ole Ham."

"D.C.," Ingersoll mused. "I could picture you there."

"And surely I'm due a nice severance package from Hoover, our next president, on account of my grief and all."

Dixie Clay and Ingersoll looked at each other, and she took the bait. "Your grief?"

"Yep, my grief, on account of my partner, my eight years' partner, ole Dead-Eye Orphan Teddy Ingersoll, being washed away in the flood. I saw it with my own eyes."

"Did you now?" Ingersoll asked.

"I did. I shorely did. The '27 crevasse at Hobnob Landing; I was there, you know."

"Were you now?"

"Same as I'm sitting here! Same as I live and breathe. Lost my partner, right after he put together what that no-good Jesse Holliver was up to, ablowin' the levee with stolen government TNT — a big whole tidal wave swept Ing seaward, him ascreamin', 'I never did appreciate you enough, Ham' — those were his last words, they were — Ingersoll's untimely death a double shame, really, as he probably woulda gotten some kinda pretty medal for that piece of detective work to go along with his bronze from the war. So his chest wouldn't be all lopsided, you know. And to make matters worse, right after that fella Holliver was snatched into the mouth of Jonah's whale, I saw that pretty little Holliver filly swept clean away. Tragedy, that. She was just about to succumb to my charms, too."

"Was she now?" This from Dixie Clay, cocking her head.

"Indeed, indeed. She thought the sun come up just to hear ole Ham crow."

Dixie Clay smiled and ran her palm over Willy's downy head.

The conversation ceased, the lighthearted tone too hard to maintain, perhaps, and probably everyone was thinking the same thing. What Ham had worked out. Death and rebirth. So that's how easy it could be.

Though there was one more thing. Dixie Clay cleared her throat, then said, "About the two revenuers." She was still running her hand over Willy's head. "The ones you were supposed to find. You're not gonna find 'em, Ham, I'm pretty sure." She lifted her eyes. "I was there with Jesse and —"

Ham held a large pink palm in the air. "Well, I reckon that's a story I don't need to know, being that everyone involved was washed away."

She swallowed, and they were quiet again.

"Here," Ham said abruptly, slapping an obscene spool of rubber-banded hundreds on the table. "You dry those bills out, they'll still work."

Ingersoll shook his head, though it was true that on the boat to the sheriff's, he'd totted up how much these ribs would eat into his remaining four damp dollars.

"Oh, don't be an idiot," Ham said. "It's hers, after all, she cooked the damn whis- key."

Ingersoll looked at Dixie Clay, and she pursed her lips and gave a tiny shrug. She *had* cooked the damn whiskey. Ingersoll looked back at the roll yet felt powerless to reach out. Finally Ham backhanded it across the table where it skidded to Ingersoll's fist. He uncurled his fingers and drummed them once on the roll and then picked it up and straightened his leg to push it into the pocket of his dungarees. He gave Ham a nod.

Broken vows and broken laws and blood and desertion and money — all that he'd needed to come to pass had come to pass. They were free to go.

The waitress came over with the coffeepot but they shook their heads. "We're quittin', sugar," Ham told her.

"Alrighty, I put it on your tab, Ham."

"Thank you kindly. By the way, I don't suppose you'd fancy a trip to Kentucky, run barefoot through the bluegrass with a big tipper like Ham Johnson?"

"And give up all this?" Her gesture took in the ramshackle room, the displaced customers, the ribs on pulleys.

"You got a point."

"Hey, I been meaning to ask. Where's the name Ham come from?"

Ingersoll sat back in his chair and reached out to squeeze Dixie Clay's knee, then turned, already grinning, to Ham.

But Ham's gray eyes were serious. "Ham," he said. He turned to Ingersoll. "It stands for Abraham."

The waitress nodded and moved on, yet the men sat regarding each other. "Abraham," Ingersoll said softly. He smiled and shook his head, a confused gesture, inadequate to convey all that sloshed in his heart.

Finally Ham slapped the table with his huge hands and the silverware jumped and the three rose.

There was nothing more to do then. Where before the men had hugged, now they shook hands, but there was so much in their grasp and in their eyes that it did not seem a lessening.

Dixie Clay stuck out her hand, and Ham stuck out his hand, and then she seemed to think better of it and raised on tiptoes to kiss Ham's cheek, the whole exchange a little awkward, but it got the job done.

Then Ingersoll placed his palm on Dixie Clay's neck and took Willy onto his shoulder, and they turned away and descended the steps. Just before Ingersoll's head passed below the floor, he looked back to see Ham, who was facing away, thick legs crossed, gazing toward the window, the late-afternoon

light making the air seem solid with the dust
of the centuries.

EPILOGUE

Hobnob was ninety miles and three days behind them. They were in Arkansas now, the farthest west Dixie Clay had ever been. Each step the horse took became its own extremity, its own frontier. This was the farthest west she'd gone. No, *this* was. *This.*

When they'd left Greenville, they could have boated across the flat Delta to Greenwood, the beginning of the hills, fifty miles and four hours away, or so people said. Instead, Ingersoll turned the boat west. They crossed the river, if you could still call it a river when it was ninety miles wide.

They knew they were boating over places where houses and farms used to be. It was houseless, farmless. Treeless. Then, westward, a few trees, like broccoli dipped in batter halfway up. Then signs of houses — concrete steps, a brick chimney. Then a copse of woods, logjam that had trapped, like the mesh pocket in a pool table, a bank of school lockers, a pair of dead calico ponies hitched to a wagon, a planing mill saw, a mailbox, a sign reading TALLULAH'S, WORLD'S BEST CATFISH. Apocalyptic, this landscape they boated through. No need to worry about trampling anyone's cotton, river had seen to that. No need to hop fences, river had seen to that. River had seen and seen. They began to pass humps of dry ground. Prosthetic leg sticking up out of the mud. Bloated carcass of a donkey beside a bloated Bible, as if he'd been reading the events of the end time when they befell him. Wild dogs circling a tree, snagged high in its branches a coop filled with dead chickens, rattling because of the buzzards that hopped and thrust their beaks in to pull out bloody cords of meat. They passed a hill with strange white arcs cresting the mud. Like baby's teeth pushing through gums, said Dixie Clay. But Ingersoll shook his head. Gravestones, he said; a cemetery. Though where the church was now, God only knew.

Willy was often sleeping on her lap, lulled by the motor of the boat as he'd always been by the rumbling of the thumper keg. Sometimes when he fussed, Ingersoll sang a bit. It didn't rain, which was another record.

On the far side of the river, they traded

the boat for a horse. They were not sad to ride away from it. The land was scraped-clean mudflats, cracked like so much poorly thrown pottery. Dark brown in low spots where the mud was thick and lightening toward the edges as it dried. They didn't talk much. They peered strangely at the strange world they passed through, Ingersoll's arms around Dixie Clay's arms around Willy. Sometimes she rested her chin lightly on the baby's head and Ingersoll rested his on hers.

Then a clapboard house rising from a mud moat, slanted but still upright, said Ingersoll, because the owners had the smarts to leave the doors and windows open so the floodwaters could rush through.

They rode up to the door and Ingersoll yoo-hooed but no one came out so they dismounted and went inside. In the kitchen Dixie Clay found two cans of carrots and two of spinach and they ate one each and fork-mashed bites for Willy. They were tired and pulled down the straw ticking that someone had wedged over the armoire to stay dry. It smelled moldy but they were happy to lie down and stretch their saddle-sore legs. And they were happy on their sides with the baby sleeping between them as they spoke in low voices. Then Ingersoll's feet on Dixie Clay's feet and then a raising-up-on-elbows-to-lean-over-the-baby kiss and then he'd rolled over her and they were making love and it was not the wild frenzied mudlove of the Indian mound but a probing tender molasseslove. Even so, Dixie Clay was not able to bite down on a cry, which woke Willy, so Ingersoll cradled him with one arm against his bare chest as they finished and Willy was rocked back to sleep, Ingersoll asleep almost immediately after. Dixie Clay thought, *Not me, I'm too happy to sleep, I'll stay up all night and look at them sleeping.* That's the last thing she recalled until waking.

They left at dawn with the sun spooling gauzy mist from the puddles. The rhythm of the horse released her thoughts, which were easy. She felt calm and unplagued by questions, even concerning their destination. They hadn't discussed it except briefly, the first night when they'd found some strange island of land and made camp. They'd gathered someone's blasted barn for firewood. When Dixie Clay dumped her fagot near where Ingersoll crouched, trying to light some tinder, she stretched her horse-jolted back and said, gazing up at the darkening cloud cover, "I miss stars."

Ingersoll looked up and nodded. "We'll

keep on until we're in star country."

"Yeah?"

"Yeah. The Ozarks. Fellow there named Jim, fought with him in the war." Ingersoll was flicking the flint wheel of his lighter and produced a small blue flame. He held it to the tinder. "Part Indian. Came home with shrapnel in his skull. No one thought he'd live. But he lives, all right." They heard the tinder begin to crackle.

"How do you know he'll help us?"

"I know." Ingersoll poked the fire a bit and smiled. "The Ozarks, Dixie Clay. Mountains so old they're just hills now."

She liked that and repeated it. "Mountains so old they're just hills now."

That was enough to know for the present. What she wanted now was a simple life. Small cottage. Books. Tidy garden with rows of peas and corn and tomatoes. Flowers if Ingersoll liked them, but as for herself, Dixie Clay preferred vegetables, hardworking, practical, her blossoms squash blossoms, honeybee wriggling its fat furred bottom down the creamy throat, then lurching drunkenly off to forge its gold. Maybe a stream somewhere so the three of them could fish. Oh, and she wanted a dog. A big dog, a big and hairy dog. A boy should have a dog. She wanted chickens again, the daily trade of feeding them and being fed by them. She wanted honest work. Go to bed with the dark, tired, and wake up with the sun, rested. She wanted to bake scratch cakes and pick blackberries and can jam and when her boy came hungry from school she'd take bread from the oven and he could tear off a steaming feathery hunk and give it a fat swath of blackberry. Ripe June in his red October mouth. Yes, she would feed her men.

She wanted to grow old with Ingersoll. Sit with him of an evening on the gallery after supper, Willy a man now, though that would take some getting used to, her pulling a book from the shelf Ingersoll had built. Then maybe listening to him strum his guitar and sing in his dungaree-spearmint voice while she did some small useful task. Shelling pecans, say, that she'd gathered into her apron from beneath the trees earlier that day.

She indulged in this vision and then realized that in it she'd been cracking pecans with the bell-end, hickory-handled hammer she'd brought to Hobnob from Alabama. But that hammer, well made and well used, freighted with the fate of ten thousand pecans, lay at the bottom of the lake that filled the gulley that used to nestle her house. The trusty little hammer knew no touch now but the fins of fishes, the undulant stroke of long grasses. She had a flicker of something — pity? For the hammer? For herself? But then it passed, the way troubling things pass when you recall they happened only in a dream.

There was the before world, and the after. It was a kind of freedom. Starting from scratch, she was. As was Ingersoll. Freed even of the silver weight of his occupation, freed even of the bronze weight of his valor. They could be anyone now.

She'd live out her days in the space his arms made.

The events that would form the great story of her life were nearing their close, and she was glad of it. She was not by nature a dramatic person, but dramatic events had befallen her, and she'd endured, had been compelled to endure. But now she was ready for what came next. Common days.

And there would come a time, when Willy was old enough, to tell him the story. She would have told him bits already, enough for him to know there *was* a story, and he'd know that she wasn't his natural-born mama. She'd tell him that from the start so he didn't have to swallow some terrible

493

truth when he was older, a truth made more terrible because it had festered in shameful silence. No, he would know already, important that he know already. So he'd understand she'd had to work to be ready for the gift of him, to work and wait and wait and work.

By the time she'd be ready to tell him the story, she'd know how her part fit into the whole. Historians would have described to her what she'd lived through. So later, when she is ready, she will be able to say, *Son, it was the greatest natural disaster our country had ever known.* How big, Willy, was the area that was drowned? About the size of Connecticut, New Hampshire, Massachusetts, and Vermont. Of course, if it *had* been those states, we'd have had help right quick. Supplies. Money. Later, chapters in the history books. Monuments everywhere. But it was Delta dirt, the richest dirt in the nation, though under the boot soles of the poorest folk. The official death toll would be reported as 313, though we all knew the real number was much higher, Willy, much higher. Coolidge never came to the suffering people. In the months that followed, four governors and eight senators would beg him to come, to turn the eyes of the nation on the South. But Coolidge did not come.

And was not reelected. Hoover, darling of the newsreels, star of the Sunday supplements, did surf the flood to the presidency, as he'd predicted. This flood, now forgotten by much of our nation, changed what our nation became.

She'll know all this then, but not now. Now, three days after fleeing, it is not yet the story of the Great Flood of the Great River. It is just their story. And so when she imagines telling it, she imagines telling it like this:

It is time to tell you a story, a story that will surprise you. The year was 1927, and Lord, the rains did rain. Your mama was a bootlegger, and your daddy was a revenuer, so they were meant to be enemies, natural enemies, like the owl and the dormouse. But instead they fell in love.

This story is a story with murder and moonshine, sandbagging and saboteurs, dynamite and deluge. A ruthless husband, a troubled uncle, a dangerous flapper, a loyal partner. A woman, married to the wrong husband, who died a little every day. A man who felt invisible.

But most of all, this is a love story. This is the story of how we became a family.

ACKNOWLEDGMENTS

We wish to thank some of the many folks who helped us write this book:

Dr. Luther P. Brown, director, Delta Center for Culture and Learning, shared his expertise on the Mississippi Delta and the flood, and the '27 Break Hunting Club allowed Dr. Brown to show us the location of the '27 crevasse. Andrew P. Mullins, chief of staff to the chancellor of the University of Mississippi, shared anecdotes of the Delta and Prohibition. Richard P. Moore, colonel, U.S. Air Force (Retired), vetted this book for inaccuracies about firearms, explosives, and World War I. Barry Bradford — librarian, historian, and cousin — provided sources and suggestions that were timely and serendipitous. Jane G. Gardner loaned us her grandmother's photos of the flood. Those, and the materials housed at the Flood of 1927 Museum in Greenville, assisted our research greatly. One String Willie provided diddley bow tips. Michael Knight, author and pal, provided helpful and only slightly smart-ass notes.

Several books were of crucial importance to our research. Those who wish to read more about the flood could do no better than to read John M. Barry's *Rising Tide: The Great Mississippi Flood of 1927 and How It Changed America,* an amazing work of research and journalism, to which our novel is indebted. *Lanterns on the Levee: Recollections of a Planter's Son,* by William Alexander Percy, is a fascinating memoir with vignettes of Delta life and landscape, including an interesting account of the flood. Other books that proved useful are *Deep'n as It Come: the 1927 Mississippi River Flood,* by Pete Daniel; *Wicked River: the Mississippi When It Last Ran Wild,* by Lee Sandlin; *Where the Wild Animals Is Plentiful: Diary of an Alabama Fur Trader's Daughter, 1912–1914,* by May Jordan, and *1927: High Tide of the Twenties,* by Gerald Leinwand. Films that provided inspiration include *Prohibition,* a documentary by Ken Burns, and *The American Experience: Fatal Flood* (PBS).

Many thanks to the Mississippi Arts Commission, which awarded each author an Individual Artist Grant. The University of

Mississippi has been deeply supportive: thanks to Chancellor Dan Jones, and to Dean Glenn Hopkins of the College of Liberal Arts, which provided a summer grant to Tommy, and to the Office of Research and Sponsored Programs, which provided a travel grant to Beth Ann. Deep thanks to our collegial English Department, especially our chair, Ivo Kamps, who read the manuscript in an early version, and Jay Watson, the Howry Professor of Faulkner Studies, who encouraged us, and our colleagues in the MFA Program. Surrounding the university community is the community of Oxford, Mississippi, home to a whole bunch of readers and writers and one of the world's best bookstores, Square Books. The authors are proud to call Oxford home. For the Lafayette County Literacy Council's Mardi Gras Ball fund-raiser, we auctioned off the right to name the two boys paddling the canoes in Greenville. Thanks to Nicholas Brown for the winning bid.

We wish to thank our families, especially Betty and Gerald Franklin and Mary Anna McNamara Malich, who encouraged and who babysat while portions of this book were written.

The folks at William Morrow/ HarperCollins have been a delight. Sharyn

Rosenblum in PR is exceptionally good at her job. The company's president, Michael Morrison, makes it look easy. Our editor, David Highfill, is always a pleasure. Liate Stehlik, the publisher of William Morrow, offered valued support. Across the pond, our UK editor at Mantle, Maria Rejt, and her assistant, Sophie Orme, suggested some thoughtful changes that prevented a few embarrassments, such as renaming the baby in the UK version because over there, " 'Willy' is a silly word for penis."

This novel grew out of our collaborative short story, "What His Hands Had Been Waiting For," which first appeared in *The Normal School,* edited by Steven Church, and was reprinted in *Delta Blues,* edited by Carolyn Haines, and *Best American Mystery Stories, 2011,* edited by Otto Penzler and Harlan Coben. It was our agents, the husband-and-wife team Nat Sobel and Judith Weber, who first suggested the story be expanded into a cowritten novel and who then read it several times along the way. We dedicate this book to them, and to another collaboration of ours and inspiration for this book, Nolan McNamara Franklin.